I0589403

Eva Rae's Song

Also By the Author

The Intruders

The Old Boys

Eva Rae's Song

Kirk Winkler

DEDICATION

For the strong women who taught me much about life:
Clara, Vera, Bonnie, Marge and Dede

And for Arlene, always

I Begin

YOU WHO MAY BE READING THIS, just keep in mind that it's coming from an old lady who's past worrying about trying to make a good impression. Consider it fair warning. If you don't like what you read, blame Evie.

Evie is my granddaughter. She gave me a Christmas present of a pencil and this Big Chief writing tablet just like the little tykes use in school and told me she wanted me to write down my life story so she could pass it on to her own kids someday.

Evie's a peach for even thinking of such a thing, which is saying something considering her momma and daddy are about as sour and quarrelsome a lot as there is on the planet. Of course, I reckon I'm to blame for some of that on account of I raised her daddy and have lived under the same roof as her momma for many a year, so if you who's reading this is the grandchild of Donald and Lydia, don't take me wrong. They're good people—good hard-working Christians, kind to the down-trodden and all that.

It's just that they ain't particularly cheerful. Maybe it's the hard times we all been through. Or maybe it's living with me. I know I can be a handful when I want to be.

Anyhow, Evie wants some stories, so I reckon I'll just begin at the beginning, and see what happens.

A Child of Missouri

I WAS BORN AT HOME in our little secesh corner of central Missouri on a wettish spring day in the year of 1868. My momma always said there was a scent of early lilacs and new grass on the air that day, with the threat of thunderstorms lurking on the western horizon. On account of all that, she knew I was going to be sweet as molasses and terrible trouble, all rolled together. Or so Ma always told me, though she was prone to coloring the facts now and again for the sake of a good story.

There's no doubt I was my momma's little darling from the first, mostly on account of I was the very last in an unruly brood of three boys and eight girls spread out over fifteen-odd years, which to my daddy's way of thinking was about eight boys shy of enough and at least seven girls too many.

When he gave any thought to me at all, which wasn't often, Daddy said he figured I was God's gift to our family the same way Mr. John Wilkes Booth was a gift to the South—too damned little and too damned late and, in the end, more curse than blessing. Of course, some of the old man's attitude towards me might of come from the fact that Daddy had no intention of me being the last of his children, him holding out for more sons to help with the chores.

But he was pure out of luck on that score.

Ma simply put her foot down.

I was going to be the last if she had to kill him to do it, which I know for a fact she considered on occasion for any number of reasons, most of them having nothing to do with children.

The truth was, that old buzzard was plumb wearing her out in so many ways there wasn't no accounting for it. An old tin-type from the year before I was born shows Ma as an old, stooped woman of thirty-two standing alongside a perfectly healthy man of broad shoulders and drooping handlebar mustache surrounded by a gaggle of kids, most of them just blurs on the image on account of they couldn't hold still. Her teeth were gone and her strength was going, but there was nothing wrong with her mind, and once she'd birthed me, she decided she was slap through with having young'uns, and that was that.

The way she always told it, she was just determined to quit making babies before she wound up like some used up brood mare, good for nothing but being sent off to the glue factory. So from the day I came into the world, if Daddy ever did relieve his male urgings, he did it in town, because he sure as heaven didn't share Ma's bed.

I know that for fact, and I swear she got younger over the years because of it.

We were Cumberlands on Daddy's side, which was where we hailed from as well as our last name, my daddy's daddy having come west to Missouri with Danl Boone when Kentucky got too crowded for either man. Of course, old Danl was famous, whereas my grand-daddy was a nobody. That's why just about everything for some miles around our place was called by that great pathfinding gentleman's name— Boone's Lick, Boone's Ford, Boone's Prairie and so forth— whereas there wasn't nothing named after our people. Truth to tell, I've always suspicioned that we must of had some other family name in Kentucky we wanted to leave behind so the law wouldn't put two and two together. Knowing what I do about some of my daddy's shady dealings, which he likely learned at his own pap's knee, I'm certain there was plenty of reason for us Cumberlands to want to stay outen the limelight, you might say.

Anyway, we took great pride in being Kentuckians, and old Danl's shining light was enough for us to live by.

In fact, the only other person on God's earth that my daddy thought more of than Mr. Boone was Robert E. Lee. Of course, old Danl was a flesh and blood mortal who was well remembered, warts and all, by some who were still kicking when I was born.

General Lee was nothing short of a god.

Jesus Christ himself didn't have nothing on Marse Robert amongst us hill people. But if Lee was God, then old Danl was at least the equal of Moses since he'd brought us to the Promised Land. We were the Israelites, glad to be living in the land of milk and honey and never mind whether anyone outside the county had ever heard of us.

Of course, keeping our light under a bushel was hard work given how many of us there were, and I don't just mean Ma and Daddy's brood. We Cumberlands were more clan than family, my daddy having come from a bunch of eighteen young'uns in three groups, his daddy having worn out three wives in succession. Daddy was christened Levi and was the middle child of the last wife, so he had a passel of nieces and nephews some years older than himself, just about all of whom bred like mice in a hay mow. We had shirttail relation all over the hills and hollows of central Missouri—so many that my Aunt Mabel, who was Daddy's oldest full sister and as mean a woman as God ever gave breath, once said a Missouri Cumberland couldn't help but marry a cousin unless he was to marry a Yankee, which wasn't likely to happen until Hell froze over.

I suppose that's why so many of us had wild red hair,

green speckled eyes and six toes on each foot.

I was lucky enough to miss that last family trait, thanks be to the Lord, but I did get the hair and eyes. I also got the family streak of pure orneriness. I've always chalked that up to taking after daddy more than it being a matter of inbreeding, though of course it could of been either. Daddy's cantankerousness likely got a shade or two worse after I was born for reasons I've already mentioned, but from everything I've heard, a sweet temper never had been one of his better points even when he was sharing Ma's bed, and gentleness of nature didn't run in that family under any circumstances.

I suppose that Cumberland cussedness is what started me on the hard road I've followed, though I'm getting ahead of myself there, and I don't want to blame Daddy for that, no matter what else he did, which was plenty. If there's guilt to be laid for the life I've lived, I'll shoulder my fair share.

But you do have to understand about Daddy.

Let's just say when I was growing up, he'd take the switch to any of us just for the exercise, and sometimes he'd swing his old razor strop so hard it'd pop like a whip. The younger boys got the worst of it, sometimes wearing scabby bandages for weeks where Daddy got carried away, but he didn't spare the rod nor spoil the child with us girls, neither. Daddy had a good side, but you generally only saw it when his pals came around, and then only between the time he started to drink and when he'd drunk too much.

Only Cyrus Robert, my eldest brother and the apple of Daddy's eye, ever got what might be called the milk of human kindness from Daddy, likely because Cy was the one who was supposed to inherit the home place when it came time for Dad to cash in his chips.

Ma was a Gosper. Adelphia was her given name, though I don't believe I ever heard anyone, even her own people, call her that except for Daddy when he was drinking or otherwise trying to sweet-talk her. "Dell" was what they called her.

Daddy mostly just called her "Mother," and even the neighbors took to calling her "Mother Cumberland" as if she was some kind of matriarch or something.

In my recollection, she, even more than Daddy, was part and parcel of the piece of ground she lived on every day of her adult life.

And what a place it was.

Looking back on it from the vantage point of all these years, I know our old homeplace was just a hardscrabble plot of a hundred stony acres in the hills overlooking the Missouri river where it came tumbling outen a limestone gorge and spilled into a broad flood plain. We were what you'd call dirt poor, living on a patch of pitiful poor dirt. But I was pure in love with our little hollow, especially the way it looked and smelled and sounded of a midsummer morning, when the ragged mist that was part fog and part smoke clung to the treetops like huge strips of gauze snagged on the fat leaves of buckeye and oak and the farther ridges paled against the brilliant greens of our own, with the tang of new-mown hay in the meadow smelling even sweeter than the sugar-cured ham frying for breakfast. Even the wet, rocky earth Daddy turned when digging a new privy was pure joy for a young'un. And there was always the call of the jays and the clank of the brass bell on our old Jersey cow as she cropped the grass near the back door, and the nervous buzz of the bees working over the petunias Ma planted like a pink carpet between the well and garden, or the racket of the seventeen-year locusts so loud in the trees it liked to drove Daddy's old coon dog crazy.

Yessir, I loved that place in the summer. I loved it just as much in the early autumn when we'd butcher and hang them big hams in the smoke house over fires of maple and hickory, and on a winter's morning when a new-fallen snow turned the world a perfect, brilliant white, and on a green and muddy Sunday in spring when folks from the other hollows came around, the women just to talk and see how everyone had survived the long hibernating winter and the men to sip whiskey outen a jar and the boys to smoke home-rolled see-gars behind the barn.

That place was pretty as a picture, but it was damn poor land for farming, which guaranteed we were going to stay poor no matter how many sons Daddy got to help with the chores. We raised just enough corn to feed a few hogs and a gaggle of geese, with a little left over for the moonshine that was our only cash crop. Even in a good year, that 'shine barely provided enough cash to buy shoes for the kids, and in a bad year the hogs rooting acorns in the woods fared better than we did. Daddy worked the fields from sunup to sundown, ran his still back in the woods by the light of the moon, Ma raised the kids, and us kids raised Cain.

Our house was built on a slope just on the Callaway County side of the Missouri River, and by the time I came along, the whole place had sort of tumbled over and slipped down toward the river a bit. With all the broken tools and pieces of junk Daddy left laying around the yard, the house looked mostly like something a summer cyclone had busted up to kindling and scattered over half an acre. It was so drafty we'd sometimes waken of a winter morning with little windrows of snow on our comforters and the house was so full of vermin Ma sifted the flour when she made biscuits mostly to get the mouse turds out. When it rained, I swear the pigs had better lodgings.

Our place was just a few miles north and east of Jefferson City, which seemed like the biggest city in the world, but looking back, I realize Jeff City was just a muddy one-horse town that happened to be the state capital. I learned some years later it was named for Thomas Jefferson, but us kids all naturally assumed Jeff Davis was the true and only namesake for our town. How else could it be in good Confederate country? If you'd clumb the chinaberry tree at the end of our lane, you could see the great gray dome of the capitol itself, and when we went to town, while Ma went to the store and Daddy had a whiskey with his cronies, we loved playing in the streets around the capitol, dodging amongst the fancy black lacquered buggies, scaring their beautiful matched teams and making the fat, whiskered gentlemen drivers blow and swear. But on our place, it was busted up democrat wagons, cantankerous mules, and a drafty clapboard house that sprawled in all directions but mostly downhill.

Of my three brothers and seven sisters, I've already mentioned Cyrus Robert. The rest of us kids hated that boy, him being Daddy's pet. Cy would get candies from town when the rest of us got nothing but sharp looks if we didn't jump fast enough to curry the horses, and one Christmas, Daddy gave him a .22 rifle, new shoes, and a black felt hat with a rattlesnake hatband while the other boys got oranges and socks and us girls got emery boards and a hank of yarn to make something with. It plumb went to Cy's head. He could be as mean as Daddy, and his beard, red as fire and growing every whichaway, came on early, giving him a wild look that could scare the be-Jeezus outen grownups, let alone his baby sisters.

Ma never could keep him in school, and she always said she figured he was headed for prison for sure, but he found God instead.

When I was still a little girl, Cy took to reading the Bible and reciting favorite verses, and I mean all the time. I swear he memorized the Book of Job. It liked to drove Daddy crazy. Cy ran off to St. Louis when he was nineteen with the intent of learning enough religion to get a collar and a proper church, but I guess he lost God as easy as he found him, because the last we heard, he was knifed during a fight over a hand of cards and was laid up with a bad case of blood poisoning. It didn't kill him, but it sure spoilt his habit of dealing from the bottom of the deck, or at least that's what some fellows who ran into him on the wharves in New Orleans said.

Seth LeRoy was my middle brother—the middle one of all us kids.

Seth didn't turn out to be the kind of child Daddy would of wanted, neither, boy or not. He was the fairest of all us children, and a sickly child with a peculiar temperament. Ma always said Seth got the vapors whenever it rained. He turned bookish on us and went to school clear to the tenth grade, moved to Jeff City, went to work in a dry goods emporium, and took up with a spinster schoolteacher. He was fifteen and she was thirty. The scandal liked to killed Ma until Seth married that woman. They had no young'uns of their own, and on account of the scandal having cost her her teaching job, they moved to California, where we lost all track. I've always imagined he turned out to be a writer or maybe worked in moving pictures when they came along, but that's just daydreaming on my part.

James Jesse was my youngest brother, just three years older than me. Ma never liked the name on account of she didn't much care for his namesake, which was the notorious Jesse James, whom Daddy had met before he got famous, when he was a young raider with that Quantrill trash, though I do believe Jimmy was Ma's favorite child in spite of the name. He was a hell-raiser like the rest of us, but he minded Ma and never sassed Daddy that I can remember. By the time he was ten years old, anybody with half a wit could tell he was going to be the only boy who was going to make something of himself no matter what it took, which was a lucky thing once Cy got the Call. Jimmy was the one who actually inherited the place, such as it was, after Daddy passed, and he did a right smart job of looking after it from what I've heard. He died of the influenza in 'Eighteen, and I heard folks came from fifty miles around for the funeral, which was saying a lot, I'll tell you. He turned out to be the one Cumberland folks respected.

Anyhow, them were the boys.

Us girls were a different bunch entirely. There was Mary

Ellen, the oldest child of all, being about ten months older than Cy; Matilda Louise, the third child; Roberta Lea, the fourth and named in a fit of patriotic fervor never mind she was a girl; Gwendolyn Marie, the only dark-haired child in the whole bunch; the twins Gladys Lucille and Lucinda Jean; Dell Christine, my dearest sister just a year older than me; and yours truly.

Mary Ellen was the dark humored child. She was almost grown by the time I came along. She would go to moping over lost loves or loves never had like some moonstruck calf at the drop of a hat, and there wasn't nobody who could sigh better than she could, sometimes right in the middle of supper. There was a grotto in the limestone bank of the creek that ran through the woods below our place, and Mary Ellen loved to go there and cry when her moods came on. Amongst my earliest memories are the times Ma would send us down to the creek to fetch Mary when she was having one of her spells. She would be all disheveled, with torn clothes and stringy hair like she'd been tramping through the woods, but it was only her pulling at herself while she wept. She was past twenty before she left home to take a job as a cleaning lady in a big house in Jefferson City. I heard she became the mistress of the man of the house, but it was a thing we never spoke of, as you can imagine, and to this day I don't know it for a fact. I do know she wound up marrying a storekeeper and having eight kids of her own, so I assume she outgrew them vapors at some point.

Matilda Louise I never knew. She was the only one of us to die as a child, which was a mighty rare thing for a brood of that size in them days. She caught diphtheria when she was eight and died within a day. Daddy buried her in the shade of a big old chestnut tree in the side yard and carved out a head-stone from the limestone of the river bluffs. All it said was

Matilda Cumberland

Loving daughter
Gone to God

There weren't any dates nor anything.

Roberta Lea—whom we called Bobbie Lea, usually with a snicker, and sometimes Marse Robert behind her back—tried right hard most of her life to be the boy Daddy wanted, and for obvious reasons she was our proud little rebel. She hung out with the Confederate veterans who came by our place and listened to their stories, generally while sitting on the lap of some old sour-smelling half-drunk heathen. She seemed not to mind. By the time she went off to school, she knew as much about the War Between the States as anybody in our part of Missouri, at least from the rebel side. She was a good student but a better horsewoman; when she was sixteen, she married Buck Palliser, one of our second cousins who raised mules and racing horses. In time, they and their three young'uns moved to Kentucky, where Buck died of the ague and she married another horseman. I heard that one did real well for himself and left her a fortune when he died. I believe she lived to a ripe old age though I can't say for sure, her and I never having stayed in touch.

Gwendolyn Marie and I never got along on account of she was the one who had to look after me when I was just a toddler and not even housebroke. Gwen was maybe seven at the time and allowed as how I was spoiling all her fun, which I imagine was true. That must have spoilt her on having kids right there, because she grew up to be the only spinster of the bunch. She went clear through the twelfth grade and took up teaching in a one-room school over in Mexico, Missouri, which I always considered odd for someone who didn't like children. In later years, I understand she took to calling herself "Miss Cumberland" even amongst the family, which didn't go over too big with that clan, and one summer she decided to take a trip to Paris to see the sights, from which she never returned. If anyone knows what happened to her over there, they ain't telling.

The twins, Gladys and Lucy, were as alike as two peas in a pod. Ma dressed them the same except for a little red bow she put in Gladys's hair so she could tell them apart, and once they caught on, them two made endless trouble for the rest of us by swapping that bow back and forth. They pretty much ignored me, which bothered me a bunch when I was little, but as I grew older I came to realize they ignored just about every-body: they provided each other with all the companionship they ever needed. From what I could tell, they just about raised each other, which was a good thing considering all the trouble Ma was having keeping the rest of us in line. She always said them girls were a blessing to her, being both quiet and gentle. They married brothers, too, the sons of a Baptist pastor, which meant they probably got more religion in the first few months of married life than they'd gotten all the while they were at home, Daddy not being much of the church type, though Ma would of been if he'd let her. Anyway, the twins and their husbands went to farming over around Sedalia and raised a passel of kids between them. They tuned out to be real church people, and I mean that kindly.

Then there was Dell Christine, named for Ma after a fash-ion, and my friend and companion. We were almost as close as the twins, though even had we been exactly the same age we could never of tricked anyone into mistaking one for the other. Dell was a beautiful child—maybe the most beautiful child I ever saw—with big brown eyes and honey-colored hair with a few darker streaks thrown in and a splash of freckles acrost dimpled apple cheeks, whereas I was a tone or two lighter and more angular. I could dress in my brother's trousers and slip on brogans and even fool Daddy into think-ing I was a boy, especially if he'd been drinking.

Dell was one hundred percent girl.

We were a team, though, and we could make doing

dishes for the threshing crews into a game till Ma and the rest of the neighboring women thought we'd slap lost our minds with our giggling and carrying on. I taught Dell how to smoke corn silk cigarettes, having learned it from watching my brothers, and she taught me how to spit into Daddy's coffee cup and stir it in with a dirty finger on the mornings he was feeling like he was going to die from a hangover and hollering for his morning brew.

We had us some times growing up on that place, I'll tell you.

Dell had a cornhusk doll some uncle had painted for her, and we'd take that doll into the woods and play house amongst the oaks and beeches. Or we'd climb the chinaberry tree and tell each other stories about what we were going to do with our lives once we grew up. When we got big enough, we'd read to each other outen the only decent books on the place, greasy dog-eared copies of Robinson Crusoe and The Count of Monte Cristo, which Daddy had bought for Cyrus in an ill-fated attempt to get him to give up his fascination with Scripture. Them books fell into other hands, namely Seth's, who practically memorized them, and then Dell and me just because we thought the language was funny and laughed to think of men running around on desert islands or chasing one another with swords and what all. It was the romance of the thing we were after.

Dell always said she was going to marry a rich man and go to San Francisco even though she didn't know where that was and live like a princess on tea and little cakes smothered in orange marmalade. She took to drinking her buttermilk with her pinky arched the way she thought proper ladies did it, and I'd like to die laughing looking at her sitting there with a butter yellow mustache and that little finger pointing to the sky. My daydreams couldn't compare with hers, so I always told her I'd be her maid, but she'd say no, I was going to run off with a sea captain and we'd go to the Sandwich Islands and look for savages like Crusoe's man Friday.

Our schooling was a catch-as-catch can affair. We went off and on to a little school about three miles down the road and learned to read and write and cipher to the rule of twelves. But school took second fiddle to work around the place. Ma would sometimes find second-hand books on her trips to Jeff City with hopes of giving us a little extra education in the wider world, but Daddy'd snag them to tear apart for the paper, which he used in the privy.

Yessir, them were fun times.

At least until Daddy joined the Klan.

You got to keep in mind that times were hard thereabouts, not that it excuses what them men did, but cash money was in short supply and there was a powerful lot of fear that the colored race, being freed from bondage, would swarm over us like a Biblical plague of locusts, eat up all the food and take what few jobs there were. Now, there weren't many coloreds in our area at the time—very few of the white folks in our neck of the woods had ever had enough holdings or cash money to make having slaves worthwhile. There had been slaves in Jeff City, of course—house servants, liverymen and the like—and a goodly number of them stayed on with their former masters once Emancipation hit. I reckon them people's lives didn't change much at all with freedom.

There were others, though, stragglers from southern Missouri and farther south, in Arkansas and Tennessee and Mississippi, who worked their way north in bedraggled bands looking for work once the big cotton plantations got busted up. Every once in a while I'd see some of them people in town, living in tarpaper shacks along the river. They were men, mostly, with some scrawny women and pot-bellied kids, and for sure they had a wild look in their eyes as if they'd gone rabid like some old 'possum. I don't know if they ever found work—probably not in them environs—or whether they landed in a big city like St. Louis or just kept drifting north. I reckon most of them died somewhere along the way of starvation or at the hands of the night riders like Daddy and his pals.

Because them blacks from cotton country purely put the menfolks round about in some kind of crazy state.

You would of thought that every ill that had befallen our country from the dawn of Creation was the fault of them poor freedmen. Some old boy would find his melon patch raided or a few ears of sweetcorn gone, and him and all his friends would go wild trying to find the culprits.

One time I remember a neighbor of ours (he lived a long mile away as the crow flies) found one of his hogs dead and gutted in a little ravine. Now, that old sow could of been brought down by coyotes or even a painter, there still being some of them big cats in the Missouri woods back then, but this neighbor took it into his head that roving blacks from Louisiana had done it to use the pig guts in some kind of hoodoo ceremony. Anyway, he whipped up the locals including my Daddy, and they went riding, looking for the culprits. I know for a fact they didn't find any Louisiana witches, but the way I heard the story, they did come upon a black boy, maybe fourteen years of age, night fishing for catfish. He told them he was the son of a cook down in Jefferson City, which would of been easy enough to prove, but that didn't make any difference. They bound him, hands and feet, tied a rope around his neck, and tossed the other end over a limb of a chestnut tree. When he'd finished kicking, they stripped him naked and rode off, leaving him hanging there as a warning to any other poor colored folk who had the nerve to be out alone at night.

It was their first lynching, but it wasn't their last.

The Kluxers were a big deal in the border states in them days, having been founded by General Nathan Bedford Forrest, a genuine Confederate hero, to guard the flower of Southern womanhood from the depredations of black men.

At least that's what Daddy's friends always said, though most of them were a passel scarier to womenfolk than any black man I ever saw. Anyway, the Klan was sort of like the Masons or the Odd Fellows, but with the extra added bonus of gang murder thrown in, and it spread like wild fire among the poor whites.

Daddy joined, along with a dozen or so of his drinking friends, the lynching of that kid serving as their initiation rite, so to speak. Next thing we knew, they were having their women cobble together robes and hoods made outen bed linens and old flour sacks so no one could see their faces when they went on their night raids. Daddy got himself elected to some job or another and took to calling himself Grand Knight Cumberland, or G. N. for short, Daddy never having learned how to spell worth a damn. He actually bought a red satin dress off a whore in Jeff City just so he could have Ma sew a cross of that red fabric onto his get-up. The rest of it he fashioned into a sort of mask for his horse, as if the old nag needed its face hid, too. The horse hated that mask and stamped and snorted and tossed its head around every time Daddy put it on, maybe because it couldn't see properly but more likely because that lady of the evening had drenched the dress in so much cheap toilet water it smelled of crushed lilacs at fifty paces even after it had soaked up a lot of horse sweat. I know for a fact that horse threw Daddy once in the middle of the night and trotted off and rubbed that mask off into some bushes, though Daddy never ever told that story on himself.

Well, before long the G. N. and his pals were out riding and raiding two, three nights a week looking for coloreds or them that sheltered them, which could be just about anyone from down-on-their-luck poor whites who hired a black hand to help bring in a crop to one of the few gentleman farmers who'd had slaves and let them stay on their place after the Emancipation. That latter bunch were special targets, since our folks didn't take kindly to rich people nohow. In a couple of cases, Daddy and his boys rode through the streets of Jeff City calling out state senators and judges demanding they turn their blacks over for mob justice. The better people just stared them down or sent them packing with a load of birdshot, but there was the occasional sissy who wouldn't stand up to them fellows and turned over their black people instead. When that happened, Daddy and the boys would haul some unfortunate Negro out to the woods, string him up, and sometimes, if they'd had enough liquor in advance, set the corpse on fire.

It was a nasty business.

Now, you would think the law would of put a stop to that, except that the sheriff of our county was one of the night riders himself, and even among the politicians there were some who, whether out of cowardice or some twisted conviction, donned the sheet and hood to help drive all blacks and them that loved them out of our country.

Whenever Daddy and his friends did an act of lynching, they'd retire to one of their number's homes toward morning, stuff their flour sack robes into their saddlebags, drink moonshine until the sun was well up, have a big breakfast, and sleep off the drunk until the middle of the afternoon, whereupon they'd all scatter for their own places. More than once Ma cooked up eggs and sausage and fried potatoes for that bunch with the certain knowledge that they had fresh blood on their hands.

It was during one of them morning moonshine parties at our place that my dear sister Dell first met Clement Handley, the youngest and handsomest of the Kluxers. Clement was blond and tall, almost six feet, which was big for a sixteen-year-old in them days, with eyes the color of a noon sky and an impish pug nose. Being barely more than a boy himself, he did most of the chores for the big shots like currying their horses and looking after their traps while they settled down to the jug. The first time them fellows came to our place at three or four o'clock in the morning, it was Clement who knocked politely on the door and asked Ma if please, ma'am, could he have a jug of water and a couple of jelly glasses since some of his more fastidious friends didn't want to drink from the communal jug. He was so pleasant and smiled so sweetly that us girls, hiding behind the old gray curtain that separated our sleeping quarters from the kitchen, set up a giggling that put Ma in a pure rage. She took after us with a paddle once that boy had sauntered off with his glasses, and that licking was enough to convince me to stay in bed the next time he came to the house looking for anything.

Not so with Dell.

She was bit by the love bug, and bit hard, and from the looks of it, he was hit just as bad the first time he laid eyes on her. Clement took to hanging around our place like a moonstruck calf most of the time, whether on Klan business or not. It got so he'd do most of the chores around the place if you'd let him, which was all right with me, but Ma took offense and more than once shooed him away with the business end of the old shotgun we kept over the lintel.

Now, I got to admit right here that I was just about as taken with that boy as Dell was, he was that good looking, slim of waist and broad of shoulder and all. I teased Dell unmercifully about him, but I had more than one dream about him myself. He, of course, saw nothing in me, being that I was scrawny and still more tomboy than growing up woman.

For her part, Ma didn't like Clement at all, partly I suppose on account of his hanging around with the Klan fellows.

Ma wanted no part of the Klan, and she and Daddy had had words about that early on: she'd said her piece and kept her tongue after that, though she usually sat thumbing her old family Bible when the men were all sheeted up and on the warpath. She didn't like black folks any more than most of the poor whites in our country did, but she didn't take to lynching them, neither, and she was mighty concerned that somebody with gumption was going to try blasting them Klansmen outen the saddle when they came calling. Of course, she didn't want to see Daddy burn in Hell for his misdeeds, but more to the point, if he was dead or maimed, he wasn't going to be much use around the place, and there was a lot that needed doing that a woman couldn't handle by herself.

Mostly, though, Ma didn't like Clement because it turned out she was a pretty fair judge of character.

She was slap certain that Clement's overfondness for strong drink was going to lead to ruin. Now, that was a failing of almost all of them fellows, except that in Clement's case, he barely had his growth and probably hadn't yet lifted a razor to his chin. Still, he'd hang around the campfire down the hill from our house and fetch and tote for the men and sip from the jug right along with them, and by the time the evening's festivities rolled to a close, he'd be retching in the grass or be passed out cold as a corpse somewhere.

The last thing she mistrusted about him was the sugary way he was always saying "yes'm" to her or tipping his hat or holding the door when she was struggling to wrestle with a tub full of wash that needed hanging on the line. What others might of seen as politeness, Ma took for mockery. We didn't see it, Dell and me, but Ma sure did.

Not that it had much effect over the long haul. Dell was smitten, and that was that. Before long, them two would start disappearing for hours at a time, and Dell clammed up to me about what she was doing on them long walks she said they took. I figured I knew, since she usually came back with bits of straw or leaf-mold in her hair and her dress all wrinkled as if it had been twisted off. I guess she figured I knew, too, because she'd wag her finger at me and make me swear honest Injun cross my heart and hope to die that I'd keep my mouth shut around Ma.

Daddy was another matter altogether. He sure as hell saw

what was going on, and although he was more or less the reason Clement had shown up on our doorstep in the first place, he decided he didn't like it one bit, which struck me as passing strange since losing Dell off the place would mean one less mouth to feed.

But he didn't like it. Not at all.

One night after a Klan raid, when ten or twelve of them men were hunkered around a bonfire, Daddy lit into Clement and started slapping him around. They were making so much noise that I could hear 'em clean up to the house, and rousing Dell, the two of us snuck out to see what was going on.

It wasn't a pretty sight. By the time we crept up close enough to see, Clement was bleeding out of both nostrils. He kept backing away from Daddy, fending off the blows with his forearms held in front of his face, but Daddy kept pressing, moving him around that fire as relentlessly as an old bull will keep after a yearling. The other men mostly sat there and took it in, pulling on their sour mash, some offering shouted encouragement to one combatant or another, some laying bets on how long Clement could keep standing against the onslaught.

Well, it was more than poor Dell could take. Even though she didn't have a robe over her nightshirt, she charged straight into that circle of men and lit into Daddy's backside as ferociously as he was lighting into Clement. Her blows didn't have any power behind them, of course, but she rat-a-tat-tatted on Daddy as hard as ever she could. It must of stung at least a little, for he turned on her, blinked in amazement as her blows landed on his chest instead of his back, and with one slow sideswipe, backhanded her acrost the mouth and sent her sprawling into the weeds.

By this time, Clement had got some wind back in him, and when Daddy started sputtering and wagging his finger at Dell, Clement tackled the old man around the legs, pitching him face first into the embers of the campfire.

You never heard such a howling in all your life as Daddy put up. He came up outen them coals like he'd been shot from a gun, kicked free of Clement, and grabbed a chunk of firewood the size of a grown man's lower leg and swung that thing straight at Clement's head. He'd have brained him for certain, but Clement saw it coming and dodged just enough to take some of the blow on his upraised left arm.

The sound of the bones in his forearm breaking was like a gun going off, I'll tell you, but it wasn't nothing compared to the yelping that Clement let out.

The ruckus seemed to stupefy Daddy for some reason. Clement crawled away dragging his arm behind him. Dell was up and circling around Dad, going for her beau to comfort him while the rest of that passel of white trash just sat there laughing their heads off. Daddy blinked, grinned at the laughing men, and dropped his club at his feet.

"Boys," he said, "I could use me a shot of the jug." Then he sat down, took the proffered keg of moonshine, drained off a couple of mouthfuls, and wiped his grimy face with his shirtsleeve. "Dell, you get that little bastard outen here before I bust t'other arm," he said to my sister, then he laughed, took another drink, and plumb forgot them kids were even there.

Dell helped Clement up to the house, where Ma set the arm as best she could and told him to get on home, and when he got there, to stay put. That boy done as he was told, but not before he kissed Dell full on the mouth right there in front of Ma, who shuffled me off to bed as fast as ever she could so I wouldn't see no more of that.

It's one of the peculiarities of humankind that we can watch one person brutalize another and not think much about it, but if two people show affection, we get all spooky inside and go to clucking about morals and such.

Anyhow, I went to bed and waited for Dell so we could talk, but it was hours and hours before she crawled under the old quilt next to me.

"I'm leavin'," she said as quietly as she could, and I knew she meant it. "Me and Clement are going to elope tomorrow."

"You're not but fourteen," I said, and she didn't even try to answer that.

Instead, all she said was "We're going to St. Joe."

And that was that. At first light, she was gone.

Ma cried when I told her Dell had run off, but after her first spell of weeping, she made her peace with it. I figure she was as sorry to see Dell go as I was, probably sorrier since she had such a poor opinion of the bridegroom, but I imagine she at least took some comfort in her daughter being away from the old man. Daddy didn't even know she was gone for a couple of days on account of his hangover kept him in his own bed, and when he did find out, all he said was something about good riddance to bad rubbish, which made Ma so mad I thought she was going to brain him with a hunk of stove wood, but apparently she thought better of it, more's the pity.

In any case, we didn't hear from Dell for the longest time, and of course Clement didn't ride with them Kluxers any more. When we did hear, it was from a drummer passing through who said he'd seen Dell and Clement over to Sedalia, and they'd told him they were on their way to St. Joe.

For my part, I was beside myself, I can tell you that. Losing Dell was like having part of me cut off and thrown away. I didn't have nobody I could talk to, nobody who'd make me laugh or help make the hours of hard chores go by. I took to pining like a sick calf until my clothes, which I never did exactly fill out, practically fell off my scrawny frame. I didn't care if I ate nor slept, and more than once, I just went to wandering and found myself miles from home without even knowing how I'd gotten there. Grief is a funny thing that way, and I was for sure grieving.

Ma said if I didn't snap outen it, I'd waste away to nothing, and she wasn't about to lose two of her girls just because one was foolish enough to run off with a damn idjit who'd sweet talked her into going to St. Joe, which was practically in Kansas it was so far away! That's what she called Clement ever after: a damn idjit. And of course she was right, the way things turned out, though I'm getting ahead of myself there.

Anyhow, I was pining one night, sitting at a little plank table out behind the house watching the summertime stars wink on and feeling sorry for myself when Daddy came outside and stood acrost from me. Now, you might think I blamed him for Dell being gone, but I didn't. He wasn't responsible for Dell and Clement doing a stupid thing just because he was a mean sonofabitch when he was drinking. The way them two were mooning after one another, it was bound to happen sooner or later, and all Daddy did was put a match to the kindling, so to speak. That's how I really felt about it.

Daddy apparently didn't know that.

"You'll be running off soon, too, I reckon. To get away from the likes of me."

He said it as he towered over me, blocking my view of the bright evening star and the first grayish smear of Milky Way.

"No sir," I said.

"Hell you won't."

"I ain't going nowhere."

"Yeah, you are, Missy," he said. He hadn't called me that more'n twice in my life, and both times he was fixing to wail into me with the razor strop.

"No, sir," I repeated. I was so low, mourning Dell and all, that I didn't even tense up for the blow I figured was coming, but the blow that fell was more than ever I could of imagined.

Daddy sniffed and spat tobacco juice into the dust at his feet. "Well, just in case you're thinking of doing such a thing, you can stop thinking about it right now, because you're getting married come Sunday."

I must of looked at him like he was speaking Chinese. I

for certain remember exactly what he said and how he said it to this day.

"I ain't getting married," I said with what must of sounded like a giggle.

"Yes, you are," he said right back. "To Jack Ross. I took a brace of mules in trade." Then he spun on his heel and went into the house and banged the door shut behind him.

Jack Ross!

The very words made my blood run cold.

Jack was a Kluxer, a pal of Daddy's, a tall, lean man with broad shoulders and mostly tattered rags for clothes and the singlemost ugly human face I had ever seen. I guessed him to be pushing forty, nearly as old as Daddy, but his face carried a lot more years than that. He had a black hank of hair that stood up every whichaway like it was sculpted outen bear fat but mostly fell over a greasy forehead the color of old saddle leather. His eyebrows were even blacker and grew together in the middle over deep-set light gray eyes that darted back and forth like a coyote's. His nose was potato shaped, having been busted in various brawls more times than he could count. But the one feature you noticed first and last was the angry red welt of scar that zigzagged from his left ear acrost his cheek to the place where his upper lip should of been. It was a saber scar, given him by a Yankee officer at Pea Ridge, and as I heard the story, he liked to died from that cut, though more from the infection than the wound itself. The blade had gone clear to the bone, and years later, when I knew him, that scar still leaked blood and pus now and again. When it did, old Jack smelled like death itself. Under that cut, he wore a stubble of beard that never seemed to grow more than a quarter of an inch and never went away, neither.

Jack Ross couldn't read or write or cipher more than just to add or subtract, and he smelled like pigs when he didn't smell like putrefaction, which only made sense on account of he kept a hog lot up against the shed he called home. He fed the hogs on the mash left over from his whiskey still, old potato peelings, rancid scraps of meat (most of which was likely them hogs' older brothers and sisters), and whatever other garbage was handy. He worked ten or fifteen acres of land for corn to fuel his still when he wasn't riding with Daddy or sharing his squeezings with whatever friends he had thereabouts.

In short, Jack Ross was pretty much the last person on earth I wanted to hitch my wagon to, so to speak, even if I'd of wanted to get hitched at all, which I most certainly did not. Hell, I wasn't but a month past thirteen!

So there I sat, looking at the place where Daddy had been, trying to come up with words to tell him what I thought of the idea. I remember thinking I ought to jump up and light out into the woods and be gone. Better to be eaten alive by a painter than be hooked up with ugly old Jack Ross.

Then I heard Ma and Daddy arguing, and my name was a part of it, which meant the old man had told her what he'd gone and done. I couldn't make out most of it, but I'll never forget the final words my Daddy spoke on the subject: "There ain't no use in arguing, woman. I sold her fair and square and that's that."

So I was sold. By my own father. To the cruelest looking human being I'd ever laid eyes on.

Oh, I should run, I told myself, but it was like I was stuck to the spot. I just sat there, not thinking because I didn't know what to think, until the very dew began to settle on me. Ma came to the door and asked me, sort of timid like, if I was all right, and when I told her I was, she let me be. I sat there until long after the lanterns were out and then stood stiffly, did my business in the outhouse, and went inside. I could of caught my death of cold and probably hoped I would, but of course I didn't, you never being able to get sick when you want to. I crawled into my lumpy bed, started to say my prayers, and then changed my mind on account of it was pretty clear that God had written me off as a lost cause, and if He'd given up on me, it seemed only right that I should give up on Him.

Right there, I was plumb disgusted with myself for not having taken off the second Daddy told me what he'd done, but lying there on my corn shuck mattress, I determined that fussing over lost opportunities wouldn't keep me from finding new ones.

I suppose I wanted to join up with Dell and Clement, though I don't recall thinking exactly that, but I know I wanted to go west, out of the reach of Daddy and what I took to be the worst fate that could befall a girl, namely being the wedded wife of Jack Ross.

I was up at the crack of dawn, even before our banty rooster decided it was time to announce the coming of the day. I had slept nary a wink, and I'd come up with a plan. I went about my morning chores, feeding the chickens, collecting the eggs, helping Ma with the griddle cakes as if nothing had happened, but all the while scheming my escape.

Now it was obvious that Ma hadn't slept much more than I had, and when Daddy brought in the morning pail of fresh milk and sat down for his coffee and corn cakes, she slapped them things down in front of him with a bang.

"What's that for?" he barked, mopping up spilled coffee with the corner of his dirty blue bandana.

She spun on him, glared for a minute, then turned her back. "There ain't going to be no wedding, you old scoundrel. Not while I got a breath in my body."

"Like hell there ain't!" he shot back.

She just stiffened and stalked outen the room.

He pushed a wad of breakfast into his mouth, slurped coffee to wash it down, and pushed his chair back. "Come back here, God damn it!" he shouted, which for all his bad traits was the first and only time I ever heard him take the name of the Lord in vain inside the house.

She hollered something back that I couldn't hear. He must of, though, for he reddened in the face, threw his chair against the wall, and pounded into the parlor after her.

Well, there commenced such a caterwauling that I wasn't sure the house was going to be standing when it was over. Them two went at it hammer and tong, each giving as good as he or she got. First one would yell, then the other, then there would be a slap, then a groan. Things started to fly, and what little decent crockery we had commenced to exploding against the walls. Through it all, I could hear my name, almost like a scream.

Then they were back in the kitchen. Daddy had Ma by the hair, pulling her toward the door. His face was so red he looked fit to bust a blood vessel. She was clawing at him, going for his eyes, but she was neither big enough nor strong enough to do much damage. A bluish welt was already coming on the side of her face.

"Damn you woman, I'll tan your hide till there's no to-morrow," Daddy was wheezing as he pulled her toward the door.

And that's when I said it.

"Leave her be, Daddy, and I'll marry Jack Ross."

Just like that. Something inside me, even at that tender age, knew it was the only way to keep Ma from getting beat so bad she might be crippled or worse.

Them two stopped stock still and looked at me as if I was someone they didn't even recognize.

Ma came to her senses first, of course.

"You'll do no such thing, child. Marry that filthy old..."

Daddy raised his hand as if to cuff her into silence, but I beat him to the punch, pulling myself up to my full four foot ten and sticking my chin out as if daring the old man to hit me instead. "I said I would and I will. If'n only to get away from you, Daddy. Any man would sell his own children and beat his wife ain't fit to be a husband nor father."

He blinked, started to say something, and lowered his hand. "You sass me like that and I'll kill you," he said, and from the tone, I was pretty sure he meant it.

"Then you'll have to give Mister Ross them two mules back, won't you?"

Where I came up with the pure intestinal fortitude to spout off like that, I'll never know. I guess it was Ma sticking up for me the way she did. I must of cut quite a figure, standing there toe-to-toe with that old man, the both of us glaring at each other. I do recall feeling the sweat come to my armpits and bead out on my forehead, and there wasn't no doubt that my fortitude was beginning to wilt the longer I stood there.

"You'll marry him?" Daddy said at last, and it was definitely a question.

"I said I would."

He let go of Ma altogether. "See, then, Mother? She'll do as she's told."

Ma started to say something, then got all white in the face and bolted outside. I could hear her retching in the yard, but Daddy just sat back down like nothing had happened and commenced to shoveling them griddle cakes once more. I followed Ma out into the yard.

"It'll be all right," I said, standing over her.

She looked up at me, wiping her mouth with a corner of her apron. "You don't have to do this," she said. "I won't allow it."

I took her hand and pressed it to my breast. "I give my word, didn't I? Daddy did, and now so have I."

We Cumberlands were a coarse lot, but our word, once given, was a sacred oath. I stood there and crossed my heart with my right index finger and kissed it to seal the bond. Then my knees gave out and I fell to the grass and into Ma's arms and the two of us spent the next hour that way, rocking and hugging and knowing the world was about to change completely for the both of us.

So it went until Sunday, with me being in a sort of trance. I did my chores, washed my face, and helped Ma hang the clothes or knead the bread without saying two words the whole day long. Of course, she did the same while Daddy went about his business as if there wasn't nothing wrong in the whole wide world.

When the Sabbath dawned, Ma was up early and did me the kindness of washing my hair and plaiting it into pigtails which she wound into a bun and piled on top of my head. She even gave me a store-bought gray velvet dress, though of course it was one she'd bought for herself second or third hand to wear to church. Somehow during that week, she'd reworked it to get rid of the bustle and snug it up to fit my scrawny frame at least a little.

At ten o'clock, we were ready. Daddy was in his one decent pair of trousers and the cotton shirt Ma always scrubbed and blued so it was white as could be for church even if he never did wear it there. He was out pacing up and down in the yard, checking his pocket watch every ten seconds.

I found myself hoping against hope that Jack Ross had forgotten about me and that somehow I was to be spared.

But at 10:15, there he came, jouncing up the road in a shabby buckboard being pulled by the sorriest swayback mouse-colored gelding I ever saw and with a pained-looking Preacher Goodnight riding alongside on a dun that didn't seem none too happy about the company, neither, though that may have been because the good pastor tipped in somewhere over three hundred pounds. Daddy grinned from ear to ear, but mostly because he saw them two mules trotting along after, their halter ropes tied to the buckboard.

My heart sank to a lower place than it'd ever been before that moment.

Daddy turned a critical eye on me and Ma. "Girl, you git a smile on that puss of your'n, or I'll slap daylights outen you," he said, as if he'd plumb forgotten our set-to earlier in the week.

Ma squared her shoulders and glared at him, her eyes flashing above the bruises still plain on her face. "Levi James Cumberland, you touch a hair on that child's head on her wedding day, and I'll skin you with a rusty knife and feed your sorry bones to the pigs. What you done to her already is punishment enough for a lifetime."

Daddy's Adam's apple bobbed up and down at that and after a couple of seconds I could see his eyes darken in anger. "Now, Adelphia," he said.

But Ma wasn't done, and if she saw that gloom gathering behind his eyes, it apparently didn't worry her none. "Don't you 'Adelphia' me. You're bound to marry off this child, and I'm standing for it only because she won't have to put up with the likes of you never again. Just like she said."

I confess I turned away from my parents to take a furtive look at Mr. Jack Ross as he clumb down from his wagon and advanced acrost our yard, a clutch of wildflowers in his huge hand. No matter what we'd said in the heat of anger, I reckoned that both Ma and me must be touched in the head to think there was any good to come of me shoving off the home place and into the arms of that blackguard.

Jack stopped a few yards short of us and touched a dirty finger to his mop of unruly hair.

"'Morning, folks," he said. Then he looked at me and smiled, his mostly missing lip widening to show mossy teeth behind a bristle of beard. "'Morning, Miss Eva."

I slunk back a few feet, but it was Ma who stopped me and gave me a little shove.

"You tell Mister Ross good morning, Eva Rae," she said. I hoped it was mostly for the benefit of the preacher, but I have to admit she suddenly had a look on her face that told me she was somehow getting into the spirit of the thing. Women just seem to go to pieces around weddings, even one as truly of the shotgun variety as this one.

Anyway, I done as I was told, though I doubt anyone could hear more than a mumble outen me.

It was Pastor Goodnight who busted up that little tableau by dang near falling off his horse and staggering up the hill toward us. I could see his face was bloodshot and guessed—rightly, it turned out, once I could smell him—that it was some of Jack Ross's white lightning that had paid for the services he was about to render. He puffed and wheezed just walking them few steps and sort of leaned on Daddy when they shook hands, then he greeted my mother but fairly ignored me.

"Are we ready to get this show on the road?" he asked once he'd caught his breath sufficient.

Jack Ross nodded. Ma didn't say a word, and I was scared to. Daddy said something about waiting a minute, and for a split second I figured maybe I'd been saved by Daddy having an attack of common sense, but it turned out he just wanted to go over to the Ross wagon and inspect the mules to make sure he was getting what he'd bargained for. Satisfied, he nodded to Pastor Goodnight, and the wedding commenced.

What can I say about them five minutes of my life?

Ma lined me up on Jack Ross's left hand and turned us both to face the preacher. He read something outen his Bible, though about all I could hear was the pounding of my own heart. At one point, Jack said "I do," and a few seconds later, Daddy poked me in the ribs to get me to say the same. Then the pastor asked us to join hands, and once again I did as I was told, letting my fingers disappear into that big grimy fist. His hand was all hot and sweaty, and it dawned on me right there that he was at least as scared as I was.

"Be damned," I said out loud, which brought the pastor

up short.

"Pardon, young lady?"

"Nothing," I said. "Sorry."

"Well, you should be," that liquored up old fraud huffed. He wiped his lips with the back of his hands as if he was too dry to continue, but continue he did.

Then came the moment: he laid his own palm on top of our two joined hands, or more rightly Jack's with mine hid inside, and turned his eyes to the heavens. "With the power invested in me as a deacon in the Baptist church and a notary public for the State of Missourah, I hereby pronounce you man and wife."

Just like that, I was Mrs. Jack Ross. I liked to peed my pants.

"You may kiss the bride."

Jack turned that ugly visage toward me, and I thought my heart was going to stop. But his eyes only met mine for a split second before they danced away toward the pole barn and the woods yonder. "No'm. We can do that later." Then he let go of my hand and wiped his on his trousers.

The rest of that Sunday morning was a blur. Daddy got out his jug and offered pulls to the groom and the pastor while Ma brought out ham and cold chicken and fresh baked bread for the wedding dinner. She leaked a few tears now and again, but when she did, she just whipped out a hankie and blew her nose and went on serving the menfolks. Jack ate like a starving man and the pastor tucked away several platefuls of victuals himself, though mostly he sucked at the jug like he hadn't had a drop to drink in a month, which even then I found right peculiar for a Baptist, that denomination being given to teetotaling and finding fault with just about every-thing a normal person considers mildly enjoyable. Of course, I wasn't finding nothing about that affair enjoyable in the least, and even when Ma brought out sliced peaches and honey and cold buttermilk a little later, that dessert having always been my favorite, just the smell of it turned my stomach.

Then, suddenly, it was time to leave. Daddy unhitched his mules and shook hands with Jack Ross to seal the deal, Ma gave me a bundle of all my worldly possessions tucked inside a clean flour sack tied up with a piece of purple velvet rope she must of bought in Jeff City as a wedding present, and Jack led me down to the wagon. My knees were like rubber bands, and it was all I could do not to upchuck down the front of my gray dress. I know I never said good-by to Ma, though I surely intended to, which was more than I was bound to do for Daddy. Right then, I didn't never want to lay eyes on that rascal again in my entire life, which I didn't figure was going to be too long, given the appearance and smell of my new husband.

Jack Ross lifted me onto the seat of that wagon, jumped up alongside, and gave that old mousy horse a crack with the whip and off we went, headed for what, for better or worse, was bound to be my new home.

I didn't look back, which is pretty much the story of my life since.

Mrs. Jack Ross

"Y OU TAKE A BATH RIGHT NOW, Mr. Ross, and use the lye soap this time!" Those were honest-to-God my first words to my new husband.

I fairly shouted it at him as I stood in the middle of that tumbledown shack of his. I was squared up to my full height, and though he towered over me, that didn't stop my tongue-lashing. Truth to tell, I was scared outen my wits by that man, and giving him sass was about the only way I could think of to fight back at what I figured was about to be my demise.

To my everlasting surprise, that big greasy hulk of a man just stepped back, blinked, and said "Yes'm."

"And leave that union suit outside so's the ants can pick it clean of nits," I was bold enough to add, though my voice quavered when I did.

"Yes'm," he said again, right politely, and with that, he turned and headed for the lean-to that made up what passed for a kitchen, porch, slaughtering pen, and laundry.

Since I'd started this thing, I knew it was up to me to finish it, so I pumped a bucket of water from the well in the front yard and carried it inside and hoisted it up onto the stove, which was already glowing cherry hot on account of Jack had promised me a wedding supper, which from the looks of the fixings in his larder was going to amount to fatback and fry bread.

"You got any decent clothes?" I called out after him.

"This here's my best," he said.

"Toss 'em in here, then, and I'll boil 'em once I get the bathwater het."

"Yes'm," he said again. There was a long pause before he added. "But, Missy, what'll I wear while they're a-washing?"

"Don't you got no other clothes?"

"Sure, but they're... a little ripe."

I mumbled something under my breath that isn't fit to write down and told him he could keep his trousers until I could get the rest of his rags clean.

Now you have to understand that we weren't hardly past my folks's front gate when I commenced imagining that he was playing all meek and mild and shy because he had his heart set on ravishing the daylights outen me, and this bathing and laundering was about all I could think of to hold off that dreaded moment as long as I could, short of murdering either him or myself. Ravishment was something me and Dell had talked about many a dark night as we huddled under the covers, her thinking it was so romantic it was something to swoon over—she having Clement in mind for doing the ravishing, of course—and me thinking it was largely disgusting. I'd seen pigs and horses doing it, and of course the rabbits we kept hutched for a quick wintertime meal when game was scarce, and as far as I could tell, there wasn't nothing romantic about it. Especially with a foul beast like Jack Ross.

The water on the stove came to a simmer, and I hauled it gingerly into the lean-to, taking care to keep my eyes averted. Even so, I caught a glimpse of bare back and buttocks, all pinkish white like a newborn piglet and pretty much a surprise compared to the grime and sunburnt leathery look of the public parts of the man. He mumbled something like an apology when I poured the water, then I skedaddled on outen there.

As that man bathed, and it was probably the first time since the previous Christmas, unless I missed my guess, I took a look around my new home.

To say it was a bachelor place would do injustice to just about any bachelor you ever met. Pure and simple, the hogs were living as well if not better outside.

The place smelled of grease and smoke and tobacco juice spit on the floor, but over it all was the odor of mice and God knows what other vermin. There were mouse tracks in the dust and grime on the floor and little mouse turds in any corner you cared to shine a light. I supposed a hole the size of a human fist in the peak of the roof was there to let out the smoke, there being no proper chimney except for the stove pipe jammed through the wall, but that hole was plenty big enough to let in bats and bugs of all descriptions. When I moved the water bucket, a roach the size of my thumb skittered for the darkness, and I took it for Gospel without even looking that the ticking on the swayback bed was alive with bedbugs or worse. It made my flesh crawl to think about lying in that infested bedding, not even counting the notion of who I was going to be lying there with.

What few belongings Jack Ross had looked to be plumb wore out, and everything in the place was covered with greasy gray filth. The only things I could spy that looked at all decent were a Sharp's carbine hanging on a nail over the door and a carefully folded bundle of muslin that appeared to be somewhat clean, and in fact only yellowed some from its original white. I lifted a corner to see what it was, suspecting that maybe he'd got me some kind of a wedding present, but it was his Kluxer sheet.

I should of known.

I confess the first thought that ran through my head was that if ever a place needed a woman's touch, this was it.

The second thought was that it would be a kindness for

the neighbors for miles around if someone burned that miserable shanty to the ground, with him in it.

I remember thinking that maybe setting just such a fire was the way I could get outen there and save myself from the vile acts I knew that man yonder was about to commit.

So for a moment, I actually considered arson if not murder, and even though I knew nothing about juries and such at that tender age, I figured there wasn't a right thinking person within a hundred miles who would hold it against me.

But murder wasn't in me that day, nor burning neither. Instead, I busied myself trying to clean up what I could with his homemade soap the color and roughness of the coarse wood ashes it was made from. I straightened the few chipped bits of crockery, rinsed the sludge outen the tinware coffee cups, and scraped the congealed grease off the sideboard where he'd last supped. Then I sat in an old straight-backed cane chair and waited, smoothing my gray wedding dress with hands that begun to tremble the minute they stopped working.

I should run, I thought. Run away as hard and fast as ever I could. Maybe I could hire on as a scullery maid in Jeff City or somewhere. If he found me there, I'd run away again, to someplace farther away. Head for St. Joe and Dell, or just about anywhere I could find civilized people.

I fancied myself with a group of settlers heading west, acrost the expanse of prairie, maybe even riding in a railroad car, listening to the sing of the rails as we moved farther and farther from the hell-hole that was my present condition.

Maybe I'd even go all the way to San Francisco and meet that sea captain of my daydreams...

"Miss Eva Rae, you certainly look nice."

Them words like to scared the be-Jeezus outen me, spoken as soft as they were. My head jerked up, and there he stood, with wet hair slicked back and his face still all whiskery and scarred but the patches that weren't covered with hair were scrubbed pink as a baby's bottom. He wore the same dirty trousers he was married in, as I'd told him to, but he'd left his faded red underwear outside, so the suspenders were pulled up over naked shoulders that were white as snow except for a few little spikes of stiff black hair. He smiled at me, showing teeth where lip ought to of been, then let his gaze fall to the floor.

"I reckon you ain't never been with a man before," he said. "I mean, not that way." He stammered when he said it.

I tried to say that no, I had not, but my mouth was suddenly as dry as an August hayfield and no words came out.

"Well," he continued, "I ain't been with a woman, neither." The eyes came up and met mine for about a quarter of a second before darting away. "Leastwise not in many and many a year. I mean, I had plenty of chances before the war, but once..." His hand drifted up to the scar, and when he spoke again, it was from behind his fingers as if he was trying to hide the cruel ugliness. "Once I got outen that Pea Ridge business with my wound, well, it never come up again, so to speak." He reddened at the neck from embarrassment and shifted his weight from one bare foot to the other.

The shyness in the man struck me as the most pitiful thing I ever did see.

"I know we're hitched and all," he said, but mostly to the wall instead of me, "but just so you know, I ain't going to force myself on you on account of I know this wadn't your idea nor your pleasure. Maybe once we get to know each other a bit..." But he let that trail off and after a few seconds, he turned on his heel. "I guess I'll take care of the pigs," he said, and hustled on outside.

"Bedamned," I said right out loud for the second time that day. I felt as if the weight of the world had been lifted from my shoulders, if only for the moment. There I was, just weeks past thirteen, one minute scared outen my pantaloons by that jasper, and the next feeling sorry for him. Besides, I'd never had a grown man treat me like a regular grown-up before, let alone a man as old and otherwise scary as Jack Ross.

So, "bedamned," I said yet again, and for want of something better to do, I unwrapped the package Ma had sent along, slipped outen that wedding dress, which I folded carefully, and into the gingham shift I wore when doing inside work. Then I commenced to seeing what decent grub there might be to fix my husband and me for dinner.

And that's how we spent our wedding night: him scrubbing himself plumb raw again after messing with the hogs, and me cooking up some sorry biscuits and a couple slices of ham. Then he helped me clean up the dishes and made a pallet of clean straw to lie on under the window where I could get a cooling breeze or two. He allowed as how I was welcome in his bed any time I wanted, though he understood I'd want to clean it up some, and anyhow he wasn't going to press the issue. With that, he outened the kerosene lantern, clumb into bed, and within a couple of seconds was snoring fit to wake the dead.

I laid there on that straw for a long time, listening to the rasp-rasp of his snoring, the whine of a couple of skeeters, and the soft scrape and shuffle of the mice as they went about their nightly business. Once again, I thought of Dell with her beautiful man and me with my ugly one. I suppose I cried myself to sleep, though I don't remember for certain, no matter how clear the rest of the memories of that day still are.

So it went for some weeks. Bit by bit, I worked at tidying up that place. My hands grew callus where they never had before, and the sinews in my arms hardened and tightened with all the lifting and hauling I did to get most of the trash cleared from yard and house. Jack slaughtered and dressed a brace of hogs and I made head cheese and scraped casings for sausage and helped him hang the hams in the stone smokehouse out near the edge of the woods close by his still. I boiled his bedding and hung the ticking over a clothesline strung up between a couple of maple trees and beat the daylights outen the blankets with a corngrass broom and let the chickens feed on the wildlife the beating scared up. I scrubbed floor until my knees and elbows felt like they were on fire and darned socks and patched trousers until Jack Ross looked like a clown but at least didn't have any holes for decent folks to cluck over.

To my surprise, my new husband proved to be a fairly industrious man, though to be blunt I figure to this day that it was because my activity shamed him into it. He helped clean the trash from the yard, built a new and better fence to keep the hogs in, put up a decent log chimney, and hoed the corn and put up a scarecrow we dressed in the tattered rags he'd once have worn to town without thinking anything of it. He took to calling me "Missus," and never laid a hand on me except to give me a boost if I needed something off an impossibly high shelf above the stove. In them first months, he never left the place to go riding with the Klan, neither, though to be honest, I've always figured he thought if he left me alone, I wouldn't be there when he came back, and in the first few weeks he would of had reason to worry, though by our second month together, I'd pretty well settled in to my lot in life. Though hardly happy with being Mrs. Jack Ross, there wasn't much I could do besides accepting the fact of it. And as he still hadn't yet tried to have his way with me, I couldn't rightly complain on that account.

Come August, when what tomatoes the raccoons hadn't eaten were about ripe and the pickles were in the crock, we made our first visit to Ma and Daddy so I could collect some jars and lids for the canning and needles and thread and maybe a half bolt of good wool to sew up some decent things for the coming cold spell. I hadn't figured I'd ever set foot on that ground again, with what Daddy had done to me, but once a body gets used to the day-to-day circumstances of living, you just make your peace with whatever it is that put you in them circumstances in the first place. Leastwise, that's the way I settled it in my mind, so when we rode up the long trail to my old home, I was looking forward to the visit without holding much of a grudge.

It was a Saturday afternoon, hottish, with the locusts putting up a hellacious racket in the woods and bumblebees working the first of the black-eyed Susies peeking outen the ditches. Daddy was waiting for us, ensconced in his rocking chair in the middle of the front yard like some lord high ruler of the manor, with a jug sitting on a milk stool and another straight-back chair waiting for my man. Daddy didn't so much as give me a "by your leave" but what he offered Jack a drink and a sit while I got on with the job of unhitching the rig and taking the horses out back to cool. Them mules Jack Ross paid for me were back there, and neither of them looked to have done a lick of work since the day they arrived on Daddy's place, which meant that they'd gotten a better end of the bargain than I had. Anyhow, I watered the horses and went inside to help Ma with the supper.

It was a pleasant enough afternoon, up to a point. The menfolk et like they hadn't had a bite of food in six weeks, which meant any conversation was left up to Ma and me. We weren't either of us much for gossip, so the talk was mostly about Sunday school, which Ma had taken up teaching (mostly to get Daddy's goat, or so I believed) and me asking Ma for recipes for pickle relish and what spices she used when she canned crabapples and such like. Then the men went outside to resume their drinking and Ma and I did the dishes. I should of noticed the way Ma was looking at me as I carried the plates to the slop bucket or stretched to fetch down a case of mason jars, but I never tumbled to what was in her mind.

Anyway, not until Daddy came to the door shortly before Jack and I were set to go and stood there, leering at me.

"So when's the little one a-coming, Sister?" he asked me

with a little hiccup. "Seems like you'd be a-showing by now."

"Ain't nothing to show," I said right back at him, and I felt the prickly heat of anger and embarrassment along the back of my neck.

"How you know?" he asked. "You two've had plenty of time to get a young'un in the works, 'specially with ol' Jack having been backed up for so damned many years he prob'ly could of gotten a knot hole in a fence post in a family way."

With that he laughed, but Ma fairly came outen her shoes. I swear she leaped at him, her fists raised to chest height. "Levi, you take that trash mouth outen this house this instant!" she barked.

He only grinned and hiccupped again. "Aw, relax, old woman. I'm just trying to figger when that girl yonder is going to make us grandparents."

"She ain't. Not yet."

"Well, why the hell not?"

"Because they've not yet slept in the marriage bed!"

Now, I have to tell you, how she could of known that just by looking at me—or maybe it was by looking at Jack—I never did know. But the effect it had on Daddy was the same as if he'd been pole-axed. He commenced to clenching his fists, and I could see the muscles knot in his cheeks like he was fit to grind his teeth down to the nubs. He tried to say something, but no words came out, he was that mortified. He looked at me, and all I could do was look back, but there must of been something in my look that told him Ma had the story right. Them jaw muscles worked some more, then he spun on his heel and headed back out to the yard at a fair lope.

"Oh, Jesusmaryjoseph," Ma said. "I done it now." And with that, she picked up a good sized cast-iron frying pan and lit out after Daddy with me trailing along behind.

By the time we got there, them two men were already going at it like a couple of bobcats. Daddy was flailing out at Jack, striking him hard with his fists, but the blows were delivered hammer-style and not the way a prizefighter would punch. Jack had back-pedaled a few steps. That poor man had a look of pure bewilderment on his ruined face, but I could see there was anger starting to boil, too, as he fended off Daddy's blows. After a couple of seconds, he swung back, just once, and hit Daddy on the side of the head with a blow that I swear would of stunned a horse. Daddy reeled, fell back, and then lit into Jack again like nothing had happened. By this time, Ma was on Daddy, hanging on his back, holding on with one arm and swinging that skillet with the other in an attempt to knock some sense into him. On top of that, she was screaming something, but in the general hubbub, I couldn't rightly tell what it was.

Jack landed another blow, then another, and what with the weight on his back and the thudding of the skillet on his skull, Daddy was slowing down some. He shrugged Ma off, but stood there glowering at Jack rather than trying to hammer him again. Ma stopped swinging, too, and tried to catch her breath.

"What the hell's that all about, ol' man?" Jack asked as the two of them stood there, their chests heaving.

"You ain't bedded my girl!" Daddy spluttered, and it sure looked as if he was ready to start swinging again.

Poor Jack looked at me as if I'd just sold him into white slavery. Ma must of noticed, for she piped right up.

"Eva Rae never said a thing, Mr. Ross. It's me that said it. It's just a mother's way of knowing."

Now, she probably should of quit without saying that last part, because it sort of perked Daddy up and he commenced moving in on Jack again, swinging his fists back and forth. But this time, Jack was ready for him. He punched out a little short jab with his left hand, and when Daddy moved away from that, Jack swung his right up with all his might. It caught Daddy square on the chin, and I'll wager you could hear the pop of teeth and bone a quarter mile away. Daddy sort of lifted onto his toes, hung there for a second, and tumbled over backward, landing with a thud on the grass with his arms splayed out to the side.

"That'll do, ol' man," Jack said, and he stepped over Daddy, grabbed me by the arm, and started hustling me toward the wagon. "Goddang you, that'll do!" he hollered over his shoulder.

I started to protest that it wasn't me that had spilled the beans, but he told me to hush, that he knew it, and I didn't have to defend myself to him. He marched me straight to the wagon, lifted me up onto the seat, hitched the horses, and we were outen there in about a minute. Ma called something after us, but Jack wasn't listening. He snapped the reins, and pushed them old nags into a canter.

Well, you can imagine my frame of mind. This huge old varmint had been beaten on by my Daddy and shamed by my Ma and I figured no matter what he'd said, he probably blamed me for it. I was certain my maidenhood was a goner, if not my life.

Funny how things work out.

Or at least it was funny when it came to Jack Ross.

By the time we got home, he'd cooled off some, but he was still so angry I could hear his teeth grinding. I went inside and began rattling pots and pans with some sort of notion that I was going to fix us some supper, though really I was just burning off nervous energy. I confess I also looked at that old gun on the wall and considered whether I ought to load it for bear and be ready in case my husband attacked me, though at that point in my life I'd only fired a weapon maybe twice, and that being Cyrus Robert's gift .22, which was a dang sight short of being as much gun as Jack had.

Anyhow, Jack stayed outside with the horses for a long time, feeding and currying them and generally giving them more careful attention than was his usual habit. It was slap dark by the time he came inside and sat down at our table. He pushed the coal oil lantern away a bit, as if he didn't want the light to fall on his face.

For a couple of minutes, it seemed like all I could hear was the soft sigh of his breath. Then he spoke. "I reckon I would of killed your Pa today if he'd of kept it up," he said so softly I could barely hear him.

"I reckon," I agreed.

"It wadn't so much that he was a-hitting me as it was the shame of the thing."

Again, I agreed.

"Shame's a terrible thing, Eva Rae."

That set me back on my heels a little, as I believe it was the first time he'd ever called me by my entire Christian name since that first night of our married life.

He lifted his hand to cover the torn lip, as he often did when speaking serious.

"You ashamed of me, girl?"

"No, sir," I said, and somewhat to my surprise, I realized I meant it.

"You afraid of me?"

"Yessir. A little."

"I ever give you reason?"

"No."

"Don't intend to, neither. A good husband don't do that to his woman. I may not be much of a man otherwise, but it's my ambition to be the best husband I can be. I got me a whale of a powerful temper, and you don't want to see what I'm capable of when I get riled through and through, which I was close to this afternoon. But like I said, a good husband don't do that, and I'll do everything in my power to keep my word on that." He cleared his throat. "Now, about this having relations business. You know I ain't pushed myself on you, which would of been my right."

I guess I hung my head a little. "I know." I wanted to say that I was right glad he hadn't, too, but I kept my mouth shut.

"Some of that's on account of I don't want to scare you."

"You don't scare me, Jack. Not now, anyway."

"Well, thankee for that." He moved the lamp again and shoved his own chair back a couple of inches. "Some of it's also on account of I ain't too sharp with the ladies. Never was, and like I tolt you once, this here war wound didn't help none. I'd come to figure I wadn't ever going to have me a regular woman, nor any other kind, the way even the whores in Jeff City sniggered at me. Forgive me for speaking plain."

"Forgiven," I said.

"But now we got to take a stab at it. You see that, don't you? Your ol' man... well, he's the Grand Knight and all, and if he sets his mind to stirring up the boys that I'm some kind of a sissy..."

He was struggling so much I couldn't help myself. I scooted my chair to a place where I could reach out and touch the back of his hand with my fingertips. He drew away as if burned, but after a few seconds he moved that hand a mite closer and let me stroke the coarse black hair of his knuckles.

He drew in a deep breath and said what must of been on his mind since Daddy started wailing on him. "Or if you want, we'll get a divorce and I'll just up and leave this country and let you go back to your ma and pa unspoilt. If that's what you want."

You could of knocked me over with a feather.

"Jack," I said, "you're a kind man. I allow as I wasn't ready to marry you, and that's for sure, but I could of done a whole bunch worse. I see that now, if I didn't before. You ain't maybe the prettiest fellow a girl could find"—I smiled so he'd know I didn't mean it unkindly—"but you're decent to me and you've been patient as well. So there ain't no reason to talk about any divorce." Of course, I didn't fancy my chances in life being a divorced woman at the age of thirteen, nor was there much chance of me moving back in with the folks, or wanting to under any circumstances, but there was no need getting into that right then.

Anyway, the air came outen him like you'd punctured a balloon. "I appreciate that, Missus. I surely do."

I traced my name with my fingertip on the back of his hand.

"Next time we go visit my Ma and Daddy, maybe Ma will see something different than she did this time," I said.

"Hope so," he said, with a tone that sounded like a little kid wishing for some shiny new toy for Christmas.

So the fat was in the fire for sure.

"I ain't promising, Jack. We just got to let things happen as they will."

"I accept that."

"But I'll tell you this: if Daddy or any Kluxer friend of yours, or even my Ma, for that matter, ever says we ain't knowed each other in the Biblical sense, I plan to tell 'em they're hoot-owl crazy."

He laughed a little. "You got spunk, Eva Rae."

Indeed I did.

So it was that Jack Ross and I commenced to living like a real husband and wife. Truth to tell, I've had pleasanter experiences, but I've had worse ones, too, and after a time, it got to be just the way it was. It sure kept Jack looking after his own cleanliness better than he probably ever had before, which wasn't a bad thing. He was right, too, that he wasn't too sharp with the ladies, at least as far as I could judge never having had the experience before myself. There was a lot of clumsiness to it, though later on I came to realize that's pretty much the way it is in life except in cheap novels and the movies, especially when two people ain't used to each other.

I expected to get pregnant right away, which was the sure-fired way of proving to the doubters that my man and I were clear-through married, but such was not to be the case. That didn't seem to bother him, though, and I never heard him comment one way or the other in them days about having an heir to carry on the family name, such as it was. Winter came on, and it was a hard one, which in time made me grateful I wasn't with child, there being plenty of bone-wearying work to do and no doctor roundabout who would brave three-foot snowdrifts just to look in on an expectant mother.

The snows also kept us from seeing my folks, which was an altogether good thing since the bad blood betwixt Jack and Daddy hadn't entirely settled down. Daddy had, in fact, tried to drum Jack outen the Klan for some made up offense or another, but it was really just because he'd been humbled by his son-in-law in a fight, which the rest of them Kluxers understood well enough, because no one ever seemed to hold it against Jack. In fact, that fight with Daddy did more to raise Jack's status and lower Daddy's in their eyes than anything else ever could of, though to this day I can't figure out why that would be. You would of thought them good ol' boys for sure would of taken Daddy's side, him being the Grand Knight and all and Jack apparently not being able to do his husbandly duty. But maybe they looked at it differently. Maybe they were peeved at Daddy for the way he tried to lord that Grand Knight business over them. Most likely they were just scared of Jack Ross's big fists and that temper he'd told me about.

Though I'd never seen it, I came to learn from the womenfolk of some of them Kluxers that they'd for sure seen it. "Like the flaming wrath of God going before Moses" was the way one of them ladies put it, and the way her eyes lit up when she said it made me think for a second that she was jealous of me for having a powerful, wrathful husband. For my part, I was just as glad that I didn't have any first-hand knowledge of what they were talking about, and I was equally glad that most of their nightriding husbands were cowards under their sheets.

Anyway, that hard winter definitely dried up the Klan

activity, the members apparently not feeling up to riding around through drifted snow. Subzero temperatures, a genuine rarity in Missouri, probably took the thrill outen drinking moonshine in some clearing in the middle of the night, too.

But spring came on, as it always does, though the ice on the north side of the house, where it never got the sun, was a long time leaving. It was almost May before the crocuses bloomed, and well neigh June before the lilacs showed their purple flower clusters. Then the cyclones were upon us, with many a night so wild from wind and lightning that I thought the house was going to shake apart. A twister hit a little village some miles to the west of Jeff City on the first of June, killing three folks in their beds and generally destroying everything that wasn't absolutely nailed down. I heard tell that them winds actually drove pieces of straw six inches into oak planking like they'd been nailed there, but I can't say for certain because I didn't see it myself.

Anyway, when the storms let up, the hots arrived well ahead of schedule, so it seemed like we went from winter to summer in about three weeks, which is also a rarity in country where spring tends to linger through the magnolia and dogwood blooms right on to peonies and wild roses. But high summer it was, and folks began getting out and mixing a little again, taking in church on Sunday morning or getting together for an afternoon of fried chicken and cool buttermilk and gossip when the spirit moved them. Ma even came over for a visit one day and invited us out for a Sunday dinner again, and in doing so, she crossed her heart and promised me that Daddy would mind his manners.

What she didn't tell me until we showed up that Sunday was that Daddy was sick.

Something, she whispered whilst we set the dinner table —the long winter indoors, losing the respect of a good deal of his Klan following, or whatever—had taken a toll on him.

Well, a fool could see that was true. I have to tell you, I

couldn't take my eyes off that man. Before that summer, it was Ma who had looked worn down to the nub, but in one season, Daddy had surpassed her. His muscles had turned all stringy, and his hair had gone a dull, wiry gray and some of that was thinning in a hurry. The spark of the Devil was gone from his eye, too, leaving a rheumy stare in its place. He allowed as how everything was fine as frog's hair with him, but he grunted getting up outen his chair when we rode into the yard, and the least exertion had him coughing into his fist so hard I thought he'd bust something.

"Looks like consumption to me," I said, having seen some cases of it around Jeff City, though of course I really didn't know what I was talking about.

Ma only shook her head.

One thing was for sure: it kept Daddy from riling Jack.

I'd never seen Daddy defer to another human being in my whole life, but he sure did that day, calling my husband "Mr. Ross" just as natural as if he was a child being respectful to a teacher. I swear that made Jack more nervous than if Daddy had been pointing a shotgun at him and breathing fire, so it was Ma and me who had to carry whatever conversation there was around that table, with most of it running to "pass the peas" and "sure is good ham."

But then Daddy let slip about Dell.

"Got a letter from your sister Dell Christine," he said around a mouthful of mashed potatoes and a hard cough. Ma gave him a sharp look that he was too occupied with the coughing to notice. "She and that bum she married have up and left Missouri and settled on a homestead in Kansas."

I confess to feeling a little weak in the knees to hearing that. Not that I'd tried to keep in touch with Dell, nor her with me, but there wasn't a day went by that I didn't think about her and swear to myself that one of these days I was going to find out where she and Clement had settled in St. Joe and talk Jack into going for a visit even if it took us a week to get there. But that wasn't ever going to happen if them two were clear off in Kansas.

"Oh," was all I said.

Daddy coughed again and shoved his plate away, having apparently had enough even though it was less than half of what he used to wolf down. "Having a tough time of it, from the sound of the letter."

I looked at Ma, and she looked away toward the window, as if she'd heard something outside.

"Real hard time," Daddy said, warming to the subject in spite of the nagging cough and a trickle of blood that he wiped off his lips with a filthy blue bandana. "They're living in a dugout. Can you imagine that? Our dainty little Dell grubbing in the dirt for a place to sleep like a badger or some such?" He tried to laugh when he said it, but didn't pull it off. "That Clement always was a dumb sumbitch to my way of thinking. This here proves it."

"Now, Father," Ma said by way of scolding him a little.

"Well, hell, woman, you're always calling him a damn idjit, ain't you?"

Just from the way she colored at the throat, she knew she was caught and pretty much agreed with him on the issue besides.

"Momma, may I see the letter?" I asked. I was on my feet without even having thought about standing up, and I couldn't remember the last time I'd called her "Momma."

She sniffled and kept looking out the window, then turned slowly to me.

"After dinner, darling. After dinner."

"Maybe it's a soddy, Daddy," I said, trying to sound cheery. I just couldn't imagine Clement being so thick-headed as to put my precious sister into a mean hole in the ground. "I know some folks say they can be real comfortable." I thought of my own home and figured having foot-thick grass-covered walls would at least keep out the winds and maybe even an occasional family of field mice.

"Ain't no soddy," Daddy said with a shake of his head. "A damn dugout. That's all. I should of kilt the dumb sumbitch stead of just busting his wing." Then he turned to Jack. "You was there that night, wasn't you?"

Jack nodded, but he was eyeing me careful, trying to judge my reaction.

I sat down slowly and tried to finish eating, but the food had suddenly turned the taste of ashes. Not only had I lost Dell, but if what Daddy said was true, she'd most likely lost touch with whatever civilization there was to be had in our part of the world. I pictured Dell holding up her pinky while she drank outen a teacup in a bare hole in the side of some cut bank somewhere on the edge of the world. It was enough to make me cry.

After we cleared the dishes and the men went outside for a smoke (though Daddy chewed instead of smoked on account of the smoking only made him cough all the harder), Ma and I cleared the dishes, then I asked her again for the letter. She took it outen the pocket of her apron and pressed it into my hands.

"Best sit down to read it, child," she said, then she turned away again.

So that's what I did. I opened the little packet and pressed it out flat on my knee. I still have that letter, and after all these years, believe it or not, I still read it every once in a while, though it's faded and torn along the creases and I don't really need to, anyway, on account of I have it memorized:

Dear Momma and Daddy (it began),

> *Just so's you know, I've been thinking of you ever so much these last weeks. I am sorry we left without telling you of our going, but thought it was for the best. We are close to settled here in a place near the Smoky Hill River*

and not too far from the Union Pacific railroad, which I believe will make our region grow in coming years. Least that's what Clement says. We got a homestead filed on a 160 acres of land that C says will grow wheat so thick a man couldn't walk through it all. The nearest town is twenty miles away, a day's jaunt on horseback and longer by wagon on account of rough terrain and there being no roads. Our home for now is a hole in a creek bank, which is snug enough.

Can you imagine that, Momma? It is better nor it sounds, however, as it is cool in the hot wind that seems to blow all the time around here, and it is a safe place to be in a cyclone, too, we having had one blow through here a week ago. It busted up our wagon some, but we was safe and snug in our little den. C promises he will build me a proper home when he can, though there is no wood to be had for miles around, so I'm not sure how exactly he plans to do that. He tells me not to worry, though, so I suppose I shant. The work is hard, but again, C promises 'twill be milk and honey by and by!

This was once buffalo country, and the skeletons of some of them great beasts are still to be found in our neighborhood. Just two weeks ago, a bone picker come by in a big wagon. C talked to him, though I did not for he was a rough looking character. He will be back in a day or two with a full load and I will trust him to take this letter to the post office in Fort Hays and from there on to you.

Fear not for us, for we are fine and will make a good life for ourselves in this wilderness. I am expecting a child in November, so will have a true Kansas baby!
Love to all, especially to Eva Rae if you see her.

Your loving daughter,
Dell

Well.

I folded that letter and tucked it into my apron without even asking Ma if I could have it for keeps. Just the thought of Dell living in some hole in the ground absolutely made my blood run cold, and her in a family way on top of it.

I had to agree with Daddy, much as it pained me: Clement Handley really was as stupid a sonofabitch as ever drew breath for taking my darling sister so far away from the people she loved. He might of been a pretty man, but it was plain that brains didn't run deep in his family, or if they did, that river had dried up for certain before it ever got to him. How could I of been taken in by them good looks? How could Dell?

"Milk and honey, indeed," I said out loud. How on earth was that beautiful girl going to handle a baby living in a mean hole in the ground, with no roads to town and ruffians all around? Even if Clement managed to pull together some kind of a decent house, which I doubted he had either the sense or the gumption to do, she was still a hard day's ride from help if she needed it.

"She'll be all right, child," Ma said. "She's strong." But of course we both knew that wasn't true at all.

I can remember making my decision just as suddenly and just as completely as if somebody'd spoken a command in my ear.

"Ma," I said, "what would you think if Jack and me looked for some homestead land out there in Kansas, too?"

She gave me a look that spoke volumes: fear, disappointment, hurt, and then a glimmer of understanding of what I was driving at that brought some relief to her tired features.

"I can't lose you, too, child," she said.

"You won't be losing me, Ma," I countered, knowing even as I said it that it was probably a lie. "But Dell needs someone to look out for her. I reckon that's me. Clement sure ain't the one to do it. You know I can handle myself—Jack and me, that is."

She nodded, slowly, with tears welling up in her sad gray eyes. "But you'll need to convince Mr. Ross of that, darling."

I believe I actually laughed out loud. "You leave Jack to me," I said. "He'll do what's right."

So it was that we commenced planning for Kansas. Jack wasn't the least bit stubborn on that account once he saw that I had my mind made up and was likely to go on my own if he didn't agree to come along, too. Besides, it wasn't exactly like there was much holding us to Missouri beyond a patch of corn, a few hogs, and a bunch of Kluxers who wouldn't miss someone they was more than half afraid of.

The trouble was, there didn't appear to be a way of making it happen before that little tyke of Dell's came into the world. The trip itself wouldn't take that long on account of the railroads if we could scrimp enough cash money from the moonshine business to come up with the fare, but figuring out what we were going to do about living in that country when we got there was another matter. It was already too late to put a crop of any kind in the ground if we did get to Kansas that year unless you counted winter wheat, which would leave us mighty hungry through the cold dark months, and what Jack knew about wheat you could put in a thimble and have room enough left over for your thumb. Corn and pigs, both of which he was passing familiar with, were out of the question, and anyway there likely wasn't much call for white lightning in them parts even if we'd had a crib full of corn to make it from what with the population being so scarce.

Jack did some figuring and said we could sell most of the hogs for maybe enough to pay the fare and even take a couple of piglets along to start a new herd, but they wouldn't fetch close to enough to outfit us once we got there, and you can't eat money once the winter weather sets in, nor too much hog, neither, if you expect to have suckling pig come spring. Reluctantly, we decided to hold tight where we were and make a go of it the following year, after we'd saved and scratched every red cent we could lay our hands on. Maybe we could time it so once we got there Jack would be able to get something in the ground for the growing season and I could manage a truck garden for table vegetables. It would mean poor Dell would have to have that baby on her own, but there wasn't no other way of it.

I wrote to Dell of our plans, sending the letter care of general delivery, Fort Hays, Kansas, and hoping against hope it would get to her before that baby came. I also checked with Ma every week or so to see if she'd heard again, especially when enough time had gone by for my letter to have gotten there and her reply to have made its way back to civilization. We didn't hear a peep, but since the mails were dependent on bone pickers and other such white trash, about the best you could do was cross your fingers and say a little prayer and hope for the best. In any event, Dell was much on my mind that summer and early autumn.

Then there was Daddy, who continued to worsen until I actually felt a pang or two of grief over his condition. The cough deepened, and when he started to spit up blood regular, Ma took him to a sawbones in Jeff City over his own protest.

It was the consumption, of course, far advanced. The doc prescribed high dry air, like in Colorado where some of the best sanatoriums were said to be, but he might as well of told Daddy to go to the far side of the moon in a sailing ship. Instead of Colorado, he went home, hid out in the woods drinking his own shine for a couple of days, and was so weak by the time he crawled home that Ma put him to bed. Pneumonia developed on top of the consumption, and it was a slap miracle that old buzzard could breathe at all. He got some better toward the first of September, when the terrible summertime humidity let up a little, but when the cold nights of November put a glisten of white frost on the grass and the windowpanes, the pneumonia came back again. Daddy fought hard, or so Ma said, but he was used up. On the sixteenth of November, 1883, my father passed away in his sleep. He was just a month shy of fifty-three years old but looked a score of years older.

Not many of his children came home for the funeral, they being scattered to the winds from New Orleans to Kansas and California and Daddy not having been their favorite person on earth, anyhow, to be honest about it. My older brother Jimmy, now the man on the place, did a fair job of taking care of what few arrangements there were, which was mostly rounding up the Kluxers to serve as pall bearers, and Ma put on a feed for the gaggle of various Cumberlands who came from all around the territory. They laid Daddy in a little patch of grass just west of the woods where he kept his still. As luck would have it, the weather had been warmish and the ground was still soft. I guess what I remember most about that day was the way the turned earth smelled of spring more than approaching winter. Daddy's Klan friends were all decked out in their sheets, and most had had more than a nip of the corn squeezings he'd left behind, but in the main they behaved themselves better than our shirttail relations and showed a fair amount of good manners toward Ma. The place where they buried Daddy got good light in the afternoon, and it was high enough that it didn't bog down in wet weather. Deer came there at night to nibble, and all in all it was as pretty a place to spend eternity as you could ask for and a good deal better than Daddy deserved.

I sat with Ma for a few days, but after the first hard grieving, she was fine.

Relieved, to tell you the truth.

Keeping that man outen trouble had taken as much toll on her as birthing all them kids, and if Daddy ever had been kind and considerate to her, I never saw it. It honest to God made me appreciate Jack Ross, and I told him so.

Anyhow, I asked Ma if she wanted to come with us to

Kansas the next spring, but she just shook her head. She was determined to stay on the place to help out Jimmy at least until he found a wife of his own.

"I belong here, and here I'll stay," she said, casting an eye toward where Daddy lay. "You just promise to come back some day and visit us, your daddy and me, up there in that glade."

I promised, of course, though it's a promise I'm shamed to say I've never kept, leastwise until now, and I'm getting a little long in the tooth to make the journey. I don't imagine she really expected me to, even then, and she's way past caring now. She knew me better than I knew myself in them days, which of course is what a mother is for when you come right down to it.

We finally heard from Dell a week or so before Christmas, when the snows had covered all of central Missouri in a blanket of white and we couldn't have moved if Moses himself had been there to lead us.

She was a momma at last, of a little dark-haired boy she'd named Caleb Levi Handley, the middle name being for Daddy even though she could not have known he was dead, nor did it make much sense that she'd honor him given the way he'd driven her husband off the place. But maybe poor Dell had taken to thinking better of Daddy now that she'd had a chance to see that her shining knight Clement had a few failings of his own.

Anyhow, the baby had come in mid-October, a mite early, but Dell said the child was near ten pounds even so, and both mother and child was doing fine once they both got the knack of feeding at the breast. She was looking forward to Christmas and hoping for a little snow, even, as long as the wind didn't come from the east since their little cave-home was somewhat open on that side. She allowed as how she was also hoping Clement would get to Fort Hays or some other outpost of civilization to buy the baby a Christmas comforter. She'd seen one in St. Joe that she couldn't get outen her mind, with a needlepoint St. Nick and holly on one side and a red sateen backside. If there was any way, that was something her little boy should have some day, she said. It wasn't practical, she knew, but then what was the use of having a child if she couldn't spoil him at least a little?

All in all, it was a cheery enough letter—too cheery to my way of thinking. There that little family was, living in what amounted to a mud cave on the edge of the world with nothing but bone pickers for occasional company and probably not a red cent to their names, and a man of the house who apparently didn't have sense enough to come in outen the pouring rain or figure a way to put his wife and child in a decent dwelling.

It made for a long winter worrying about Dell and that baby. I wrote two or three times, but only heard back once long about the first of March, when we still had plenty of dirty old snow left on the north side of our place and in the woods where the sun didn't get to it. We'd had a passably hard winter, and from the sound of Dell's letter, theirs had been worse, with bone-cracking cold and winds that howled offen the Colorado plains (fortunately from the west), driving blizzards of dirt and snow mixed. Still, she kept up the good cheer. Or so she said.

Then real spring came, and it was time for us to go. We sold our place to my brother Jimmy for a dollar an acre, that being about what we needed for train tickets from Sedalia to Fort Hays, sold the hogs separately to our nearest neighbor so's we'd have a stake once we got to where we were going, packed up the few things we could carry, and gave away what we couldn't to various of my relatives.

On the first of May, a gray and drippy day with a moldy smell to it, we hitched Jack's broken-down old horse to the buckboard and rode out to my old home place one last time.

Ma was in her garden planting onion sets and sowing carrot seeds. She clumped up through the yard in a pair of Daddy's old shoes, wiping the mud offen her hands as she came. In spite of the weather and the hard work, I swear she looked years younger than I'd ever seen her. She shook Jack's hand just like a man would of, and didn't even scrape the mud off her shoes when she led us inside.

"Your brother is down to Jeff City buying supplies," she said, pointing out the chairs where she wanted us to sit. "I ast him to stay and see you, but he said he had work to do."

"I understand," I said, though of course I didn't. Maybe Jimmy was a little afraid of Jack, or maybe he just couldn't abide seeing another member of the family slip away.

Ma put on a teakettle and shoved a plate of sugar cookies our way. "You eat up, and what you don't eat, put in a sack to nibble on your trip."

Jack thanked her and took a couple of cookies and shoved them into his mouth. Ma smiled.

"I'll write you as soon as we find Clement and Dell," I said.

"Course you will," she said, but there was a look on her face I couldn't quite cipher. Then she turned her back to us and fiddled with the tea until the water was boiling and the leaves steeping. When she turned around again, there were tears in her eyes.

"You be careful, child," she said. "Mr. Ross, you take care of my baby."

"Yes'm," Jack said around a mouthful of cookie.

"And the both of you take care of Dell Christine. She ain't strong like you."

"Yes'm," he said again.

Once again she turned her back. "I ain't good at good-bys, so you better git."

"Momma," I said, but she waved over her shoulder at me.

"Git. You hear me?"

***

So we did.

We rolled on down the hill, crossed the river by ferry, and headed west for Sedalia. I don't believe Jack nor I spoke again that first day, and maybe most of the second. Ahead of us lay the unknown. What I was feeling was something like what Columbus must of felt when he set them three ships westward from Spain: excitement, anticipation, and dread of the unknown in somewhat equal measure.

I do recall the words I spoke to Jack once we'd sold the rig and horse in Sedalia and sat waiting for the westbound train that would take us on our way.

"You're a good man to do this," I said. "Not every man would sell all and leave his home just so his wife could rescue her sister."

He sniffed and put his hand up to cover his mouth, then apparently thought better of it and lowered the hand to his side.

"Not every man has a wife like you," he said.

Just then the train whistle blew, but I could swear I heard him add "And I love you for it, Eva Rae."

Before I could ask him to repeat it, the whistle blew again and the cars slid to a stop not thirty feet away with a great screech of steel wheels trying to grab purchase on the iron rails and the hissing of steam.

And that was that. For good or ill, we were leaving Missouri behind and heading for Kansas.

Gone To Kansas

YOU HAVE NO IDEA WHAT IT'S LIKE not seeing a tree for days on end when you've lived all your life a stone's throw from woods so thick a squirrel could live two lifetimes and never touch the ground. And when I say no trees, I mean it. By the time we were a few miles west of Topeka, the only greenery higher than a blade of grass was a few scrubby bushes and a slip of a willow or two along whatever passed for streams, and well before we hit the Smoky Hill country, even them things had disappeared altogether.

It wasn't that the land was flat—far from it—but with nothing growing taller than knee high in all that land, you had the feeling that if you could just climb up onto a high step-ladder, you could see the far end of the earth.

Then there was the color. When we left Missouri, the grass of home was so green it almost hurt your eyes to look on it, but the buffalo grass in that far, high country was still brown and dead-looking, as if winter had been so hard on it that it didn't have energy left to send up new shoots in the warm spring sun.

Not that I minded all that much, at least at first. I'd gotten so accustomed to the rolling brushy green of home that this change to a brown, scalped, treeless landscape was practically intoxicating. Exotic is the only way I can describe it:

something so new and different that I was plumb swept away in amazement.

I think it made Jack nervous, though, to tell the truth. He'd traveled some in his early years, having been born in Tennessee and only coming to Missouri to fight in the war, but in all of them places he'd been a woodsman, living on the edge of the hardwood forests.

In time, it dawned on me as we traversed that great stretch of open country that there was more to his discomfort than just never having been a plainsman.

Jack liked being hemmed in. Maybe it was that war wound or the way he got it, but I think he liked the notion of being able to hide behind something, and there sure as the devil wasn't anywhere to hide in that country unless you laid flat on your face.

As our train belched and rattled its way acrost them miles of emptiness, he took to muttering about how great the land would be for farming and how wonderful it would be to plow and plant without grubbing stumps or stones, but he sure didn't sound as if he was convinced, like he was saying it mostly for my benefit. Every time we took on wood or water, he'd jump down and scuff his toe into the grass that grew right alongside the cinder bed for the track.

"That stuff's as tight-wove as a good piece of homespun," he'd say, or "Going to take a breaking plow honed sharp as a razor to slice through them roots, let me tell you, and even then it'll be a tall order," or "We may just skip hogs altogether and go straight to cattle, that grass is so good."

Like I said, in spite of the words, his eyes had a troubled look about them, and the farther we went the closer it came to something I judged akin to fear. He kept hold of my hand sometimes, or patted my knee, but always more to reassure himself than to comfort me. Or so it seemed.

As we journeyed on, I was at least as interested in that train ride as I was in the way the landscape changed, on account of that was the first time in my young life I'd ever been aboard a railroad car, and while it wasn't much for comfort, being about as bumpy a ride as Jack's old buckboard and a bunch noisier, it was a true experience. There was glass in the windows, which you could raise and lower with just a little work (though when they were open the cinders and smoke from the locomotive tended to blow in something awful). In spite of them cars being hotter'n the hubs of hell when the sun beat down on them, each one had a potbelly stove just like one of the mercantiles in Jeff City, which was mighty useful at night when the cars turned cold as the grave. The seats weren't nothing but flat wood slats like church pews only not as comfortable, except that they had some kind of coarse padding and a red velvet cover nailed onto them, which mostly just made them lumpy.

Them cars smelled vaguely of manure, too, which led me to surmise they must of been cattle cars before they were turned into coaches, though it might just of been too many unwashed folks sitting on that lumpy velvet for too long.

But it was the sheer speed of the thing that like to bowled me over. There were stretches where we must of been doing upwards of thirty miles an hour, which was lickety-split for someone who'd never got anywhere much faster than a brisk walking pace in her whole life. Of course, that train didn't keep up that pace for too long at a time, what with there being stops in every town big enough to have a depot, and when you consider that most of them towns were only there because of the train and not the other way around, that was just about every burg we came to. The engine had to take on wood and water every once in a while, too, and when that happened, they'd let us out to stretch our legs or have a bite of lunch. In some places, the locals had set up shop providing sandwiches or little tea cakes and coffee, and in a couple of towns like Topeka, the Harvey Company had their eateries with them so-called Harvey Girls bustling about. Of course, us being poor as church mice, we never ate in the fancy joints. I'd brought a hamper full of cold fried chicken, bread and cookies and a jar of applesauce Ma had given me as a going away present along with the princely sum of twenty dollars she said was a loan from Jimmy, though I knew better. Anyhow, while the other folks partook of the Harvey fare or homemade sandwiches in the little towns, we lived off the contents of that hamper while it lasted and did without when it was gone.

We got off the Kansas and Pacific Line at the little village of Hays, which lay about a half a mile from old Fort Hays, which was already well past its prime and running to seed. We were still sixty-odd miles short of our goal, but from what we'd been told, this was about the last place where we'd have hope of finding a buckboard, horse, plow, and whatever other truck we could afford with the gift from Ma and what few dollars we'd managed to scrape together when we sold off our place. Even with the little wad of cash money I had stashed away from Jack's selling off the last of a good crop of moonshine, we knew we'd have to dicker pretty close on the stuff we needed.

We weren't wrong, neither. The local merchants were plenty sharp enough to know that a body couldn't get what they were selling anywhere else, and they set their prices sky high accordingly.

The town of Hays itself wasn't much more than a couple of streets running betwixt a bunch of rattletrap buildings that didn't look much sturdier than some of the lean-to's back home. Ma and Daddy's place, not to mention Jack's, would of fit right in. Some places that passed for buildings were just tents with clapboard false fronts held up with long poles, and the saloons, of which there was an astonishing abundance given the fact that the sale of alcoholic spirits was strictly illegal in the entire state of Kansas, generally didn't even bother with the false front.

In that dry spring, Hays was as dusty a place as I've ever

seen in my life. Fort Street, where we went looking for a place to stay while we did our business, was ankle deep in yellow dust as fine as flour except for the spots where somebody's horse or team had made water. You just knew them streets would turn to mud the consistency of Ma's potato soup with the first rain, which unfortunately came before we were able to get our business done and skedaddle outen there.

We found a room in a boardinghouse, where a gaunt old spinster landlady let us stay for fifty cents a night as long as we found our own victuals, which meant that we didn't eat, our hamper being empty. That rude old woman also made it a point to tell me to keep my "father" away from her other paying customers on account of his messed up lip might put them off their feed. You can bet that I straightened her out, though I did it as politely as I could since we needed the place to stay.

Once we were ensconced in that boardinghouse, Jack went out to see about buying the essentials, meaning a horse and buggy and a breaking plow, that being the kind of device a homesteader needed first to cut through the tough buffalo grass wool before you could hope to turn it over. I offered as how he ought to look at a brace of mules, too, but he said he had his heart set on a real working horse if he could find one, so I didn't push the point. Instead, I gathered up six bits and went looking for bolt cloth and the food staples we'd need, meaning dry beans, coffee, and flour.

That night, it rained. Or rather, I should say it flooded. The thunderheads had been building up all afternoon, and sometime shortly after dark, they cut loose. Now, I'd seen lightning before, but never anything like that. Seemed to me like the whole world had turned electric green in the flashes, and the thunder made that old flophouse creak and rattle like the wood itself was chattering in fear. When the rain came, it was in sheets, and mostly sideways the way it was blowing. The roof over our heads wasn't much better than cheese cloth it leaked so bad. We had to spread an oilcloth poncho we'd brought along over the bed to keep the straw ticking dry enough so's we could sleep. Jack spent most of the night outside trying to keep the big gelding draft horse he'd bought from tearing loose its picket pin and running away, which would of put us in mighty dire straits. That man was so soaked and cold by the time he came inside that I was slap sure he was going to die of pneumonia before we ever got a chance to find Dell, but he was made of sturdier stuff than I supposed, and after a little nap in a mercifully dry bed and a bowl of oatmeal I begged from our hostess mostly by shaming her over the leaky condition of her roof, he was fit as a fiddle and itching to get going.

I tell you, the mud slowed us down some getting outen town. The wheels on the used wagon Jack had found sunk down almost to the axles when we moved, which wasn't much and was excruciatingly slow when it happened. Of course, the weight of that breaking plow in the back end didn't help any, and that poor gelding seemed to sink ever lower in the mire just standing in one spot. I swear he was sunk in to halfway between his fetlocks and his hocks, and you could see the muscles strain and hear a sucking sound every time he managed to pull a hoof free. Once or twice he'd start to panic, his eyes rolling white in his head, and if he'd been free to run, I reckon he'd of kept going until he'd pulled that wagon all the way to the Rocky Mountains. But Jack would calm him and somehow he'd eventually pull himself free of that ooze, only to get bogged down again forty feet farther on.

Finally, though, we managed to get outen that town, and fortunately, the road that ran parallel to the railroad tracks was a good deal easier to traverse than the town streets on account of it hadn't been traveled enough to get pounded into powder.

It took us three days to make the last part of our trip from Hays to the Smoky Hill where I hoped to find Dell in good spirits and health, the first day being the easiest along the railroad right-of-way and the next two being far harder as we angled acrost open country.

It wasn't exactly empty of people, but it sure came a lot closer than anything I'd ever seen before. What passed for towns was little more than a saloon and a handful of ratty canvas tents that Jack said must of been leftovers from the Army at the end of the Indian wars. When we left the railroad near the little burg of Grainfield, we aimed southwest, into progressively wilder and wilder country.

It was, to quote Jack, some of the by-God-damnedest country either one of us had ever seen, with spires and columns of sandstone and deep gullies, canyons almost, that looked like they'd never had a drop of water in them. Overhead, red-tailed hawks and more than a few golden eagles soared, as if keeping an eye on us intruders.

Anything a normal human would consider a genuine road had petered out within sight of little Grainfield and turned into what I took for a cow path, though Jack straightened me out on that, somebody having told him that they were trails the buffalo had followed in the old days when the great herds of them beasts still roamed free.

About all we saw of buffaloes was a couple of skulls near a low muddy spot that a great many of them creatures had probably used for a wallow in the olden days, and one place where forty or fifty skulls and an odd assortment of other bones were strewn over a half-acre of brown grass. Jack allowed as how that must of been one of the places where the old-timey hunters had killed and skinned a whole stand, the coyotes and other such varmints having scattered most of the carcasses so the bone-pickers hadn't yet found this place.

How that man knew all these things when he hadn't been but ten miles from home in the last eighteen years was beyond me. He said it was because he paid attention when people talked, and he'd asked a lot of questions in Hays.

Anyway, we camped under the stars and ate cold corn

bread and molasses we'd bought off the Hays boardinghouse keeper. Jack could of shot a plump prairie chicken or two, but there wasn't anything to serve as fuel for a fire and the grass was dry as tinder, anyway, the gully-washer that had swamped Hays apparently having missed this country. We figured we could of set the plains afire with the stump of a day old Lucifer match if we'd wanted to, a fact which gave me the heebee jeebees when a dry lightning storm blew up overnight, once again forcing Jack to spend several of the dark hours trying to calm that horse. Another night, when the moon came up, so did the yodeling of the coyotes, which frankly made the hairs on the back of my neck stand up. I'd heard coyotes back home, but they hadn't seemed much worse than the yapping of the family dog. Here, it sounded like they were so close I'd be afraid of tripping over one if I left the cover of the wagon to relieve myself. I guess I cuddled Jack pretty close them nights.

There were other critters to worry about, too. On one stretch near what I later learned to call Hackberry Creek, we saw three rattlesnakes bigger around than my arm sunning on a sandstone ledge, and more than once that old Belgian gelding side-stepped to get away from the buzzing at his feet. Jack killed one with a stick and skinned it and threatened to make me turn it into stew, but of course he was joshing and only wanted the skin for a hat band.

We forded Hackberry Creek with no trouble, its bottom being a dang sight firmer than the streets of Hays had been, but the Smoky Hill was another matter. That was the sorriest excuse for a genuine river I'd ever seen, though of course up to that time my main experience with rivers was the Missouri, which is a powerfully big stream by the time it cuts through the limestone benches near home. The Smoky Hill was upwards of a quarter mile wide, maybe more in some spots, and from what I could tell, less than six inches deep and meandering so slow I swear I saw water striders moving upriver on the surface. But the sand bars that studded that river like jewels on a fancy lady's necklace were soft as quicksand and likely to shift and disappear as if they were as fluid as the river, and once we nearly lost the horse for real. We wound up scouting for hours along the north bank looking for a good place to ford, and when we found it, we sat in the short grass a few yards away from the stream for the better part of a day planning out how we were going to get acrost. It was a measure of our lack of confidence that we decided the only way was to take off the wheels and float that old wagon acrost, or rather pole it, pretty much letting the horse fend for itself.

So we unhitched right at the water's edge, set the axles on the handle of the plow to jack the box up just enough for Jack to wrestle the wheels off and toss them into the wagon, then the two of us together shoved with all our might to push the whole contraption into the river with Jack holding onto the Belgian's harness to coax it into what little current there was.

Well, wouldn't you know, we'd picked us a hard-bottomed ford after all, and while we worked like demons to haul that rig across the river in a half-a-foot of water, that horse strolled across without much more than wet hooves and enjoyed a peaceful rest on the south bank while we unloaded wheels, hoisted the box, and got hubs on axles again. It cost us a full sixteen hours of hard labor when we could of ridden acrost as easy as crossing a bridge back home! We'd of laughed about it but we were too blame tired.

From there, we turned more westerly, following the southern bank of the river toward where we hoped to find Dell and Clement. Jack kept a lookout for decent land to homestead, too, and there wasn't any doubt that we could have our pick when the time came: in all that country from Grainfield to the Smoky Hill, we hadn't seen but two human habitations, and one of them was abandoned. South of the river, we didn't see a one.

Leastwise not until we came on to a series of cut banks

running perpendicular to the river and had to follow the largest southward on account of the ravine was too wide to cross. I was thinking it would be days before we could get around that ditch and find our way again, and I wasn't so sure about even that from the way the sandstone cliffs and buttes rose on the other side like stone chess pieces some three hundred foot tall giant had flung to the ground. It was like something out of a fairy tale or a bad dream all muddled together.

Wouldn't you know, that's where we found them, though we probably would have missed them altogether had she not been smoking a venison ham, for it was the wisps of white grass smoke that gave the place away.

At first, I thought it was a dust devil, to tell the truth, and when we got closer I considered that maybe it was the work of some other passerby who'd set a fire and forgot about it, because the first thing I saw was a wagon box on its side leaning up against the bank with slats and wheels missing and the leather springs all torn to shreds and the smoke rising from a little mound of yellow soil ten or fifteen feet away. A handful of scrawny chickens pecked at the hard earth.

Then I saw a flash of faded red cloth behind the wagon, and a human arm pushing the cloth aside.

What stepped out into the sunshine didn't hardly look human at first. Its hair was wild, the color of old grease and woodsmoke, and the skin that showed was burnt to a brownness that matched the dirty shift and apron it wore. To tell the truth, it took me a few seconds to realize it was a woman as she raised a hand to shade her eyes against the blazing sun that stood high overhead.

"My God in Heaven," I said aloud as recognition set in. That woman was thin as a rail and aged by the circumstances of her life to the point she would have passed for Ma's older sister.

"I b'lieve that'd be your sister Dell," Jack said matter-offactly as he reined in twenty yards short of the end-up wagon. He turned to me with a grin that was both relief and embarrassment. "Leastwise, I think so."

I clumb down offen the wagon and headed toward her. I'd imagined our greeting a thousand times, with me running into her arms and us hugging and laughing like we had in the olden days, but now I couldn't make my feet move faster than a shuffle toward that scarecrow of a woman.

"Who's that?" she hollered at last, her voice coming out in a sort of raspy croak. "You keep your distance, now. We ain't got nothing for you here!"

I tried to shout back, to tell her who I was, but my voice got stuck in the dry muck of my throat.

"Don't you recognize your own sister, woman?" Jack shouted out. "This here's Eva Rae and Jack Ross, come to visit!"

I could see her features twist up as she peered under that shading hand. Then: "Oh my God! Eva!" And she took a step, then another, and commenced running for me and finally my feet caught the wind, too, and in a half-dozen paces, we were together, our arms around one another.

"Eva, Eva, Eva," she said, almost in a chant, as we danced around that pitiful yard. She pushed me away just far enough to take a good look, then hugged me and danced some more.

It was almost more than I could bear, for the smell of her, all earth and smoke and rancid grease, would of made me sick to my stomach had I et more than two chunks of stale cornbread in the last twenty-four hours, but when she took my hand and led me around that mud hole that passed for a yard, it was like we were kids again playing ring-around-the-rosy. Jack must of found it powerful amusing, because he commenced to laughing so hard I was half afraid he'd choke.

When we stopped to catch our wind, she held me out at arm's length to take another look, which of course gave me a chance to do the same.

My, oh my, what a couple of years had done to that girl. She'd gone from girl to woman to old lady in about the time it takes to tell it. All the baby fat was gone from her face and the skin that had stretched over what had once been plump and soft sagged in the creases like old stretched-out leather. Her eyes had lost their luster, too, and there was a hint of wildness in them that I hadn't never seen on a human being before, like she was touched. There were wisps of gray in her hair though she was not yet out of her teens, and them golden locks, now darkened and grimy, had lost all their sheen till they looked mostly like some old animal pelt. I could see her teeth, for she was smiling, and they'd gone dark, with gums that were an unhealthy purplish color that reminded me of an old man we'd seen around Jeff City who was said to have the scurvy.

"Come in and see the baby," she said at last, and tugging at my hand drew me toward the embankment and the up-turned wagon. She slipped behind that contraption, lifted the red cloth that served as a doorway, and bid me to follow.

Of course, I couldn't see a blamed thing for a full minute it was so dark in there. But I could sure as hell smell it, you'll pardon the language. Like dead things, it was, and mold and stale smoke that had nowhere to go. The pungent smell of the earth itself was the best odor I could pick outen that place. When my eyes adjusted, I could see why it smelled the way it did, too: skins hung everywhere—pelts of coyotes and what I took to be badgers and more than a few skunks, and from the way they were curled on themselves, they hadn't been properly scraped nor cured, so whatever flesh was still attached on the meat side had putrefied. Made me wonder what it was that was cooking in that smoky little oven out front, I'll tell you that. And even on that hot day, embers glowed on a hearth that wasn't much more than a scraped-out ledge on a far wall. Wispy smoke curled upward and some of it leaked outen a little slit in the sod, but most collected like a fog along what passed for an earthen ceiling.

"Here he is!" she cried, and pulled back a fur cover from a rough-hewn cradle pushed up against the far wall. "Here's my little Caleb." She bent over and scooped that child up and held him out to me with a look of pride on her face like she was showing off the Grand Duke of Russia or some such.

That child.

I don't know what I expected, but it wasn't that filthy starved-looking thing that looked back at me from his momma's arms. He had wispy dark brown hair plastered to his scalp like it was slicked down with grease, and his momma's big brown eyes. The rest of him was sort of puckered up. His mouth was clean and pink, but there were black smudges like soot elsewhere on his face, and when he held out his little hand, I could see black under his tiny fingernails. The rag he was wearing around his middle was soaked and stinking, though Dell seemed not to notice. I reached out and touched his cheek, and he turned toward my finger almost violently as if to suckle. Dell giggled at that and held him to her own breast, which he commenced to rooting for, never mind her filthy shift. She looked down at him and began to rock back and forth, crooning softly. I recognized the tune as one that Ma had sung to us kids when we were little. All in all, it gave me the shivers in spite of that hot, fetid air.

"He's a beautiful child," I said, sounding as happy as I could.

"Yes," she said, "he certainly is."

We hung around the place most of that day, and I pitched in as best I could to get some sort of a start on cleaning up that pigsty. First order of business was to get water het over a good outside fire, and that presented the biggest challenge on account of there was so little wood around the place. We actually busted off a couple of pieces of the wagon that served as front wall and doorway to the dugout, it being fairly obvious that Dell and Clement had done the same a time or two, and probably for the same reason. Then, once we got that burning and the water hot, I took rags and wiped down everything I could find inside that hole. Grime and grease coated everything like it had been sealed in wax. Having done the best I could there, I took a cool rag to mother and child both, and she let me do it, too. She just sat there crooning her songs, and I came to realize that my first notion had been more right than I knew: Dell was, indeed, touched. It like to broke my heart.

Then I boiled what passed for the baby's diapers and hung them on a makeshift line Jack strung from our whole wagon to the other busted up one. For his part, Jack picked up trash including gnawed bones in the yard and buried them far enough away that if the coyotes came back for the marrow, they wouldn't be right there amongst the chickens and that baby boy.

Along about dusk, here came Clement, riding in on a tall horse with several dead animals of various descriptions tied over the cantle behind him. He swung down and greeted Jack and me like he'd expected us to be there all along. Other than being darkened by the sun and wind, he didn't look much different than the day Daddy busted his arm and drove him off our place, which is to say he looked a dang sight better than his wife. It pained me to remember that once upon a time, I'd looked on him as some kind of white knight come to take Dell away from the troubles on our home place and even lusted after him a bit myself, or as much as a twelve-year-old could. Now, just looking at that mother and child, I recognized Clement for what he was: a stupid, selfish oaf who couldn't even see what he'd done to a fine woman.

Damn you, Daddy, I said under my breath. Damn you for being right about Clement.

"Got to get some greens into them folks," Jack whispered to me once my brother-in-law was out of sight, confirming my own fears of scurvy.

We shared the meat from one of Clement's kills that night, trying not to think too much on exactly what kind of varmint it was, and talked with him of decent land around about that was still open for homesteading. There wasn't any getting around the fact that Clement didn't have a clue. He was satisfied living in a hole in the ground and trapping or shooting whatever he needed, even if it meant slim pickings of coyote roasts, which I figured was the equal of cooking up somebody's mangy old yard dog back home. Even prairie dog would of been better, it being about the same as squirrel, but Clement fancied himself a wolf killer for some reason. When I asked whether they had chicken often, he snorted and said my heavens, no—they were brood hens so he'd have pullets to sell later in the year. I thought Jack was going to choke on a tough bite of supper over that, there not having been any sign of a rooster on the place!

Jack and I elected to stay the night a hundred yards or so from the Handley's crude home, with the notion of Jack searching in earnest for a claim of plowable land the next day while I went about the business of furthering the clean-up of Dell and her little boy. We agreed that what she needed most was vegetable matter in her diet. Fortunately, we'd brung along a couple of hundredweight of oats, mostly for the horse, so I knew I could make up a little porridge for now, and some dried beans mixed with whatever chicken I could catch— Clement be damned—would make a hearty soup. There were a few packets of seeds tucked away in the truck Ma had given me that might yet produce a few string beans or a pumpkin or two before the summer was out, though I reckoned we'd have to pray for rain. Beyond that, I'd bought some dried apples I'd planned to put into a pie, but applesauce was quicker and might do the trick getting my sister back onto her feet.

That's how it went our first weeks in Kansas—me nursing Dell, getting a little nourishment into her, which in turn she passed along to that child—while Jack scouted for land, eventually finding a high, flat hundred and sixty acres that looked fairly promising about three miles east of Dell's place. A little spring bubbled up near the center and cut a brushy creek acrost one corner, so we knew we had plowable land and sweet water to boot. After talking it over, we decided that was about as good as it was going to get in this part of Kansas.

The first order of business for Jack was to turn enough sod to start building a shelter and break enough ground to get oat seed and a vegetable garden into the ground. When he wasn't engaged in that back-breaking labor, he was out hunting, bringing home venison and partridge when he found it, and chokecherries and little bulbs that he said tasted like the wild ramps of his childhood. On them trips, he spent about as much time searching for wood as he did for game. There were willows and scattered brush in the bends of the streams, but he said he could have worn out two horses to find enough windfall firewood to light his pipe. In some places, old buffalo flop so dry it would crumble at the touch still littered the ground, but it burned, and Jack hauled home more than a ton by the time his rambles were through. What we'd do when winter set in we did not know, though Clement had some vague notion that families roundabout might hire a train to bring firewood from back home, such was his idiocy.

God's own hand was with us in one respect, and that was the rain. We got a steady day-long drizzle a couple of days after I'd put in the truck garden, and that softened the ground enough to make it easier for Jack to turn the sod for planting. Without it, I don't know as we'd of had a crop at all that first year, given the work it took just to get the plow blade through that buffalo grass wool. Jack sharpened the plow until I thought he'd file it plumb away, but it'd be dull as a butter knife the very next day, and both he and the horse liked to kill themselves pushing and pulling that hunk of iron acrost enough ground to rightly say they had a furrow. But then, the very day after the oats were in, it rained again, not for as long as the first time, but harder, and it was a warm rain that turned the whole world roundabout emerald green by the next morning. Little purple flowers on spiky stems that I came to know as "blazing star" appeared in the creases of the hills, and hairy plants that reminded me of tomatoes that in later times I learned were weeds known as "buffalo bur" produced round yellow flowers in the old wallows and cut banks. I'll never forget laying out our soddy and putting up them walls of dirt and grass in the midst of all that beauty.

The flowering of the hillsides and warm spring breezes that had neither the cutting fierceness of winter nor the searing heat of summer even perked up Dell, who by then was halfway presentable and showing signs of being more like her old self. The baby started thriving, too, once it got cleaned and fed.

I was glad to see that, but for my own reasons, because I'd been feeling poorly and knew I needed the rest. It was on the very day that Jack and I were set to head back to Grainfield to file our claim that I told him the news: I was in a family way myself.

Well, you never saw a man react the way Jack did. You'd of thought I was the first woman in the history of the world to get herself with child. He whooped and hollered like a crazy man, then stopped long enough to set me on a cushion out of the sun, only to commence his little war dance all over again. It purely tickled me just to see him so happy. He even forgot to cover his mouth when he told Clement our news when we detoured by their place on our way to town. Clement didn't seem to quite understand what he was being told, which didn't surprise me much, but Dell's reaction did. She just stood there with a blank expression on her face while she held her own child on her hip like he was a sack of potatoes.

Never mind, I said to myself. This was my business, not hers. If she wasn't going to be happy for me, then I'd have to get my happiness elsewhere. And I knew exactly where that was. I confess that I gave my man a little hug when he snapped the reins and turned our old plow horse north.

Now, filing the homestead claim was both our business, but it mostly came down on me, because in them days you had to take a loyalty oath to file for a homestead, the idea being you had to swear that you hadn't never taken up arms against the United States of America. It was the government's way, I suppose, of keeping unreconstructed Rebs from taking the free land. Jack, of course, couldn't make that oath in good faith, and so he wouldn't. I'd come to appreciate that for all his other faults, this man of mine was about as pure honest as a human being could be. Ordinarily, I found that comforting, but in this case, with our life and livelihood hanging in the balance, I thought he was being plain stubborn. I figured if I was willing to bend the rules, he should, too. I argued till I was blue in the face that he should just say he'd never fought for the Rebs and let it go at that, because how in God's name were they going to figure out any different? There probably wasn't any record that he'd ever even been in the Confederate States army, and if there was, nobody in the wilds of western Kansas was likely to be able to find it. But Jack had his pride and his principals.

"I fit 'em, and I ain't entitled," he'd say over and over. "Their rules, not mine."

So in the end I was the one who had to file, which would put the land in my name once we'd proved up on it after five years. We trundled on up to the fledgling town of Gove, slap in the middle of what was proposed to be Gove County come sometime the next year, and there I gave my oath, and we spent the absolute last of our cash money for a couple of crates of pullets and two roosters, planks to make a door and a cupboard or two, timbers to shore up a roof for our soddy, and to hire a surveyor to come out and mark a proper plat of the ground we were claiming. That night, we stayed in town and went to a dance at the biggest wooden building in town not counting the two-story hotel then under construction. That dance hall was mostly a Methodist church, though it served as town meeting hall as well. Jack wasn't a dancer by any stretch, and I could tell his lip and scar made him nervous around the townfolk, but I had a grand old time meeting people, some of whom had lived in the environs for upward of three years, which made them old-timers enough to look down on us, but they didn't. We watched the unmarried young'uns—some of whom was a good deal older than me—do the schottische and polka and other such lively dances, and we sipped lemonade and ate sugar cookies and slept that night in the wagon bed on account of we had not a red cent to our names to rent a room.

The next morning, we collected the surveyor and headed home. That gentleman talked up a storm all the way out to our claim, stopping only to sleep the one night we had to camp on the way, and once we got to our soddy he pronounced it the best claim in the whole Smoky Hill region. He went about his business with his little tripod and spyglass, drove corner stakes to mark the boundaries, proclaimed our spring was going to be known as Ross's Creek from that day forward, handed Jack the slip of paper with the details on it, and rode off, still hollering back over his shoulder at us until he was plumb out of sight. Once he was gone, I swear both Jack and I didn't say a word for a full day we were so glad for the silence.

So here we were, citizens of soon-to-be Gove County, with our claim filed and our house mostly up. Jack rode over to Dell and Clement's to enlist some manly help with the roof while I stayed behind to hoe and weed my little truck garden. I don't think I'd ever been happier in my entire life than I was in them early summer days, even if it was Kansas.

You should of seen that soddy once we got it done. It wasn't but about ten by fifteen feet, with a door and two square holes cut for windows on the south side. We stretched muslin over the holes to keep out the flies for the summer, and Jack commenced to scraping and tanning some doeskin hides to make a somewhat sturdier window covering for cold weather. He promised me that if we had some spare grain to barter after the harvest, he'd see about ordering at least one honest-to-God glass window! Anyway, I mixed up a slurry of earth and water and a little animal glue and used that to plaster the inside of the sod blocks to keep the chunks of dirt from constantly flaking off. It wasn't perfect, but it made a cleaner, better wall than we'd had in Jack's cabin in Missouri, to tell the truth, and it was a sight cooler during the summer hot spells than Ma and Daddy's tumble-down place ever had been. For the outside, we mixed a thicker mud and added plenty of dried grass to it for an even better plaster. It baked hard enough to shed water except in the heaviest downpours, which didn't happen too often in that parched land, and even then it only required a little patching. Overhead, we let the grass grow on the sod blocks of the roof, that living grass being the best way we knew of for soaking up rainwater and keeping it from leaking into our living quarters. Of course, that sod was home to a passel of critters, but they mostly stayed where they belonged and didn't bother us much.

Inside, we built a fireplace and a decent chimney outen sandstone at one end and put up a bed at the other. Jack cobbled together a small table from what was left over after he'd fashioned a door and a small cupboard. Our few belong-ings went into that cupboard or else we hung them from hooks in the posts that supported the beams and the great weight of sod overhead. The floor was bare earth, the side walls having been dug up in that very place, which I swept a half-dozen times a day until between the sweeping and our walking on it, it became hard as brick. Outside along a low hill just north of the house, Jack carved a sort of half cave to provide a bit of cover for the horse, and near the house but away from the spring, he dug a hole for the privy and turned the wagon on its side to offer a little privacy.

All in all, it wasn't much, that was for sure, but we could see that in a couple of years, if we could add on some real lath and plaster walls and maybe put in a cook stove, it would be snug enough to be considered a proper home even back in Missouri and an honest-to-God mansion compared to what most folks lived in in our part of Kansas. It was a regular palace compared to Dell and Clement's cave.

Once we finished our soddy, Jack volunteered to help Clement put up one on their claim, too, but Mister Handley would have none of that. His cave was snug, he said, and wouldn't melt in the rain or get blown over in the winter winds like ours would. He seemed right proud saying that, too, as if bedding down every night in a mean hand-hewn cave was the highest form of human habitation, but it was a lead pipe cinch that he never noticed the look on his wife's face when he said them things.

"Can't force a man against his will," Jack would say as we rode home from a Sunday visit, both of us riding bareback on our plow horse so we didn't have to up-end the wagon. That critter's back was so broad that Jack's legs practically stuck straight out, and I sat side-saddle behind him, holding onto his belt for dear life. But the horse was slow and gentle, and once we got used to his gait, it never did bother us.

"But can't he see what it's doing to his wife?" I'd ask. "Poor Dell looks like she's seen a ghost when he starts talking about winter."

"Maybe he's right, you know. Ain't no north or west wind that's going to get into that hole."

"But it is a hole!" I'd say.

At that, Jack would only laugh lightly. "You paid attention to your own place?" he'd say. "That ain't much more than an above-ground cave with a door."

"Well, I like it," I'd say back. I still felt proud of our place and good deal more secure there than I ever would of in that mean dugout. I know Jack felt the same, too, though he wouldn't say so.

"And I like you, Eva Rae," is what he'd retort. "I shorely do."

So summer went on. The truck ripened in the garden and I put up what I could working with kettles over an open fire of dry brush from our creek. We had sweet corn and cucumbers, what I didn't turn into pickles, and peas, which made for wonderful eating along with a chicken or two spared from our first crates of livestock. For the coming winter, I bagged up onions and carrots and potatoes and put them in a deep hole Jack dug and covered that with some oat straw from our first grain crop and enough dirt to maybe keep out the mice and voles. We even had a little left over to take up to Grainfield to trade for a few small household implements and the like. I believed we were set for the winter.

As the days began to shorten toward real autumn, we sat many an hour at our plank table talking about what lay ahead. Jack had big plans for the coming year, with hogs and a corn patch to feed them—though not enough to tempt him into putting up a still, he said. He drew up a diagram for a smoke-house to be built out of sandstone quarried outen the badland country to the west where he'd gotten the blocks for our fireplace and chimney, and he nailed that picture to the wall just so he could look at it and make additions when the spirit moved him. He promised me that stove and window, and figured he'd add a goat or two to help with milk for the baby, goats requiring less forage than a cow. We even sketched out ways we wanted to expand our house once the baby came.

After I got past the morning "punies," that pregnancy seemed to go as slick as ever I could of hoped. The thrill of being able to feel that life inside me was the greatest I'd ever known, and when my tight-waisted sun dresses got too snug to wear, I'll admit I took pride in doing my daily work in a pair of Jack's trousers held up by suspenders and covered with one of his work shirts. He laughed to see me with the sleeves and trouser legs all rolled up, and he'd stop and pat my stomach and give me a kiss on the top of my head.

It was about then that I realized that I really did love Jack Ross, or at least I'd come as close to it as a body needed to under the circumstances. He was good to me, he worked hard, and never had a cross thing to say unless it was grumbling about how little Clement worked when the two of them pitched in together on some chore or another. He for sure wasn't the prettiest thing that ever drew breath, but I figured Dell had a pretty man, and look what he'd turned out to be. I guess I knew right then, even at that tender age, that it's what's inside a man that counts the most.

As I got bigger and took on that rosy glow that was part sun and wind burn from the Kansas out-of-doors and part pure joy at being with child, Dell seemed to turn more and more sullen. Sometimes when we'd ride over for a visit, she wouldn't say ten words, and other times, I'd catch her looking at me the way she did her husband, as if I wasn't treating her decently, neither. It troubled my mind when I had the time to dwell on it, but fortunately, that wasn't often.

And then Marcellus Robinson came into our lives.

I was standing in the yard one day, chopping what kindling Jack had dragged up from the creek, and he was out in the garden, working to bring in the last of the potatoes and pinching bugs off the pumpkins and a few other squash plants. He would of been the first one to see the little plume of dust kicked up by horse and rider, but he didn't take much notice on account of it was the dry season, and dust devils had fooled us more than once into thinking someone was coming. I watched it for a bit and was on the verge of thinking it was just dust myself when a pale horse and rider emerged from the gray cloud and came riding our way. A quarter mile from the house, that rider halted, clumb down, and led his mount forward on foot, though the animal balked some and appeared to want to crop the grass rather than follow.

I shaded my eyes against the sun and watched him come on. He wasn't a big man, at least not tall, and from the way he walked with a rolling gait that said he had bow legs, I took him for a cowboy. His trousers bunched at the calf over top of his heavy boots, and he wore two or three shirts and a torn canvas duster in spite of the heat of the day. Both him and the horse looked pretty much played out.

When at last he was within hailing distance, he stopped, pulled a bandana from his pocket, and mopped off his face.

Well, I have to say it surprised the daylights outen me to see the gray trail dust give way to a face near as black as a hunk of coal.

"Pardon, ma'am," he called out, "but I am purely in need of a square meal. I ain't eaten in two, three days."

"Well come on, then," I answered. "We ain't got a lot, but I can fix up some cold corn bread and a cucumber salad."

"That'd be pure wonderful," he said.

"I can fix you some eggs, too," I added, "or you can wait for supper. That'll be chicken and biscuits."

I saw him grin, his big white teeth gleaming in a black face that even from that distance I could tell was handsome in a broad sort of way, but then just as fast as a snap of the fingers, that grin faded.

"Come on, Mister," I shouted again, and started to wave him in, but Jack, who had snuck up behind me, caught my hand.

"You go on!" Jack hollered louder than he had to. "Git!"

The man just stood there and scuffed a toe in the dirt. "Sir, I'm neigh on to starving."

Jack glowered and waved a fist. "I said git!"

"Oh, Jack," I said, "we got plenty to give a man a bite to

eat. Whyn't we give him a decent meal?"

"He's a nigger," was all Jack said.

"He's a hungry man," I said.

"I used to hang niggers from oak trees for sport."

That set me back. It had been a spell since I'd thought about them days. "I reckon you did. You and Daddy and the rest of you Kluxers," I said. "But that war's over and that man wants a bite to eat. Now, you ain't going to let him starve."

He rubbed his jaw and gave me a look I'd not seen before. "You'd feed a nigger?"

"I'd feed the devil himself if he was starving, and you look at the way that fellow's clothes hang on him, I believe he's starving."

Jack shook his head. "No'm. I won't."

"Then I will."

"I won't let you."

"How you plan to stop me?" I asked.

That stumped him. He started to say something, wiped at his lip, started again, then sort of slumped. "All right. But bring him his victuals out here. I won't have him eating in our kitchen."

I actually laughed at that. "Jack, our kitchen ain't much better'n a hole in the ground. Some days, I'd rather eat out here!"

"Aw, hell," he said, "have it your way." With that, he turned and stumped off somewhere.

I waved at the black man. "You can come in for a proper meal," I shouted. "I'll fry up some eggs."

He grinned again at that, though I suspect he was still keeping a weather eye out for that man of mine. "Thankee," he hollered back, and commenced walking toward our soddy. He stopped some yards short, though, and I could see he was puzzled. "You got a back door?" he asked. "Be happy to use the back."

I laughed. "Front and back's the same. Wash basin's over

yonder. Once you've used it, come on in." And so he did, though he was real nervous about it.

Turned out his name was Marcellus Junius Robinson, which was quite a handle for someone who'd been born a slave in Alabama. He told me he got pulled into the Union army during the war when he wasn't but twelve or thirteen years old and had come west to fight Indians with the buffalo soldier outfits after the war, they being squads of black troopers who earned that nickname on account of the Indians thought their woolly hair was like that of the buffalo. All in all, Marcellus said he stayed in the army for better'n ten years and when he got out, he was so far from original home and there being no particular prospects for a young black man in the Reconstruction South anyhow, he stayed on in the West and worked at whatever kind of job he could find, mostly cowboying or doing menial labor for the railroads. He'd hit a patch of bad luck when some Irishman who didn't like him took a swipe at him with a pick ax and busted his wrist, so he hadn't worked for some months even though he was healed up.

All that came out in between bites of cornbread and runny eggs. What he didn't tell us that day, though we came to learn it later, was that in spite of the pain of a broken wrist, he'd grabbed that ax with his good hand when the Irishman swung again, wrestled it loose, and brained the Mick with it. Had he not been fleet of foot, they'd of probably lynched him on the spot. It kept him from getting too near to towns, and so he'd just been riding circuit, so to speak, trying to keep body and soul together. He'd not been able to find game for several days when he came upon our place, which accounted for why he was so hungry.

Now, Jack still wasn't too happy about having Marcellus anywhere near our claim, let alone eating at our table. He wouldn't even come inside until after that black man had finished up his meal and gone outside to tend to his horse.

"I'll tell you what, he ain't staying," Jack said while we ate our noon meal. "'Tain't fitting."

"Oh, he's staying," I said. I could see Marcellus outside sitting Indian style with his own plate in his lap while he gobbled down a second meal in just about as many hours.

I could also see the black anger gathering at the corners of Jack's eyes, and for a moment, it had me a mite scared. I remembered what he'd said about his temper.

"No ma'am. He ain't," he said. Before I could argue any more, he'd slapped his bandanna acrost his mouth to wipe off the crumbs and stormed outside. He didn't say a word to Marcellus, but the look he gave him would of sent shivers through a hunk of stone.

So Marcellus left that day, riding off east in the general direction of I don't know where. But he was back the next week, taking care to approach the house when I was outside again. Jack stormed and swore, but didn't put up too much fuss when I fed him. This time, Marcellus chopped kindling and hauled water in payment for the victuals, too.

"Good riddance to bad rubbish," Jack said as he watched him go.

That time, Marcellus stayed away for two weeks, but when he came back the next time, it was with hat in hand.

"I need work," he said from his usual place thirty or so yards shy of the house. "Real work, not just chores. Be glad to do whatever you need for a meal and place to pitch my tent." To tell the truth, he looked as if he hadn't et since the last time he was by the place.

I took the request to Jack over our midday meal. He fumed some more, but I reached for his hand and stroked it. "Marcellus insisted on doing some work to pay for his cornbread and molasses..." I said.

"You know that boy's name?" He seemed stunned.

"Marcellus Robinson," I said, "and he ain't no boy. He's near as old as you are, for heaven's sake. Anyway, he says he'll work for food. You know there's a powerful lot of work to be done around here. Getting the ground ready for winter wheat, for one. Digging a new privy, for another. And you ought to finish a proper sod barn for that horse."

"We can do it our ownselves," he said.

I shook my head and moved his hand to my swelling belly, which right then was rippling with life. "Not me, husband," I said. "I can cook and wash, but the heavy work has pretty near passed me by. You really think you can get all that work done yourself?"

"I'll ride over and snag Clement for a day or two."

I actually laughed out loud, and he reddened some. "Jack, I know you don't cotton to colored folks, but that man out yonder can do five times the work ten times as well as that worthless brother-in-law of mine. You can tell that much just from looking at him!"

He was caught betwixt the devil and the deep blue on that one. "But Eva..."

I let him pat that belly again, and the fight went outen him.

So it was that Marcellus stayed, though the notion was he'd be around only as long as the hard work lasted. I struck a deal that very afternoon that we'd be more than happy to feed him supper and breakfast every day if he'd take care of some of the hard things for us, especially the digging since the dry summer had baked that earth about to the hardness of granite. He agreed on the spot.

Jack harumphed and muttered for the rest of the day and even pointed his shotgun in Marcellus's direction a couple of times, but I reckon Marcellus had faced worse, for that didn't seem to faze him. Jack finally allowed as how he'd let a nigger dig a privy. Marcellus only nodded and tipped his hat, stripped off his shirt, and commenced digging.

That night, he pitched a little canvas tent out near where we kept the horse, which got Jack all nervous again on account of he was sure our guest was going to try to steal that animal, but I shushed that nonsense with the observation that he already had a decent enough saddle horse and what on earth did he need a plow horse for? And as it turned out, Marcellus was a whiz with horses, too. When Jack got up the next morning, Marcellus was already at work filing down one of our horse's hind hooves that had split where Jack hadn't nailed the shoe right. Jack didn't talk to him that day or the next, but sometime on the third day, I was hanging wash and heard them two swearing a blue streak. Thinking they were on the verge of killing one another, I lifted my skirt so I could run and hurried on down to the creek, where last I'd seen them. Turned out they were on the far side taking turns on a long-handled crowbar trying to grub a rock outen a patch Jack wanted to turn for crops. Them two were stripped to the waist, sweating like stokers in the fires of hell, cussing at the top of their lungs, and laughing in between when that rock would budge a little, then fall back into place just when they thought they had a purchase on it.

They got the rock, and Marcellus ate at our table that night, though Jack still wouldn't talk to him directly with me present, it being "Ask Mister Robinson would he please pass the spuds" and such like. Over the next week, though, meals became less tense affairs, and the two men finished a proper sod barn and tacked on a lean-to of sod and Marcellus's old tent to make a passable room for a hired man, for such by rights he had become.

Now, Clement and Dell didn't think much of that arrangement, I'll tell you, and I thought Clement and Jack would come to blows over it, which I found almost comical on two scores—first that Clement would dare challenge a man as powerful as my husband, and second that blood-thirsty old nigger-killer Jack Ross would stick up for a good man, no matter the color of his skin.

And so it was that our first summer disappeared into a gentle autumn and that crept on to winter. We were snug in our little home, we had another hand around the place for the hard work, and so far Kansas had been bountiful to us. I was swelling by the day and looking forward to a baby soon after Christmas.

It snowed Christmas week, but just enough to turn the world a pure white. Jack surprised me with oranges he'd bought on his and Marcellus's last trip to town for supplies, and I gave him a blue scarf I'd been knitting in secret for weeks, then I made chicken and dumplings, cooked carrots, and a mock apple pie for both men.

I was sixteen years old and on my way to seventeen, I was eight months pregnant, and other than I missed seeing my Ma once in a while, I figured life couldn't get much better than that.

Then it turned January of 1885, and it all changed.

Dell

R OBERT JOHN ROSS decided to come into the world on the second day of January, 1885.

The new year came on with a blizzard that sliced in outen the northwest with a ferocity I never did see back in Missouri. January 1 had dawned warm and almost wettish, with a sweet east wind and hazy blue skies that I'd of taken for spring had I not known better. By noon, the winds had turned to the north, and the western and southern horizons were lost in mountains of gunmetal gray cloud. It commenced to rain about the middle of the afternoon, and that had turned to sleet by the time we sat down to supper. The full force of the wind hit shortly before midnight, and the snow with it, driving against our snug sod house so hard I swear the very earth rattled.

I'd been feeling poorly most of the day but chalked it up to the change in the weather. When I awakened soaking wet in the middle of the night with a feeling like every muscle in my body was ready to tear in two, I finally knew what was happening.

Dear Jack did the best he could, but about the most experience he'd had birthing anything was pigs, and this lone child trying to come out of its momma was a whole lot different than a litter of piglets. I worked and sweated through the night and on through most of the morning while Jack tried to make me comfortable, but there wasn't nothing he could do that would really help. Toward midmorning, I just gave a grunt and felt something give and then it was over, with me shaking like a leaf and Jack doing a little dance like a five-year-old kid about to wet his pants.

"It's a boy," he said, and he actually clapped for glee. "Oh, Evie, it's a boy!" His breath was smoking it was so cold in that soddy, but he stripped off his shirt and waved it around his head like some battle flag.

"I'm glad, Jack. I surely am," I said between clenched teeth to keep them from chattering with fatigue.

First thing we did was name him Robert John, which was Jack's daddy's Christian name, then I cleaned the both of us up as well as I could, and drifted off to sleep with that wee thing tucked under the blanket with me. I never did hear the worst of that storm as it blew itself out over the next twenty-four hours, for I was sleeping the sleep of the just with that warm, sweet-smelling body cradled against me.

But that was the best day that my son, my husband and I had together.

By the second day of my baby's life, his father was plumb wearing himself out trying to dig a path to the barn through three feet of snow and drifts three times that high to make sure Marcellus and the livestock had survived the blow. I was busy trying to get Robert John to suckle, which was a chore since neither one of us had any experience at making it work, and at the same time I had to be up cooking oatmeal and eggs for my man. As for Little Rob, as I called him, once he found the teat, he worked it right hard, but in a little while he'd spit up most of whatever he'd sucked down. He took to crying almost constantly in between feedings, and I began to worry about whether he was all right. By the third day of his life, he was so colicky I thought he'd drive me crazy. Jack at least had a chance to get away outdoors, but there I was with that tyke crying so hard he broke blood vessels in his scalp and me not knowing what on earth it was that I could do to quieten him down. I never in life imagined that something so tiny and frail could put up such a fuss.

"Jack," I said over the caterwauling, "maybe I need to have you get Dell over here to see if she knows what will stop this crying." I confess that racket was making me nervous as a cat in a roomful of rocking chairs.

"What would that woman know?" he asked. "She barely pays attention to her own boy."

"But she must of got him through this stage."

Jack looked from me to that tiny red face and back again. "The drifts are terrible, but I'll see if I can fetch her," he said.

By the time Dell and little Caleb had shown up riding bareback behind Jack on our plow horse, Little Rob was asleep, though I could tell more from exhaustion than comfort. Dell stripped off her coat and laid it next to the hearth, where it commenced to steaming, planted her little boy there, too, to warm him up, and came to peer at me and mine.

"Looks peeked," she said to me with her back turned.

"Yes," I agreed softly.

"He et?"

"Some. Not much. He spits some of it up."

She clucked a little and looked back at her child, who was sitting up on a blanket. Satisfied that he was all right, she scooped up Little Rob and held him tight. He stirred and made a face, and she gave him back to me. That was when I noticed the deep purplish bruise on the side of her face.

"What happened to you?" I asked, touching my own cheek.

"Nothing," she said, and she brushed at the bruise as if she could wipe it away. "Nothing to trouble your head over, anyhow." She nodded toward Little Rob. "Any fool can tell what the trouble is with that child," she said in the same tone of voice that Daddy would of used to say the same thing. It right startled me.

"What's that?" I asked.

"The child is touched by the devil."

I recollect actually smiling at that, though I'm certain it was a nervous smile, her words having made the hairs on the back of my neck stand up. "Now, Dell, don't josh," I said.

"Ain't joshing," she said. "It's on account of you've had a free nigger in your house. The good Lord looks on that as sin."

"Oh, come on."

She whirled on me, and I swear her eyes were blazing like fire. I'd never seen a look like that before, and it terrified me. "It's true," she said with more of a hiss than the soothing voice I remembered from childhood. "You've broke God's law. Clement says so, too. Having that man eat right at your table..."

"Dell, don't," I said, and I hugged my little son close. He stretched and started to whimper again, and I knew he was fixing to cry hard. If there was evil in my house, it seemed to me that it came from her, not me. "You know that's foolish talk."

"'Tain't," she said, and she leaned close. I could smell her stale breath and see the little live things crawling in her unkempt hair. "You've done evil, and it's touched the child. Ain't nothing for it but that you baptize him in the river right away."

"The river's froze over," I said, though at that moment I'll tell you my heart was as cold as that water.

"Can't be helped. Chop a hole, dunk the child, say the words, and drive that wicked black man away. 'Tis the only way to save the child."

Well, that was just about the end of that conversation, I'll tell you. She fixed supper for Jack and fussed around the place a little, pretending to clean up a few things even though she and Caleb were dirtier than anything in our home, then she insisted on getting back to Clement even though it was coming on to night and bone-chilling cold outside.

"Get that child baptized in the river," she said as she wrapped Caleb up and prepared to leave. She hadn't paid her own little boy any mind at all since first she'd arrived, and he was stinking from soiling whatever sort of rag she had him wrapped in. "Else his soul will burn in eternal damnation."

I cried myself to sleep that night, and I commenced again when Jack came home sometime near on to midnight, half frozen from riding both ways. He stoked the fire with a few pieces of scrap wood he had left over from the timbers he'd hauled from town, banked it so it would burn as long as possible, and slid under the covers next to me and the baby.

"I won't touch you on account of I'm froze stiff," he whispered. "Maybe once I warm up."

Little Rob stirred and tried to cry, but he was too tuckered.

"She's crazy, you know," Jack added. "Crazy as a damn hoot owl. Wouldn't talk about nothing but how we was committing mortal sin having a black man on the place. I'll run Marcellus off the place if that's what you want, but he's doing most all the work these days. Been sharpening the plow to get ready for spring."

"You leave Marcellus alone," I said.

"If that's what you want."

"You know it is. It's what you want, too. He ain't the cause of our troubles."

"No, I suppose not." He rolled over. "Well, good night, then."

"Jack," I said.

"What?"

"This child ain't well."

I could feel a shudder run through him which was more than a shiver from the cold. "I know."

"What are we going to do?"

"Wait it out, Evie. Say our prayers and wait it out."

And so we did. After a couple of days more, Little Rob rallied and commenced to eating better, but the terrible colic never did go away. I made every poultice I could think of and some that Jack concocted that he said his own momma made when he was a boy. Along about the end of January we had a nice thaw and I took baby Rob out for some fresh air when there wasn't any breeze. Clement and Dell both rode over on one of them warmish days, but I couldn't hardly stand to be around either one of them the way they harped on getting Little Rob baptized. I was actually afraid they were going to snatch him up and haul him to the river and do it themselves, although Dell wouldn't touch the little tyke on account of she was so sure he was touched by the devil. Clement got his rifle and threatened to take care of the nigger problem, too, although Jack calmed him down by saying Marcellus was our nigger and Clement would owe us all Marcellus's labor if he did anything. Our friend stayed well outen the way that day, but of course I knew Marcellus well enough to know that he would of blown Clement to Kingdom Come if that idiot had actually tried anything. Too bad he didn't, the way it worked out.

After that spring-like day, the weather turned brutal cold again, and Little Rob started to lose ground. He lost interest in nursing after more than a few minutes, and that soft skin began to sag where it should of been stretching over plump-ness.

On the fourteenth of February, little Robert John Ross slipped away from us in his sleep without ever having been baptized, though I have to say that any God worth praying to wouldn't make that poor babe burn in Hell just on account of his folks didn't get around to getting him sprinkled. Anyway, it liked to broke my heart, but as strong as he'd seemed for the six weeks we'd struggled to keep that child going, I could tell it hit Jack worse. He wrapped the baby in a piece of blue blanket and sat with him on the edge of the bed for hours, just rocking while tears poured down that craggy, broken face. Little Rob had been a miracle to Jack, coming fairly late in life and all, and now he'd been snatched away.

Marcellus paid his respects, then went down to the barn where he took a couple of boards off the bed of our wagon and planed them until they were smooth as silk, tacked them together into a coffin, and left it there while he rode out onto the plains for a couple of days, leaving us to our grief.

We wrapped the body tight in his blanket and filled the tiny coffin with clean straw and laid him in it. Then Jack went up near the high corner of our claim and dug a grave. I don't know how he did it, that ground was frozen so hard, but he scratched and clawed at it with a pickax until he got through the sod and into drier dirt and carved out enough of a hole about three feet deep to lay the coffin in. We buried our boy, just the two of us, on a gray day that spit snow at us, and I recited the Twenty-third Psalm best as I could remember it while Jack gathered up enough broken bits of sandstone to put a little cairn over the grave to keep the prairie wolves away. He promised me we'd put up a permanent stone marker when the weather turned, then we trudged home and held each other until we went to sleep.

Spring did come on, though only after a cold and cruel winter made worse by our grief. I've never known such a time of ache and loneliness, and before the first greening on the hillsides, I thought Jack aged ten years. His hair began to sprout hanks of gray that stuck out like it was made of wire, and the torn, scarred cheek seemed to shrivel up. His clothes hung on him the way they had before we were married, and sometimes he shuffled when he walked. I suppose I wasn't doing much better, for Dell's charge that Little Rob's death was our fault—mine, really—hung over me like a sword. I knew it was a lie, and just the notion that she'd had the gall to say it rankled me more and more every time I thought about it, infuriating me in my calmer moments and filling me with dread and guilt in the dark of night when I missed that babe's warm mouth on my body most of all. No matter how I tried to get shed of it, Dell's accusation was always there, planted in my mind like some tough weed that only grew stronger the more I tried to chop it out.

With the first warm days, Jack and Marcellus commenced going about the necessary farm work. The winter wheat would be coming soon, and with luck we'd have a cash crop at last that would let us buy some livestock and a stove and things to make our place more truly our home. At first, Marcellus did most of the hard labor on account of he could see how it was with Jack even though he stood to gain nothing from it beyond what he was already getting, namely a roof over his head such as it was and two hot meals a day. But later, with the warm sun shining on him and the heft of honest tools in his hands, Jack began to rally a little, taking his own turn at the hard work, and bit by bit he began to shed the grief that had come so close to causing him to waste away.

As for me, the rhythms of women's work around the place helped some, and seeing Jack get a bit of spring back in his step lifted more of the burden from my own heart, though I knew for a fact that I'd never be entirely the same again. I'd been a girl, and now I was a woman with a heavy load of sorrow to show for it. Jack insisted I go in to Grainfield with him to pick out the truck garden seeds, and I went, though Dell's charge was still so burdensome I stayed as far away from the church as I could and only nodded in passing to the women townfolk I'd met before, as if there was some mark of Cain on me that them ladies could of seen.

It was April before I laid eyes on Dell again, when she and Clement and little Caleb rode over for Easter dinner. I hadn't wanted to do it, but Clement had stopped by the upper acres while Jack was working there and invited themselves over, avoiding any mention of our dead child as he did so. Jack shot a doe and a big white whooping crane in the breaks along the Smoky Hill and carved up a couple of big roasts and plucked that bird, saving the feathers to sell to the milliner in town. I cooked everything up into a kind of stew with the last of our potatoes, though that bird smelled pretty gamy, and Marcellus contributed two big cans of peaches he'd managed to buy in town on his last trip and some green coffee beans even though he knew he wasn't going to be sharing our table.

"That's all right, Miz Eva," he said as he handed over the coffee so I could parch and grind it. "You just have a good day with your sis. I been thinking about riding over to Hays to see the sights, and this is as good a time as any." He grinned and tipped his hat, and you'd of never known there was any hurt or anger in him over being shunted aside for Dell and her family.

But hurt and anger wasn't the half of it when it came to the Handley clan, and none of it had to do with Marcellus, who didn't even get a mention that whole day.

I'd never seen Clement so out of sorts. He stomped around, sniffing like he was searching out a polecat, and he actually booted his own child outen the way whenever that poor boy happened to come too close. At more than a year and a half, Caleb Levi was toddling around and getting into everything, sticking fingers in the slop jar, playing in the ashes on the hearth, picking at bits of root that held a sod block together. I confess I enjoyed watching him, and for the first time in two months, that innocent young child sort of took the sting outen my own grief. But Clement was having none of it. He'd cuff the boy or swear at him, and once he picked him up by one arm, dangling him at chest height, and slapped him a good one on the bottom. When it came time to eat, Clement sailed into the crane, only to spit it out right onto the serving dish, spoiling it for everyone else. It did taste like roots or grubs or some such, but that was no reason for him to do like that. Dell wouldn't even touch that bird, and when she took to mumbling how it was a sin to kill a creature like that, it being the reincarnation of lost souls, I scooped it up and took it outside and threw it in the garbage heap behind the privy.

After that, Dell sort of withdrew. She sat at our table making small talk mostly to herself and ignored both child and husband. She ate daintily, lifting her pinky the way she had as a child, and once, she even turned to me and called me Lucy Jean after one of our twin sisters. It brought tears to my eyes. Whatever had caused the sharpness over poor Little Rob appeared to have given way to a deeper, sadder sort of craziness.

"Lonely, that's what it is," Jack said after they'd ridden off into the lowering sunset. "That husband of hers ain't there but once in a coon's age, and when he is, he's drunk as a skunk and hits her."

"Clement drinks?" I thought instantly of that ugly purple bruise on Dell's cheek.

Jack laughed, but there wasn't any humor in it. "All the time. Not today, of course, on account of they were coming here, which is probably what put him in such a foul mood."

"I worry for the child," I said.

Jack wrapped his arm around my shoulder. "At least they got one," he said softly.

"Maybe that's all the more reason to worry," I said.

He didn't answer, but I knew he felt the same way I did.

I spent some of the next days sitting alongside that pile of sandstone where our son was buried. Clusters of little purple wild onion blossoms washed the ground in color, and meadowlarks were already warbling their bubbly song. From where I sat, I could watch the soft breeze ripple the emerald green fields of winter wheat so thick I could hardly walk through it, just the way Jack had promised when first we came to Kansas. We would have a good harvest in a few months. I missed my child terribly, but it was impossible to grieve as deeply as I had with the bountiful spring around us. Or, perhaps, the necessary part of grieving was behind me now and I was ready to begin living my life again.

Which was more than I could say for Dell. What Jack had said about her being lonely worked on me. I had stayed away from their place during the latter days of my pregnancy and through the winter. Our only two times together in months and months had been spoiled by the business about baptism and Marcellus and by Clement's churlishness. If I was to be any help to my sister, I couldn't let that go on. So I told Jack one evening that I wanted to go spend a few days with her, and after some arguing on his part over not wanting me to have to put up with that husband of hers, he relented. He needed to go to the new town of Gove City, which was soon to be officially named our county seat, to make arrangements for delivery of the wheat crop once he and Marcellus had it sheaved and thrashed, so he allowed as how he could drop me off with Dell and pick me up a couple of days later on his way back. That suited me fine.

What I found when we got to that mean dugout was even more shocking than what I'd seen a year earlier. How it was them three people could live in that mess was more than I could fathom. Filth was everywhere, from rancid scraps of meat and fat lying on the table and already crawling with maggots to spilled slop jars that had the place smelling worse than a two-hole outhouse on a summer day. Little Caleb crawled around mostly naked through all that muck, and Dell might of done better for herself if she had been naked as well, her dress and apron were that crusted with grime. One eye was swollen shut, too, which she said was on account of getting a splinter, though there wasn't enough wood on the place to amount to a toothpick. Her husband was nowhere to be found, neither, which was all right by me. Bits and pieces of broken tools lay scattered around the yard, and a pile of what appeared to be guts hummed with a shimmering blue-black crust of flies. How in God's good name them folks had cleaned up well enough to come visiting on Easter was absolutely beyond me.

"You can't stay here," Jack said to me from where he stood beside me in what passed for a doorway to that place. Dell heard him, though from the blank look on her face, it didn't register.

"I've got to," I said. "Look at all that need's doing!"

"You can't fix this problem, woman."

I pushed him outside and away from that door, beyond where my sister could hear us in case any of it was getting through her addled brain. "Jack, she needs me. You see how it is. I can't leave her alone any more."

"Then I'll stay."

I shook my head. "No, you get on to town and do your business and come back tomorrow or the day after. That's soon enough and will give me the time I need to see to cleaning the place up."

"I don't feel right about it."

I patted his arm and steered him toward the wagon. "I can take care of myself."

He whirled on me, his face suddenly dark with something I took for anger for a moment, until I realized it was concern, or perhaps grief in a different way than he'd grieved over our child. "Eva Rae, there's lunacy hereabouts. Look at that eye of hers. It ain't safe."

"She says it's a splinter."

"Splinter on her husband's knuckles, maybe."

"I'll be all right, Jack. You go do your business and I'll see you tomorrow or the day after."

His jaw worked while he thought on it, then he turned and tugged me toward our wagon. Reaching in under the seat, he pulled out a wrapped oilcloth bundle. I knew what was inside.

"You take this and keep it with you every minute, awake

or asleep," he said as he untied two leather strings holding the bundle together. The oilcloth dropped away, revealing his Navy Six, an old revolver he kept stashed away except when he was traveling. Jack had told me once he'd taken that gun off a dead Yankee, but I'd always supposed that Yankee got strung up by the Kluxers rather than being involved in some battle or another on account of Jack couldn't have kept that gun through his long convalescence after Pea Ridge. Anyhow, he pressed that heavy old weapon into my hand.

"What on earth would I need this for?" I asked.

"Clement," he said, and just the way he said the name made me shudder. "If he comes back drunk... if he tries to lay a hand on you..." He let the thought trail off. "If you're bound to stay, don't be afraid to use it. Nobody would blame you," he added, and he pulled himself up onto the wagon seat, took up the reins, and rattled on down the road toward town, though I could see him looking back over his shoulder at me until the wagon topped a rise and dipped down the other side out of view.

So there I was. I dropped that gun into the pocket of my apron, where it commenced to banging against my hip as I walked. I determined that I had to find a place to hide it since I couldn't very well lug it around while I cleaned and fetched, but I took Jack's admonition to heart, too: Clement Handley was a dangerous man. He had to be, for what decent person would let his wife and child live in such total squalor? I found an old bread box that Ma had given Dell as a wedding gift unbeknownst to Daddy and slipped that gun inside it with the few ancient crumbs and mouse turds. Wouldn't nobody look in there.

I spent all that day trying my best to clean that place up, starting with the boy. He seemed even-tempered, and yet boy child enough to put up a fuss at being washed. His momma appeared not to notice, as if she was deaf to his noises. Once I'd finished with him and got him into the cleanest rags I could find, I got a pot of water boiling for the laundry and threw everything that looked like a piece of clothing into it. There wasn't a bar of soap to be found anywhere, but that water was hot enough to do what most needed doing. The lice came bubbling to the surface like scum.

Dell didn't help one whit as I straightened and scrubbed. She seemed amused by something I couldn't see as she watched me lift the clothes outen that boiling vat with a long stick, and she actually giggled as I scrubbed her table and swept the dirt floor and hauled the bedding outside. I laid the latter over an ant hill like I'd done my first week of married life and hoped the ants would clean up the vermin.

"How'd you get this way, sister?" I asked her when it came time to clean her up. She was docile enough as I ran my own comb through her tangled hair, plucking out lice with my fingernails. The nits would have to wait until I could get some good lye soap. The only time she seemed to pay any real attention was when I accidentally bumped that swollen eye. She winced and pulled away. Jack was right: it sure wasn't any splinter. But then she seemed to forget about it, and when I used a rag and hot water to scrub at the grime on her body, she mumbled a snatch of song that sounded like one we'd sung as girls.

That's when I noticed what I should of seen at Easter: Dell was in a family way again, and far enough along to be showing, though when I asked her about it, she gave me a blank look. I might of been speaking Chinese for all she appeared to comprehend.

Well, I vowed to do my best to look after her, or more precisely to look after that child she already had, since the longer I was there the more I was sure she pretty much paid him no mind. I'd already seen him stealing scraps off the table when I pulled together some lunch of stale cornbread and half spoilt side meat from some wild critter, and the longer I watched his momma, the more sure I was that he was mostly looking out for himself, and him not yet two.

It made me fairly weep to see what my sister had become, and it dang sure made my blood boil thinking about how much Caleb's daddy ignored the both of them. There was my precious child cold in the grave in spite of having the lovingest father a babe could have, and here was Caleb, with neither parent acting as if he was even alive.

So it was that I was in a genuinely foul mood when Clement came riding in at suppertime, sitting on that tall horse of his like he was king of the country. He had a brace of ducks thrown over the saddle horn and a jug in his hand, and it took him a spell to climb down off that horse on account of he was having trouble balancing himself and juggling that whiskey both at the same time. When he spied me, he gave a little snort and unhooked the ducks and tossed them in my direction. They landed a few feet short in the thick dust.

"Clean them up fer supper," he said with a slur, and I swear I could smell the drink on him even though we were fifteen feet apart.

"Clean 'em yourself," I said, and I turned my back on him.

I have to tell you, that man crossed that distance in the blink of an eye, and drunk or not, he hit me square in the back so hard it knocked the wind right outen me. My feet went out from under me and I flew a good six or eight feet with him coming along for the ride. I landed hard, and before I could even wiggle, he was on top of me. I twisted around in time to see a big fist come my way, and to this day I can't tell you how I got outen the way of it. I heard the knuckles crack when he slammed into the dirt by my head, and he winced with pain, but not enough to stop him. When he reared back for another go at it, I shoved his chest, and that threw him off balance for a split second, but he recovered and swung again. This time he connected with the side of my face. I could feel the blood rush outen my head at the blow, and I saw stars, but before he could connect again, I reached up and clawed at that face, catching nose and lip and bringing a gusher of blood. He bellowed and backed up and lifted off of me just a mite, and as he did, I brought my knee up into his privates as hard as I could.

That did it. The bellow died in a squeak, and he rolled off and crumpled into a ball, holding himself where I'd kicked. I scrambled to my feet and raced for that bread box, retrieved my gun, and took it outside, wagging it in Clement's general direction.

"You pick your drunken self up and get off this place!" I screamed at him, and I used both thumbs to pull back the hammer on that old Navy. It clicked into half cock, and I thumbed it again to full. "You git, Clement Handley, or I'll put a hole the size of a July watermelon right through you."

He was still rolling on the ground in pain, but when he saw that revolver, I could see him sober up some.

"You like to killed me," he mumbled, and I could see he'd thrown up, because he was lying in a pool of brownish mud.

"I'll finish it, you ever try anything like that again," I said.

He tried to stand, but apparently the pain in his crotch wouldn't let him. "Shit," he said, and slumped back into a ball.

"You git," I said again, and I stood there pointing that gun at him until he finally clumb to his feet and stumbled off to find his horse.

"It's my place," he whined as he eased into the saddle. Somehow or another, he'd managed to get the jug up there with him. "You can't shoo me offen my own place."

"Can and did," I said, and I waggled that gun. "You come back when you're sober and fit to take care of your family. Otherwise, stay away."

He sat there considering for a moment, then he turned the horse, kicked it in the slats, and rode away into the darkening night. I listened for the receding sound of his horse's hooves for several minutes before I eased the hammer down. My hands were shaking so hard I was half afraid I was going to blow my own foot off, but I vowed right then and there to keep that weapon in my apron, no matter how much it banged against my hip.

And I vowed to use it, too, if need be.

Then I turned around, and there was Dell, on her hands and knees, plucking the forgotten ducks like nothing had happened, with Caleb kneeling beside her, watching in silence. I confess I sat down right where I was and cried for the two of them.

Jack appeared late the next afternoon, having hurried through his business to get back to me, and I told him all that had gone on. By that time, Dell was conversing a little, though it was just small talk—"hot enough for you?" or "my, that duck was tasty" or "reckon I oughten fetch a pail of water" and such like. Sometimes she called me Eva Rae and sometimes Lucy or Gwen, and once she even called me Ma, though she tittered when she said it, as if she was laughing at some private joke I wasn't privy to. Jack took me outside while Dell cleaned up after we finished a bite of supper.

"She's tetched," he said. "Real bad, too."

"Oh, I know it. Must of come on awful sudden."

He shook his head slowly. "Now, you know that ain't true. She was probably already on her way when you was still kids at home. Didn't you tell me she was always play-acting the lady?"

"Child's play doesn't make you crazy," I said.

"No, it don't. But thinking you're a lady... believing it... and then leaving family and friends and coming to... this." He waved his hand around at their place. It was whole lot tidier than it had been when we first arrived what seemed like weeks before, but there was no getting around the fact that it was still just a hand-dug cave and a few battered old belongings spread out above a dry creek bed.

"Badgers live better than this," he said. He pointed to a stack of skins as stiff as boards stacked against a wagon wheel that the iron tire had come off of. "And badgers get rid of their own garbage to boot."

I couldn't disagree. "What can we do?" I asked.

He scratched his head. "Dang if I know. Maybe have her and the boy come live with us?"

"Clement would have a fit."

"To hell with Clement," Jack said, then added "Pardon my way of speaking, Missus." He scuffed his toe in the dirt. "But I mean it. That man's living half wild because he wants to, but he's turned that woman more than half crazy in the process, and it's probably only by the grace of God that child's even alive."

I saw his Adam's apple work at that, and I knew what he was thinking.

"Anyway," he went on, "you want to take her to live with us, it's all right with me. I doubt Clement Handley will even miss 'em after a day or two."

"She's in a family way," I said just so's he'd have all the facts.

"You don't say."

"She is."

"Well, it don't change my way of thinking any. In fact, it makes me even more convinced she's got to get some help, which would be us."

I reached up and touched the cheek above that awful scar ever so lightly. "Thankee, Jack. You don't know what that means."

I swear he blushed. "It's the least a good brother-in-law would do."

So it was that I tried to convince Dell to leave that mean hole and bring Caleb Levi to live with us. At first, she seemed excited by the prospect the way a young child is excited to go visiting, but her excitement didn't last long enough for me to get their few poor rags together into a bundle. She started mumbling and grew fidgety, and when I tried to get the boy ready to travel, she snatched him outen my hand and tried to hide him behind her skirt the same way a child would hide a doll. The more I promised her that we'd take care of her, the more confused she seemed to get, and she commenced mumbling about Clement and what he'd do and how she'd miss him. In the end, it was pitifully clear that if we were ever going to get her outen that cave, it was going to take more convincing than we could pull off on short notice. Jack and I stayed the night, and in the morning we headed for home, though I promised to come back to see her every week and made her promise to have Clement bring her by our place, though I figured that she'd forget that promise before we were well out of the yard.

Which was, apparently, the way of it. I never did see Clement the rest of the spring and even into summer. I did manage to get over to see Dell most every week, usually having Jack take me over in the early morning, which gave him time to ride back home and put in most of a day's labor before it was time to come get me. It meant four or five hours of bone-rattling travel for him from well before sunup until way past sundown with hard work in the middle, but he never complained.

During them visits, I thought Dell was making a little progress of sorts. She started calling me by my right name, and there were days when I would of sworn she was her old self. She was keeping the place picked up, and after another bout or two with lice, we got them nasty things pretty well taken care of. Her cooking wasn't much, but with the warm weather and occasional showers helping my truck garden along, I managed to take them early greens from the garden and eggs and cold fried chicken, which beat the wild things that Clement brought on the days we weren't there. Little Caleb was doing better, too, and she was certainly keeping him cleaner. His toddler jabber was giving way to clear words and a sentence or two now and again, and he began calling me

Teva, which was his way of saying Aunt Eva.

Then came the stretch when I couldn't get over to see her for almost a month. It was brutally hot, and Jack and Marcellus both were working like demons. I thought they'd kill themselves cutting and thrashing our winter wheat. I'd helped winnow, and Jack had hauled the first load to town while I spread a canvas tarp over the rest and stood guard against the birds and ground squirrels until he came back for a second load. Then, with that work done, the men commenced working from dawn to dark digging ditches to carry water from our little spring to the fields they'd planted in corn on account of there suddenly wasn't enough rain to keep much of anything green.

There was just slap too much to do for any galavanting over to Dell's place.

I must admit, all that hard work was good for me—was good for all of us, I believe—to get our minds off the loss of our little child last winter and the struggle we knew still lay ahead with Dell. The cash money we earned from the wheat was good too, and I'd never been as thrilled as I was when Jack came over the rise after the second trip with a new horse in the harness, a regular cast-iron stove swaying in the wagon box along with a barrel of flour, cans of lard and other such luxuries, and a dozen piglets snug in a burlap nest at his feet. He was singing as he rode in, and though it wasn't a pretty tune nor a pleasing voice, it made me laugh right out loud to hear it.

We spent some days getting that stove inside and hooked up to the tin chimney, and once I got it to draw so it would het up without filling our soddy with smoke, I baked white bread and a gooseberry pie that we ate with capon and wild onion relish. That stove turned the soddy into an absolute furnace, so we had our big feed out of doors, Marcellus sitting right there with Jack and me, and it was as good a feast as ever I had in this life.

It was after that meal, as he sat patting his belly and picking chicken outen his teeth with the point of his pocket-knife that Jack said it was probably time to look in on Dell again. Too much time had gone by, he said, though I knew in his heart he was glad for the break, as was I. So early the next day we hitched up our new horse to the wagon and headed west toward the Handley place just as the late summer dawn began to gray out the stars in the eastern sky.

It was as if we'd been gone a year, so much had changed, and none of it for the better. The trash was back, compounded by new stacks of animal skins so badly dressed they weren't much more than boned carcasses. The flies were thick, and both of us could smell the place a quarter mile from the door. Caleb was half wild and rooting around in all that filth, and I wasn't sure Dell had bathed since last I saw her. Once again, I set myself to cleaning up the mess, and this time Jack stayed, though more to stand guard against Clement's return than anything else.

Good thing, too. We hadn't been there more than two, three hours when I heard Jack talking in a loud voice. I stuck my head outside, and there he stood, his old shotgun cradled easy in his arms, but his feet spread apart and his hands on the grip of that gun in such a way that he could bring it to bear in a split second. Ten yards away, Clement sat on his horse, his own weapon resting acrost the saddle horn. He looked like I'd always pictured the mountain men or the woodsmen of Boonesboro who'd crossed the Cumberland wilderness with Danl. He wore leather in spite of the heat, and head to toe he was slick with grease. If he even saw me, he made no sign of greeting. He growled something at Jack, and my man said right back:

"You're doing a wicked thing, treating your woman this way."

There was another growl, and then he wheeled the horse and galloped away. At the top of a little rise, he turned, held the gun in the air, and discharged it, the sound reaching us a second or two after we saw the white puff of smoke. Again he turned, and was gone.

Jack opened the breech of his gun, extracted the shells, and slipped them into his pocket, but still he stood there, keeping guard.

Dell didn't say ten words to me that whole day. She didn't help as I washed and combed her hair, and she seemed not to notice when I cleaned and fed her child. Her belly was swelling, but when I asked how her pregnancy was going, she just got a funny look on her face and said nothing.

I couldn't help but conclude that my sister had gone away to some place where I could not and would not follow.

Late in the day, I tried to talk her into coming home with us, but she wasn't hearing me. Once, I saw her sitting in the corner, raising her pinky in the air and talking softly to herself, and it hit me like a thousand of brick that she was having an imaginary tea party. Right then, I decided the only sensible thing was to take that child with us to get him away from that situation with a daddy gone plumb wild and a momma so far gone in craziness that she couldn't rightly understand what was real and what was dreaming, but when I tried to get Caleb loaded onto the back of the wagon with promises of candies and pie, she seemed to snap outen her reverie and came running straight at me with her head down like some crazed cow trying to protect her calf from wolves. Try as I might to step aside, she hit me hard and low, and before I could collect myself, she had us rolling on the ground while she snapped at me with her teeth. Jack pulled us apart and tried to hold her while I finished loading the boy, but that woman was strong— far stronger than she had any right to be as malnourished as she was. She tore away and whirled and started snapping and clawing at him until he had to raise his hand to strike her to keep her away. I yelled, but all that did was distract him for a second, and she sank her teeth into the heel of his hand up to the bone. He yelped and danced away, and she started after him again.

Well, it was plain to see that we weren't going to get out of there in one piece unless I let that child stay, so I lifted him onto the ground and he ran straight for her, as wild as she was, and hid behind her skirt. It took a second or two for her to comprehend what had happened, but when she did, she quieted right down. I moved toward Jack to dress his hand.

"No, Missus," he said, pulling the hand away from my grasp. "We best get outen here right now, before she starts in again."

"But what'll we do about the child?" I asked.

He shrugged. "Danged if I know. Come back here every day, I suppose, until maybe she gets used to us again, or you can get her to see reason."

"She's way past seeing reason, Jack."

He nodded. "Then I guess we'll just have to help that child as best we can however we can. Right now, though, we got no choice but to leave him with his ma."

"Maybe I should stay."

"No," he said flatly. "Clement will be back, and I'll not have you here alone when he does. He's as moonstruck as she is and a powerful lot more dangerous. We'll come back tomorrow."

"You can't be spending all day every day here."

"I will if I need to. Marcellus can do what needs doing around the place."

"That ain't fair to him, Jack."

He glowered at me. "Fair don't enter into it, Eva Rae. Your sister needs you, and I won't let that brother-in-law of your'n come anywheres near you. Marcellus is a good man and he'll do what needs doing to help us out. And that's the end of it." Then he lifted me up onto the box, swung up beside me, and we took off.

I looked over my shoulder, though, watching that mean

hole until we topped the rise to the north, then dipped down into the swale on the other side and lost them to view.

"What's the matter with her, Jack?" I asked as we rattled along. "What's made her so crazy?"

He shook his head and considered my question for a long time. "Can't say. The lonelies, I suppose. I've heard in town that many a homestead woman has given in to loneliness."

"There's no reason for her to be lonely," I said. "I'm here for her."

"Reason don't enter into it, neither," he said, and he chucked the reins over the horse's back to get it moving a little faster.

"Maybe we can get her up to Gove to a dance," I said hopefully, but Jack said nothing, and I realized he really didn't have to.

It rained the next day and the next after that, which was unusual for the dry season in late summer, and though we tried to make that trip, the freshets running off the bluffs and mud thin as flapjack batter in the flats kept us from getting there. We were thankful for the moisture for our crops, but I surely feared what Dell would be like if we let too many days go by betwixt our visits.

On the third day, the rains let up, but the mud was still bad. I was beside myself with worry, so Jack mounted us double on the horse and we went that way.

Clement was there when we arrived, so we sat in the yard, with Jack holding the shotgun at the ready.

"Git," Clement hollered out to us as soon as he saw us, and he moved to a spot behind what little was left of that up-ended wagon, grabbing his rifle from where it leaned against the dugout entrance as he did so.

Jack backed the horse up a mite, though hardly far enough to be out of range of that rifle.

"I said git," Clement shouted again, and he fired once. I could hear the zip of the bullet pass close above our heads.

"We just want to see is Dell all right," I shouted back to him.

"She's fine," was all he said, and even at that distance I could hear the metallic click of him cocking his piece.

"Let us see her!" Jack let out.

The next shot came so close I swear I could smell the gunpowder. I was amazed my own man didn't fire his piece.

"All right, we'll go," Jack said, as calm and even as if he was talking to a child, and he backed up some more, turned the horse, and kicked it into a gallop to get as far away as he could as quickly as possible. As he did so, I looked behind. There wasn't any sign of Dell, but that child Caleb had come outside and was squatting to do his business the same way a dog would.

"I thought you'd shoot," I said when we were far enough away to slow the horse to a canter.

"Would of if he hadn't been standing right in front of their doorway," he said. "Couldn't risk what a stray buckshot or two would do."

We rode on for another mile or so. "We need to go back again, Jack, as soon as we can," I said. "For Dell's sake."

"I know, Missus," he said, but I could tell his heart wasn't in it.

Still, he was good as his word. We tried again two days later, and I confess I had a bad feeling about what we'd find before we'd even left our own yard. It was a windy day, with the kind of brittle, dry heat that sucks the life from your very bones and makes you hate August, and as we rode along, my dread worsened. I believe Jack could read my mind, or perhaps he was having the same misgivings I was, because he usually chattered about the crops or his hopes for getting a decent wooden house on the place, but that morning he sat glum and silent beside me. He had a tight hold on his shotgun, too, as if he expected Clement to waylay us before we ever got to the dugout.

Anyway, that ride seemed to take twice as long as usual, until it was almost like one of them dreams where you're running toward something that's so near you can almost touch it yet you can't ever quite get there.

But of course we did.

The yard was empty except for a couple of rangy looking chickens pecking at bugs in the dirt. Clement's horse stood picketed in the yard, and he'd been there long enough that he'd cropped all the grass he could reach down to the roots. Jack reined in, cocking the hammers on the shotgun against the likelihood that Clement would appear, and I called out for Dell.

There wasn't nothing but silence.

I called again.

"This ain't right," he almost whispered.

I looked at him. "What do you think we should do? I don't want to bust in on them, not the way Clement is."

Jack squinted at something on the rise behind the dugout, and then he pointed. "There."

I sighted down his arm. "Crows?" I asked.

"Maybe. You stay here." He reached under the seat and produced his Navy Six, which he cocked and handed to me carefully. "I mean it, Eva. Stay put. Don't go inside. Don't go nowheres." Then he clumb down and loped toward whatever it was he saw up on the rise, keeping low to the ground to make himself a smaller target. He slipped once in the grass, but caught himself and kept climbing. When he reached the top, he stood up and sure enough, three or four big black crows took wing with a chorus of perturbed cawing. I thought maybe he'd wave to me to come on, but he didn't. Jack just stood there for a minute or more, then turned and scooted down the grassy slope.

"What is it?" I called out.

He held up a hand to shush me as he walked around to the filthy blanket covering the entry to the dugout. Pushing it aside, he stepped inside. A few seconds later, he came out and headed my way.

I'd never seen a look like the one he had on his face. The color was so drained outen it he looked like a corpse.

"Jack, what is it?"

He came to the side of the wagon, took the revolver from my hands, and let the hammer down carefully. "Eva Rae, you don't want to go in there."

"What is it, Jack?" But I was already clambering over the side. He took me by the shoulders, and when I looked up at him, he nodded in the direction of the rise. "Clement's up there."

I wasn't sure I'd heard him right. "Clement? What's he doing?"

Jack took a deep breath. "He has a butcher knife sticking outen his back, Eva. He's dead. Been dead a while, actually. The crows..." But he let his voice trail off and didn't finish the sentence.

I was dumbstruck. Then it hit me. "You mean someone come by and killed him?"

"No," he said, shaking his gray head. "She did it."

"Who?"

He actually shook me. "Eva, you know who. He beat her pretty bad, and I reckon she'd had enough."

I let that sink in for maybe half a second and then pulled away and raced for the dugout. He tried to grab me, hollering at me not to go in there, but I was fleeter of foot than my man. I got to that blanket, ripped it down, and stepped into the fetid darkness.

Before I could see anything, I could hear the soft whimpering of the child.

Then I made out the body of my sister, swaying slowly, like some heavy pendulum, from a length of rope tied to a rafter they'd cobbled together to keep the roof from collapsing. A few inches under her feet, a rickety chair rested on its side, just the way it had landed when she kicked it over.

"Oh, my God in Heaven," I said as I sank to my knees. Her bare feet were just about at my eye level. They were gray and cold and swollen with the blood that had settled there, and her dress and legs were smeared where she'd soiled herself.

Jack took me by the shoulders and gently moved me aside, took her around the waist with one arm, and stretched toward the ceiling with his pocketknife clutched in his other hand. I could hear the hemp fraying, and it snapped with a little twang like a slack guitar string being plucked.

Jack laid her down softly on the dirt floor.

Little Caleb Levi, naked as the day he was born, shuffled out of the darkness and sat down next to the body of his mother. Her face was black from the strangulation, but the deep welts on her cheeks and chin where her husband had hit her were still obvious. Her nose was flattened over to one side, and dried clotted blood smeared her forehead underneath a cut along her hairline.

"He did that to her, and she kilt him for it," Jack said softly, as if trying to figure it out for himself. "Then she came back inside and did this."

I felt myself trembling so hard my teeth began to chatter in spite of the wicked heat of the day. "Why, Jack?"

"Like I said, Evie. They're tetched. Ain't no answer to your question other than that." He stepped around Dell's body and reached down for little Caleb's hand. "Come on, sonny," he said softly. "Let's get you away from here." The boy cried out and tried to pull away, but Jack lifted him up as gently as he could and carried him outside. The child's crying grew to a wail, and I could hear him kicking. Then they were gone, and it was just me and the battered, dead body of my favorite sister. For the first time, I noticed the way her belly was all stretched and lopsided from the dead child inside her.

So there were three of them dead, and for no reason at all

that a sane person could decipher.

I do not know how long I stayed with her, though it was coming on to night by the time Jack convinced me to come outside and sit with the boy a while so he could dig the graves. I remember stroking that poor child's head while Jack scouted out a soft place and commenced digging on the rise not far from where Clement had died. It was full dark before he was done, so we decided to wait until morning for the burial. We took a few bites of the cold chicken and gooseberry pie I'd brought along to feed Dell, but only little Caleb had any appetite. He ate like he hadn't tasted food in a month, which I realized from feeling the bones beneath his skin wasn't far from the truth. Jack hauled Clement's body down to the dugout and laid it out alongside Dell's, then built a big bonfire from whatever he could collect around the place that would burn to keep away the night-feeding creatures. Sometimes as the night wore on, I could see the twin yellow lights of a prairie wolf's eyes as it circled that miserable place, hungering for the bodies but kept at bay by the fire. Morning couldn't come quickly enough.

At last it did, of course, and by the red light of an early morning sun, we laid Dell and Clement out side by side in the grave Jack had dug and covered them with dirt and sod. We could only hope he'd dug deep enough to keep the scavengers away.

I offered a few snatches of Bible from memory, then we bundled up the child and carried him to our wagon. He kicked and fussed, but once we were moving, with me holding him tightly, he fell into a fitful sleep that deepened the closer we got to home.

Jack

So IT WAS THAT I LOST A CHILD and a beloved sister in the space of eight months and took on the raising of my sister's child, all at the age of seventeen. Still a child myself, I was, but with the burdens of a full-grown woman.

Even after all these years, it still rankles my heart that I wasn't able to save poor Dell from neither Clement nor herself, and I took it especially hard right after the fact. The letter I wrote home to Ma telling her of Dell's passing was the saddest I ever wrote, though of course I left out a good many of the details, including Clement's murder. Him I mentioned not at all. For all Ma knew from what I wrote, Dell had died in childbirth. I didn't try to explain why I had taken on the responsibility of Caleb Levi, but just stated the fact of it. Whether Ma could tell from the tear stains on the page how much grief I put into that missive, I'll never know, though I've always believed that my mother simply understood things in her heart whether they were told to her or not.

Little Caleb seemed not to know what had happened to his folks, nor did he understand the circumstances he now found himself in, though who could expect that of a boy not yet two? He spent most of the first few days huddled under blankets in spite of the searing heat, and it was all I could do to keep him clean and fed, for he had no better toilet manners than a puppy. Truth to tell, he reacted better to Jack than he did to me, actually smiling occasionally when Jack talked to him or carried him around the yard on his shoulders. Jack's ugly war wound seemed to fascinate that boy rather than scare him. He did not talk, which I took for shyness at first, but then it became clear enough that even though he'd been calling me Tevie and seemed to be learning to talk, he'd somehow forgotten all that and now couldn't manage to form even the simplest of words. I thought he was slow, but then it came to me that perhaps for months that poor child had not been talked to or cooed over while whatever madness it was that had destroyed his momma and daddy had worked its way through that family. It was likely that as much time as his dead pa had spent away, he'd heard very little human speech, anyway, and what he had heard was the ravings of lunatics. It like to made me heartsick all over again.

Turned out it was a difficult autumn for us in other ways, too. Marcellus had been talking of filing for his own homestead claim on a quarter-section adjoining ours, but he hadn't done it, and finally decided against it, at least for this year, when the weather turned from the late-summer dryness to peevish and wet with the onset of autumn. Hard rains came just at the time when the men should of been preparing the ground for winter wheat, turning the fields to muck and mire and rotting the late summer truck in my garden. What didn't rot was attacked by mice, which must of been waiting for cool weather to breed, for we hadn't seen many of the little gray creatures through the summer (though of course the red-tailed hawks, which were in great abundance in them days, kept them in check), but once the rains came, they were suddenly slap everywhere. A body couldn't step outdoors without a mouse skittering inside to get away from the wet. Jack grumbled and worried about the wheat, counting the days before we could expect the first frost and hoping beyond hope he could get the crop planted and sprouted before the hard freeze without the mice nibbling away the seed and shoots. I tried to can what I could and put away squashes and pumpkins in the root cellar, but the black mold got to almost all of them, meaning we were going to have to live off potatoes and onions through the winter.

The rains were followed by cool and windy weather that dried the fields quickly but gave a few of our chickens pneumonia, and try as I might to separate the sick birds from the rest, that disease ran through the flock like greased lightning. Before it was over, all our roosters and all but a handful of our laying hens were dead, which meant our hopes for spring pullets were dashed. The pigs were doing well, fortunately, and with a few dollars he'd managed to save, Jack bought some more and an old cow off a neighbor who'd homesteaded eight miles to the east and had more livestock than he needed. That cow was still fresh, which meant the child would have some milk at least for a while.

Jack and Marcellus finally got the wheat in the ground, but just barely before the first heavy wet snow fell, which kept us housebound for two days before the warm southerly winds returned and melted it off. Since it was only early October, Marcellus said that didn't bode well for the winter ahead, and we believed him. As if to prove the point, Jack dropped an anvil on his foot while trying to carry it from the barn to a new shed he'd added beside a little corral, and a brace of broken toes had his foot swole up so bad that I was afraid for some days he would lose it. Naturally, that didn't put him in any kind of good humor.

Once the crop was in and the snow was gone, we did take a jaunt into Gove for what we figured would be our last trip of the year. I bought yard goods on credit to make work shirts for Jack and little outfits for Caleb, and Jack bought board lumber and a keg of nails for various projects including the summer kitchen he promised to build behind the soddy so our place wouldn't get so hell-fire hot in the warm months. I even stopped by the post office and mailed off a much delayed letter to Ma with somewhat cheerier news than I'd sent upon Dell's death. I confess I lied a mite about how little Caleb was prospering under our care.

That boy did draw some attention on that trip, I will admit, for folks in Gove knew I'd lost a babe the previous winter and were naturally full of curiosity about where I'd come up with another, older child. Now, they hadn't any of them ever laid eyes on Dell, she and Clement having arrived on the Smoky Hill before the town was even founded and Dell at least never had a chance to ride into town for the barest scrap of human companionship beyond what she got from her husband and my occasional visits. I explained the situation as simply as I could to the curious old shrews, but you could tell they weren't necessarily believing it. Not that I cared, for what were they to do?

I will say that Caleb seemed to enjoy that trip about as much as a child could. You'd of thought he was seeing the sights in Paris or Rome the way he stared at them claptrap buildings. For some reason, the plank sidewalks fascinated the daylights outen him, and he'd pick up little handfuls of dirt or rocks to drop through the gaps between the boards just to see them things disappear. The old upright piano at the Stark Brothers drinking emporium absolutely made him so wild with delight that if a body didn't keep a tight rein on him, he'd up and skedaddle off to that low den just to see that musical contraption. Jack had to fetch him a half-dozen times, being careful, I have to add, not to imbibe of the spirits himself.

In that way as in so many others, Jack Ross was a far different man than the one I'd married four years before. He wasn't any prettier, of course, but he surely was hard-working, clean, and temperate—three things I believe any woman appreciates in a man. He was even less concerned about that scar, being quicker to smile and slower to hide the gash behind his upraised fist. Folks who didn't know him still stared, which he took in stride, but them that knew him seemed to forget about his disfigurement the same way I did.

We headed home from Gove on a lovely late autumn afternoon with the bolts of cloth, nails, boards, and sundry other things tied securely under an oilcloth tarp. We'd charged the whole lot against what we hoped against hope would be a decent wheat crop next spring. Caleb dozed on the seat betwixt the two of us, and for the first time in a long time, I felt like singing. I must of started to hum a tune, for Jack pitched in and rattled off "The Yellow Rose of Texas" in his rough baritone, and I followed with "Aura Lee," and before you knew it, we'd sung half the songs we knew and made up some of our own into the bargain. The child wakened to the racket, but even at just two years old, I swear he tapped his foot in time to the music and laughed every time Jack reached down for a low note. I actually told Jack that if that child liked music so much, we'd have to buy him a piano soon as our ship came in!

It was the happiest I could remember being since first I'd told Jack I was going to have a baby, and this time, I promised myself it was going to last.

And happy we were, in spite of the way the weather turned wicked on us yet again. For Marcellus was surely right: winter came on hard and strong a good deal earlier than it should of, with howling winds and bone-cracking cold. Marcellus actually had a mercury thermometer he'd bought someplace in his travels, which he kept tacked to the side of the horse stall. One morning long about the first of December, there wasn't any mercury at all in that little tube, and the scale bottomed out at twenty-five below. That morning and the next and the next after that, the mercury stayed out of sight. Just stepping outside would cause the lining of your nose to freeze, and even indoors with the stove stoked up and burning almost cherry-red, you could see your breath on the other side of the room. Jack and Marcellus worked cruelly hard to keep the stock alive, but the old cow caught pneumonia and died and actually froze solid as rock before the two men could haul her away. One of the pigs lost an ear to frostbite, too. And the chickens... well, what few we hadn't lost in the earlier sickness froze or just plain vanished, likely blown away on the fiendish winds.

After the cold snap, Christmas week seemed a blessing with daytime temperatures pushing freezing, and we enjoyed a day of rest on the 25th with as much of a feast as we could muster up and even invited Marcellus to join us, that being the very first time that Jack had invited him into our home as a true guest and not just a hired hand. The men played checkers and cribbage—Jack beat Marcellus at the former, but my man wasn't a great one for figures and couldn't best our friend at the card game—while I sewed and played with Caleb by rolling him a ball of twine. Come evening, when Marcellus bid us good-night, there was already a tang of snow in the air, and the big flakes started falling sometime before Jack and I went to bed.

It snowed that night, the next day, and into the next night so hard you couldn't see acrost the yard. The wind built with it, too, first from the east and then the north and west, blowing a full gale that turned them little crystals into icy knives that stung exposed flesh like a million little bees. The drifts built up around the front of our house, which faced south, and Jack was out there every hour with the garden spade just to keep a space clear enough to let us open the door. Getting to the privy was out of the question, for trying to walk ten feet in that blast would of gotten any grown-up lost. The one time Jack tried it, I had him tie a piece of clothesline rope to his waist while I tied the other end to the stove. He didn't get more than fifty feet from the front door before he had to turn around and fight his way back, the whole excursion taking nearly a half hour, and when he was back inside he looked like some gigantic snowman with ice crusted in his hair and ears and eyes and his clothes so covered I practically had to chop him out.

When that storm finally let up, the cold returned, this time even worse than it had been before. We were separated from our livestock and Marcellus by drifts eight feet high, and it was several days before we were entirely sure he'd even survived. Our pigs were buried in the drifts, and it took almost a week for the two men to find them. When they dug them out, several were dead, and two were still alive though partly frozen. I'll never forget looking on them poor dumb brutes as green pus ran from their noses and they stood there unable to move on account of their hindquarters being frozen. I've never enjoyed seeing an animal killed, not even for meat, but the rifle shots that put them pigs outen their misery truly were a blessed relief. The men butchered out what they could, but whatever had kept them animals alive while buried had put a taint on the meat that made it sour to the taste.

If there was anything good that came outen that awful weather, it was our chance to get to know our son, for that was the way we thought about Caleb now, and in some wonderful way he truly did replace the ache still left over in our hearts from the loss of Little Rob. In the long, cold days when there wasn't anything for Jack to do but worry, that boy was our one true source of wonder. Though he'd been so very slow to talk, somehow the dam finally broke, and a positive flood of language came outen him. He would sit on our earthen floor and chatter up a storm, talking to himself or us or the table leg. It seemed he was learning three or four words a day, and putting them into sentences that made sense, too. Sometimes he'd get a faraway look in his eyes and get still and quiet, as if some part of him was remembering something it wasn't good to remember, but then he'd sort of shake himself off and go about his business.

Caleb took to having an absolute fascination with whatever Jack was doing to take care of the implements around the place, whether it was repairing harness or fixing the stove pipe where it came loose from the wall or spending hours moving our knives over the thin sheen of warm lard on the whetstone. Caleb would huddle nearby, his dark eyes so alive I thought I could see fire in them, just watching his new daddy. Sometimes he'd ask a question, which usually started with "how come?" and sometimes he'd just sit, silent as Jack, his mind working while Jack's hands did whatever task it was that he'd set before himself.

When it came to me, though, Caleb didn't seem to take much notice when I went about the household chores. I swear, I could dust myself with flour and dance a jig in front of him and he wouldn't pay the least bit of attention.

Our time was at night, just before I tucked him in. Whether he'd been starved for affection before he came to live with us, I can't say, but the first few times I tried to hug and kiss him, he'd pull away and holler, until one night I just grabbed him and held him tight until the fight went outen him. He was like butter slowly melting in my arms, and as he relaxed, I crooned some snatch of nursery rhyme I remembered from childhood and rocked him back and forth.

Well, that did it. From then on, every night he'd climb into my lap and nestle down into whatever soft places I had like some burrowing animal and wait for me to sing. It didn't matter that I didn't know but two or three tunes, of course not counting the bawdy ones or war ballads that Jack said he was willing to teach me: I could of sung "Yankee Doodle" ten times through every night and he would of been plumb satisfied. Then I'd put him to bed, making sure to tuck in his old wool blanket good and tight, and he'd be asleep before I could step away from the bed. He started to housebreak himself about that time, too, though he was only a shade over two and I've always heard that boys are notoriously slow at that particular endeavor. It seemed like we'd turned some corner for sure.

It made a difference in Jack, too. He'd grown right

pleasant to be around over the pretty near five years we'd been married, and I'd sure come to appreciate the solid, hard-working way he lived and the decent way he treated me every single day we'd been together. But humor was always in fairly short supply with Jack, probably on account of he'd never had much cause to think there was much humor in the world, not with what he'd seen in the war and what his life was like in the dark years before he traded for my hand—years when he'd lived on strong drink and whatever hateful things them Kluxers could think up of a given night. He always told me that I was a Godsend to him and that I'd turned him from an evil path to an upright one, and I could tell that he meant it.

In all honestly, I'd harbored some secret worries that taking on that boy so soon after the loss of Little Rob would only remind Jack that his own son was dead and turn him evermore sorrowful than he already was.

I needn't have worried.

Caleb brought out the sprite in Jack. Once that child took to watching his new daddy so diligently, Jack returned the favor by watching the boy when he was at play, and then getting down on all fours and entering in. Or Jack would toss Caleb onto his back and crawl around our place on his hands and knees making neighing sounds until the boy squealed with delight. They'd make up games or even play with invisible things that I swear both of them could see.

Part of what did it, I suppose, was Caleb having no fear of Jack's looks. He stared at that scar, but in the curious, unafraid way of a child seeing something interesting for the first time. Or, sometimes when he was on Jack's knee, he'd reach up and trace the line of the scar with the tip of his little finger and smile or giggle when he did it. The first time I saw that, I swear I was more than half afraid that Jack would lose his temper, but instead, he just smiled back without trying to hide that missing lip at all.

It was after that that Jack started calling Caleb "Sonny,"

which actually cut me to the quick the first few times I heard it on account of I still wasn't completely over my grieving for Little Rob, but the truth of the matter was that Caleb was our son now. Even if I couldn't quite get him to replace my baby in my secret heart, the fact that Jack could and did became a comfort to me, too.

At last the winter waned and spring came on, though it was almost as fierce as the winter had been, which is the way of it in Kansas.

March winds turned the prairie to dust that caught in the nose and made the eyes burn with alkali, and by the time April arrived, even though there was a spattering of rain, it didn't do any more good than making little mud circles in the dust. Lucky for us, there was a bit of moisture in the soil from the snowstorms, so most of the wheat revived, though with a permanent sideways slant from that west wind. Jack commenced to worrying about the crop, which I understood since most of what we'd bought over the past year was laid against that wheat, and if we had a poor crop or no crop... well, we didn't want to think about where we'd find the money to pay our creditors.

In spite of the drouth, the weather turned humid late in April, with that close feeling that made a body almost certain a cyclone was coming on, and after a long week of the muggies going into Easter, with thunderheads building to the west every afternoon only to blow over before dropping their load of rain, we told each other we were actually ready for a good storm.

Then came Easter Sunday itself, which dawned hot and got hotter. By midday, we could see the towering white storm clouds somewhere off toward Colorado, and by mid-afternoon, hammer-headed clouds were bearing down on us so fast you could actually watch them move, only they weren't white anymore, having turned gunmetal gray with swirling rain-heavy flat bottoms streaked with blue-white flashes of lightning. Jack and Marcellus were playing checkers in the barn when the first crack of lightning hit, and it wasn't but a couple of seconds before all hell broke loose, with claps of thunder and greenish lightning bolts, some of them so close you could almost taste that peculiar burnt air smell that Ma always said was the odor of brimstone. The hail started as little pea-sized things that went pocketa-pocketa off the door and oiled leather windows, then quickly turned to sharper cracks and thuds, and dust began to sift down outen the ceiling above my head.

That was when I heard it, above the racket made by rain and hail: a low moan that grew and grew until it was a wail and scream like a dozen railroad trains racing side by side and all bearing down on our place. The sky lost all hint of light except for the flashes of lightning, and the twisting wind of the cyclone hit with such force that our window tore outward, the door blew open and pulled loose of the hinges and went sailing like a piece of paper acrost the yard while whole chunks of the sod roof lifted up, bounced down once, and then were gone. I hardly had time to scoop up Caleb and slide under the bed before pieces of stove pipe commenced to flying around in that house, then table and chairs joined in as if tossed by some invisible giant, and even the bed itself.

I said my prayers, I'll tell you, and I reckon I screamed, though that wind snatched away any sound other than its own passing.

Then it was gone, just as fast as it had come. I crawled out from under the bed, and holding Caleb's hand, we ran outside and down to the barn to see about the men. It was still pelting down rain, but the day was already lightening up some, and I could see the snaky tail of that cyclone moving on to the east, churning up a black cloud as it went.

The only trouble was, there wasn't a barn any more. Sod and lean-to and rail fence and all were gone as if they'd never existed, except that an upended crate still stood with the checkerboard and pieces right where the men had left it!

Well, I was more than half frantic seeing that, and no men, but then I heard a rustling behind me, and little Caleb and I turned around in time to see them two crawling outen the root cellar, both of them soaked to the skin and covered with mud so's you could hardly tell which was the black man and which was white except that Jack was the taller of the two.

When they saw me and the boy, Jack took off running and grabbed us both up and lifted us off the ground.

"Oh, thank God!" he shouted, and swung us around like he was hoorawing me at a dance. "I thought sure I'd lost you!"

It turned out, them two fellows were so intent on their checkers that they'd plumb ignored the storm until the hail started, but once they heard that roaring sound, Marcellus knew right away that it was a genuine twister, so they'd started off for the house with the intent of looking after Caleb and me and getting all of us squeezed down in that root cellar, but they didn't make it all the way and had to dive into that hole like a couple of prairie dogs when our front door came flying at them like some scythe intent on mowing them down.

We spent that whole next week trying to get our place back in order. Fixing the house wasn't that tough. What was left of the barn we used to patch the holes in the roof. We'd found the door, busted up but fixable, though we did have to board up the window until we could get to town for the piece of glass Jack had promised me, which I thought was plain foolish given what Kansas weather had just done, but he said never-you-mind, a promise is a promise.

But the barn would take stripping fresh sod and starting over, and we'd have to do that without a draft horse on account of our animals had disappeared along with the barn. Marcellus's riding horse was spared, and so he went looking for our horses as soon as he could, but came back glum with the news that the cyclone had picked up that big old draft horse and flung it headfirst into the Smoky Hill, where the flies were already at work on the carcass. Whether our other horse had gone flying as well or just run off from terror we couldn't say, but it was gone for sure.

That put us in a bind, I'll tell you. A single saddle pony couldn't wrestle a breaking plow, nor could he pull a wagonload of grain when the time came to take our crop to town—even that small part of it that wasn't destroyed by the hail. There was nothing to be done but that one of the men ride into Gove City to see about buying or hiring at least one proper draft horse. The job fell to Jack for the sensible reason that he'd also have to see what he could do about arranging credit for the things we'd need to buy to finish the necessary repairs on the house plus all the halters, horse collars, and such that had vanished along with the barn.

Jack left us on the Thursday morning after Easter, and I recollect in spite of the seriousness of the mission how both Marcellus and I laughed to see him sitting on that small horse, with his legs dangling down nearly to the ground. Caleb ran along behind, begging at first to go along, then for a ride at least as far as the wheat field, but Jack just blew him a kiss and kept riding.

Well, you would of thought that Jack had decided to vanish from the face of the earth the way that child took on. Caleb cried for the better part of the day and would not be consoled on account of his daddy had left him, and once he'd pretty much worn himself out from crying, he just sulked. I tried to sing to him or tell him stories, reciting nursery rhymes as best I could, but it wasn't any use: he was half mad and half sorrowful that Jack was gone, and was slap determined not to get over either of them emotions. That was all there was to it.

Finally, I gave up and told him he'd just have to live with it, that Daddy would be back in two days, tops, and he'd simply have to wait.

But Jack wasn't back in two days. Nor in three.

By the morning of the fourth day, Marcellus and I both

agreed that we had to go look for him, or more rightly Marcellus would while I stayed home and tended the place as well as I might. So our friend prepared to take off on foot on what would be a cruel long walk to town for a bow-legged man accustomed to sitting horseback and whose only shoe leather was a high-heeled pair of riding boots. No sooner had he clumb the long slope behind the house, though, than I heard him shouting. I ran out to see his pony, riderless, trotting toward him. Even from where I stood, I could see the saddle twisted off to one side. Marcellus led the beast to the yard, conferred with me while the animal ate up some oats, then adjusted the cinch and hauled himself into the saddle.

"I'll find him, Missus," Marcellus said.

"Do," was all I could manage. "Oh, please do."

I puttered around the place the rest of the day pretending not to worry. Although by that time I had been in a fret for a day and a half, it was nothing to what I felt now, knowing as I did that Jack had had some sort of real accident. By that evening, I was almost as sullen as Caleb, and the two of us skipped supper and instead squatted Indian-style in the front yard watching the sun set in the west and the sky fade from red to pale rose to lilac until the twinkling on of the stars washed out even that last little bit of color. Then I put Caleb to bed and waited some more, rocking in the darkness and waiting.

They appeared the next forenoon, coming slow on account of the two-man burden the little horse had to carry. Jack was sitting the saddle, though his head was down and he appeared asleep while Marcellus rode bareback behind the cantle, holding Jack on.

"Found him a couple miles north of the Smoky Hill," Marcellus said as he slipped off the horse's rump. Jack teetered and began to slip to the right, but Marcellus danced around and caught him and eased him to the ground, taking great care as Jack's left leg dragged acrost the saddle.

That was when I saw what had happened. Jack had tied his own red kerchief around his left leg just above the knee to stanch the bleeding, and he'd even tried to push the piece of leg bone back inside the skin, but a jagged end still poked through an inch or so below the knee. The flesh around the tear was oozing pus and smelled like putrefaction.

"Horse must of thrown him," Marcellus said, keeping his voice low. "Maybe saw a rattler or something, or just stepped wrong. Anyway, Mister Jack had pulled himself up against a little outcropping of sandstone and was smoking his pipe as calm as could be when I come along, but any fool could see how bad hurt he was."

Jack sort of came to and opened his eyes. When he saw me, he smiled thinly. "Busted my leg, Evie," he said. He didn't even try to hide that lip when he said it, and I could tell from the shine in his eyes that the pain and maybe the fever were eating at him. "Hurt like hell for a while, but it don't hurt so bad no more." Then his eyes glazed over and he slid into unconsciousness again.

Together, Marcellus and I lifted and carried him into the house and laid him out on the bed, propping the leg up with blankets and a clean pillow.

Caleb, perhaps understanding the seriousness of what we were doing, slipped to the side of the bed and stared at his daddy with wide, sorrowful eyes.

"He'll be all right, sonny," I said as cheerfully as I could manage, but of course I had my doubts.

"Can't save that leg," Marcellus said, as if reading my own thoughts.

I turned to him. "Ride to town fast as ever you can and fetch a doctor."

He shook his head. "Ain't time, Missus. Been too long." He sniffed, as if to call my attention to the smell. "'Sides, the only doc I know about's all the ways to Hays. Might as well be on the dark side of the moon for all the good that'll do us."

"But we need a doctor," I said, knowing it came out like a whine. Jack actually opened his eyes a little at the sound of it.

Marcellus waited until Jack's eyes drifted shut, then he shook his head. "Got to do it ourselves, I'm afeared." He licked his lips and said the next so soft I scarce could hear him. "Else he's gone die."

My legs went weak and I had to grab on to the bedstead to keep from falling.

"I..." My tongue was thick in my throat. "I mean, how..."

Marcellus took a deep breath and scratched the crown of his head with a long black finger. "I seen it done in the war, more times 'n I care to count. Bloody bidness, but I watched. My job was to clean up after. Reckon we can do it, too." He swallowed hard. "Reckon we gone have to."

So it was that on that beautiful spring afternoon, we commenced to taking Jack Ross's left leg off. Though it was the lower bones that were broken and the gash where the bone stuck out was a good four inches below the knee, Marcellus was pretty certain that the only way to save Jack's life was to take the leg off three or four inches above the knee, where the flesh still seemed sound. At any rate, Jack didn't appear to be in too much pain there when I poked him with my finger, and it wasn't swole up too bad.

Marcellus slipped outside to gather up what implements he could find and get a good fire roaring in the yard to heat water and whatever heavy piece of metal he could use to cauterize the blood vessels we were going to have to cut. For a long time, I just stood there, looking at my husband and the dark-eyed boy clutching the bed clothes beside him, then I pulled myself together and started to work.

"You takin' the leg?" Jack asked, scaring the be-Jeezus outen me as I bustled around the bed, gathering up whatever I could find to use for rags. It was my turn to swallow hard against the dry lump in my throat. I found I couldn't look him in the eye.

"'S all right, Evie," he said through the shine of fever. "'S all right. I knowed this was comin' soon's I busted it. Got to be. Course, I'll cuss you once I heal up for makin' me a cripple." He tried to smile, but even that much exertion exhausted him. "Damn you all to hell fer makin' me a cripple," he repeated as he drifted away. Then suddenly he sat bolt upright in bed. "They're a-comin' boys!" he shouted. "God-damn bluebellies is a-comin'!" He started in on a wavering shriek that I took for some kind of rebel yell, but he broke it off and started mumbling to himself. His eyes were wide open and focused on something I sure couldn't see. After a time he quieted, and then his lip would move once in a while and he'd try to say something else, but the effort was too much for him and he'd slump backward onto the bed, going all limp like he'd passed away.

The first time that happened, I confess I really did think he'd given up the ghost right then and there, but after a few seconds I could see his shallow breathing make his shirt rise and fall ever so slightly. He was alive, but wouldn't be for long if we couldn't get that fever outen him.

"Come on, sonny," I said, tugging Caleb away from the bed. "You can't be watching what's about to happen." I led the child outside and found some splinters of wood for him to play with. He kept staring back into the house, and I kept trying to distract him.

"What you plan to do with the boy?" Marcellus asked from thirty feet away. He already had a fire building and my biggest kettle hung from a little tripod. I could see he was honing his jackknife on a small whetstone.

"Don't know," I answered. "Can't let him watch."

"Well, maybe you can keep him inside. We'll have to move Mister Jack out here to take advantage of the light, anyways. I can do the worst of it while you sit with the child indoors. Like I said, I seen it done during the war."

"You'll need help," I said.

Marcellus just shrugged.

So that's exactly what we did. For me, the moving was the hardest part on account of Jack was a big man, and the delirium settling on him made him mostly dead weight except when he'd jerk or thrash out in pain.

Marcellus had set up several long planks on saw horses to make a sort of table, and we eased Jack onto that as best we could, then Marcellus started dosing him with a jar of moonshine he must of kept for himself since I'd never seen it before. Jack threw up the first mouthful, but then he managed to hold a little of it down, and as it went to work, he began to relax some. At Marcellus's orders, I brought out a spool of the heaviest thread I had and a thimble and a couple of precious needles, what rags I could find, and an old blanket we tore into strips, which we used to tie Jack down to that table. Then Marcellus brought out Jack's fine-tooth saw and a crow bar and the tongs Jack used to heat horseshoes when he had to do his own blacksmithing. He waved the saw through the flames to scorch it a little, but the iron he pushed deep into the fire.

"You go inside now," Marcellus said. "He'll holler some. Don't mind that. I'll call you if I need you."

I must of stood there, practically dumbfounded, for some time, because he told me to go inside again. This time, Jack raised up his head. "Do what he says, Missus," my husband said. That startled me, coming so clear from a man who was half outen his head with fever and the other half clouded with drink. Then Jack looked square at Marcellus. "You may be a black man," he said, "but I trust you with my life. You do what you have to."

Well. That was about more than I could take.

I turned and went inside, stopping at the doorway long enough to look back at the both of them. Marcellus took a good swallow of that white lightning for himself, then put a strip of rawhide into Jack's mouth for him to bite down on. I went inside and closed the door behind me and waited for what I knew was coming.

Holler some he did, though it was more a combination of wail and moan muffled by that chewed piece of leather. Caleb heard it and froze stock still where he was standing, looking at the closed door as if he expected Satan himself to come busting through at any moment. I couldn't help but wonder how many times he'd heard similar noises from one or the other of his parents. I busied myself around there as best I could, pretending to tidy up things that didn't need tidying, and pretending not to hear. It was a long time before I heard Marcellus calling my name.

I whirled on Caleb. "You stay put, boy," I said, wagging my finger at him. "I mean it. I'll tar you good if you move."

His dark eyes just got wider and he stood as if rooted there.

I hustled outside.

Blood and pus were everywhere. All the rags I'd brought were soaked and stinking with the yellow poison that had drained outen that leg once Marcellus cut into it. The very air was salty with the tang of blood. The leg itself was detached now, lying under the table in a heap like some piece of meat dropped accidentally on a slaughterhouse floor. Marcellus was squeezing the stump in both hands.

"You got to cauterize it," he said, nodding toward the crow bar now glowing cherry red in the fire. "I done some of the vessels with thread, but he gone bleed to death if you don't cauterize the whole end whilst I hold it."

I gulped, tasting the contents of my stomach rise into my throat. "Me?"

"I got aholt of him," Marcellus said. "You got to do the burning."

I recollect shaking my head and backing away from that awful sight.

"Got to, Missus," he said. "Else Mister Jack gone bleed to death right where he is."

I remember looking again at that leg, tossed idly away, and at the pleading brown eyes of our friend who had done the worst of the job with knife and saw.

I must of done what needed doing with that hot iron. All I remember is the sizzling sound and the smell of cooking meat and poor Jack's screams of pain even though he was asleep. I do not remember what I actually did, nor what it must of looked like as I put that iron against my husband's stump, and for that I am forever grateful.

When it was over, and the blood stopped flowing even when Marcellus let go his hold on the leg, I stumbled back inside and left our friend to finish up whatever needed finishing. Little Caleb, still rooted where I had told him to stand, took it all in without a sound.

We spread a coverlet over Jack mostly to keep the flies away and left him on that table through the afternoon and into the soft evening. Marcellus cleaned the whole place up, soaking up the blood with yard dirt and sawdust, then he took that piece of leg he'd cut off and wrapped it in burlap and carried it up to the little makeshift graveyard on the hill and buried it beside Little Rob. After a time, I managed to rouse myself enough to make a poultice of lard and herbs to put on the wound, and I tore up the hem of my old gray wedding dress, it being the finest fabric I had, to use for bandages until I could get the blood and poison washed outen the rags Marcellus had used in the amputation.

Around dark, Marcellus and I picked up that table and carried it and Jack inside as carefully as we could and settled it onto the bed. We untied Jack and eased him onto the ticking. He moaned and opened his eyes and asked for a drink, though whether he meant water or whiskey I couldn't tell. I fetched a dipper, but he was already asleep again before I got to him.

It was touch and go for several days as the fevers washed over poor Jack in waves. He'd be outen his head and trying to get up from bed one minute, then so sound asleep the next I was certain he'd died. His forehead practically burned my hand when I touched it. When I tried to bathe him a little, just the touch of a damp cloth set him to shivering so hard I worried that he'd crack his teeth against one another. I kept the stump smeared with the poultice and wrapped in whatever clean cloth I could manage. It oozed yellow fluid and some pus, but progressively less with each change of linen.

Finally, after more days than I cared to count, he started to get better. One morning he announced he was hungry, and he wolfed down the cold cornbread and molasses I fetched for him. Later that day, he explained to me as calm as if he was talking about the weather that he could still feel the missing foot, which seemed to amaze more than trouble him. His color, which had been as flat and gray as old wood ashes, started to improve, and he took to sitting in the sun of an afternoon, with a blanket wrapped carefully around his stump and Caleb sitting on the other knee.

If that boy worshipped Jack before the accident, it was a double dose of adoration afterward. There was just no getting around that. He wouldn't let that man outen his sight for more than a few seconds at a time from the moment he waked up in the morning until it was time for bed at night. He'd just sit on the dirt floor, Indian style, watching. When Jack would move, so would the boy. When we went outside for the sun, he'd come along and stand next to Jack's chair until he lifted him up and put him on the good knee. Come suppertime, boy and man would sit side-by-side and sometimes sip from the same bowl of porridge or whatever sort of soup I could cobble together in that mean season, the summer truck being not yet available and the spring storms having pretty well cleaned us out of edible livestock. Marcellus shot some prairie chickens and a doe for meat, which I put together with dumplings and a few wild onions and tough old turnips left over from last year.

Little Caleb was fascinated by Marcellus, too, staring for

what seemed like hours at our friend's dark skin and tracing the patterns made by the dark lines on the paler palms of his hands. That would get Marcellus laughing, and his happy bubbling baritone would put us all in a better mood. But it was Jack that Caleb seemed to live for.

As the days went by, Jack even started talking about fashioning some kind of peg to replace that missing leg, and oftentimes at night he'd sit at the table by the coal oil light making drawings of how it would be carved and figuring what kind of attachments he could make. He had Marcellus bring him an old harness that hadn't been lost to the cyclone so he could fiddle with the straps and buckles to see how he could rig them to strap onto his upper thigh. The leg itself was still too tender to try to cinch anything to it, of course, and the size of the leg itself had begun to shrink some now that the awful swelling was going out of it, so there wasn't any point in trying to build the contraption he was designing until the healing was complete.

One night late in May, Jack lingered outside as I put Caleb down for the night, then I joined him. It was a beautiful evening, as lovely as any I'd ever seen back home.

"I miss the lilacs, Jack," I said as I settled onto a chair next to him. The last light of day had turned the edge of the western sky a similar color to them fragrant blossoms, but overhead the stars were already winking on and a fat moon, nearing full, rose in the east. Overhead, bats and nighthawks competed in crazy dances for the nighttime insects.

"Then you shall have lilacs, Evie," he said softly and reached out for my hand. "I'll plant them here by the door and up the slope, where our boy rests."

"That would be nice," I said, though I wasn't at all sure that lilacs would grow in the fierce Kansas weather.

"What else would you like here?" he asked.

"I don't know," I said. "Apple trees, maybe. A cherry tree for sure so we could have one good cherry pie a year."

"On the Fourth of July."

"Why, Jack," I said, "I didn't know an old unreconstructed rebel like yourself even recognized the Fourth. I sort of figured in your mind the month went straight from the third to the fifth."

He laughed softly at that. "Tell you the truth, Evie, I'm reconstructed for sure. Here I sit, letting a free black man who turns out to be more like brother than friend look after my place, and with my onliest child buried in Union soil. The way I look at it, I'm damn near a Yankee."

We both laughed again, and I gave him a peck on the cheek.

"I believe I love you, John Arthur Ross," I said.

He liked to broke his neck he turned so fast. "You ain't never said that before."

"No," I said, "I suppose I haven't. Forgive me?"

He swallowed hard, and when he spoke, there was a crack in his voice. "Nothing to forgive."

"Jack, there is one other thing I'd like," I said.

"Name it, Missus."

"I'd like us to put up a proper house for Marcellus. Another soddy would do fine, but I think he's earned not having to stay with the livestock."

Jack laughed deep in his chest. "You think so, huh?"

"I do."

"Well, whyn't you call him up here and let's discuss it."

Which is exactly what we did. Marcellus sat with us for a long time while we talked over what kind of a little house we could pull together, how we would get the sod stripped without our old draft horse, and so forth. By the time we were done, Jack had promised Marcellus a place near as big as ours and with its own glass window, too! Then them two men shook hands on it, and I wondered what must be in Jack's heart about the murders he and the Kluxers had done what seemed like so very many years ago. But if he was thinking on it, he made no sign.

"I feel like singing," he said at last. "You care to join us, Marcellus?"

Our friend grinned. "You know I love to sing, Mister Jack."

"Just Jack'll do."

The grin only widened.

So there we sat in the dark of evening, me with my high scratchy voice singing "Yankee Doodle" and a few other tunes, Jack's croaky baritone offering up a version of "Dixie" that even made Marcellus laugh, and then our friend commenced on some spirituals that almost brung me to tears they were so beautiful.

It was a perfect evening.

We did it again the next night, and then the next, though on that third evening Jack said he wasn't interested in singing and was feeling a mite puny, having spent much of the day helping Marcellus repair harness and sharpen tools, which mostly meant scraping the rust off that had accumulated from lack of use over the winter.

"Well, let's go to bed, then," I said after we'd watched the stars for a while.

"I b'lieve I'll just stay out here a spell longer," Jack said.

"Don't sit out here too long, Mister Ross," I said, running my index finger through his wiry graying hair, "lest the night vapors get you."

"No'm," he said. "I won't."

Then I went inside and readied myself for sleep. When I had my nightdress on and hair combed and had run some baking soda around inside my mouth with my finger, I went to the door to call him in.

Jack was lying on his side in the dirt where he'd toppled from the chair. I ran to him and tried to sit him up, and when I touched him, I could feel his whole body shake almost as if he was having a fit. I pressed my cheek to his forehead. It was burning up. Ten minutes earlier, he'd seemed fine as frog's hair, and now he was in desperate straits.

"I'm sick, Evie," he said so softly I could barely hear the words. "Been feeling it come on this evening, like I said, but it just hit like a ton of bricks." And with that his head lolled over sideways and he passed out.

Somehow, I got him inside without running for Marcellus to help, got myself dressed, and then went for our friend.

"Poison must be back," he said as he knelt beside Jack's bed. Caleb, aroused from his slumbers, stood in the shadows at the head of the bed.

"Can't be," I said. "He's been getting better." As if to prove my point, I begun to unwrap the rags bandaged to Jack's stump, but as I peeled the last one away, the smell of putrefaction reached my nose. How could I not have smelled it before? Marcellus and I just looked at one another.

I kept cool rags on Jack's head, and toward midnight, he wakened.

"Poison?" Jack asked, as if he'd heard us earlier.

"Poison, all right," Marcellus said without looking.

Marcellus asked should he go for the doctor, but we all knew the answer to that wouldn't be no different than it had been when Jack first got hurt. Besides, Jack didn't have any more leg to give, and if the gangrene had spread far up into his body, all the doctors in the world couldn't do a thing. All anybody could do would be to tend to him while he fought it by himself.

I've never been prouder of a man in my whole life than I was of Jack Ross them next few days. He fought so hard against that fever and the way his own body was decaying on him. He slipped in and out of consciousness, but when he was awake, he seemed content, almost jovial, even. He'd whisper to little Caleb or try to tickle him, and more than once I caught him trying to teach that boy to sing "Dixie" as if they were going off to war together.

But Jack's fighting days were over.

He died peacefully, in his sleep, on the second day of June in the year of our Lord 1886, three days shy of our fifth wedding anniversary and two weeks short of what would of been his forty-fifth birthday.

How did I get through the days that followed? To this very day, I am not sure. There I was, left behind for the third time in a year-and-a-half by the kin I cherished most in the world. Now I was a widow with an orphan to raise on my own, and me only just barely eighteen. But I didn't dwell on my worries in them days, leastwise not beyond the indescribable sadness I felt at Jack's passing.

What was it that had made me come to see that poor man as so much more than the filthy old rebel I'd been forced to marry? Had he changed, or had I? Probably a lot of both, to tell the truth. Surely, I'd grown from green girl to woman, and he'd grown from awkward suitor full of explosive anger to something akin to a gentleman willing to make friends outen perceived enemies, and with a soft spot in his heart for little children to boot. And he'd always had a soft spot for me. For certain, I knew the man I had once assumed was a lazy ne'er-do-well had proved himself to be a hard worker and good provider.

I laid him out in his best brushed and pressed clothes and combed his hair. Marcellus shaved him. Then we buried him next to Little Rob, in the very spot where Marcellus had buried Jack's leg so few weeks before. I remembered a piece of Scripture outen Ecclesiastes about how there was a season for everything, then sat up there in that place with my dead son and husband until way after dark, listening to the far-off coyotes and the closer sounds of owl and field mouse and cricket.

In some ways, it seemed as if I'd lived with Jack all my life. I truly had come to love him, not for his youth or beauty or all them other trifles that young girls the age I was then usually think of as love, but for his basic decency and strength and most of all for his consideration for me, from that very first day of our life together in that old ramshackle house of his in Missouri.

But here I was, deeply in debt, with nothing standing betwixt starvation and me and my orphaned son but a kind-hearted black man and a hundred and sixty acres of Kansas soil that was better suited to raising cattle than corn or oats even if I ever could prove up on it.

It must of been near midnight when I lifted myself up from the grass and staggered down the hill toward home.

Jack's home.

Little Caleb was sitting up in bed when I went inside, his eyes dark and shining. He'd not shed a tear from the moment Jack died until then, but when I sat beside him and took him in my arms, he let out a sort of howling sob that liked to rend my heart. As I squeezed him close, his whole body shook with the sorrow that welled outen him like some pent-up river bursting through an earthen dam.

Then it was over, almost as quickly as it started. He pulled away, tucked himself under the rough blanket on his bed, and burrowed in like some night creature trying to get away from the day. I curled up on the bed atop the covers beside him and slept myself until well past dawn.

When I awoke, it was to a home as empty as ever I've seen a place, for Jack's spirit had left it at last. I washed my face in the basin, brushed the wrinkles outen my dress, and went looking for Marcellus to tell him what was on my mind. I found him in the lean-to he'd cobbled together where our barn had been, shoeing our one remaining animal—his horse.

He heard me out without comment, and when I was finished, he went about his business. I sat there for a couple of minutes, watching the way that man handled the horse, then I got up to leave.

"Can't do it," he said with his back to me. He was bent

over, gripping the right pastern in his left hand as he filed at the hoof with his right. "Your place, not mine."

"I'm giving it to you, Marcellus."

He put down the hoof gently and stroked the animal's side. The horse's hide rippled under his touch, and the animal nickered. When Marcellus turned to me, I could see his eyes welled up with tears. "No'm. Can't do it. This your place. You and Mister Jack's."

"You know I'll never be able to prove up on it. We'll go to town and I'll sign whatever papers we need to put it in your name. I'll pay you back the borrowed money as I can. I just can't stay on the place."

"But you gots people buried here."

I took two steps toward him and reached out a hand. "Marcellus, there ain't no way I can make a go of it here, not even with you to help. Even in good times, it's enough to wear two strong men down to the nub. If there's drouth or hoppers or another cyclone..."

He shook his head. "No'm. You gots people here."

"That's why you need to file for the place," I said. "So someone who knows them—who cares—will look after them for me."

Tears spilled down his dark cheeks. Before he could say anything, I turned away and hurried to the house where I could hide my own.

So it was that a week later to the day, I packed up my earthly belongings in one tattered old carpetbag, hitched my friend's horse to the wagon that now rightly belonged to Marcellus along with everything else on the place, and headed for town. Marcellus drove while Caleb and I sat in the back. The boy sat beside me but not touching, silent and not looking back at the hill as we passed. Nor did I. I'd made my peace with that: Jack would of agreed that I was right, that we couldn't stay, that it was unlikely if not impossible for us to make a go of it, but perhaps Marcellus could, turning the hundred and sixty into a bit more with luck and hard work and maybe in the fullness of time running a few head of cattle. Anyplace would be hard for a free black man to start a life without hassles, but maybe the empty wilds of western Kansas would be as good as it got. And he knew the history of our little piece of that wild country, from the hill that held my husband and my son to the lonelier stretch to the west where Dell and Clement, star-crossed from the beginning, rested above that cut bank that had been their mean home.

Marcellus was right that they were my people, the only ones I'd truly cared about in my young life. Still, Jack and Dell and Little Rob would of wanted me and the boy in my care to live and thrive. I knew that. We weren't likely to do neither in that harsh land.

"You look out for them, you hear?" I said more harshly than I meant as we rolled down the far slope and lost sight of the little burial plot.

"You know I will, Missus," he said. "You know I will."

That was all I could hope to hear.

We rode on to Gove to do our business, where Marcellus insisted on taking on the debt himself and giving me two twenty dollar gold pieces for the right to transfer the claim, which I suppose was all the cash money he had in the world. From there, he took us on to Grainfield where I planned to buy a one-way ticket back to Missouri.

At the depot, though, I saw a handbill that said the Atchison, Topeka and Santa Fe railroad was looking for help, including laundresses and cooks for track being laid in southern Kansas and the Indian Territories. Now, I never had given any thought whatsoever to being a working woman, especially in the rough and tumble of a railroad camp, but the truth was that Marcellus's forty dollars was going to be gone in the blink of an eye, and if I went home to Ma, Caleb and I would be little more than a burden. Better, I reckoned, to earn a few dollars and find my own place in the world.

So the ticket I bought wasn't to Jeff City, Missouri, at all, but to a place I'd never even heard of before, a place called Chautauqua, Kansas, and the rail yards of the A T & S F.

Just like that, Caleb and I were going railroading.

Railroads and Indians

I HAVE OFTEN WONDERED why it was that I turned away from the green beckon of Missouri for that wild A T & SF country down along the southern border of Kansas, near where Missouri, Kansas, and the Indian Territories all come together. At the time, I truly believed it was to save my poor widowed mother the burden of having to take on two mouths to feed, though I have come to understand in later years that it was much more than that.

First off, as I already mentioned, I never had told her about Dell taking her own life and that of her good-for-nothing husband, and I wasn't much in the mood for breaking her heart on that subject. Ma was a Christian through and through, especially if you judged her by the way she treated folks instead of how many hours she spent warming a pew, and the thought of her dear child burning in Hell on account of committing two murders—three, if you count the child she was carrying—would of made her waning days pure misery. With all Ma had been through, mostly including living with Daddy, who sure as the devil was burning in Hell himself, it just wouldn't of been right to cause her additional grief over the soul of the fairest of her daughters.

Then there was the child. Ma would of gone off the deep end over that boy, slathering attention and whatever presents or sweet edibles she could spare on little Caleb like he was the King of Egypt or some such in an attempt to take away the sting of orphandom, no matter how misguided. She would of tried to do all the right things by him that all of her own children had missed, but of course the more she would of done, the more just plain wrong she would of been.

In the first place, I'd been around Caleb enough to know that he just wouldn't thrive under that kind of attention. After Jack's passing, that quiet child only grew quieter and more withdrawn. Imagining what he'd seen by the time he was two years old made my own blood run cold, and if ever a child had reason to be touched in the head, it was that one. Just having lived under the same roof as Clement Handley and dear crazy Dell—if a couple of yards of Kansas clay can rightly be called a roof—would of weakened stronger minds than any toddling child could possess. Then to be cooed over and coddled by a doting grandmother... well, it was just impossible to think about.

Besides, there were my own concerns. To go back to Callaway County, to the bosom of home and hearth, would of set me back to being a child again, at least in Ma's eyes and probably in some ways in my own, and with all I'd seen of life since the Sunday Jack Ross and I got hitched in Ma and Daddy's yard, I just couldn't let that happen. I was a woman of eighteen with most of a family buried and an orphan to raise, and I wasn't going to be able to do that if I was Ma's little girl again.

So there it was: I had to earn my own living in my own way, no matter what that meant.

Which left Caleb and me on the road to somewhere called Chautauqua, which was a highfalutin word I surely didn't know the meaning of, to tackle a job I'd only seen advertised on a handbill in a railroad depot. They said they wanted cooks and laundresses. Well, I could do both them things, couldn't I? I'd cooked for farm hands as a girl at Ma's side, and I didn't figure railroad roustabouts could have much bigger an appetite. As for boiling clothes... well, Jack Ross could get a pair of dungarees just about as dirty as they could get, so the sweaty old rags off a gandy dancer couldn't be much more of a challenge. If they were paying cash money, I was ready to give them a day's hard work in exchange.

That was the sum total of my knowledge of what I was about to commence, which only goes to show you how ignorant I truly was as we headed south from Topeka toward the end of track.

Now, Kansas in the eastern parts is about as different from the Kansas of Gove County as I suspect the moon is from England. Whereas our homestead on the wide openness of the buffalo plains was dry and brown most of the year, that eastern region of the state, edging as it did toward the Ozarks and the Missouri woods, was green and wet. We could practically feel the stickies increase with every mile we clattered down that track, and Caleb actually broke out in a rash because of it. But what I really noticed was that it was smaller country. Both parts of Kansas were mostly flat, with some rolls near the creeks, but the cutbanks in the southeast were no more than a few feet high, and the deepest ravines no bigger than a man could cross in a minute or two of brisk walking assuming he could fight his way through the snags of brambles and brush, whereas the bluffs and banks out west were towering naked things, high enough for human beings to burrow into and make a crude home of (as I well knew) and polished by winds strong enough to prevent any native vegetation taller than a man's knee from gaining purchase in the soil. Sandstone monuments reminiscent of great stone buildings, and named such by weary travelers, marked that western country, while cottonwoods and whitebark sycamores and thickets of Osage orange and red cedar and blackjack oak fairly choked the landscape in the southeast. Where there was soil to see, it was rich and black, loamy and smelling of worms, the kind Daddy had always said he'd give his right arm for back home.

The people were different, too, or seemed so as much as a body could tell from the windows of a passing train. All about, the land and the people showed an industriousness that bespoke long years of living in one place, something I'd taken for granted back home. Nobody I've ever known in my whole long life worked harder than the homesteaders of the West, but all that work didn't usually generate much in the way of outbuildings or herds of livestock or the other trappings that said prosperity to any and all who chanced upon them. Instead, it was just hard work to stay alive, pure and simple. In eastern Kansas, though, tidy farms and fat cattle and barns painted red as ripe cherries, black lacquered buggies pulled by high-stepping walking horses, and fields of oats so green they hurt the eye made me think of a veritable Garden of Eden. Such things had existed in Missouri, of course, but being born there, I had never noticed them until they were absent, and seeing them afresh liked to tear a hole in my heart. I thought of Dell, and how she'd lived out her last years in that hell of a cave her idiot husband had dug and wondered what her life might of become if Clement had had the brains to settle in such a rich and comfortable land as this. But he had not, and after all, Clement was Clement: I suspect you could of put that idiot down in New York City and he would of found a way to kill his wife with loneliness.

Of course, not all of eastern Kansas is like that verdant country we rolled through. Some little ways south of Topeka, we entered the Flint Hills, the long rolling grasslands that aren't much different from most of Texas, or so I'm told, being about the best cattle country on God's earth but right poor for crops. But then, through the hills to the south, we moved on to the Arkansas River drainage—and just before we would of crossed over into the Indian Territories themselves, we came onto what was in them days one of the roughest little one-horse towns in all of creation, set in one of the very prettiest spots.

Chautauqua.

Nowadays, Chautauqua's a sleepy little village that folks in a hurry to get somewhere would call a wide spot in the road if they even gave it that much notice, which is all right by them of us who don't cotton to the traffic and clutter that too many human beings bring. The fact that it's been steadily getting smaller for most of the last fifty years is all right with me, too. When my time comes, let the oaks and scrub have whatever place they lay me—that'll be as fine a monument as a body can have. As for Chautauqua itself, some day soon it won't be nothing but a ghost town after all the young'uns have moved to bigger places like Wichita and Tulsa.

But in them days, it was a pure rip-snorter of a town, and growing bigger every time the train pulled up at the siding. You could just feel there was a real chance of Chautauqua becoming something big and important if enough decent folks decided to stay a while, which of course was exactly what the town fathers hoped the Atchison, Topeka and Santa Fe would do for them.

Now, originally the town had been founded as Chautauqua Springs on account of a mineral spring some of the locals said was good for health, but by the time we got there, them waters were playing second fiddle to the railroad, and that's a fact. Before the train came through and set up an end-of-line roundhouse, repair shops, and barracks for the track layers, the town hadn't been much more than that old spring and a buffalo wallow or two nestled amongst a few hills on the edge of the bur oak woods. The "town fathers" I already mentioned were mostly men who'd followed the railroads in the hope of getting rich, buying up sections along the right of way and encouraging others to homestead the rest. In them days, you understand, the government allotted alternating sections to the railroad companies to sell or use as they saw fit, which encouraged the railroaders to push on mile after mile because they could get richer than Midas by selling all that free land the government gave them. Who they usually sold to, at least in my experience, was the speculators, who then turned around and sold it all again to anyone who had a few dollars and didn't want to have to wait for the five years it took to prove up a homestead or who wanted to live in town rather than on some hardscrabble farm. In that way, the country got its railroad, the railroad boys made money, the speculators made money, and once in a great while the poor folks who bought the parcels managed to squeak by, though of course a lot of them latter types went bust, which to my way of thinking is just about the story of America.

But let me get back to describing Chautauqua the way it was when Caleb and I first clumb down outen the day coach and stood there blinking in the white light of noon on that railroad platform so new the green planks were still oozing sap.

The whole place wasn't more than maybe a half mile square, with a sprinkling of buildings around the railroad shops and the flimsy barracks. Farther away, tents and rickety buildings cobbled together from scrap lumber, canvas, and tar paper dotted the landscape. Tree stumps were everywhere, most of the building lumber having been cut from the native trees that dotted the whole area and plumb choked the rolling country to the south. The streets were mostly dirt tracks leading from one building to another, and depending on the volume of travel, they were either rutted affairs given to ankle-deep dust (which of course turned to greasy mud when it rained) or fairly smooth grassy paths not unlike cow trails back home.

It seemed like the people we saw that first day were all moving at once, going in every possible direction and getting nowhere. They were a strange mix of just about every type of human being you could of imagined, too—cowboy, Indian,

Chinese, business man, Irishman, and on and on—as long as it was male.

Women, at least at first glance, were as scarce as hen's teeth.

The most impressive building in town was the Chautauqua Hotel, which boasted a whitewashed false front, a full three stories, and a porch wide enough for gentlemen to be able to sit in rocking chairs and watch the world go by and narrow enough that them same gentlemen could spit tobacco juice right from their rockers and have a goodly share of it land in the street.

It was to that edifice that Caleb and I repaired once we'd gathered our wits. To this day, I remember thinking how strange it felt not to have the clacking of the rails in my ears or the constant sway of the train under me as we walked the long block from the depot to that hotel, being careful to dodge the horse apples that seemed to cover most of the ground. About all I could think of was getting a washbasin full of water to scrub off the dirt and a fresh bed for me and that boy to lie down in.

Well, we were sorely disappointed on both counts. The hotel was full up with various trashy types including more than one lady of the evening, that being the predominant occupation of the few women who did live there, and some railroad fellows who claimed to be bosses but looked for all the world like Irishmen straight from some slum or another. The hotel desk clerk was a weasel-faced little woman with a rheumy eye who stared at me and Caleb like we were something the cat had dragged in. She told me flat out there wasn't a room to be had in her place, but for five dollars she would put me up on a spare bed in her own room until her shift was over, at which time she would boot me out. I was free to take it or leave it, and that was that.

Needless to say, I left it, though I confess to a sinking feeling wondering where we were going to light.

Back outside, I surveyed what of that town I could see and decided to try the only building other than the railroad barracks that looked the least bit substantial. It turned out to be a boardinghouse (mostly for railroad men, of course) run by an Irish woman named Francine Maguire, with a laundry out back owned by a family of Chinese who provided a little opium den along with their cleaning services, although I didn't learn about that right away.

The house was a two-story rambling affair along a creek bank that somehow reminded me powerfully of my old home place, though it was on the flat and didn't run downhill the way Daddy's place did. It turned out to be decent enough, too. At least a couple of the boarders truly were railroad bosses, and though they were a rough lot, they proved to be a good deal more gentlemanly than the hammer and shovel men who shaped the rail beds and drove the spikes. Anyhow, after sizing up Caleb and me and judging us to be at least some-what satisfactory, Francine agreed to take me and Caleb in for room and board if I'd help her with the cooking, which she admitted wasn't her strength, and whatever of the cleaning I could manage. At the time, I didn't think cooking was my strength, either, what with most of my experience running to stews and dumplings, but after one helping of her boiled beef and sauerkraut, which tasted more like old grease and spoiled cabbage than anything else, I knew I could do a sight better, and since I'd come all this way to work for the railroad, anyway, this figured to be as good an introduction as I could have.

What really sealed it was that Francine had a boy named Rufus who was a year or two older than Caleb, and from first appearances, them two hit it off well enough. Leastwise, they didn't tear each other apart at first sight, which was good enough for me.

Francine kept a clean house, I'll say that much for her. The sheets were washed once a week, and she aired and beat the ticking just as often and checked for bedbugs. It turned out that no matter how solid her house appeared from the outside, though, it was a drafty, rickety affair with gaps in the plank walls you could throw a shoe through, but that didn't matter much given that it was the middle of summer. She made her other boarders toe the line, too, in terms of being polite at table and picking up after themselves. Just about all the men chewed snoose, but she wouldn't allow them to spit in her parlor or at the table, and there was a standing rule that everyone had to clean out their own nighttime slop jar, which made the tidying up a whole lot more pleasant.

I found out soon enough that Francine had her weak points, though, the main one being she was willing to trade her personal favors for an extra bit of pocket change. She did it mostly with a big ugly fellow named Guthrie. Fortunately, she didn't make a fancy deal of it the way the painted ladies of the illegal saloons did, Francine being discreet enough that a body could ignore it if you just took care to look the other way. Turned out she'd run a boardinghouse near the railroad yards in Topeka for some years and had known Mr. Guthrie then, as he'd been a boss for the A T & SF up there, which accounted for the fact that Francine's Rufus had the same flat nose and crossed eyes as that gentleman.

Well, I was more than a little worried at first that maybe I was going to have to follow Francine's lead in keeping one or another of them bosses happy between the sheets, but luckily for me, none of the railroad men (with but one exception, which I'll get to shortly) ever bothered me on that score, which is to say that they didn't press the issue once I'd told them no the first time. It turned out that though they weren't evident from the vantage point of the rail siding, there were plenty of ladies in that town—at least the sort who bedded in the hotel and various other tents and lean-tos to service the men's needs. And to be honest, most of them gals had a little more meat on their bones than I did.

Of course, helping Francine took care of room and board, but it didn't put any silver in my apron pockets, neither, and I was determined to make something of a stake for Caleb and me, so I set out to see what else might be available by way of work in that town, principally the advertised railroad jobs that had brought us there in the first place. Unfortunately, the Chinese more or less had the market cornered on the laundry business for the railroad just like they did at Francine's. Cooking was another matter, so I signed on at the roundhouse to help feed any railroad man who needed feeding. Mostly I worked early mornings—the middle of the night, really—to midafternoon. I'd show up at three-thirty or four and from then until I went home, I was slinging that grub as fast as I could. Them laborers had appetites, I'll tell you, and there wasn't any set meal times. When they wanted to eat, they et. It'd be beefsteak and potatoes and eggs by the hundreds in the mornings, with enough coffee to positively float a steam engine. Sometime along about the middle of the forenoon the fresh eggs would run out and we'd add slices of ham and cornbread and pickled eggs and maybe chutney or succotash to the mix, but the coffee would keep flowing. Then I'd start chopping carrots or slicing onions or turnips for stew, and by the time I left around three or three-thirty, the nighttime cooks would have them huge stew pots slung over the fires and bubbling away while they plucked chickens and stirred up dough for more dozens of biscuits than I could count. I'd drag home, knowing that I still had work to do around Francine's place to earn our keep there.

That cooking for the railroad was truly hard work—as hard as any I've ever done in my life—and the pay wasn't nothing to write home about, I'll tell you, though I could take home day old biscuits or soup bones and the like, which Francine would buy offen me for six bits a week, which was money for the rainy day fund I put straightaway into an old cigar box tied up in my underthings.

***

I have to explain about Chautauqua in them days. As I said, it was a mean, low-down hell-hole in a lot of ways, but set on the prettiest parcel of land I think I ever saw. Several creeks cut through the town site, with willows and alder and such lining the banks, and water as sweet and pure as any I ever tasted, being neither muddy nor alkaline, at least if you dipped it upstream of the various fords the mules and ox teams used. The grass, where it hadn't been chewed off by livestock or pounded flat by hooves and wagon wheels, was almost waist high to me and of a color that gave it its name of big bluestem. North of town, wild roses grew everywhere on the rolling hillsides. Groves of blackjack and bur oak and towering cottonwoods provided plenty of shade, and on hot nights when I sat outside with Caleb, the big leathery cottonwood leaves made a sort of swooshing sound that seemed to be God's own accompaniment to the squeak of crickets.

Now, it is true that the soft rustle of the wind in the trees couldn't much compete with the rumble and snort of the trains. Even in the middle of the night you'd hear the pounding of the drivers and the screech of the wheels as a train slowed to a halt somewhere shy of the roundhouse, then the bang and clatter of uncoupling, more rumbles as the train eased into the roundhouse, then all the same noises in reverse once they'd turned the engine around and pulled it out on a different piece of track and headed it off in a new direction. Even more than the noise, the smoke from them big engines spoiled at least some of the view in every waking hour, and the cinders they spewed out always threatened to do serious damage to some dwelling or business. The big stacks on the engines had cinder catchers, but they were imperfect things, and there was always hot ash on the wind.

As you can imagine, fire was a constant in that town that summer. I'd never seen a real full-scale conflagration before, but I sure got my fill of them during that hot, dry season.

Most were smoky little grass fires along the right-of-way that the work crews beat out with wet gunnysacks, but occasionally something would catch in a yard or on a building or tent. The worst I saw was when a tarpaper shanty near the tracks caught fire one night. Inside were barrels of tallow, which the railroad used to grease the drivers on the engines, and several casks of pure alcohol, which I believe was contraband bound for the Indian Nations, which as I said wasn't but a few miles away. That white lightning burned so bright and hot it was almost like a roman candle, and the grease spread the fire out for fifty yards in every direction. The local fire crew pulled up the water wagon and tossed a few buckets on the blaze, but any fool could tell it wasn't no use, so they just backed off and stood with the rest of us, watching the whole thing burn. That fire was so bright you could of read a newspaper by the light of it two or three blocks away, and the heat scorched the whitewash off of walls and charred tent canvas fifty yards away. Luckily, there wasn't any wind that night, or the whole dang town and miles of prairie and oak woodlands to boot would have burned. As it was, a mile or more of right-of-way was singed, with ties burnt up and that newfangled barbwire twisted over piles of ash where the fence posts should of been. Luckily, the only things that died in that fire were a handful of chickens that got caught inside their coop when it burst into flames from the reflected heat.

Caleb was with me watching that night, and the look of wonderment on that boy's face would have tickled the hardest heart had the circumstances been different.

My day off from the railroad was Monday, which was a real blessing since I had to do all the cooking for the Sunday evening meal at the boardinghouse even though I'd slaved over them hot stoves at the railroad for a full twelve hours, Francine having taken the Sabbath off. By the time I'd washed dishes in an old tub out in what passed for a backyard by the light of whatever moon there was, I was about as tuckered as a body could get.

Not that I begrudged Francine her Sunday. She worked plenty hard during the rest of the week, and she needed her time off same as me. She wasn't exactly a church woman, but she did take her boy to what passed for a religious meeting at the hotel on Sunday mornings on the notion that putting a little fear of God into any youngster was never a bad thing. She always volunteered to take Caleb with her, saying they had a good Sunday school even if it was run by a saloon keeper who usually had bleary eyes and a swollen tongue of a Sunday morning. I let him go once, but I could tell when they came home that he'd been more than a handful for the barkeep if not for Francine, and he sure never asked to go back.

Anyhow, Monday was my day off, and as the summer wore on hot and dry, I tried to think of things to do to get away from the outdoor ovens at the railroad or the closed-in heat of the boardinghouse. I took to borrowing Francine's buggy and taking Caleb for a drive in the country just to hear the meadowlarks and bobwhites or look for a flash of goldfinch in the high grass near the road.

We usually went north or west, that being where the country was more open and there was less chance of straying acrost the Line into Indian country. Sometimes we'd stop along a creek and Caleb would wade in the shallow water and try to catch little suckers in his bare hands. It was our chance to glory in that beautiful country together, and truth to tell, it was a chance for me to get to know that boy a little better. He was growing like a weed and turning into a right beautiful child, with dark hair and eyes and a skin color that would of made me think his people were Gypsies or some such if I didn't know better. Where he got them dark looks, given the light coloring of his folks, I'll never know, but he sure had them.

And sakes alive, he was a quiet child, with a serious face

that always made me think he was deep in thought like some full-grown person might be.

I'd talk on them little trips, telling him about my home in Missouri and how his ma and I had been best of friends as well as sisters, and he'd just sit there, looking at me like he was absorbing every word but staying quiet as could be. Each Monday, I'd venture just a little farther than I had the previous week, in part to stretch out that bit of alone time with him, and after some weeks I turned my attention to the more wooded country south of town just to see something different.

So it was that one late September Monday, when the days were beginning to grow noticeably cooler and the sumac was just turning its fiery red, I discovered that I'd managed to get some miles into Indian Territory.

How I found out was that what seemed like a whole tribe of Indians jumped us one afternoon after we'd stopped along a little creek for a picnic lunch. Well, they didn't jump us exactly, but rather just kind of appeared out of nowhere, as I discovered Indians have a way of doing. And not a tribe, exactly, but more like an extended clan of brothers and cousins and such.

I have to tell you that to be laying back in the weeds of a little meadow, daydreaming about nothing in particular while the bumblebees buzz in the black-eyed Susans and the horse is cropping grass just as slow and contentedly as ever you please, then to look up and see a dozen or more dark faces staring at you from not more than twenty feet away when you thought you were as alone as could be is about the most startling thing that can happen to a body.

To see Caleb standing there amongst them as if he belonged to them rather than to me was more surprising still, but there he stood just the same with his trouser legs rolled up and his feet still wet from the creek, with one hand lost in the fist of a tall Indian dressed in dirty dungarees, a shirt that must of been red once upon a time but was now the color of dry earth, and a broad-brimmed black hat with a hole in the crown to allow a long white feather to stick out.

I tell you, I jumped up and ran to that boy and fairly snatched him away and tucked him behind my skirt, though in truth he didn't look exactly disturbed to have that tall dark man holding his hand, and my skirts wouldn't of protected him for one second, anyhow, had that red man had evil on his mind. Instead of scalping the both of us, which I more than half expected, that tall Indian just grinned, tipped his hat like a gentleman, and, with a wave of his hand, turned his family gathering around and led them away.

Which absolutely flabbergasted me.

My heart was beating practically outen my chest, and before that clan was lost from sight, I had Caleb up in the buggy, our picnic things gathered and stowed, and headed back to town as quick as ever I could.

When I told Francine about the afternoon's events, she clucked in sympathy and gave me pretty clear instructions to stay away from the Nations, not so much for my own sake but to make sure nobody swiped her buggy. She said the red men south of that invisible border that lay somewhere between Chautauqua and the muddy waters of Caney Creek were liable to steal just about anything that wasn't nailed down, though primarily they were fond of stolen horseflesh.

"They're Osages," she said, saying the word as if the very sound of it alone would explain everything. I must of looked puzzled, for she drew herself up to her full height and tilted her head back as if to lecture me. "They think they own this country, don't you see," she added. "Positively own it. There'll be hell to pay unless the Government sends us some soldiers to deal with them red rascals."

"But they do own it," I offered. "At least that country in the Nations, south of the Line. Ain't that right?"

I might as well of said the streets of Chautauqua were paved with gold. She shook her head sadly at what she must of presumed was my total ignorance.

"You just stay north of the Line, hear?" she said. "They steal horses and rape and murder women."

Having no reason to misbelieve her, I shuddered to think of what might of been and determined to take Francine's counsel to heart. North would be the direction I'd go from then on.

Except that after that first encounter, Caleb was absolutely goggle-eyed over them Indians. That child's silence suddenly gave way to one constant stream of jabber. He asked me a thousand questions about who they were and where they were from and why they looked the way they did, none of which I could answer, of course. I turned some of his questions to the men around the supper table, but changed my mind on that tactic when the tales they offered up were terrifying and bloody enough to curdle milk, being along the lines of what Francine had said but with a lot more gruesome detail. They seemed to enjoy outdoing one another with yarns about lifted scalps and burned homesteads and violated virgins—passed on with many a "begging your pardon for the language, ma'am"—and while I reckoned at least some of that must of been true based on what we'd heard up in Gove County about the Comanche raids of yesteryear, I began to get the notion that the clan Caleb and I had run into most likely wasn't the type to do that. If they had been, then the way I figured it, Caleb's and my scalp would be hanging in some hut down there in the Nations already. When I put it to Francine that way, she just clucked and told me again to stay as far away from that country and them red devils as ever I could, leastwise whenever I was using her buggy.

So that was what I did, and in time, Caleb let up on the questions, though when he did, he commenced to retreating into silence again. In any case, I'd pretty well put them Indians outen my mind when, out of the blue, one of them came to town.

It must of been a Monday on account of I wasn't slaving over potatoes or plucking chickens. It was late October or early November and cool, but in the bracing sort of way that makes you think that if every day could be that crisp and clear, life would be wonderful. I remember I was standing on the boardwalk in front of the hotel talking pleasantries with a weathered old railroad man who took his evening meal at Francine's when this old democrat wagon rattled to a stop in the middle of the street and a tall man clumb down off the box. For a second or two, I didn't pay any attention, but when I realized that the gentleman I was talking to wasn't listening to me anymore but was staring at the wagon instead, I turned my head for a second look.

What I saw was that hat with the top cut out and the white feather sticking straight up.

"Be Goddamned," my friend said under his breath. "Begging your pardon, ma'am. But what in blazes brings that trash to town?"

"Who's that?" I asked.

"Reuben Whitesnake," he said, and he made a face as if just saying the name had left a bad taste in is mouth.

"Who's he?"

"Orneriest sonofabitch in the Nations is all. Thinks he's the law down there. Osage, or some such."

"What's he doing here?"

"Now there's a question, little lady," the gentleman said. He spat tobacco juice, dribbling most of it onto his own boots, and turned on his heel to go. "You watch yourself, now," he said by way of parting. "Ain't no white woman safe around them red bucks." And with that, he clumped off.

So much for him saving me from ornery red sonsofbitches. The men of that town were sure worried about protecting the flower of womanhood as long as it wasn't none of them that had to do the protecting.

Now, most all of my life I'd been raised to believe exactly

what that man had just told me—that no white person was safe where Indians were concerned. I remembered as a girl hearing about how the redskins had slaughtered General George Armstrong Custer and his boys at Little Big Horn, and even if he was a Yankee, most folks around home considered him a hero because he'd died trying to rid the nation of Godless Indians. We had nightmares for weeks about how we were going to be butchered in our beds by renegade savages, never mind there wasn't a live wild Indian within a hundred miles of Callaway County. And for certain the tales I'd heard around Francine's table hadn't done nothing to disabuse me of them lifelong notions about Indians. But there I stood, looking at a man who had had ample opportunity to harm me and Caleb already and had not done so. It dawned on me like a bolt of lightning that everything you're told in life just isn't necessarily true.

Besides, now that I could study him a little without fearing for my life, I could tell this red man was a fine looking specimen.

He was tall, nearly six feet, with a waist and hips so slim there wasn't no way he could of kept his trousers on without the red galluses that ran up over his wide shoulders. There wasn't an ounce of fat on him that I could see, and strong shoulders and arms rippled with muscle under a gray homespun shirt. His face was broad, but with the prominent nose of his race, and from where I stood, it was impossible to tell whether he was twenty or forty years of age, though I came to find out that he was just about slap dab in the middle.

While I'd been sizing him up, that Indian had tethered the mules pulling his wagon and was wrestling something outen the back end. At first, I thought it was a big sack of spuds or something, but then I saw it wiggle and it hit me: there was a person inside the gunnysack Mr. Reuben Whitesnake was fighting. He upended that sack, and whoever was inside must of been standing on his feet, for the sack didn't topple over.

"Ben Green!" that Indian shouted at no one in particular and everyone in general. "This is Ben Green, caught red-handed delivering liquor into the Nations!" With that, he pushed the sack hard, and this time it did sway and fall. "Next time, I will turn him over to the U.S. authorities, and they can string him up for all I care. If that don't do it and he comes back onto our land, I'll string him up myself for trying to poison my people!"

It certainly struck me that he had a wonderful command of the English language for a savage.

Anyway, by this time, Mr. Whitesnake had drawn something of a crowd, as you might imagine, and this last brought a collective gasp outen the group. He only laughed at that and toed the gunnysack, rolling it away from himself and his wagon. Then he hauled himself up onto the wagon box with the grace of an athlete, clicked the reins over his mules, and made a wide turn in the street and headed out the direction he'd come. Some fellow about my age whipped out a heavy old revolver and pointed it at the Indian as he rode past, but some other fellow grabbed that raised gun and pointed it skyward. Within a few seconds, the wagon had rattled on past the crowd, whose attention now turned to the man struggling to get free from the gunnysack.

Two or three boys rushed to his aid and tackled the jute string tying the sack shut. One produced a pocketknife and began sawing away, which must of stabbed that Ben Green fellow, for he commenced to wailing fit to die. At last they got him loose and more or less shook him outen the sack and dumped him like so much garbage into the street.

Now, I will tell you plainly, that old boy was much the worse for wear. If Reuben Whitesnake had foreswore hanging him for whatever offense he'd committed, he sure hadn't fore-swore dragging him through every wild rose patch in two counties, or whatever passed for counties south of the Line.

That Ben Green gentleman stood there, rubbing his eyes and oozing blood outen more places than I could count, though the only bad cut he had was one on his upper arm that his pocketknife wielding rescuer had inflicted.

"Boys, I'm purely glad to see you," Mr. Green said, "even if you did stab me."

"You trying to sell whiskey to the Indians again?" someone called out from the edge of the crowd, and everybody laughed.

"Naw, hell, you know I wouldn't do that," he answered. I could see he was licking his lips and looking in the direction of the hotel, which I may not have mentioned had the best saloon in town, or at least the only one that was completely indoors instead of under canvas or in some lean-to that threatened to blow away in any bit of wind. "Any a you boys willing to buy me a drink?" he asked.

Laughter rippled through the crowd again. "'Tain't legal," someone shouted, and "Ain't you got your own?" came from someone else as the laughter grew louder.

Ben Green licked his lips again. "Not hardly. That wily redskin poured it all into Flapjack Creek."

"Must be some happy suckers and catfish down there," another offered.

"Or dead ones, given what ol' Ben calls liquor!" yet another answered.

"Come on, fellas, buy me a drink!" Green pleaded. He'd pulled a filthy old bandana outen his trouser pocket and was working to stanch the blood leaking from his knife wound.

"Only if you tell us how ol' Whitesnake got the drop on you," somebody else said.

You could kind of see the air go outen Ben Green at that point, but he nodded finally. "Sure, I'll tell you the story. Only you got to buy me a whiskey."

Well, it was about all I could do to get outen the way of that stampede as them fellows raced for the saloon, pulling

Mr. Green along like a bit of fluff on a flood. As they passed, I could smell him, and it wasn't good. Not all of his whiskey had found its way into the creek, that was for sure, and there was other smells, too, as if Reuben Whitesnake had put a skunk along with Ben Green into that gunny sack. The other men seemed not to notice, though, on account of they had an excuse to treat each other to whiskey and it wasn't yet noon. I found myself wanting very badly to follow them into the saloon to hear how Reuben Whitesnake had, indeed, gotten the drop on that old reprobate, though of course I could not, it not being seemly for a decent woman with a small child to be seen in a drinking emporium. Instead, I went home and picked up my room and looked after Caleb and found myself daydreaming about taking another outing come the next Monday, this time somewhere south of town.

You see, just like that, I was smitten. Me not six months a widow, and here I was fascinated by another man, and a red-skin to boot.

Doesn't life beat all sometimes?

Of course, I didn't go south again, at least not for some time. First off, I was fighting that natural womanly feeling as hard as I could. I wasn't exactly in widow's weeds, but that was mostly on account of I didn't have the money for a proper black mourning dress, and whenever I got to thinking about that Indian, I'd finger a locket I kept around my neck at all times—a locket filled with a snippet of Jack Ross's hair. Jack had been good to me and I'd come to love him for real, and it just didn't make sense that I should take an interest in another man so soon, especially someone who wasn't even white. I even took to reading the Bible, especially the Old Testament passages, to get my mind right.

It helped, in a peculiar sort of way, that I lost my job with the A T & SF right about then.

Track laying was moving on to other locales, principally

down in Texas, and though the roundhouse stayed for the time being, the big crews of laborers were moving on. What men were left could get their meals at the saloons that offered free lunches of pickled eggs and ham sandwiches for anyone buying a beer or two, and Francine took to putting together lunch boxes for the engineers and conductors who stayed with her, though I know many of them fellows weren't especially fond of the gristly roast beef and cold boiled potatoes she'd heap into their tin pails. But the truth of it was that the A T & SF didn't need my services any longer, nor did they particularly want women on the end of the line, they having found out that a handful of single women living cheek-by-jowl with several hundred tired laboring men sometimes caused more trouble than it was worth.

So unless I found something else, there wasn't going to be any more silver clinking into my cigar box.

I spent some days going door to door in Chautauqua, seeing what I could do to improve my situation. It was coming on to winter, and I have to tell you, I didn't relish the prospect of spending the cold months without real work. Most folks were polite, but they weren't exactly flush with cash themselves, so whatever needed doing they were prepared to do on their own.

However, the week before Thanksgiving, I paid a visit to the home of the roundhouse manager, Mr. Herbert Wilbertson, who was about the last of the important railroad men permanently settled in Chautauqua, and after looking me over and asking about a thousand questions about what did I cook and could I sew and was my child quiet and housebroke, he allowed as how he needed a woman to look after his home. On account of I was a widow woman with a double-orphan child to look after, he agreed to hire me on for five dollars a week and room and board, of which he would deduct only two dollars a week for Caleb as long as the child didn't cause any ruckus around the place. This was some better than the deal I was getting from Francine since I'd only have to cook and clean for two people not counting myself and Caleb, and after I'd met his wife, who was an invalid with a crooked spine and what I took at first to be a real sweet disposition, I agreed to sign on.

Well, that turned out to be one of the bigger mistakes of my life, and I've made a few, I can tell you.

I doubt that it would of been any harder to keep a hundred gandy dancers from laying hands on my person than it was keeping Mr. Herbert Wilbertson at bay. It became a sort of dance, the way I had to scoot outen his way and keep myself at arm's length while not giving offense.

And that was just during the daylight hours. At night, after his wife had turned in, Mr. Wilbertson would stalk me like a coyote hunting rabbits. After the first night, when I was afraid I'd have to kill him to keep him offen me, I took to propping a chair up against my bedroom door just to prevent him from barging in and demanding whatever favors it was that he thought he was paying for at five dollars a week, and that only worked because he couldn't rightly bust the door down on account of it would make so much noise it would waken his wife. It got so just the sight of the man gave me the shivers.

Of course, that woman of his wasn't much better as it turned out, and it was just as hard to stay outen her way.

What she wanted was someone to whip. I had some fellow feeling for her, she being confined to a wheelchair and all and her husband being little short of a tomcat, but that sympathy only went so far. If the spuds weren't done to her liking (and they never were), she'd try to slap me or poke me with the knitting needles she carried around more for weapons than for knitting. If I was a second late bringing her a lemonade or a cup of tea (and I always was, at least by her lights), out would come them needles again. If her husband gave me one of them looks that said he had something on his mind other than supper (and he always did, right there in front of her), she'd set to shrieking about how I was trying to bust up her happy home.

Now, I was never a quitter, but I knew in about three days that I was going to have to quit that job or kill the both of them, and quit I did at the end of the third week. To get even with me, Mr. Wilbertson paid me just half my wages due while withholding the full amount for Caleb's keep, saying that it would cost him the difference to find a new girl. So I had just six dollars and fifty cents to add to the cigar box in spite of all the shenanigans I'd had to put up with.

Anyhow, there I was with no gainful employment and nowhere to go except right back to Francine's, only in the interim she'd taken in a Negro girl to help with the cooking, so to pay my way, I was relegated to the Chinese laundry, and I have to tell you, the Chins weren't much happier about being forced to take me on at three dollars a week than Mrs. Wilbertson had been, the difference being the Chins were reasonably polite people who didn't knit.

It was the lowest moment in my life up to that minute, I'll tell you that. Even the grief over Jack's death, as intense as that had been, didn't have the bleakness to it that my life did in them weeks. I worked like a coolie for a coolie, stirring men's clothes in soapy, boiling water for hours on end, and I didn't see there was going to be any end to it, neither. When I didn't have my arms in scalding water up to the elbows, I was generally making lye soap, which was an even nastier business. The Chins would gather up the ashes from the fires they used to heat the kettles and trickle water through them, using wooden bowls to collect the lye that leeched out, then they'd send me all over town begging for whatever bacon grease or tallow or lard folks could spare on account of Francine didn't have enough herself in spite of all her cooking, and then I'd heat all that fat and grease and strain it through cheesecloth to get out the brown, crispy bits. Once that was done, I'd stir it together with the lye and let it set up into cakes, which we'd shave into the hot water or rub straight into some garment or another that was particularly soiled. I have to tell you, rubbing some old fellow's nasty longjohns on a washboard is enough to scrape your knuckles off under the best of circumstances, but when you do it with a hunk of that caustic soap in your hand while you're standing outside in a whipping wind and the thermometer at pretty near zero...

Well, let's just say it ages you some. I've never been afraid of hard work, and by the time Jack died my hands already had the big knuckles and calluses of an old lady, but my hands looked mostly like a skeleton's claws while I worked at that Chinese laundry.

The Chins—I never did learn to pronounce or spell their first names—had worked for the railroad before they started their own business, and from what I learned over time, it had dang near killed them. The father of the brother-and-sister pair I worked for had come over from China to work on the Central Pacific the year I was born, and his son and daughter had come over the next year. They'd worked as powder packers, stuffing explosives into granite holes hammered out by other Chinese on their crew. That both father and son had survived at all was something of a miracle, since so many of their kind died in premature explosions or rock slides or just from the sheer hard labor of the thing. The old man was deaf as a post and blind in one eye from where a splinter of granite had struck him, so by the time I met him, about all he could do was sit and smoke while his children slaved along with yours truly over the washtubs. Anyhow, his son had stayed with the Central Pacific project all the way to Promontory Point, where that road joined the Union Pacific, whereupon he'd been fired and told to get on back to China where he belonged as he and his kind weren't wanted in America now that the hard work was done. So he settled into a new line of work instead, one that seemed to draw the Chinese like a candle draws moths.

The sister had been a laundress for the railroad crews as they built eastward acrost the California mountains and the Nevada and Utah deserts, so they had a ready made trade to fall back on, so to speak. They'd washed white men's dirty underwear in Utah and Colorado before coming to Kansas, and they were thinking about moving on to end-of-track again before long, so they hadn't yet finished the journey they'd started at Shanghai or wherever it was they'd lived in China.

I learned all this from the sister, as the brother either couldn't or wouldn't speak English. He was so tiny I was a half a head taller than he was, but that man was powerful. Hammering steel spikes into granite will for certain build muscle if it doesn't kill you. I will say this for him: he could work harder than any living soul I've ever seen, before or since.

Them three, brother and sister and their old father, lived in a tiny little tarpaper hovel at the back of Francine's property on account of she couldn't rightly have a Chinese clan living alongside the white folks. They ate rice flavored with whatever bits of this and that they could come by, mostly scraps of chicken or pork left on the bones that Francine threw out after she'd boiled them down for soup. It didn't seem to me that a single person could live off what the three of them had to eat, but live they did, if that's what you call it. And they did make some extra money providing opium to whatever railroad man had that particular hunger, so come nightfall, you'd see the occasional gandy dancer slip into their shack, and you'd see him leave the next morning looking like he didn't rightly know where on earth he was. I presume the younger Chins never smoked opium themselves on account of how hard they had to work, but I certainly can't say that about their old man.

Anyway, there I was, slaving alongside them two Chinese folks, with Caleb getting wilder and wilder as lingering autumn disappeared into hard winter.

I didn't know what I was going to do with that boy, he was so prone to running off at the drop of a hat, and I was too busy minding the washtubs to keep an eye on him like I should. One time, I didn't even know he was gone, and here came old Herbert Wilbertson, crunching through the snow dragging Caleb by the ear. Seems the boy had showed up at the roundhouse, and Mr. Wilbertson, being the nasty old coot that he was, took it upon himself to bring the child home in the most punishing way possible. There was blood running down the side of Caleb's head, and that ear was dang near twisted off. Old Wilbertson huffed and harrumphed and acted like I was supposed to give him a dime or something for the safe return of the child, but instead I gave him the toughest steely look I could muster, splattered soapy water on his nice wool trousers without even an apology, and snatched up the boy and took him inside to doctor. The strange thing was, that child never once whimpered—not from the twisted ear, nor the dab of witch hazel I put on it to stanch the bleeding, nor when I threatened to tar the daylights outen him for running off like that. He only sat there, glum and silent, with blood and witch hazel running down his cheek and into his shirt collar. Afterwards, I made it a point to find Herbert Wilbertson's laundry and rub a couple of holes in his best shirt on the washboard, but that couldn't make up for the humiliation my strange, quiet boy had undergone.

Anyhow, we got through that winter and into spring somehow, then from spring to the following summer. When we marked our first full year in Chautauqua, I pulled out my cigar box and counted out my savings. It didn't come to thirty dollars, which meant I had less than I'd started with. All I had to show for that year, it seemed, was raw hands, a silent, willful child, and absolutely no prospects.

So it was that, on a perfect early autumn day of 1887 with geese and ducks flying overhead, I decided to borrow Francine's buggy and go south again, on another picnic. I had no notion that I'd find Reuben Whitesnake, but I had no notion I wouldn't, neither, and it was clear from the way Caleb commenced to smiling and laughing as we jounced along that road into the Nations that he was thinking much the same thing that I was.

We had a splendid picnic, the two of us, with cold fried chicken and a jar of lemonade and biscuits that Francine's little Negro cook had made especially for Caleb. That girl could flat find her way around a kitchen, and her chicken was a real specialty. We fished along some creek or another, pulling in a sucker or two with poles made outen willow switches and baited with kernels of sweet corn hooked onto bent pins, and laid in a patch of grass and watched the clouds sail by overhead. Caleb found an abandoned meadowlark's nest, a sort of grass bowl with a roof over it, which he made me promise to let him take home, and I told him stories of his mother's and my childhood, being careful to leave out any-thing about Daddy and the Klan on the assumption that hearing that Kluxer stuff wouldn't exactly be good for such tender ears. He'd listen, then turn and look over his shoulder, then I'd feel compelled to do the same. I know we both half expected to see red men materialize outen the long grass, but such wasn't our luck that day. Along about dusk, we hitched up and rode home, both of us tired and happy but, I suspect, more than a little disappointed.

So we did it again the next week, and the week after that. By then, the days were more than a little crisp. The autumn tang in the air made picnicking downright uncomfortable if there was any wind blowing at all, and if you know Kansas and what's now Oklahoma, you know for certain that the wind blows pretty near all the time. The leaves were falling, cre-ating big dusty windrows that horse and buggy crunched through, sending up clouds of little lacewing insects.

And then even they were gone.

At last I decided that we'd make one final trip down to the Nations, and that would be that for the winter.

The truth was, I was thinking about abandoning Chautauqua and going home to Missouri, as I'd started to do nearly a year and a half before. The track crews were gone, the roundhouse wasn't busy but once or twice a day now that we were no longer anywhere near the end-of-track, and Chautauqua itself was beginning to dry up. Even the Chinese laundry wasn't as busy as it had been, which was something of a relief to my lye-blistered hands, but I could see the handwriting on the wall, too. One of these days the Chins would decide they couldn't pay me but two dollars a week or maybe wouldn't need me at all to help scrub the dwindling piles of union suits and dungarees.

Which made that last planned picnic more than a little sad. Going back to Callaway County would be a blessing on one level, but it would sure enough be everlasting proof that I'd failed on my own, and of course there was still that nagging worry about being a burden to my mother and having to tell her about what had happened to her darling Dell.

But that day, the countryside still showed a few traces of autumn color amongst the brown of approaching winter, which picked up my spirits as we followed the single wagon rut south of Chautauqua and across the invisible line that separated the United States from the Indian Nations. A few bumblebees and yellow jackets still worked at what was left of the milkweed and heavy sunflower heads looming over the road on browning stalks. Where the oaks hadn't plumb taken over, clumps of grass almost as tall as the sunflowers swayed and rattled in the light breeze. Overhead, skeins of geese and other migrating water birds streaked the sky. I don't think I've ever seen a prettier day in all my life.

And then, appearing as suddenly as angels dropping down from heaven, there they were, maybe a hundred yards off on the far side of a clearing.

This time, it seemed there truly was a whole tribe of them—several families, at least, with men and women and little ones. Reuben Whitesnake was one of them. I counted fifteen Indians of various ages, yet it was as if they had just appeared outen thin air, right there in the high grass with no more sound than smoke makes. The men were mounted on ponies, but the women and kids were walking. From the looks of them, I figured they weren't going anywhere in particular, but were maybe out for a weekend stroll much the same as I was.

Of course, they had seen me, probably long before I had seen them. They were stopped still as statues, just watching Caleb and me.

I stopped the buggy and stared back.

Reuben Whitesnake raised a hand like he was greeting me, but before I could do anything, Caleb raised his hand in reply. For some reason, that was apparently enough for them Indians, for they began to move along the same path they had been traversing when first they spied me and the boy.

For my part, I just sat there, watching. What I saw mostly was a young woman hardly older than me walk up alongside Rueben Whitesnake's pony and hand a bundle up to him. He took it and cradled it and pulled a corner of cloth away from it. Even at that distance, I could see he was smiling at a child wrapped tightly in that hunk of cloth. My heart sank about to my knees, though it plumb made me ashamed of myself, and I forced myself to finger that locket of Jack's hair to remind my-self of my obligations as a widow woman.

Caleb watched them go for a moment, then he jumped down from the buggy and took off after them through that tall grass. In the couple of seconds it took me to come to my senses, that boy had slap disappeared, with nothing to show for his passing except the slight rustle of shoulder-high grass.

"Caleb!" I shouted, but there was no answer.

He was gone.

Indian Territory

THERE I SAT, wondering what on earth I was supposed to do next. In no time at all, them Osages were lost to view, and I had no idea where Caleb was in that sea of chest-high grass. I clucked to the horse to get him moving and commenced to hollering at the top of my voice for that boy.

Absolute silence greeted my calls. Even the bumblebees had gone quiet.

To say that panic began to settle over me would be more than a little of an understatement. I don't believe I'd ever in life experienced the sheer terror I felt at that moment, on that beautiful autumn day. I stopped the horse, jumped down, and started through the tall grass afoot, hoping beyond hope that Caleb was playing hide-and-seek with me, though I knew in my heart that wasn't the case. I cut as wide a swath as I could through the grass where I'd seen him run, almost getting myself lost in the process, so thick was that bluestem, then I doubled back and tried it on the other side of the track in case he'd gone over that way. I didn't find a thing except a gopher hole that liked to break my leg when I stepped into it and brambles enough to rip the lower part of my skirt to shreds.

But nowhere did I find that boy. I called some more, then clumb back into the buggy and stood on the bed to get as high as I could.

Nothing.

In the blink of an eye, that child had run off after them Indians. If I was going to find him, I realized I was going to have to do the same.

For about a second and a half I considered going straight back to town, both because I knew Francine would expect her buggy and horse back and because maybe I could get some of the men at the boardinghouse to help me in my search, but I gave that up as a crazy notion. In the first place, I didn't know a single man in that town with the intestinal fortitude to go into the Nations searching for my boy. They'd blather and blow about how somebody had to teach them redskins a lesson and suchlike, but they'd leave any of the doing up to somebody else and simply claim the boy was lost for sure, which meant that nothing would get done. And it was a lead pipe cinch that Francine wouldn't let me take either horse or buggy again if it meant I was going to take them south of the Line.

So that decided it for me. I was already where I needed to be, with the only transportation I was likely to get and with no real chance of enlisting any help. If Francine missed that beast... well, let her charge me with horse stealing if she wanted to. I had the only excuse I needed, which was a missing son, for so I'd come to think of Caleb even if he did mystify me on most counts.

I headed that animal south, hoping I'd come upon my boy, and if I didn't, I'd eventually wind up in whatever kind of town the Osages kept.

I must admit, that country sure didn't seem like a foreign land, though by right and law that's what it was in them days. It just seemed like more of Kansas, though a bit wilder on account of nobody had settled there, at least nobody of the white race. Except for the rutted track I was on, which began to peter out the farther south I rode, there was no way to tell that humans had ever even been in that country. In point of fact, I didn't see another person for hours, nor any sign of them, neither. How that party had disappeared so quickly and where they'd gone I could not say any more than I could say where poor Caleb had wound up.

The sun was well down and the cold night air settling on the countryside before I saw the first human habitation, which appeared to be a small farmstead on the edge of a rolling meadow surrounded by thickets of bur oak. Dim yellow light shone through a tiny window and leaked around a door frame, but it was far from bright enough to compete with the rising moon. I summoned up as much courage as I could muster and flicked the reins to get Francine's horse moving just a little faster and rode straight into that yard.

An old dog of about the size and shape of a coonhound came out to greet me with a couple of low yodels. The horse shied and whinnied and the dog growled, and if I'd had any notion of keeping my presence a secret from whoever was inside that little dwelling, I'd sure as heaven lost the chance.

The door swung open on sagging leather hinges, revealing a stout man about my height standing in the doorway. I could see he cradled an old shotgun in his arms.

"Begging your pardon," I said with as calm a voice as I could manage, "don't mean to disturb you, but I'm lost and looking for a child that run off just north of the Line." That last part was a bald faced lie, of course, but I figured it was best not to admit to trespass just yet.

The man just shook his head and kept standing there.

It dawned on me that maybe he didn't speak English, and it goes without saying that I sure didn't speak Osage or whatever language it was they used in them parts.

"There anyone here who speaks English?" I called out, sort of standing up in the buggy as if that would help me throw my voice a little farther. The dog growled deep in its throat and slunk back a few feet, crouching down as if both afraid of me and ready to pounce just the same. I wished I'd brought along Jack's old Navy Six, not that it would of been much competition for the blunderbuss that fellow was holding, but I'd left it wrapped up in the very last piece of my gray wedding dress and stuffed under the mattress back at Francine's.

The gentleman in the doorway scratched at himself, and after a couple of seconds he turned and shut the door.

I guessed that was that. I'd struck out for sure in my first contact with the Osages.

But I was wrong. Before I had a chance to get the horse turned around, the door opened again, and a woman came outside carrying a smoke-darkened lantern with the man sort of covering her from that doorway. She was even shorter than the man but about twice as big around, making her old gingham dress look like an overstuffed sack of potatoes. She lifted that lantern as high as she could and spilled some of its weak light onto the horse and me.

"You're white," she said in a halting sort of way that told me English wasn't her native tongue.

"Yes'm," I said. "My boy run off. We were picnicking just north of the Line and he saw some of your people..."

"Didn't see any boy," she said.

"Well, yes'm, but like I said, he run off and I couldn't find him, and I'm right worried that something happened. Do you know Reuben Whitesnake?"

There was a long pause, and I could feel her studying me. "Didn't see no boy," she said again without answering my question, and with that she turned on her heel and strode back into her house. The man stood there for another heartbeat, then followed her and closed the door after and pulled in the latch string.

There I sat, alone in the dark once more. "Please," I said in a sort of a shout, but then I gave it up and slumped back onto the buggy seat. I must of sat there for some time, wondering what to do. I remember an owl swooshing by, nearly scaring me outen what wits I had left, and sometime later that old dog lit out after something, which he must of treed judging from the way he howled, but them people were slap not going to come outside again while I sat there. After a long time, I realized I was beginning to take a serious chill with the dew settling on me, not to mention Francine's poor horse might catch its death from the night vapors, and I just gave up and turned the wagon around and headed north.

I don't think I'd ever been that low in my life except maybe for the days Jack and my little baby boy died.

I got back to town shortly after midnight and rode right into a hubbub I sure never expected.

Half that town was looking for me. All the men in the boardinghouse were still up and dressed and gathered around the front porch discussing the merits of putting together a posse when I pulled up. Francine had set all of that commotion into play mostly on account of her horse, I'm sure, but just to prove she was a decent Christian woman, she asked after my health as soon as I rode into that pool of torchlight, and she brought me a blanket even before she gave me hell for keeping her animal out on such a cold night. She paid some kid or another a nickel to rub her horse down and give it some oats, and then she let me know that I owed her that nickel plus interest unless I paid up right quick, though out of simple decency she wasn't going to charge me for use of the horse and buckboard unless the horse caught sick and died.

Meanwhile, the members of the erstwhile posse were peppering me with a million questions about where had I been and didn't I know I'd scared the bejeebers outen Francine and didn't I realize it wasn't safe for a woman to be out on the prairie alone at night and suchlike foolishness. Of course I told them I'd been looking for Caleb, but that just started them going on with a bunch of new questions about where had I seen him last and what was he wearing and did I think that bunch of savages had made off with him and what was a woman of my age and inexperience doing taking a child out so close to the Line, anyway? I could tell they thought even less of me than they had before, and that hadn't been much.

Then the sheriff and his chief deputy showed up, having had to ride all the way down from the county seat town of Sedan, which I gathered hadn't put them in too good a mood. The sheriff was a colicky man named Cummings with big ears and wispy brownish hair and a complexion like boiled beets who occasionally kept company with Francine, though only late at night when her usual man Guthrie was out of town on railroad business and no one else was likely to notice except maybe me. His deputy was a big fellow by the name of Horace Taylor, whom I was to get to know him a whole lot better, though that night I was so wrought up I didn't hardly notice him. He just sat there on his horse, giving me a kindly look while his boss asked me all of them exact same questions over again, except that he asked them slow and one at a time rather than the way the boardinghouse posse had, all jumbled together.

"So you believe your boy—your nephew, is that right?" Sheriff Cummings said after I'd explained everything I could. When I nodded, he finished the thought. "You believe he's with Reuben Whitesnake?"

"I don't rightly know. I certainly hope so," I said.

That sure got the attention of some of the other fellows. They'd been talking and chewing snoose and spitting on the boardwalk, but when I said how I hoped Caleb was with them Indians, they liked to twisted their heads off they spun around so fast.

"You better hope he ain't!" one of them exclaimed.

"Why's that?" I asked.

"Them Osages are notorious child killers," he said, and some of his friends nodded in agreement. "All redskins are, but them Osages are by far the worst, not counting the Comanches, but then this ain't Comanche country. They prize the scalps of white children, them Osages do. Use 'em to decorate their harness and such, and I heard they'll even dash the brains outen their own babies when they're drunk."

I thought of the look of pure loving kindness I'd seen on Reuben Whitesnake's face as he looked on that small bundle in his arms. If them gentlemen were right, at least about what strong spirits did to the Osage temperament, maybe that was why he was so intent on keeping whiskey peddlers like Ben Green outen the Territories.

"I reckon I'd rather little Caleb was with them than alone out there, lost in the woods or fallen into a creek or something," I said, and just the thought of him freezing to death in some patch of weeds or stalked by coyotes just ruined what composure I had left and set me to bawling like a baby. On all that long ride home I had tried real hard not to think about it that way, but I sure did now.

And that's where matters stood for what was left of the night. The sheriff hushed the other men but didn't exactly contradict what they'd said about child murder, then he promised me him and his deputy would start looking for Caleb at first light, the night being too far gone for it to make much sense to do anything else. We milled around in the street for a while longer, then the men repaired to Francine's parlor where somebody produced a bottle of schnapps to take the chill off, and pretty soon the whole front of that house was full of cigar smoke and various man noises. Francine brought me tea with a little honey in it and tucked me into bed and told me that she was sure we'd all find Caleb in the morning, though from the tone of her voice I knew she was fibbing on that score. After a little bit, I could hear her and Sheriff Cummings going to it in her room, though more discreetly than usual on account of the other men still nipping at the bottle in the parlor. I dozed some but didn't sleep and was up shortly after four o'clock with the notion of helping Francine's Negro girl make breakfast for the posse. However, due to the late night and a full bottle, that posse decided to a man to sleep in, so Francine and I sat alone at her table with steaming bowls of oatmeal and crisp bacon and a platter of biscuits made from Francine's own recipe, which meant they were heavy as rocks and just about as hard, though I wouldn't of had an appetite if she'd been serving angel food cake and honey. I explained to her how I couldn't help with the laundry that day on account of I had to join the search, and to her credit she said she absolutely understood. Then I went outside and broke the news to the Chins, who didn't take it near as well, not that I cared one whit.

By the time the first faint streaks of color marked the eastern horizon, Sheriff Cummings had slipped outen Francine's bedroom window and snuck away so he could reappear coming down the street with Deputy Taylor in tow. When he got to the boardinghouse, he stomped up on the porch and banged his big fists on the door and announced for all the world to hear that he was ready to go, and them slug-a-beds in the posse had better get up and be ready to join him in ten minutes flat unless they expected to get left behind.

As it turned out, I had worried myself sick for nothing, for before even one of them hung over gentlemen showed up, Reuben Whitesnake did, riding in tall and straight on a handsome American horse, and to my everlasting joy, sitting right up there with him was Caleb looking for all the world as happy as a child could be. He grinned and waved but showed no inclination to slide down to me, so that Indian lifted the child gently and handed him down.

Reuben nodded to the sheriff, who nodded back. "The boy followed us yesterday," he said to me, and that was all.

"I know," I said. "I looked and looked for him."

The tall Indian laughed lightly but low in his throat. "This child has a mind of his own. You best keep him in

Kansas if you don't want him to disappear." And with that he tousled Caleb's brown hair, spun his horse around, and cantered out of town. Caleb tried to run after him, but I held him tighter than I'd ever held a person before or since.

That beet-faced sheriff, who seemed both annoyed and amused, just scratched his head, then turned and clumped into Francine's and plopped himself down at the dining table and tucked into Francine's biscuits, smacking his lips like they were pure heaven. I fed Caleb, ignored the stares of the gentlemen beginning to gather, and put my boy to bed and sat with him until I was sure he was asleep on account of I wasn't entirely certain he wouldn't take off again the minute my back was turned. Then I trudged down to the laundry and took my place at the washtubs.

The Chins were in a foul humor having had to start their work without me, but I didn't care. My boy was home, safe and sound, and on top of that I knew what a good man Reuben Whitesnake really was.

I learned much later that Caleb had been playing hide and seek with me in that tall grass for some time, staying quiet and just outen my sight until I took off, thinking he'd gone deeper into the Territories. Then he'd made a beeline for where he'd last seen the Whitesnake clan, found the tracks as slick as if he was an Indian scout himself, and followed them for several miles to their little village, which was far closer to the line than that lonely cabin I'd found long after dark.

I considered that quite a feat for a child barely four years old.

Anyhow, Reuben recognized him right off when he showed up and only kept him overnight because he rightly didn't think it would be too healthy to carry that boy into town in the dark hours when the good citizens of Chautauqua would be most liable to shoot at an Indian first and ask questions later. If it hadn't of been for that, Caleb would of gotten home hours before I did.

But right then, I didn't know how Caleb had gotten away from me so clean, and I determined never to let that happen again, which meant I vowed to watch him like a hawk and never take him anywhere near Indian country.

It was a punishment for both of us, though of course since it was plain Mr. Whitesnake had a child and likely a wife, I figured I needed to put my daydreams behind me.

But try as I might to get that man outen my mind, Caleb's moping made it slap impossible.

Whatever he'd seen and done in the Whitesnake camp—and he wasn't telling, even when I asked—had clearly been the highlight of his young life. Though he talked little, whenever he did string together more than two or three words, it was about them Indians, and most of it was questions. How come their skin's so brown? How come they don't live in a boardinghouse? How come they have so many horses? How come Mister Reuben's so tall? How come this and how come that, until I thought my head would explode just trying to think up some answer or another that would satisfy Caleb for more than five minutes. Francine cluck-clucked that the Indians had spoiled him for sure, turning him even wilder than he already was, and the men at table would join in, allowing as how I maybe thought I was lucky them rascally Osages hadn't killed the boy but that I'd most likely feel different later when I found out whatever evil things it was that they'd done to him in the hours he'd been in their clutches. They'd laugh and spit food when they said it, for there never was a moment when they weren't shoveling that Negro girl's victuals down their gullets, but that didn't make what they said any easier to take.

On top of all that, Horace Taylor, the sheriff's deputy, decided he wanted to keep me company. I tried to put him off, but Francine swore he was the best catch in Chautauqua County on account of his late wife had had money, and she saw to it that he was invited to town whenever Sheriff Cummings came down to visit.

Turned out Horace's wife had passed some years earlier in childbirth. He was gruff and bombastic, given to talking about himself a lot, telling me how he was going to run for sheriff himself come the next election and his pals in the Masonic lodge were going to vote him in on account of Sheriff Cummings wasn't a Mason and suchlike things that didn't particularly interest me. The locals did respect him, though. You could see that by the way the men would nod and say hello and the ladies would smile and look away shyly whenever he rode by.

By the third visit, he was trying to hold my hand and calling me "Miss Eva" and how much I'd like Sedan.

All of it liked to wore me out.

Winter came on early and stayed late, which was a blessing in that it helped me keep Caleb in town and made it more difficult for the sheriff and his deputy to come calling.

Ice was our problem that season, which just about stopped everything including the railroad. Nothing and no one could move, and if a body did, he'd like as not wind up flat on his back in the street. Some miles north of town an engine jumped the rails when the big driver wheels lost purchase on an icy curve, which made a terrible mess for some days for the A T & SF hands still in town. Francine's friend Mister Guthrie got one of his ears and two fingers froze off working that job, and Mr. Herbert Wilbertson fired him because he couldn't work while his hands were so swole up he couldn't get them into mittens. That riled the other workers and for a time it looked as if there might be some kind of strike, though of course none of them fellows had the gumption to do that for real. Guthrie left town, vowing to send for Francine when he found work, but he never did, or at least I never heard of it, and to tell the truth she seemed a mite relieved.

By February, Sheriff Cummings was outen the picture

altogether, his wife having apparently decided that she was going to slit him from crotch to gullet if he kept sleeping around—Francine not being his only nighttime friend, from what I heard later—and being a practical man with a decent head on his shoulders, he believed her. At least that was what the biddies whispered at the general store, and if I heard it, you can bet Francine did. Anyhow, she didn't seem to mind much either way, and for the time being, at least, she was more or less without a man.

To tell the truth, it suited her.

But that winter did wear on.

Caleb chafed under the confinement, and during one spell of particularly bleak weather he came down with a case of the measles that I was afraid was going to carry him off he was so sick. During the quarantine, which the two of us spent in the drafty old summer kitchen behind Francine's boardinghouse that was so cold our breath fairly smoked, he and I would play imaginary games, most of which involved Indians, with Caleb always pretending to be a tall Indian chief, which I took to mean Reuben Whitesnake. I tried to get his mind offen it, and when that didn't work, I said things like how we ought to leave them poor people in peace and stay on our side of the Line where we belonged, but of course that went right over his head: he'd been with the Indians and wanted to be with them again, and that was all there was to it. I was mighty relieved when his convalescence was over so he could play with the other youngsters in town and get involved in their games, though he had a knack for convincing them to play Indian, which I'll tell you left me with a sinking feeling when winter at last turned to spring and I knew there was no way I could keep that child indoors much longer. No doubt about it—any rides my boy and I made out into the country were going to have to be to the north.

Not that I ever got much of a chance.

Spring turned almost overnight into summer, which

seems to be the way it mostly is in Kansas, and when it did, it became crystal clear that the only way I was going to keep Caleb from running off was to chain him up and slap a padlock on them chains. That boy was determined to see his Indian friends again, and I do mean determined. I'd take him north, as was my plan, and once I even asked Horace to ride along, thinking that a man's presence would take the boy's mind offen the Indians.

That turned out to be a mistake, as Horace Taylor had no interest in the boy, so I didn't do it again.

The long and short of it was I'd do my level best to entertain Caleb on them picnics, but it didn't do any good at all. He'd just go plain sullen until I gave up and took him home, then he'd go more days at a time without smiling or saying a word. Sometimes I'd catch him just standing in the front yard, looking south, as if hoping to see that tall Indian and his American horse come riding up over the horizon to rescue him from his sorrows.

Francine said he was touched in the head, and I could tell from the way she said it that Caleb—a five year old boy—frightened her. Maybe he frightened me some, too, though not because I was afraid of him as much as I was afraid *for* him without knowing exactly why. I didn't think he was touched, but given his family history, it wouldn't of been too big a surprise.

Then the next thing I knew, Francine started dropping hints about the lunatic asylum and how maybe that was the place for a child who'd been through everything he had, not to mention it would be a precaution for the community. I knew she was planning on adding a third story onto the boardinghouse, and she let it drop that the only way she could pay for that kind of expansion was to add boarders, and boarders wouldn't want to spend the night in a place with a crazy child.

After a time, I realized her threat was real. She was being as kind as she knew how, but what with Caleb's constant moping about how he wanted to be with them Indians, I knew I had to do something or risk either being out in the street or having the good citizens of Chautauqua conspire to send my boy to the insane asylum.

So I gave in, but to the boy, not them small-minded town-folk.

I reckoned I was going to have to take Caleb to see some Indians.

I rented a horse and saddle at the livery stable with what amounted to most of my cigar box savings as I didn't want to hear Francine's lecture about how I'd nearly stolen and killed her horse last autumn, and this time we rode straight to the Line and right acrost it with the full intent of finding the Whitesnake camp so that boy could run around like a wild Indian with the folks who really were wild Indians and get it outen his system.

At least that was my plan.

It didn't quite work that way, and I suppose deep down I'd known it wouldn't from the start.

I certainly had no trouble finding the Whitesnake place. The truth was, they found me, as they had twice already.

Reuben himself met us a mile or so south of the Line just like he'd been expecting us, pulled Caleb up behind him on his horse without a single word passing amongst any of us, and led me another few miles to where he and his family lived. Why I hadn't stumbled acrost it on my ride the previous autumn, I'll never know, because it wasn't like it was tucked away in some hidden place.

It was a decent enough little village, plunked down in a sheltered hollow hard by a small creek, with timber and brush on three sides and a patch of corn and squash already coming up. The huts were arranged sort of every whichaway, except that they more or less lined up along a dirt path that ran straight as a string from east to west, which is the way I believe most Indian camps are laid out on account of that's the path the sun makes every day. Anyway, that Osage village reminded me of some of the hollows of Callaway County where two or three generations of the same family would all live together in a jumble of houses, except that the meanest shack back in Missouri would of been an absolute palace compared to the five or six little log huts along that creek. Jack's and my soddy in Gove County was a sight roomier than the biggest of them homes, and for danged sure less drafty.

Anyway, as we rode into that clearing, I could see two or three women working on some kind of pole contraption that appeared to be set up to dry meat, and another who looked some bit younger was hoeing the seedling corn. The men, of which there were several, were doing what I subsequently learned most Indian men did most of the time, which was as little as possible, these gentlemen being ensconced in home-made rocking chairs in the shade of their cabins.

I decided right then and there that Osage society and our white society wasn't too much different from one another, at least when it came to who did the work.

A pack of mongrel dogs greeted us while we were still a quarter mile short of the place, but they were puppies, mostly, rolling all over each other and dancing around. Reuben stopped so Caleb could slide off the horse and get right in the middle of them dogs.

"Now you be careful," I said, which made Mr. Whitesnake laugh.

"Boys and dogs go together," he said with yet another chuckle, then he tapped his knees into the ribs of his horse and led me into the village, leaving Caleb and the pups to come along behind when they felt like it.

We dismounted in front of one of the little cabins nearest the patch of squashes. My host hitched my horse to the handle of an ax stuck in a huge old flat-top stump, which I took to be a chopping block for kindling, though some darker stains on that wood made me think maybe they lopped off chicken heads on that thing now and again, too. He stripped the saddle blanket off his own animal, there being no saddle to remove, and led it into a pole corral where maybe a dozen other horses grazed. Then he bent low and went into that cabin through a doorway that was a good foot or so shorter than he was and covered with a worn skin instead of a proper door. As he'd not beckoned me to follow, I just stood there. After a few seconds, the young woman hoeing corn commenced to tittering, and one of the older women joined her.

It was plain enough that they were laughing at me.

I could feel the color rising to my cheeks, and I had a powerful urge to light into them, but of course I didn't, both on account of it wouldn't of been good manners and because I figured if I got their blood up, they'd undoubtedly turn bloodthirsty enough to put me outen my misery. It wasn't that I believed any of the stories the men at Francine's had been telling, it was just that I didn't exactly disbelieve them either. So I was determined to keep my guard up and my powder dry, you might say.

Which was the beginning of my education among the Osages.

I wasn't sure how long we would stay that first time, though I wasn't in any hurry to leave, what with Caleb rolling around with them dogs until he looked like one of them. Reuben set me up outside his hut on a hand-built chair made outen small branches stripped of the bark and leaves so I could keep an eye on Caleb, then he just went about his business visiting the other men or poking his nose into one or another hut to see what was going on inside, all of it as if I wasn't there. I figured maybe I'd get to meet his wife, but there was no one inside his hut, and no baby, neither. Late in the afternoon, as the shadows started to lengthen, one of the women offered me a bowl of stew that tasted of roots, some kind of strong meat, maybe 'possum, and lots of grease. She was tall and favored Reuben but a good deal older, and I supposed maybe she was his mother, or at least an aunt. She gave Caleb chunks of fried bread, which he wolfed down just like the dogs did the scraps that had fallen to them. Suddenly I was less concerned about the boy turning Indian than I was having him turn prairie wolf on me. Then that woman squatted on her hams outside the doorway to the hut and closed her eyes, and I swear she was asleep in seconds. I thought about asking her about Reuben's wife, but I didn't want to waken her on account of that would be rude, and besides I didn't even know if she spoke English. I was already thinking it was past time to be getting back, but there I sat, as if rooted in the spot, unwilling or unable to make a move.

Well, come full dark Reuben reappeared. He touched the old woman lightly on the shoulder and she awakened, stood, and went inside.

"She your ma?" I asked.

He nodded. "She looks after me."

"What about your wife?"

He looked away from me toward the darkening woods. "I have no wife," he said.

"But I saw you with a baby. That day when Caleb followed you and got lost..."

"Ah," he said, and he smiled. "My daughter."

That was a head-scratcher. "But you just said you didn't have a wife."

"I did. She's buried under the ground now."

"I'm sorry to hear that," I said, and at least part of me honestly was. "I lost my own husband."

Again, he nodded. I didn't know it at the time, but he had just told me all he ever would about that first woman of his. I learned later that she had died giving birth to their daughter, which of course was pretty common in them days no matter what your color. "Our daughter lives with my wife's sister," he said after a time. "A man can raise a son, but a daughter needs a woman's care. Do you not think so?"

"I suppose," I said, though all my motherly experience, which wasn't much, had been with boys.

He turned his back to me and stared out at the peaceful village. A few small cooking fires burned near several huts and the thin light of candles shone around some of the skins covering the doorways.

"Under our custom, the sister would be my wife if I wished it, but I do not," he said.

"That seems an odd custom," I offered. "No offense meant, you understand."

He didn't respond, and for a long moment I thought I had, indeed offended him. Then he turned and stepped to the doorway of his own hut and pulled back the covering. "You will stay the night and I will take you and the boy back in the morning."

I confess I hadn't thought about that. The night had sort of crept up on me, I was so fascinated just being in that village.

"You will sleep inside with the boy and I will take my robes and find a place under the stars," he added, as if to explain he meant no harm.

"Oh, I can't take over your home. Caleb and I can get by out here if you just have a blanket for us."

"No," he said. "It is decided."

And so it was. Reuben showed us inside, pointed out the skin robes we should sleep on, and took up his own parcel and departed. Caleb, who was about as tired and happy as a little boy could get, wanted to follow that man, but fell asleep on a piece of bearskin laid on the dirt floor of that tiny home before I could get him properly tucked in. I settled down on a much worn hide of some sort and pulled a fine piece of soft doeskin around me for warmth and just sat there studying that place by the light of a guttering tallow candle.

The room wasn't but maybe eight by ten feet, with a simple table and some skin and canvas bags hung on pegs in the wall. There were no other furnishings to speak of, with various hides and such arranged around the wall opposite the door. Some of them were pouches with fancy beadwork and stitching of porcupine quill which I presumed held Reuben's clothes or maybe some kind of mysterious ceremonial regalia. A few blackened cooking utensils rested on a shelf near the door. That was all there was. If the place had ever enjoyed a woman's touch, there was no sign of it, yet it wasn't the least bit slovenly the way most of the white men I knew would of kept it.

Mostly it just seemed sad.

After what may have been a few minutes or even a couple of hours, I drifted off to sleep.

The first light of day, along with Caleb's tugging at my clothes, wakened me. It was cold in that hut, and damp from the dew that had settled over everything, me included. I stretched and crawled out from under that doeskin and rubbed sleep outen my eyes. Once Caleb saw I was up, he grinned so wide it liked to make my face hurt just looking at him, then he darted outside like he'd been shot from a gun, leaving me to follow. When I did, I was astonished to see that whole village appeared to be up and at it. Cooking fires filled the air with drifting smoke and the smells of frying meat and something like coffee. Dogs were dancing around the kettles, arguing over scraps the women tossed them. The men sat on the ground smoking pipes, their backs braced against the walls of their huts. Reuben was there, leaning against his own house, and I wondered suddenly if he'd been there all night.

He looked up at me, nodded once, then looked away.

"We best be getting back to town," I said. "Before Francine and the rest of 'em take me for being lost or kidnapped." I tried to make it sound light and cheery, but it occurred to me when I said it that the townfolk probably had given me and the boy up for dead or lost already and likely didn't care which. On the off chance they did, I didn't want any madder-than-hell posse charging in thinking the Osages had taken me and Caleb captive.

"We will eat. Then we will go," he said, and he pointed to Caleb, who was busy playing some sort of game of stick ball with a bunch of other boys of various ages.

"I suppose you'll want me to fry something up?" I said, making it a question.

"No. My sister will do that for us." He patted the ground next to him. "Sit."

So I sat and watched the other women work. It gave me a peculiar feeling, like I was both an honored guest and somehow taking advantage of a situation I shouldn't. "I'd be happy to help your sister," I said after a time, of course having no idea as I said it what I'd be expected to do.

He just sat there. It dawned on me that he was watching Caleb play, and a little half-smile was the only sign that he was tickled with the way my nephew-son and the others were getting along. That is, until he said: "Your boy would make a good Osage."

Well, I allowed as how that was probably more right than Reuben knew, as fascinated as Caleb was with them Indians and their ways. To that, he just smiled, more broadly this time, and rose. "Now we will eat, and then we will go back to your town."

And once again, that was that.

Well, my friends in town, if friends they could be called, were as outraged at my behavior as if I was a scarlet woman. Worse, in fact, for they generally treated the dance hall girls and them that kept to the cribs near the rail yards with at least a little respect, like that due to unfortunates who couldn't help their miserable circumstances. I, on the other hand, had walked right into my evil ways with the ability to avoid my sin.

The cluck-clucking wasn't behind my back, neither. Them "civilized" folks would say pretty much whatever was on their mind right to my face, and more than once it took all my intestinal fortitude to keep from telling them straight to their faces exactly what they could do with their opinions. Francine told me how disappointed she was in me, and pointed out that a decent fellow like Deputy Sheriff Taylor would never pay court to me now. Even Herbert Wilkerson and his nasty wife would go far outen their way to avoid me if they saw me coming, which of course I considered something of a blessing.

We visited Reuben two or three more times after that, each time staying the night, and each time the society ladies' disapproval grew worse. Francine scowled at me and took to worrying out loud that I was getting a reputation for being a lewd woman, which was something coming from a woman whose own son looked a lot like a former boarder and whose late friendship with the county sheriff was well known.

Even so, I felt like I should explain myself. I thought about telling her that what I was doing was just for the welfare of my boy, but it was plain to see pretty quickly that wouldn't wash—not with her, and certainly not with the town biddies. No matter how much I assured Francine and the others that I still had my honor—and I pointedly told Francine that I considered my honor a sight safer with Reuben Whitesnake than ever I had with Herbert Wilkerson—she'd just furrow her brow and give me a look that said she felt sorry for me and ashamed to boot. The only folks I had regular acquaintance with who didn't seem bothered by my Indian friends were the Chins, probably because they had their own problems with the white folks of that town and figured whatever I had to put up with wasn't a patch on their miseries.

The strange thing was that after a little while, the more Francine would shake her head and the more the good women of Chautauqua would take to crossing the street with their noses stuck up in the air as if they smelled something rotten when they saw me coming, the happier I felt. What had bothered me something powerful at first begun to roll off me like water offen a duck's back. For reasons I couldn't explain, I was walking a little taller and prouder each time Caleb and I would come back from that Osage village and the more I felt as if our lives were on the right track at long last.

Caleb, of course, was having the time of his young life for absolute certain. That boy was well on his way to becoming a genuine Osage, and from what I could see, that wasn't a bad thing at all. Now, don't get me wrong on that score: I knew I was supposed to be raising him as a Christian, with proper schooling and a measure of discipline, and I took him to the Methodist church for Sunday School most weeks and even sat there and listened to them Bible stories with him, but watching him mope around when we were in town and then seeing him light up like a Christmas tree as soon as we crossed the Line and came in sight of that little village just set me to thinking that maybe it wouldn't hurt a thing if we put off his proper education, religious and otherwise, for a bit. The other little boys in town didn't seem any brighter nor any more well-mannered than them brown Osage youngsters, and there wasn't a child in town who was any happier. For certain all the hymn singing in the world didn't make the grownups any kinder. The Indian children had the absolute run of the village, darting in and out of every hut when the spirit hit them, and none of the adults seemed to mind in the least, whereas the folks in town tended to look down their noses at most all the children who weren't their own, especially the boys, and some of the men would just as soon give the back of their hand to a passing child as say good morning. I never saw an Osage strike a child, no matter what it had done. Whether that's a better way to raise a child I cannot say, but I can tell you without any fear of contradiction that it makes for a happier child.

Then there was me, or I should say my feelings on the subject of being in that village.

Or, to put it plainly, being with Reuben.

Now, I truly never planned on falling in love with him, even if I had had to read the Old Testament to get my mind offen him in the beginning. If you had asked me on the front end, I would of been just as shocked as the good ladies of Chautauqua, I suppose, though for reasons that had nothing to do with the color of his skin or where he came from. I just didn't feel the need of a man, or thought I didn't, being pretty well decided that I was going to spend the rest of my life as the widow of Jack Ross.

But from the first, Reuben Whitesnake made me feel all fluttery inside. In the beginning, I actually thought maybe I was sick from something the Osage women put in that stew they were always serving, because I'd never felt that way around any man, having come to appreciate and love Jack Ross over a matter of years but never having had that kind of flighty romance that had sent sister Dell down the wrong path from the moment she met Clement. Then, once I figured out the truth of it—that I was developing some pretty strong feelings for Reuben and maybe that's what that fluttering was—I tried real hard to squelch it. Honest to God in Heaven, I did.

I told myself that in the first place, he didn't think of me any different than he would any other white woman. He was just a naturally kind man, and he was being kind to me on account of his interest in the boy, and that was that. After all, he didn't know the first thing about me, and I'd come from a place he'd never even seen and likely never would. I should be as foreign to him as the Chins were to me.

Then I tried really hard to convince myself that any feelings I did have would only bring me to grief, so I should just swallow them and go on with my life. After all, wasn't it enough that I was a widow woman trying to raise an orphan nephew without I should get mixed up with another man, and an Osage at that? I even tried to convince myself that Francine and the other biddies were right.

The trouble was, talking to myself like that didn't work. Not one whit. Nor did Francine's nagging. And seeing the look on Herbert Wilkerson's face when he saw me coming, as if I was a pile of horse apples he needed to take care to come nowhere near, just made me laugh. Who did that fat old man think he was, anyway? If the women wanted to act that way... well, that was the way some women were, but it just flat infuriated me that a lecherous old fogy like Mister Wilkerson would do that, too.

Of course, where Reuben stood in all of this I did not know on account of he wasn't the talking type, and I was far too nervous to ask. For all I knew, he didn't consider me one way or another. Maybe I was just a cipher in his life, someone to be tolerated because I came along with the boy.

At least there was no doubting where Reuben stood on that score: he took such delight in Caleb that you'd of thought watching them that they were father and son, especially with Caleb's dark complexion and long, dark hair that turned nearly black when he took to greasing it the way the Osages did. Whatever that boy wanted to do, Reuben saw that it was done. So Caleb learned to ride bareback when he was still small enough that his legs stuck out straight to the sides on even the smallest pony, and when Reuben would pull him up to sit in front of him on an old paint, his little fist clenched over that coarse mane hair, he'd just be grinning from ear to ear. Reuben taught him to swim, too, the two of them jumping buck naked into that creek near the Osage village and catching suckers in their bare hands and laughing like a pair of lunatics. Caleb would bring them little fish to the cooking fire like the finest trophy any hunter ever took, and Reuben would roast and eat them with such dignity and pride that it made my own heart swell just to watch them.

Yessir, maybe I was just along for the ride, so to speak, a necessary complication so Reuben could enjoy that boy, but as long as that child was happy, I wasn't about to complain.

And then one day, fresh outen the blue, Reuben asked me to marry him.

Or didn't exactly ask so much as he just said something about how we needed to get married, then went on about his business as calm as if he'd been discussing the weather.

"Pardon me?" I said, tugging at his shirtsleeve. I was more than half afraid I'd misheard him.

He turned and looked at me, all puzzled like.

"Did you say we should get married?" I asked.

He nodded but didn't say a thing.

"Why on earth should we?" I asked, though in my own head I was already thinking of the fifty reasons it made sense.

"Why wouldn't we?" he said, though he took what seemed to me to be a long time answering. "You. Me. The boy. We are already like a family. It's the right thing to do."

"Well, you and the boy, maybe..."

He cocked his head and squinted as if he couldn't quite see me. "Do you not want to marry me? Is that not the custom among your people?"

"Well, yes. I mean, it's the custom."

"But you do not want to marry me." The puzzled look had quite suddenly given way to a smile when he said it, and it hit me like a load of bricks that he knew exactly how I felt and was just having some fun.

"I do!" I said, and I swear I stood up on tiptoe when I said it. "Absolutely I do."

His smile didn't grow so much as there was just an extra sparkle in his eyes. "Then we will. It is decided."

And with that, he stood and went to talk to a friend at the next hut like nothing in the world had happened.

Well, I don't think my feet touched the ground for the

rest of that day, and I know I didn't sleep a wink that night, neither.

Of course, you can imagine the reaction when I told Francine when we got back to town the next morning.

"Oh, heavenly Father, I forbid it!" she exclaimed before I'd even finished.

I actually laughed out loud at that. "I don't hardly see how it's your place to allow or forbid, either one," I said.

"But think of the child! You can't have a boy like that— already as wild as wild can be—growing up Indian!" She crossed herself, Catholic that she was even though pretty much fallen away.

"Why not?" I asked. "He's happy there, and I don't see how him growing up amongst the Osages is any worse than growing up here in town where half the men he sees are drunks or lechers."

That shut her up for a second or two on account of it was one of her favorite complaints that her own son had to witness such behavior, but it only slowed her down until she could think up a new argument. "If you want that boy to grow up to be a good Christian gentleman, you'd best not take him south of the Line again is all I'll say on the subject. He'll burn in Hell if them redskins turn him away from the Path."

"Them Osages is more Christian than the folks in town to my way of thinking," I said.

She was truly shocked. "That's blaspheming, Eva Rae."

"I don't care. It's the truth."

She rolled her eyes heavenward and stomped outen the room, throwing back over her shoulder as she went "It's that boy's soul you'd best be thinking on."

Well, it was true that I hadn't considered God or the church, so I had a talk about God and religion with Reuben our next trip to the village. White man's religion as I explained it to him seemed to amuse him more than anything else, but he said he sure didn't want to do anything to harm

Caleb, so if I wanted to raise him a Christian, he allowed as how he wouldn't stand in the way. As I learned later, most of the Osages were more or less Christian already, though with quite a lot of their old religion mixed in. At the same time, Reuben said he didn't see what harm there would be in teaching Caleb about the Osage ways, which he went on to explain at some length, though about all I gathered at the time was some hazy notion about something he called the great Wakonda above and Wakonda below, the father sky and the mother earth and the cycles of life that proceeded in given rhythms, like the darkness of night and the brightness of day. Things like that. I don't suppose it was any harder an idea to grasp than burning bushes and the finger of God writing in fire and a heavenly Father allowing his son to be crucified and all the rest, but it plumb made my head hurt trying to think through all of it.

So I just let it go at the simplest level I could: when Reuben told me them things, he was so earnest and clear, at least to himself, that it was just like listening to an old blind woman back home, a friend of Ma's who was so touched by the Spirit that when she got to talking on religion, it brought a feeling of peace to all her listeners. I maybe didn't know the least part of what he was saying, but I knew in my heart I was doing the right thing turning Caleb over to that man. I figured Caleb would go to church in town when he had a chance—if the townfolk would let him—but the whole world would be his Osage church the rest of the time, and if he came outen it with half the comfort in his beliefs that Reuben had, he'd be all right. And when it came down to it, I figured it wouldn't hurt me none to learn a few things about the Osage way, neither.

Of course, I for sure knew I could never explain it to Francine and the rest of the biddies, but that was more their loss than mine, so I didn't even try.

Francine still huffed and puffed, and the rest continued to

shun me outright, but it was like a great weight had been lifted off my shoulders just the same. Once I'd made my peace with the simple fact that I loved Reuben, the flutters left, and all the worries I'd been holding in about how Caleb and I were going to get by went with it. I figured maybe I'd be up in the middle of the night to fix breakfast by an outdoor fire in a half-civilized Indian camp, but that wasn't any worse than getting up in the middle of the night to stir other people's union suits in a pot of boiling water and knowing that without I did that, Francine would put me out on my ear, friend or no friend.

Now, getting ready for that wedding proved to be both an exciting and exasperating time. Exciting because I was simply in love in a way I never had been before and hadn't ever expected, and exasperating because there was so much to do and so little help was forthcoming from my erstwhile town friends.

At least it wasn't going to be any big church wedding, which of course wasn't all that common in them days, anyway. Most folks just stood up in front of the minister and said their "I do's" and that was that, except that you could count on your friends throwing a chivaree, after which the bride was expected to put on a big feed. Not having to face one of them things I counted as a pure blessing.

Still, there was one thing that I put off and put off and put off until I was slap ashamed of myself, and that was writing a letter to my mother. I hadn't been very good about keeping in touch with her since we left Gove County, to say the least. For that matter, I hadn't done much by way of letter writing ever since Jack and I left for Kansas because so often in them early days the news had been bad, and by the time Caleb and I got to Chautauqua, I was more or less outen the habit. But I knew the time had come. I figured she'd want to know that her baby daughter was getting married again—needed to know, whether she wanted to or not—and surely she must be concerned about the welfare of her grandson Caleb. I also figured I probably needed to explain in some detail why it was that I was marrying an Osage man, which I was sure would worry her half to death. Ma had never known any Indians that I know of. She probably hadn't seen more than a handful in her life, and those were chiefs coming down the river on their way to St. Louis or Washington City or some other far off place. An ordinary Indian man was about as far from her daily experience as the man in the moon was from mine, but she'd grown up in the company of folks who had fought Indians in Kentucky with Danl Boone and then fought Indians again when they got to Missouri. The battles on the northern Plains betwixt the Army and the Sioux and Cheyenne tribes had kept most of the folks in our part of the country on pins and needles for years, and most—Ma probably included—subscribed to what that little banty rooster General Phil Sheridan said about the only good Indian being a dead one.

So I wrote, and laid out my case as carefully as I could.

As I started out, I didn't know what to tell her and was half afraid the whole blamed letter would only be a couple of lines, but by the time I was finished, it was pages and pages long and I'd completely wore through a couple of pencils and a whole sheaf of paper. I told Ma about Chautauqua and how that town compared with Callaway County. I told her about the railroad and how there weren't as many railroad men around as there had been when we'd first arrived, but how there was still too many for my taste. I told her what I did to earn my keep for Francine and the Chins and how what I'd be doing after the marriage wouldn't be so different except I'd be doing it for a man I loved instead of a Chinese brother and sister who usually looked at me like I was some kind of inferior. I told her how Caleb was doing—leaving off some of the things about him and Reuben skinny dipping and such— and how the little Osage village reminded me so much of the glade back home. I confess I even told her that one day the Osage lands would surely belong to the white man, since them crazy Boomers had already staked a claim to a big chunk of land south and west of there that spring, mostly to ease her mind about me living amongst the red men. I told her how beautiful the country was in the fall and how the whistle of the train carried for miles and miles. For some reason, all the need to talk to my mother that had just been bottled up for years came spilling out in the letter, and I swear writing it took so much outen me that when I finished, I laid down and slept for three hours even though it was only the middle of the day.

When I awakened, I folded it up and carried it down to the post office and gave it to the postmaster, who squinted at that bundle, then at me, and then back to the bundle.

"What's the matter?" I asked.

"You got kin in Missourah?" he asked.

I nodded.

"I growed up in Jeff City."

"You don't say."

He squinted again. "You do look a mite familiar, to tell you the truth."

"Well, I should," I said. "We've known each other pushing three years."

"No. I mean like someone I knew back home."

"Well, I'm a Cumberland," I said, nodding at that parcel in his hands. "That's going to my ma."

He let out a whistle. "A Cumberland, you say." He turned the package over in his hands. "I knew a Levi Cumberland when I was a pup. Him and my pa were friends."

"You don't say."

He leaned acrost the old plank counter that had been polished smooth by the letters and parcels passed acrost it over the years. "I b'lieve they shared a nip now and again."

"That'd be my daddy," I said.

"Wore the sheets together, too."

Again I agreed.

He tossed the package into a bushel basket behind him. "You're the one marrying that big Indian buck, ain't you?"

From the way he said it, the hairs on the back of my neck stood straight up. "Yes."

"Too bad. I'll bet you're daddy's rolling in his grave over you pulling a blame fool stunt like that. Marryin' a Indian's almost as bad as marryin' a nigger. The good Lord don't look with favor on such like, I'll tell you."

I forced myself to smile as sweetly as I could. "I appreciate your concern, sir," I said, hoping he could tell I was just about mad enough to rip his heart out. "By the way, you'll be happy to know that my best friend—other than my betrothed, that is—happens to be a black man. I ain't seen him in years, but he's the best soul I've ever known not counting that 'big buck' you were referring to, and either one of 'em's got it all over any of the rednecked old sonsofbitches my daddy hung around with, your pa included."

And with that I spun on my heel and marched outside. I said a silent prayer asking Jack to forgive me for leaving him outen that list of 'best souls,' though I was slap certain he wouldn't mind.

The point was, postmasters being the same the world over, I knew that last comment of mine would be all over Chautauqua by nightfall.

I didn't care.

I'd never felt so free.

Reuben

S O BEGAN THE BEST TIME in Caleb's life and mine.

Reuben and I were married in that little unnamed Osage village on September the 7th of 1889, an absolutely beautiful late summer day without a hint of cloud in the sky.

The Reverend Sylvester McGee, the Methodist circuit rider who showed up in Chautauqua every month or so, performed the ceremony in that little bit of yard in front of Reuben's tiny cabin, though he was attended by several of Reuben's sisters who I think wanted to make sure he didn't do anything that would run contrary to their own notions of how to splice a man and a woman together. The reverend hadn't seemed too keen on the marriage when I asked him, but being a decent man and better Christian than most of the pious townfolk in his flock, he'd agreed to do the honors if I'd make a small donation to his church. I guessed it was the least I could do, so I pretty much emptied my cigar box into his hand on the assumption that I wasn't going to need much money from here on out, anyway. Caleb was ecstatic that we were going to live south of the Line for real, of course. Though he wouldn't be six for another month yet, Reuben solemnly asked him if he would give me away after the Christian fashion, and of course he'd been delighted at the prospect. Francine even showed up for the wedding, being a good soul and good friend when you got right down to it, though she was as nervous as a raccoon in a pack of hounds amongst them Osages, and it was pretty plain that all she really wanted to do was get back to the safety of town before some heathen scalped her or worse. I've always figured she mostly wanted to get away from Chautauqua for the day since her boarders were in an ugly mood over the sawdust and noise generated by the men putting up another floor on her place. It would of been easier for her to tear down the original house and start over, but being frugal, she wouldn't countenance that.

Still, she was there, which pleased me.

Once it was time for the shindig to begin, we all lined up in that sunny meadow, with the dogs running in and out amongst our legs. When the reverend was finished reading the necessary passages from the Good Book, my new sisters-in-law commenced saying some prayers of their own with pointing at the sky and earth and such, and Reuben paid real close attention to that, though I could not tell what them women were saying. To his credit, Reverend McGee was properly serious, too, though he appeared to be clutching his Bible pretty tight to ward off any evil spirits that might come his way, and Francine crossed herself about every ten seconds. The mood I was in that day, it just made me laugh.

I couldn't of asked for a better wedding. I was twenty-one years old, and my new husband was just a touch past thirty. As fond as I'd been of Jack Ross toward the end of his life, I knew it was pure love that I felt for Reuben, and this was the marriage I'd been waiting for without even knowing it. In my heart, I believed that Jack would of approved. Reuben was good, strong, kind, and absolutely the smartest human being I've ever known, white, brown, red or otherwise. His being three-quarters Osage didn't matter a whit to me even if it did to polite society in Chautauqua, who figured a drop of Indian blood plumb spoiled whoever had it for any chance of being civilized.

Besides giving me away, Caleb was best man, or what passed for it under the circumstances. That little boy stood there beaming through the whole ceremony as if he understood what it was all about. Just being in the presence of Reuben Whitesnake and his family was probably enough for that child, though my being happy probably added to his own pleasure, too. At least I hope so.

Anyway, when the Indian prayers were over, Francine gave me a little peck on the cheek, shook Reuben's hand about like she was taking hold of the business end of a rattlesnake, and took off outen there with Reverend McGee bouncing in the back end of her buggy. He waved and raised a hand in blessing, and then it was just me and my new husband, our adopted boy, and all them sisters, who slap took over the proceedings at that point.

Food showed up in quantities that would of fed a crew of railroad gandy dancers, and although some of it was stuff I'd never tasted before (and didn't particularly want to know what was in it, neither), it turned out to be good enough. Of the stuff I recognized, there was succotash, and dried and cooked meats of several kinds including squirrel and 'possum cooked tastier than my own ma ever had, a sort of pudding that I believe was made from dried berries and animal fat, fried bread sprinkled with the brown sugar which was one of Reuben's presents to me, he having bought a cask of it on his last trip into town, and something that passed for coffee but was probably roasted wild herbs of some sort boiled strong enough to take the enamel offen your teeth.

Then them ladies cleaned up and took off, packing up Caleb along with the leftovers. How they got him away from Reuben I'll never know for certain, although I believe bribery with a good deal of that precious sugar had something to do with it.

Which left me alone with my husband in that tiny hut of his.

Now, you'd think I would of known what to do under the circumstances since I'd been with Jack Ross those several years, but looking back on it, right at that moment I felt I was about the greenest soul that ever drew breath. Scared doesn't begin to tell it, for though I was surely in love, it struck me that I didn't have the first idea what I was going to do with that man. With Jack, whatever I did—and however bad I did it—was so far beyond his previous experience that I suppose it couldn't help but be miraculous in his eyes. With Reuben... well, he'd been married before, and I was so smitten that I naturally wanted to be the very best wife I could be for him.

Of course, it turned out all right. I won't go into details, but let's just say Reuben proved to be the tenderest person alive, never mind how big and strong he was otherwise. I was nothing short of amazed and gratified both. But as I say, I don't believe I'll go into it.

I will say, though, that it was hard getting used to living in that little bitty cabin. Where my first home with Jack Ross in Missouri had been full of holes big enough to throw a shoe through, Reuben's cabin was snug and tight as a tick, since after he'd proposed, he'd even fashioned a proper door so we had something better than a skin hanging there to keep the field mice and other assorted critters out. The trouble was, it was so blamed small that just turning around could be a chore if two of us were indoors at the same time. Though I wasn't a big person, Reuben surely was, and he pretty well filled that space all by himself. Plus we had Caleb to think about. We had to rig a trundle bed for that boy, there being no other spot than under our own bed where a third person could sleep. We'd pull it out at night, but if one of us had to get up to use the slop jar, like as not we'd step on him or kick him or something. Fortunately, he was a sound sleeper in them days on account of all that fresh air and running around.

Most all our belongings were hung from pegs in the log walls, and there absolutely wasn't enough room for any more than the barest few of my town possessions, most of which I'd had the good sense to leave in a trunk at Francine's, anyway.

Every bit of the cooking was done out of doors even in the wickedest weather. I'd had practice keeping a fire going from the earliest days of my childhood, but that was in a fireplace indoors, and usually in a proper stove with all the dampers and chimneys. An outside fire, open to whatever weather there was, created an entirely different challenge. When the weather turned cold and brought with it the ferocious ice storms common in them parts, keeping a blaze enough going to cook stew or het water for the wash became one of the cruelest challenges of my life. The women of that village, me included, would haul deadfall branches and whatever bits and pieces of kindling we could find, then get a roaring blaze going and add greenwood to it to make a slower, smoky blaze, and once we had a nice bed of coal, we'd lay in the biggest creek stones and slabs of limestone we could find—anything to hold the heat—then bank the whole thing with skins stretched taut on willow frames to keep the pelting sleet outen the fire. Some of the greenwood would turn to charcoal from the heat, and we'd save that as carefully as we could because we could set it afire more easily for cooking. But labor as we might, sometimes on them wet and windy days there just wasn't nothing could be done, and all our work would be for naught. When that happened, and we knew it might be days before we'd get another proper fire going, we'd just settle in and stay snug as best we could and try to ignore the hunger pangs that was sure to get to us before long. I learned that the Osages always dried plenty of meat in the good times to tide them over when there wasn't nothing else to eat, so we didn't starve, but squirrel or 'possum—or even acorn fed venison— dried and smoked to the consistency of a pair of your daddy's boots isn't always the most appetizing, even if your stomach is growling with hunger.

Anyway, it took some practice to keep the cooking fires

going in the winter and the spring wets, but it also took some doing to keep from setting the entire countryside afire when a dry season windstorm would blow hot cinders every which-away. I can say with pride all these many years later, though, that I learned fast, and in no time I was the equal of any of them Osage ladies who had been doing it all their lives. I believe to this day I'd have a better than even chance of keeping an outdoor fire going well enough to bring it back to life in the middle of a blizzard. I wouldn't want to do it, mind you, but I'm positive I could.

Them sisters-in-law of mine proved to be more help than ever I would of imagined, and they were a lot less nosy than white women would of been into the bargain. Not that they didn't gossip. I think Indian women, at least the ones I've known, are the biggest gossips in the whole world, but there's nothing malicious about it, and most of the time you wind up giggling with them even if you're the object of their chatter. Snooty, they ain't, unlike some others I could mention.

What they did for me in the early days was beyond measure. First off, they found things for Caleb to do when I wanted to be alone with Reuben, and they helped cook until I got the hang of the fire and some notion of how to prepare the traditional Osage food for my little family. They showed me where I could find wild onions to flavor my stews, and they showed me how to skin and clean the little critters that Reuben brought home from his hunting trips. Now, when I was a girl, it was the menfolk who cleaned their kill, taking a nip or two of the jug while they did it, but not so the Osages. Reuben's sisters thought it was right funny the way I'd gag over the entrails. I'd watched butchering since I was a baby, and I'd scraped casings for sausage and chopped cheek meat for head cheese and all them other nasty jobs, but I hadn't never scooped guts outen a critter still warm to the touch. They said I learned that real quick, but I've always suspected they were just humoring me on that score.

As for Reuben's daughter, I volunteered to have her come live with us on the sensible grounds that I was surely as much her mother now as I was Caleb's, but the one of Reuben's former sisters-in-law who was looking after that girl flat refused. There was nothing mean spirited about it—she and the girl had just grown attached to one another, and besides, there would be other little ones coming who would need a corner of our small hut, she said. I'm certain that statement made me turn every possible shade of red, for my sister-in-law and the other women who overheard it had a good chuckle at my expense, though of course I knew what she was implying was a distinct possibility. Anyway, much to my surprise, Reuben agreed with his sister about his child. That little girl would always be his daughter, but now his first wife's sister was her mother, and so that's the way it would have to be.

If it made sense to them, who was I to see it any different?

I will also admit that it took me some days to get used to being in such an out-of-the-way corner of the world. Of course, for being lonely, it wasn't nothing like Gove County, first on account there were other families right there, and second that it was only a part day's ride to Chautauqua, which I'd gotten used to over the past couple of years. But precisely because it was sort of hemmed in—you could come within a quarter mile of that little village and never know it was there unless there was a drift of smoke from the cooking fires—it seemed more isolated. And, I realized, I'd lived in town long enough to get used to having folks I didn't know bustling about and the clatter and clang of the railroad interrupting the quiet of the middle of the night.

Now, that's not to say them Osages hadn't done a right wonderful job of locating that little village, because they had. As time went on, I learned that a lot of why they were there and how they'd laid out their town was by way of following the precepts of their religion. Reuben's people, believing there are mysteries on the earth and in the sky both, had situated their village in the perfect spot to see the dawn and sunset each day, yet with enough trees to provide reasonable shelter from the wind and hide them from any enemies they might have, too. There was sweet spring water nearby, and they'd dug some shallow trenches to a small bog that provided water for the truck gardens when it didn't rain, which was a real smart thing because drouth is always a concern in our country. Wildflowers bloomed in profusion in the meadows where the horses grazed, and I saw more butterflies that first month after we married than I believe I'd seen in my entire life up to that moment. At night, we didn't have a horizon-to-horizon view of the sky the way I had along the banks of the Smoky Hill, but still I could lay flat on my back in the grass and watch the great wash of the Milky Way pinwheel over-head, all while listening to the gurgle of the brook and the low chatter of children playing inside their own huts.

Once I got used to being with the Osages instead of white folks, I came to love that place and appreciate them people, even if I did (much to my surprise) still secretly miss my little adopted town of Chautauqua.

And I loved Reuben, too, more than I thought was poss-ible. To put it as simply as I can, I was at peace with that man. That's all I can say, and having that measure of real content-ment made me realize how little of it I'd had all the rest of my life up to that point.

Now, I know the popular thinking is that a good Christian woman isn't supposed to find life in an Indian camp or marriage to an Indian man anything but pure terror. Well, I'm here to tell you that's just hogwash.

In the first place, this was a settled village, and though it was far smaller than Chautauqua, which, truth to tell, wasn't more than a one-horse town even in them days, there was a permanence to it that I believe exceeded anything I'd ever known, saving Jeff City itself. The Osages had lived there for generations, and they planned to keep right on doing it forever. Them folks purely loved that little patch of ground. In that regard, it wasn't a bit different than the way Ma and Daddy felt about their glen in Callaway County, Missouri.

In the second place, them people were gentle. That's the only way I can put it. They were decent, hard-working—leastwise the women were—considerate of each other, and kind to the two strangers Reuben had taken in, meaning of course me and Caleb. Life wasn't easy, but in my experience, life never is, no matter whether you're in a fancy city or a mean dugout within spitting distance of the end of the Earth.

And of course, there was Reuben.

What more can I say?

The only thing that made me the least bit upset with him was his choice of professions. I confess I had hoped that once we settled down together, he'd give up lawing and become whatever it was that other Osage men were, which was mostly a combination of gentleman farmer, story-teller, and loafer, there being no wars to fight with the civilized tribes anymore. We'd of been poor as church mice, but then being a lawman for the Osages didn't pay much beyond the provender folks brought by out of gratitude for whatever service Reuben had rendered, and all in all, it would of been a comfortable life.

But that life wasn't for Reuben. In some way I couldn't understand, he felt responsible for the safety of his people. He took his duties as a lawman very seriously, and thanks mostly to our white neighbors, there were for sure enough crimes to justify the position of policeman for the Osage Nation. Reuben wasn't the tribe's only lawman, of course, but he was in charge of keeping the peace as best he could in the northern part of the Nation, where it came into direct contact with the white man's land, which nearly surrounded us now since the U.S. Government had decreed that the western half of all the Indian lands would be Oklahoma Territory, and that included the Osage Nation. So we were part of an Indian country within a U.S. territory. The land belonging to the so-called civilized tribes, meaning the Creeks, Cherokees, and the like, was still theirs, which meant that it could get right confusing who was running the show on any particular piece of ground.

And it was ironic that some of the Indian tribes outside Oklahoma Territory hired white men in them days to serve as lawmen, while the white settlements wouldn't of thought of having a red-skinned lawman. In any case, the Osages were right happy to have a man of Reuben's caliber looking after their interests up near the Line, and the "civilized tribes" were even happier having a red man of his abilities keeping his own folks on the straight and narrow.

All of which meant there was plenty for him to do. If it wasn't white men trying to sell rotgut whiskey to the Indians, it was the Indians getting all crazy on stuff they managed to cook up themselves in little backwoods stills that would of done my Daddy proud. With a cupful of that poison in their systems—no matter where they got it—they truly did turn into wild Indians, stealing, fighting and even murdering. Plenty of white men can't handle their liquor, either, but there's something about an Indian that sends that whiskey to their brain a whole lot faster. And beyond the liquor problems, there was always some dispute or another over stolen horseflesh, most Indians seeing nothing wrong with trying to add to their horse herds at the expense of their neighbors, except that when them neighbors was white folks or other tribes, the situation could get ugly in a hurry.

So his main job was to keep things like that from blowing up into real violence, and he was good at it. Most of the white farmers and ranchers thereabouts knew him, of course, and some of the old-timers had known his daddy, who was half white, being the son of a trader who'd plied the Santa Fe Trail in the old days. According to what Reuben told me, his daddy had gotten a year or two of education in St. Louis, but he'd come back to his momma's people, taken up her name, and spent his later days trying to be more Indian than all the rest of them put together, except that he'd made his own son—meaning Reuben—learn English on account of he knew the Osages were going to have to live in a white man's world.

Anyway, I know for a fact that not many of the folks living north of the Line liked Reuben very much, what with he was mostly Indian, after all, and I'm sure they would of preferred dealing with the white marshals and policemen the tribes hired, even though most of them jaspers were usually working both sides of the law at the same time.

But I'm getting ahead of myself.

As for Reuben, I know for a fact that the smart folks in southeastern Kansas respected him for being an honest and hardworking man who could be depended on to bring back their stolen stock as long as they had a brand to prove it was theirs or take care of some poor drunken Osage passed out in a ditch. The whites—the good class of whites, I mean—usually admitted he was a good man for an Indian, which is about as close to a compliment as you're liable to get, grudging though it may be.

Still, going after trouble-making cowboys or riding into other Osage camps to retrieve stolen livestock without knowing whether the thieves were liquored up surely put him in harm's way more often than not, and that didn't please me one bit. He had a couple of ugly scars on his body from various scrapes he'd been in, including one little blue-black dimple in his hip that still carried a .44 slug he'd taken when some drunk fired a pistol at him. But he didn't talk about the dangers, and when I'd worry out loud, he'd just shrug off my concerns. He had a job to do to help protect his people, which more often than not meant protecting them from themselves and their customs, and that was all there was to it.

"It's what I have to do, Evarae," was all he'd say, putting my two names together into one. Then he'd give me a big smile showing them perfectly white teeth of his and scoop up Caleb and toss him around until that child nearly passed out from giggling.

You can't argue with a man who does things like that.

Now, life in that village wasn't all peaches and cream that first autumn, in spite of what I've said. Not by a long shot, and not just because I had to clean game and keep the fires going and worry about my husband.

All the work was hard, and there wasn't any of the niceties that can make town living seem comfortable. It was up and at 'em well before dawn each day, earlier than I ever had with the Chins or Francine, though I had no real notion of the time since the Osages didn't seem to understand clocks and anyway wouldn't have them on the premises. They lived in rhythm with the sun and moon, and not some machine.

Work, whether cooking or washing or patching clothes or shooing the critters who made it past the door outen our little house, took pretty much all the day from well before dawn until nightfall. Once darkness set in, the only light we had was the cooking fire outside or a candle or two made out of tallow so rough it still had bits of gristle and cooked meat in it. Them candles gave precious little light, sometimes they stunk from going rancid or just from whatever animal the fat had come from, and they were so scarce that burning one for an hour seemed like the height of luxury. In truth, a moonlit night offered up a passel more useful light than them tallow candles did, and of course once the sun went down, it was pretty much time to go to sleep, anyway.

Then there were the victuals. I have to be honest that I never really did quite get to like Osage provender. The feast Reuben's sisters provided on my wedding day wasn't typical, I'll tell you for sure. Not that the usual fare was bad, but it was long on root-and-'possum stew and roasted small game and the various squashes they grew in the garden plot nearby and mighty short on baked goods and sweets, which I'd come to admire at Francine's, especially once that little Negro girl went to work for her. None of them Osage meals was bad exactly, but they weren't good, neither, both from lack of seasonings and variety. For instance, the stew usually came with little bits of stuff that most cooks throw away without giving it a second thought. Let's just say that when it came to meat, the Osages didn't waste none of it. Seeing a squirrel's head floating in the stew—and watching my man suck the meat off it like it was some kind of delicacy—put me off my own feed more than once. Some of them greasy dishes sat on my stomach like I'd et a stone or at least a plateful of Francine's biscuits, and I took to picking at them, which was about the first time in my life I'd been fussy when it came to mealtime.

But Caleb plowed through that grub like his stomach was a pit with no bottom.

Of course, I suppose some of what put me off my feed and made all the work that needed doing even more tedious was the fact that I was with child.

Them sisters of Reuben's had it figured, I'll tell you.

It couldn't of been but a few weeks after we were married that I started feeling puny in the mornings, and of course I knew right away what that was about. I didn't tell Reuben for a spell, though I suspect he knew it as well as I did. Maybe better, in fact, since he seemed to have a sense about them things, as I came to understand most Osages, male and female, do.

Anyway, the thought of having a baby made me right nervous, mostly on account of how I'd lost little Robert John. Things like that happen, of course, but I suppose a body is just naturally prone to worrying on it whenever there's an opportunity.

At least I knew when it came time for that baby to be born that I'd have plenty of help, which was something I'd sorely missed the first time around. Every one of them Osages sisters was a dyed-in-the-wool first class midwife. It was like they'd taken turns helping each other have babies for so long that it was second nature to them. They tended to look on childbirth—whether they or someone else was doing the birthing—as just an ordinary chore, and not a very difficult one at that, but in my case, they seemed to take a special interest, probably on account of they were concerned for their brother's happiness. Anyhow, once they figured out what my condition was, they all took to hovering over me and patting my belly and grinning from ear to ear like they'd had something to do with it. I wasn't crazy about that at first, but as I got to know them better, the less it bothered me. One of Reuben's sisters, who went by the Christian name of Helen though her Osage name was something I never did learn to pronounce right, was my particular friend and just the sweetest thing I've ever known in my life, though she could be a rip-snorter when her man came up short on bringing home game or let one of his ponies wander off. We'd have long talks about kids, of which she had a passel, while we worked side-by-side in the garden or at the cooking fire. Helen spoke English almost as well as Reuben, which was unusual for them women and maybe accounted for why we become friends so quickly.

As fall turned to winter and winter progressed toward Christmas, I did find myself beginning to fret about how I was going to get through the holiday season with Caleb. I'd promised myself and the Reverend McGee, too, that I would raise Caleb as the best Christian I knew how, which of course meant Methodist in the good Reverend's eyes, but there weren't any churches close by, and for certain no circuit riding Methodist preacher was going to waste his time in the Nations, or so I thought. When I brought it up to Reuben, he'd scratch his chin and say maybe we could take the boy into town for services, but when I'd mention it to Caleb, he'd howl like I'd stuck him with a hot poker. It wasn't so much that he was opposed to the religion of it. It was just that he slap didn't want anything to do with town. The thing I missed more than I cared to admit, he was utterly tickled to be shed of. He was living what he considered the perfect life, and he wasn't about to lose a single minute of it, Sunday morning or no Sunday morning.

Still, we tried it one Sunday in late November. Fortunately, it was one of them warm, golden days that sometimes make you think winter isn't going to be too bad after all. Reuben and Caleb rode together bareback while I rode sidesaddle on an old Texas style rig that Reuben had found somewhere. I had to hang on to that big old saddle horn for dear life and would of been a sight more comfortable astride that horse, the way I'd learned to ride as a girl, but I was wearing a dark skirt I'd brought with me when I'd married Reuben, so that just wasn't possible. Even though I'd let it out as much as I could, that skirt barely covered my swelling belly.

We got to town a good hour before services were about to start, so I went by Francine's to say hello, then hurried on over to the school house, which served as whatever church was meeting on any particular Sunday. The Reverend McGee was part way through the Sunday school lesson when we walked in, and he was right kind about introducing Caleb to the other children, most of whom already knew him anyway, and he patted my boy on the head and kept on talking about Noah and the Flood, which was that day's topic for his regular sermon as well. I stood in the back of the room and watched, though I confess I was there at least in part to snag my boy as he went by if he tried to bolt for the door.

Caleb listened real intently, though, and when it was over, he asked me what seemed like a million questions about cubits and animals and gopherwood and rainbows, none of which I could answer. The trouble was, Caleb kept asking them questions right out loud once the regular service started, and what amused the churchgoers for a few minutes made them right peevish once the hymn singing was over and it was time to listen to the preacher. I'd shush him, then ten seconds later, he'd come out with a "Momma Eva, how come..." and I'd have to do the shushing all over again. Before they even passed the collection plate I'd had to take him outside. Reuben, who'd been waiting with the horses all this time on account of he assumed, rightly enough, that them Methodists wouldn't of appreciated having him set foot inside, was so tickled he laughed out loud, which was a major display of emotion for any Indian but especially that one.

When the families finally piled outen that schoolhouse, shook hands with the preacher, and went back to their homes, I pulled Caleb by the collar up to the good reverend so we could both apologize.

"Best you keep him outen church," Reverend McGee said before I could even get the words out.

"Pardon?" I said.

He turned all red and tugged at his shirt collar. "Keep him home. Some of the folks from around here..." He let the thought trail off.

"Pardon?" I said again.

He nodded in the general direction of some of the good folks of Chautauqua as they disappeared into their various dwellings. "A few of 'em... that is, most of 'em..."

"They don't want us here," I said, suddenly catching his drift.

He didn't look me in the eye. "That'd be about the size of it."

"What on earth for?"

"They just don't think it's right that a Indian..."

"Caleb's not an Indian!" I said, and I fairly shouted it, too.

He licked his lips. "No'm, he's not. But that baby you're carrying is." He let his eyes just sort of dip down to my belly and then come back up.

To say I was shocked is to understate the truth by a whole lot. "How do you know I'm carrying a baby?" But of course I knew the answer, what with how tight my skirt was and all.

"Oh, it's been all over town," Reverend McGee said with another tug at his collar. "Folks been talking about it for a while. Anyway, most of my flock don't think it's right, and..."

"Francine. She's told, didn't she?" I'd confided to Francine my last trip to town for supplies, and see what it had got me?

"I wouldn't know about that," he said, looking right uncomfortable. "But people can tell just looking at you, you'll forgive me for saying. Anyhow..."

I didn't let him finish. "Well, you tell them biddies they won't have to worry about coming face to face with no Indians on my account. Not now and not never!" I took Caleb by the hand and turned to go back to where Reuben was so patiently waiting.

"Now, I could come south of the Line, maybe," Reverend McGee called after me, trying to sound helpful. "Be glad to do it."

"That won't be necessary," I snapped over my shoulder and kept walking.

"Now, Missus..."

But I didn't respond.

And so ended my plan to get Caleb right with the Christians. It made me so mad I could of spit snakes, but it only seemed to amuse Reuben, who of course had faced that kind of stupid attitude all his life and didn't let it bother him anymore.

It took a long time for me to make up to Francine, I'll tell you. I knew right off that she didn't mean nothing by telling folks I was in a family way, but still I figured if she'd had the brains God gave a goose, she'd of known that them women around town would turn that fact against me. It just plain hurt—that Francine was a blabbermouth, I mean, because I had no problem ignoring the attitude of the biddies—and that kept me from talking to her for the longest time, which meant I was pretty well exiled from Chautauqua altogether.

Fortunately, I had Reuben's sisters, especially Helen, to give me some female companionship, but it just wasn't the same on account of their ways and my ways were still so different that I couldn't help but want to talk to one of my own kind whenever I got the chance. Many a night, I longed just to be able to chat about ordinary things with a woman who understood what I was talking about. Even Helen, who as I said was about as knowledgeable on the subject of children as any woman I ever met, didn't have any notion of the world much beyond the Line, and when I did try to tell her about Ma and Daddy and the big cities I'd seen, meaning mostly Jeff City, she'd just look at me with a blank stare that told me whatever I was saying was so far outside her experience that she couldn't comprehend it.

That was when I missed Francine. I missed her at Christmas, and through the long cold winter, and through the spring, and on into summer.

Finally, when my little Donald was safely born, I couldn't stand it any longer, on account of I was itching to show him off to my only white friend. I swallowed my pride, told myself I just had to forget about her blabbing ways, and took my child north to her place.

She plumb fell all over herself apologizing, having known all along how mad I was, and I accepted, and just like that, we were back to being friends.

Of course, Francine was having her own troubles in them days. As I've already mentioned, around the time Reuben and I got married, she'd started adding on to the boardinghouse. Then she got some grand notion that she could use it to sort of put Chautauqua on the map in a way that hadn't happened before. With the help of a nitwit railroad boss who fancied himself a town builder, she decided it was time to get Chautauqua back to its roots, so to speak. She gave a newspaper man from Sedan an IOU to print up about a thousand fliers talking about how healthful Chautauqua's springs were and how the best waters was only available at her boardinghouse, which of course was pure nonsense on account of her house was a good half-mile from the medicinal spring. Her own well wasn't but twenty or thirty yards from her closest neighbor's, and half the time the water that came outen it tasted like soap because the Chins dumped the laundry water right there in the yard, which just leeched down into the well water in nothing flat.

But that wasn't going to stop Francine.

Her notion was that them fliers would bring folks from as far away as Arkansas and Nebraska who wanted to take the cure—the railroad man was hoping for permanent settlers and not just tourists, of course—and that was really why she'd finally added that third story onto that rattletrap old building of hers.

Where once it had reminded me of a somewhat taller version of Ma and Daddy's place in Callaway County, now it looked something like a real hotel, only one that you were looking at through a cheap window that distorted the view. It leaned over to one side, and try as she might, she couldn't never get that top story level. A body could drop a marble at the north end of the narrow upstairs hallway, and that thing would start moving, and it would still be picking up speed when it slammed into the wall at the south end. The whole place sort of settled, too, though not until she had the construction completed, which caused some of the timbers to come apart, and in spite of the patching she had done, the clapboards she'd paid a pretty penny for never looked right.

That place drew a crowd, all right, but mostly it was local gawkers who came by to point and make fun, and when they found a dead child drowned in that nearby creek she claimed she took her medicinal water from... well, that was pretty much of the end of Francine's grand town-building adventure.

The newspaper man hounded her for his cash, and I've heard tell that it wasn't no time at all until she was reduced to giving him special favors, if you follow my drift, even though she'd tried to put that kind of life behind her when the sheriff and Guthrie, the railroad man, skipped town.

It was a sad thing to behold.

But I stayed her friend, and for a while there I was maybe the only one who did. Other than letting her mouth run, she'd never done me any wrong, and I had to admit that she'd done plenty to help me when I needed it.

Anyhow, there we were—a boardinghouse mistress with grand ideas that nobody else on earth would of thought were grand, and an Indian buck's white squaw, to use the phrase whispered loud enough so's I could hear it every time I went to town. I guess it came down to nobody else wanted nothing to do with either one of us, so Francine and I decided that if we were ever going to have fast friends, we were going to have to be each other's.

But once again, I'm getting ahead of myself.

I said that Donald was born without trouble, and that's the truth. That boy came into the world on the Fourth of July in 1890. All his life he's made jokes about what a firecracker he must of been, but that's just Donald's way of trying to turn attention away from the fact that he was born in a one-room cabin south of the Line on a date that didn't mean nothing to most of the people we were living amongst even if it was by then part of Oklahoma Territory, and on top of that he was brought into this world with the help of his Osage aunts.

What I've never been able to figure out is why Caleb, who didn't have a drop of Indian blood in him, turned out to be such a fine Osage, at least up until the time when his troubles just got outen hand, while Donald, who's just a drop or two shy of half Indian, has spent his entire life trying to figure out ways to keep folks from finding that out even though he lives within spitting distance of what is, to this day, Osage territory.

What's helped him, of course, was that even from the beginning, he didn't look Indian. There was Caleb, dark haired and dark eyed in spite of his fair-skinned parents... and there was Donald, with sandy hair almost exactly the same as mine, and except for brown eyes and a certain prominence of cheekbones, looking for all the world like just another Cumberland. To tell the truth, I've always thought it would of been better if he'd looked—and acted—Indian instead of the way he turned out, but that's just my opinion and one I'm certain he'd disagree with.

Anyway, he was a sturdy child from the get-go, which was a good thing since we weren't anywhere near a medical man of any description, even including a horse doctor. I never had one worry after I laid eyes on him the first time that he'd turn out sickly like his poor dead half-brother Robert. He took to the teat like nobody's business, and made it known when he was hungry with a cry that I swear would of curdled milk at two hundred yards, which startled his Osage aunts and uncles on account of their own babies tended to be quiet.

Reuben was as proud as a man could be, I'll tell you that, and the boy's fair look didn't bother him one whit. He took an old piece of cottonwood stump he'd wrestled outen the ground and carved a deep bowl into the top that, once I snugged in a piece of blanket, cradled that child to a T.

At first, I wanted to give the boy some Indian name, but it was Reuben who wouldn't hear none of that. He wanted his child to be able to live in both worlds, I think, and since he'd been given a white man's name, he said it was only fitting that he would do likewise for his own son.

So Donald James was the choice, though neither Reuben nor I had ever had a Donald in our past. The first name just came to Reuben on account of some Scotch peddler he'd known some years earlier was named Donald, and the middle name came to me as a way to honor my brother Jim, and that was that. Many's the time I've wished I'd named him Little Eagle or some such foolishness just to take some of the starch outen his whiteness and make him 'fess up to his genuine heritage more than he ever has, but I didn't, and it's surely too late now to do anything like that.

Anyway, my having that little boy to take care of morning, noon and night freed up Caleb for spending even more time with his Osage cousins, and I was only too happy to let him go.

Since he was having such a good time, I didn't worry on it much, but it was slap true that that boy was getting wilder and wilder by the day. It tickled Reuben to death—he told me once that Caleb was going to be a better Indian than any other Indian alive if he kept at it—and he sure didn't do anything to discourage the boy. Of course, like I said before, the kids in that village were pretty much left to do whatever they wanted, anyway.

Having a chance to be with Reuben was about the only thing guaranteed to get Caleb away from them other young ones. Reuben thought every bit as much of that boy as Caleb did of him, and it was a pure pleasure to watch the two of them. He taught him things I wouldn't of ever even imagined—how to make the call of a mourning dove just to see if that gentle bird would answer, or how to tell the track of a skunk from a weasel. They started going on hunting trips together, which didn't amount to much from a grown-up point of view, most of the game they brought home being rabbits and 'possums and suchlike, but for a six year old boy, it might as well of been big game in far-off Africa. He'd bring them critters right into our little hut to show me, and then he'd stand outside and watch while one of the aunts skinned and gutted them. You could tell from the look of pure concentration on his face that it was just about the most fascinating thing he'd ever seen in his entire life.

He was growing like a weed in them days, too, getting

taller by the minute, it seemed like, and losing his baby teeth and getting his full-grown teeth, and suddenly it was easy to see what he was going to look like when he became a man.

Now, I'll admit that except for his darker complexion and hair, that was too much like his natural daddy for my tastes. He was going to be the spitting image of that sonofabitch Clement Handley, begging your pardon for my choice of language. Of course, I couldn't begrudge the boy looking like his father, but sometimes the way he'd hold his head or the profile I'd see against the morning sky would positively take my breath away they'd remind me so much of his real pa. That he should favor that man in mannerisms mystified me, since by the time Caleb was born, Clement was mostly gone hunting or whatever it was that he did while sister Dell tried to make do in that little cave.

Anyway, considering what might of been, I was more glad than ever for having Reuben in that child's life, I'll tell you.

When Donald was about a month old, Reuben announced one day that he had to leave home on business for a week. Caleb heard him tell me and asked if he could go, but Reuben told him no, and fairly gruffly at that, which a blind man could see about broke that little boy's heart. He moped that whole day, and the next, and when it came time for Reuben to leave, I had to conspire with Helen to get Caleb down to the creek skinny dipping with his cousins so I wouldn't have to worry about him trying to follow his new daddy.

Turned out that Reuben needed to go chasing after an Osage man who was accused of having his way with a white woman, and of all the dangerous work he'd done before, that took the cake. The woman was a mean old biddy who ran a house of ill repute in Pawhuska, which more or less passed for the capital of the Osage Nation, so there was plenty enough reason to suppose that she had brung the trouble on herself, but even so, when the white folks north of the Line found out about it, they managed to work up a pretty good head of steam, and once they commenced to threatening to put together a posse to string up the offender, Reuben knew it was going to be up to him to calm the passions. He would, too, if anyone could. He actually went to Coffeyville, another little town almost right on the Line, and stood up to a mob of liquored up homesteaders and promised to bring the miscreant to justice if that posse would just stay home. I'll never know what that must of been like, with one lone Indian trying to convince a bunch of drunken cowboys to do the right thing. It's an absolute testament to my man's reputation that the good citizens of Coffeyville finally agreed, though with plenty of grumbling and more than a few "nays" when it came to voting on the subject.

Then, of course, Reuben had to do exactly what he'd promised: find and arrest whoever had done the deed.

Anyhow, it goes without saying that on such a mission, there wasn't any room for a little boy with a talent for running off.

Reuben was gone for the better part of two weeks, what with the miscreant giving him a run for his money all the way to the Ouachita Mountains, which was practically to Arkansas, and during that time, I had more trouble with Caleb than ever before in our years together.

First, he moped.

Then he sassed.

No matter what I said, whether it was "mind your manners" or "come to supper," he had a response guaranteed to get my hackles up. When I was busy with the baby, he'd get into some fix or another that would require my attention. When I needed peace and quiet, he was under foot. When I needed help hauling water, he grumped and grumbled and sometimes outright refused. He sulked, sitting for hours on end with a glum look on his face while letting out an occasional sigh just to make slap certain I knew how miserable he was. And all of that was just in the first few days. Finally, when I couldn't take it any more, I gave him a paddling with the flat of my hand that set up such a yelping you'd of thought I was murdering him.

I have to say, my sisters-in-law didn't think much of that. From what I could tell, the Osages never raised a hand to a child no matter what it had done, so I suppose this was their first experience with that kind of punishment. They didn't interfere, for which I was grateful, but I could tell that if it hadn't of been for Reuben's importance to that little village, more than one of the folks around there would of politely asked me to leave.

Given how their own kids were turning out, I could see that maybe there was something to the way they raised their young'uns, sparing the rod and all, but then it didn't appear that they had any problems with their kids running off, neither, and I surely did. With a newborn to look after, there wasn't any way I was going to be able to chase after Caleb if he decided to high-tail it for somewhere else.

Fortunately, Caleb didn't skedaddle, but mostly because I didn't take my eyes offen him for ten days straight, which like to wore us both out.

In due course, Reuben returned, his mission having succeeded with the peaceful surrender of the renegade and a change of heart on the part of the woman in question, who now claimed the whole thing was just a misunderstanding betwixt sweethearts, never mind how close she'd come to sparking real trouble between the whites and the Osages that might of gotten both her man and mine killed.

Anyway, I'm sure one or another of the older men in our little village told my man that I'd spanked Caleb. He never said a word about it directly, but several times over the next couple weeks, he'd make it a point to talk about how violence never worked to make folks mend their ways. He'd couch it as a lesson he wished he could get through to the whites north of the Line as well as some of his Osage friends, but it was pretty plain that he was talking directly to me—and about me. So one night, just after he'd snuffed out the tallow candle and crawled into bed beside me, I brought it up.

"I didn't mean to strike the boy," I said softly, so Caleb couldn't hear in case he wasn't already asleep. "I wouldn't of done it under ordinary circumstances, but he was just so... so churlish with you gone. I was at my wit's end."

"Ah," Reuben said, and waited so long to go on that I thought that would be the end of it, or that maybe he'd drifted off to sleep. Then he added "You thought that would make him be happier."

"Well, no," I said. "Of course not. I reckon I just lost my temper." I confess, right then I was thinking back to the days Daddy would whip one of us kids so hard and for so long that it'd plumb knock the wind outen him.

"So you thought that by losing your temper, you would teach him not to lose his."

"No, of course not," I repeated. I could see where this little lesson was going. But before I could say another word, he rolled toward me and wrapped me in them strong arms of his and kissed my eyes, each one in turn.

"It's over, Evarae," he said softly. "The boy will be all right. We need not speak of it again." Then he kissed my mouth, rolled away, and I swear he was asleep before I had a chance to take a breath.

I laid awake for some time, trying to come up with an argument I could use on him the next morning, but the harder I tried, the more I knew it was wasted effort. He hadn't scolded or lectured me, yet he'd delivered a powerful message. Whether the Osage way is the right one, or whether the way good Christians punish their children is correct, I knew right then and there what I had to do to stay in the good graces of my husband and his people, and I'd learned it in the most gentle way possible.

It was just one of the many lessons about life that I

learned from that man.

And so it was that Caleb's and my first year amongst the Osages and Donald's first summer of life came and went. Autumn came on wet and cool after a typical hot, dry summer. When the rains did come, a positive explosion of mice came with it. The Osages kept dogs, but no cats, and I'd of given my eye tooth for a good mouser that season. Donald thought they were fun to watch, and he'd sit on that dirt floor just laughing at them as they scurried to and fro while I chased after them with a broom. That is, he thought it was funny until one of them crawled up into his cradle in the night and nipped his cheek. The racket Caleb made when I paddled him wasn't but a puff of wind compared to the screeching that baby let loose over that mouse bite. For days on end, the sight of a little gray rodent scampering acrost the floor would set off a positive screaming fit, until I was sure even Reuben was going to lose his temper. He never did, but I believe to this day it was a near thing. I'm certain the other villagers at first thought I'd taken to whipping the baby since their own young ones didn't hardly never cry, and when they did it was just a squeak their mommas could muffle with a hand. But no one ever said a thing, and after a time, they took turns coming by to look at Donald when he was squawking like he was a real curiosity. Reuben must of told them the baby was yelping because he was mostly white is all I can figure.

Fortunately, in late October, we had one of them freak ice storms that plague our country, which put an end to the mouse infestation and Donald's hysterics at the same time. From then on, it was mud we had to deal with, since once the ice melted, a steady string of days filled with rain and sleet followed. We just hunkered down and got through it, staying as warm and dry as we could.

Reuben still had to go off to Pawhuska every now and again to see to the lawing business, but mostly he'd just do whatever chores he had to do like rustling up some fresh meat or tending to the horses, then spend the rest of the day right around our little cabin, playing with Caleb or holding Donald. In a way, he was acting pretty much the same as them other Osage men, who as I've said didn't exactly overwork themselves, but I couldn't think of Reuben that way on account of how hard he could work when the circumstances called for it.

Anyway, those were the days when I felt like a real married woman at long last—more so than ever I had with Jack Ross, to tell the truth, which I don't mean as any criticism of Jack. It's just that Reuben was my lover and friend from the very beginning. Life was just plain good. We didn't have nothing to speak of, but neither did anyone else in that village, and I knew enough about life in Chautauqua to know that except for some of the railroad bosses, nobody in town had much more than we did, leastwise not anything that counted for anything.

I had my man, I had my boys, and though there was plenty of work to do, it was work done in the fresh air and with other women who never complained.

Most of all, of course, I had my man.

That Christmas—1890, it was—I didn't even try to take Caleb to church, having learned my lesson the previous year. But still I saw to it that the boys and I celebrated the season. I wrote the first letter to my own mother that I'd penned in nearly a year, telling her all the news, and asked Reuben to carry it to Francine for mailing. Then I found some red yarn somewheres and knitted little matching mufflers for both Caleb and Donald. They weren't very good, my having just begun taking knitting lessons from Ma when Daddy decided to up and marry me off to poor old Jack, and the needles I had to use were just bits of the straightest thin stick I could find, which meant the yarn was constantly getting twisted or snagged. Still, the boys didn't care. It was the color that caught their eye. For Reuben, I made a pair of slippers from rabbit skins turned inside out so the soft fur was next to his feet. One of his sisters showed me how to do that, and while I didn't do close to as good a job on them slippers as any Osage woman would, you'd of thought I'd given my husband the fanciest pair of boots in the land.

Of course I didn't get nothing from any of them, Christmas not being of much account to Reuben and the boys knowing next to nothing about it—after all, Donald was only six months old—but that didn't matter to me. I was just as happy as a hog in a mud puddle being able to make them things to give to my menfolk.

Except for the weather, that was the most beautiful time in my entire life.

In fact, that whole year and the one after seemed to be about as good as a body could hope for. I even got some used to Reuben's lawing and believed his troubles with the white trash bringing liquor into Osage country would work themselves out. Donald grew like a weed, though he couldn't seem to get past squalling and squawking to beat the band over every little thing, and Caleb continued to have the time of his young life.

That child learned so much Osage that he and his new daddy could talk for hours without a single word of English, though Reuben generally wouldn't do that in front of me on account of I hadn't learned much Osage and he didn't want to leave me outen the conversation. Caleb learned more about horses than just about any grownup I'd ever known, too, and before long he was riding like he was born to a horse's back.

In fact, the whole of 1891 came and went in a blur, with my man and me and our boys living about as good a life as four people could. To me, it was like living in a heaven on earth, no matter we were poor as church mice and there was plenty of hard work that needed doing. But Donald had started walking and talking, and Caleb was spending even more time amongst the horses, and clearly having the time of his life doing it. He'd still disappear sometimes, which worried me half to death, although Reuben seemed generally more amused than concerned. I did get up to see Francine now and again, and once or twice, she even drove down to see me, the Line not having much significance anymore what with the Osage Nation now being officially part of the United States of America and all, though she was jumpy as a cat in a roomful of rocking chairs just being in our little village.

Then it was Christmas again, and once again I kept my sons from the pious folk in the Chautauqua Methodist church.

Mercifully, the weather was warmer and drier than what we'd had for the past few years, and autumn had lingered. I could work outside and the boys could run around almost the way they had during the bright cool days of October, and when it did turn cold in the evenings, we stayed snug in our cabin. I knitted Christmas mufflers for my men outen some coarse gray yarn Reuben's sister Helen had spun from the wool of the sheep she tended. Them mufflers weren't the handsomest things ever made, but I knew they'd be warm enough when the wintry blast hit at last. Oh, yes, it was a marvelous time—so good, in fact, that it seemed downright impossible that trouble would ever again find me and mine.

Wild West

I SHOULD OF KNOWN BETTER.

The spring of 1892 arrived later than normal, thanks to what turned out to be a cruel and icy winter. But warm up it did, with soft green shoots growing in the ditches and thick mud where the frozen roads had been and, on many a day, great blue-black thunderheads swallowing up the afternoon sun. We had hail and cyclones till I thought we'd be pounded to death or blown plumb away, one or the other, but the Osages just seemed to take it in stride. Their little cabins were snug enough, and if a twister were to hit, well, they'd either survive it or they wouldn't, so there didn't seem to be much point in worrying.

Then the wild weather was over, leaving us with a spring so beautiful it practically took a body's breath away. Little white and yellow and purple flowers carpeted the ground everywhere, and the new leaves on the blackjack oak were so green I swear it almost hurt a person's eyes to look at them. When the April and May rains came, all of that new life soaked up the water fast, and even when the mud along the roads or where the horses had worn down the grass seemed to grab and hold a body like it was quicksand, the sweet breezes and the absolute hum of life more than made up for it. Then, in a flash, the hots of real summer came on till I thought we'd positively fry any time we were out in the sun.

I had discovered I was again with child about the time the last dirty snow on the north side of our little cabin had a chance to melt, and once again, it was plain to see that Reuben knew it almost as soon as I did. He took to patting my stomach when we were alone and talking to it like he was talking to a real person. I thought that was a peculiar thing for a man to do, especially an Osage who was otherwise about as quiet as a body could be, and it was something he hadn't done when I was carrying Donald, but I confess it tickled me nonetheless. Then he commenced having Caleb talk to the baby growing inside my stomach, too, and that practically drove me into laughing fits.

Them men of mine were slap something! Even Donald, as little as he was, would watch the other two and smile and bubble.

It seemed that Reuben was home more than usual during those sweet spring days, too. I took it to mean that the farmers and ranchers and their hired hands north of the Line were just too busy getting ready for the growing season or tending calves to cause any trouble. The Osages, who didn't practice the farming arts the same way the whites did, were just as busy getting in their corn and squash and cleaning up the trash that accumulated every winter, no matter how hard or easy the weather had been. It was like nobody had time or inclination to cause trouble.

Or so I assumed, although I suppose I should of been aware that my husband was acting a bit skittish. Looking back, it was like he knew what was coming.

And just like that, it started.

It was the train robberies we heard about first, which you wouldn't of thought would affect us much, on account of I was long past my railroad days and Reuben shouldn't of been involved in anything having to do with the railroads since most of the lines bypassed the Osages.

But there was one robbery, then another and then another on the A T & SF spurs, with mail cars looted and passengers robbed. No one got shot, but there were pistol whippings in some abundance, leaving postal clerks and conductors with cracked heads or broken noses and a fair number of passengers scared plumb outen their wits. It didn't take long for the word to get out that them hold-ups were the responsibility of a family of brothers from up around Coffeyville by the name of Dalton. To say that them boys were wild would be just about the understatement of all time. They were well known as troublemakers by most everybody on both sides of the Line, including my husband.

Of course, you have likely heard of the Daltons, but what you may not know is that before the Daltons turned to a life of crime, several of their number had actually been peace officers, working both sides of the Line during a good bit of the 1880's. They most assuredly didn't do it out of the love for the law or concern for the downtrodden, but they did in fact carry badges, and they were well known to my husband. The Dalton brother by the name of Bob had actually been a federal marshal working outen the Osage Nation. Seems that although Bob had convinced the United States government he was a trustworthy sort, what he really wanted was to peddle whiskey in the Nations and run stock his brothers had stolen down in Texas up to friends in Kansas. Some of the Daltons' pals must of claimed all their heifers were dropping twins and triplets their herds were growing so fast. Anyway, rustling and bootlegging both put Bob seriously at cross purposes with my man. I learned later on that it was right touchy business between them for a while, until Bob got in trouble north of the Line over some shenanigans involving stolen horses. To make a long story short, he turned in his badge and lit out for greener pastures in California with half his clan, and Reuben figured we were shed of them, all of which happened before I came on the scene, so to speak.

The trouble was, the Daltons didn't stay in California.

It wasn't but a couple of years later that Bob was back again with his brothers and a couple of other mean-as-weasels ruffians and ne'er-do-well cowboys. This time, their former familiarity with lawing apparently made them feel above the law whenever it suited them, which was most of the time. At first, they'd just seemed like hot-heads who took pleasure in spreading their tales about how they'd kill a man without giving it a second thought or butcher somebody's old cow for the fun of watching little kids go hungry. All of that was probably more brag than fact, but it did the job of scaring the bejeebers outen ordinary folks.

But things turned serious when they started holding up trains all over the territory, and it wasn't but a matter of a month or so before they added bank robbery to their list of crimes.

Well, the good citizens of Kansas had looked the other way for a long time when the crimes involved poisoning Indians with rotgut whiskey or taking beeves from Texans, but stealing folks's hard-earned savings outen the local bank was a whole different thing. In a flash, they decided they'd just about had enough of the Daltons, and for once they weren't above asking for help from the red man. One morning Chautauqua County Sheriff Horace Taylor actually showed up in our little village to ask Reuben real nice if he could please put together a posse of dependable Osages with the idea of tracking and trapping the Daltons if they crossed over into Oklahoma Territory.

Sheriff Taylor never dismounted, though he tipped his hat to me and asked after my health and reached over to tousle Caleb's hair while Reuben went around to some of the other men to see if they would ride with him after the Daltons if it came to that. Turned out that none of the other Osage men were much interested, mostly on account of the Daltons hadn't done anything to them lately and what experience they'd had helping out the white race hadn't made any difference in the way they were treated if ever they happened to go north of the Line.

Still, Reuben promised to do what he could, so the sheriff rode away knowing there was only one Osage he could count on.

Of course, nothing appeared to come of it, the Daltons being a cagey lot who managed to stay a step ahead of just about everybody, white and red alike.

Then, just when Reuben thought the trouble had blown over, his own trouble with them boys began.

It was the middle of a hot June, just about the time Reuben got little Caleb to start talking to the baby inside me.

We had moved into Pawhuska for a few weeks on account of Reuben had agreed to take on some extra duties for the tribe. All he told me was he figured it might take some weeks, and I decided I'd rather be with him than stuck in our village with nothing to do but hoe our patch of corn and try to keep the raccoons outen the pole beans. Besides, Pawhuska was a nice little town, sitting as it did in a nestle of hills with open grasslands on two sides, so a body could see a lot farther and have more a feeling of being in the open than in our village or even in Chautauqua, where sometimes the scrub oak seemed to press in from all sides.

There were more folks to chat with on a warm summer's day, too. Not that Reuben's kin weren't good company, leastwise the women, but in the end, I just didn't want to be away from him.

I could tell he wasn't much for the idea, but Reuben wasn't the kind to forbid me to do something, so off we went to Pawhuska with our two boys in tow.

We moved into a little two-room lean-to shed behind what passed for the Osage Police jail, which was itself not much more than a hut made outen cottonwood logs. Compared to our cozy little home cabin, the lean-to was huge but drafty and forever crawling with bugs that wanted in outen the sun. The mosquitoes liked to ate us alive at night, too.

As for the jail, the front room was a sort of office barely big enough to hold the locked cabinet filled with weapons and two empty 25-gallon kegs with a green oak board laid acrost that served as a desk. There was a rough plank wall separating the office from the jail proper, with a door with an iron hasp and padlock on the outside and a crude hole about the size of a muskmelon with a couple of rusty iron bars jammed into it to serve as a window. There was a boardwalk out front, though, and it offered a fine view of the town. The boards were rough sawn cottonwood and about as warped and cracked as wood could get, but they gave the boys somewhere to play where they wouldn't smother in the track of thick dust and horse apples that passed for a main street.

Anyway, it was right on that boardwalk that I first came to fear that Dalton gang the day them brothers rode into Pawhuska with their pal Bill Doolin.

Now, I'd seen one or the other of the Daltons a couple of times when I was still living in Chautauqua. Then, the brothers hadn't seemed especially dangerous even if they did have a reputation as scofflaws. Sometimes they'd tip their hats to ladies and make like they were being polite, though they'd cut up and make fools of themselves in the process.

Not so Bill Doolin.

For my money, he was plainly the worst of the bunch—the pure meanest human being I ever run acrost up to that moment, and I knew it from the moment I laid eyes on him.

Doolin had narrow-set eyes and a weak chin he kept covered with a scraggly growth of beard, and he smelled worse than just about any cowboy I was ever around, which was saying something. I'd seen him knock old men down just for the sport of it, and once he spit tobacco juice all over a young mother, then laughed about it. Had that woman's husband tried to make Bill pay for his misdeed, Bill probably would of killed him and spit on him, too. He was that mean.

On the day in question, I was visiting with Reuben and trying to knit a pair of socks while little Donald played at our feet. I remember that Caleb had turned surly that day, probably on account of he was in town instead of home with his pals and the horses. Of course, even when we were at home in the village, he'd begun having spells where he could go for days at a time without saying more than a half-dozen words. Sometimes he wouldn't even talk to the baby inside me. Reuben acted like he didn't notice, and he'd josh the boy and try to turn doing the chores into a game to cheer him up, but I confess I couldn't figure out what to do or say to make Caleb talk or smile.

Anyway, that day, he'd decided to hole up under Reuben's desk with a pair of dull scissors and an old newspaper. He was cutting out shapes of various animals, and since he was quiet doing it, we let him be.

I remember it was hotter than blazes, with air so heavy you could of wrung it out for drinking water. In spite of how glorious spring had been, we'd just been through a spurt of stormy weather and suspected there was more to come. Of an afternoon, a body would begin half expecting thunderheads to appear practically outen thin air and turn the sky green and boiling. Weather like that put everyone out of sorts, especially a little tyke, and Donald had the heat rash so bad he'd busted little blood vessels in his scalp from crying, which gave him a splotchy appearance and naturally worried the daylights outen me.

Anyway, Caleb was inside under that desk and the other three of us were sitting on the front porch of that decrepit old jail trying not to move more than absolutely necessary except to try to fan up some breeze. For a time, we joked and swatted flies and Reuben jounced Donald on his knee to see if he could get him to stop fussing, when suddenly I saw him go all serious and sort of stiffen.

Reuben actually sensed their coming before I could even see the smear of dust from them horses trotting along the road. He went from playing and joshing to being all quiet and out of sorts, and after a time he handed Donald to me and got up and went inside to fetch a shotgun, which he propped up beside his chair. That was something he almost never did, and it set me to worrying.

"What's the matter?" I asked, but he just shrugged and kept his eyes on the northeast, toward the main road into town. Even Donald seemed to catch his daddy's mood and quieted down on my lap.

We sat in silence for several minutes.

"Maybe you and the boys best get on home, Evie," he said after a time. "The village, I mean. Take the buggy." He picked up the shotgun to check the load.

"You done that already when you brung it out," I said, nodding at the weapon.

"Guess I did," he said, but then he gave it another check just to make sure. He put the gun back against the wall and peered into the distance, shading his eyes with his hand. "Maybe you best get home," he said again, like he couldn't remember from one minute to the next that he'd already said it.

"Why?" I asked, but he didn't answer. He just peered, and after a couple of minutes checked the gun again.

I think it was actually a relief to him when them cowboys finally showed up. When he saw for certain who it was, he stood up. "You and Donald get inside, Evarae," he said so softly I barely heard him. "Don't leave the office for anything, and keep the boys quiet if you can."

"But why?" I asked, taking a look at the men. I hadn't recognized them yet from a distance. There was no sound except the jingle of harness and spurs and the soft thudding of horses' hooves, but suddenly I just knew there was going to be trouble. They had brought an electric feeling into town with them, the sort of feeling that makes a body's hair stand on end right before a bolt of lightning splits the sky.

Then I saw it was Bill Doolin who was slouched over the saddle horn like he was fast asleep. That man was positively weighted down with iron. A long scabbard held a carbine just where he could get at it in a hurry, a shotgun rested acrost the pommel, and he wore a brace of pistols in holsters that rode high up on his hips and flopped with every step of the horse. Two large bandoleers loaded with enough bullets to kill just about every last soul in Pawhuska twice over crossed his sunken chest, pulling him even lower in the saddle. Behind him, the other boys carried similar caches of weapons. The whole shooting match—men, horses, tack, and weapons—was all the same dun color from the trail dust, with a few splashes of mud thrown in.

Reuben gave me a grim look outen the corner of his eye. "Woman, do as I say."

That was as much of an order as he ever gave me in our time together, and along with the sight of them men, it made my blood run cold. I picked up that baby and trooped inside and pulled the door closed behind me. As I went, Reuben picked up a holster that had been lying on the porch next to his chair, strapped it on, and slipped the revolver in and out to make sure it would pull free. Then he took up the shotgun deliberately in his left hand and stepped off the porch and down onto the scorched hardpan in the blazing sun.

I'd had my doubts about Reuben's choice of professions for a good long spell, but that was the very first moment I'd known real fear for his safety.

Of course, I went to the office window to see what was happening, and Caleb crawled out from under the desk and joined me, the two of us peering out between them rusty bars like we were prisoners.

Now, it was hard to tell them Daltons apart on a good day, what with they all sported brushy handlebar mustaches and wore their floppy hats pulled low over their eyes, so with the dust and all, I had to look close to figure out who was in the party. As best I could tell, Doolin rode that day with three of the Dalton brothers, Bob and Grat and Emmett.

But it was plain as day that Doolin was running the show.

Reuben moved to the center of the street and planted himself splay-legged with the shotgun slung up on his shoulder the way a hunter might who's not planning on shooting any more birds but wants to be ready, just in case.

Doolin's horse snorted and backed up as if it smelled something that scared it. Reuben raised his hand slowly and held it out palm first, and the horse quieted, but I could see Bill Doolin's back stiffen.

"Who the hell are you?" Doolin barked loud enough for just about anyone in town to hear. He had a scratchy, sort of high-pitched voice more like the whine of an old spinster than a tough killer, but it carried.

"Tell him, Bob," Reuben said as easily as if he was talking with a couple of old friends.

Bob Dalton shifted in the saddle and slapped at the duster he was wearing in spite of the heat of the day. The dust he stirred up just hung there in a cloud around him. "That's Reuben Whitesnake, Bill. He's sheriff for the Osage Nation. You heard of him, ain't you? How you doin', Reuben?"

"Fine, Bob. Yourself?"

Dalton just shrugged, hawked phlegm, and spit into the street.

Doolin laughed and rubbed a dirty glove acrost his stubble of beard. "Osage Nation, hell," he said, just as loud as before. "Just a ragtag bunch of redskins squatting in the middle of nowhere if you ask me. Ain't that right, Grat?" he asked, turning ever so slightly in the saddle.

"Seems like," Grat said, trying to copy brother Bob in spitting, but it fell short and dribbled down his boot.

I could see Reuben shift his weight slightly from one foot

to the next. "You fellows need to keep on riding." It came out as an order, not a statement.

That sort of straightened Doolin up, and he put his hand on the butt of his carbine, which positively unnerved me. It was dangerous enough just to be on the street with a bunch like that, but it was something else entirely to challenge them in any way.

"You better not cause us any trouble, Mr. Whitesnake or whatever your name is," Doolin croaked. "Be a good nigger and tell us where we can find a bottle of rye whiskey and then just get the hell outen our way."

"There is no rye whiskey in this town, sir," Reuben said evenly. I could tell just from the dry tone of his voice that the comment about nigger had gotten to him. There wasn't a prejudiced bone in that man's body, and one of the great regrets of my life is that Reuben never got a chance to meet Marcellus Robinson because I know them two fine gentlemen would of hit it off famously. But any time a white man slurred a red man, or any color of person for that matter, Reuben took it personal.

Doolin just squinted and rubbed at his whiskers yet again. "The hell you say."

"My people don't handle whiskey very well, so we keep it where it belongs. Amongst the white trash north of the Line. Isn't that right, Bob?" When he said it, he made no attempt to turn toward the Daltons, and instead stood looking right into Bill Doolin's squinty little eyes.

"So you say, Reuben," Bob offered with a chuckle.

I could see my husband's fingers tighten around that shotgun, and I found myself wishing I had a carbine of my own to back him up. I actually looked around the office for one, figuring Donald could take care of himself on the floor for a few minutes if it came to that, but the only guns in the cabinet were secured by a piece of chain and a rusty key lock. Reuben had all the working firearms in the place with him at that moment.

Anyhow, Doolin just looked at Reuben, and Reuben looked back. I don't know how much time passed, but it seemed like hours and hours that them two just stared at one another. Finally one of the Dalton boys—Emmett, I think it was—shifted in his saddle and turned his horse. "Aw, let's get outen this hell hole. Nothing here but trouble."

Doolin smiled but didn't take his eyes off Reuben. "That true, Mr. Sheriff? Is this a hell hole?"

"Could be, cowboy," Reuben said evenly. "For you, anyway."

I thought that was tempting fate a sight more than a man should. I surely expected Bill Doolin to grab for his pistol, but his smile just widened and he actually laughed.

"Another day, Sheriff," he said, and with that he wheeled his poor weighted-down horse, raked his spurs cruelly along its ribs, and rode off lickety split, with the Daltons trailing along behind.

Reuben watched them go, then trudged up the front steps of the jail and opened the door. Quick as a flash, Caleb squeezed past him and darted outside. I started after him.

Reuben caught my arm. "It'll be all right, Evarae," he said. "He just wants a good look at those fellows." Sweat was trickling down either side of his face, washing little tracks in the dust. He gave me a lopsided smile.

I stared hard into his eyes, wondering if what I saw there was real or just a reflection of my own concerns. "I didn't think Indians were supposed to get scared," I said as brightly as I could.

"A person would have to be simpleminded not to be afraid of that bunch," he offered. He put the shotgun away and unbuckled the holster and dropped it onto his desk, then he turned and went back outside. I followed.

Caleb was standing in the exact same spot Reuben had been, with his hand on his shoulder as if holding a shotgun.

The look on his face was hard to discern, but it wasn't any little boy face, I'll tell you that. Something about it made me shiver in spite of the heat, and then I recognized it: Caleb had exactly the look on his face that Bill Doolin had showed.

If I'd of known then what I know now...

But we never do.

I turned my back on him and trudged inside. I was sick at my stomach, and it didn't have a thing to do with the baby I was carrying.

From that day on, the Dalton brothers and Bill Doolin weren't too far from my thoughts. Reuben informed me that Bob Dalton was, indeed, back to his old tricks of supplying rotgut to the Indians along with robbing trains and banks, so I knew it was only a matter of time before my man crossed paths with them again even if he never was called upon to assist the law north of the Line.

For his part, Reuben just pooh-poohed the notion that there was going to be trouble. The Daltons were a bad bunch, and he said there wasn't any doubt that they'd come to Pawhuska that day with an eye toward getting into some serious mischief, but one well armed man determined to stop them was all it had taken to turn trouble away, and that would be true the next time and the time after that, if that's what it came to. Still, I noticed he never went outside without a weapon close by, usually his shotgun, and he took to looking over his shoulder sometimes in ways that positively spooked me.

I reminded him that it wouldn't pay to press his luck any farther than he already had with that bunch.

"A peace officer has to keep the peace, Evarae," he would say whenever I brought it up, and then he'd change the subject. I allowed as how he was right, but still I let it be known that was he to change his profession to something less dangerous, I wouldn't be unhappy.

"Think of the boys," I'd say.

Finally, one day he just stood right in front of me and crossed his arms over his chest. "I am thinking of them," he said. "I want them to grow up in a decent, law abiding place. I don't want them to spend their lives being afraid of bad men with evil ways. So we'll talk no more about it."

And we didn't, though I still worried, and I still puzzled over Caleb's reaction to that face-down in Pawhuska. What-ever it was that that boy had been thinking that June after-noon as he watched Doolin and the Daltons ride away stayed with him for the longest time. His quiet spells seemed more frequent as summer wore on, and though he'd climb up in Reuben's lap in the evening and answer whatever questions Reuben had about what he'd done that day, or the two of them would talk of their horses and how to take care of them as they brushed their animals down after a ride together, whole days went by when that boy and I wouldn't touch or exchange a single word.

I found myself wondering if there was something in the meanness of a Bill Doolin that reminded that child of his daddy—Clement, I mean—or if the possibility of real violence made him recall the last horrible hours he'd spent in the Gove County dugout with a murdered father and a mother who killed herself. Of course, he'd been so young there really wasn't any way he could remember that. But still...

For a while, I fancied that things had settled into the usual bustle and buzz of summer. Reuben seemed to relax, at least when he wasn't being called off to try to run down some-body bootlegging rotgut to the Osages or settle squabbles betwixt neighbors over who owned what pony, and he certainly took extra comfort and pleasure in them sons of his. He'd made Caleb a bow outen a greenwood stick with a piece of sheep sinew for the string, and the two of them would go off and practice shooting at bits of old leather or whatever Reuben could find that would suit him as a target. Pulling on that bow wore blisters on Caleb's middle fingers, but instead of whimpering about it as most children would, he just begged me to wrap them in bits of soft cloth so he could go back out and shoot some more.

Donald's time with Reuben was in the evening, when the last light of day faded from the sky and the stars came out. Them men of mine would sit outside then, with Donald on his daddy's lap and Caleb alongside while Reuben told stories from the Osage myths about how the world began, how the Osages came to be, and so on. Oft times I heard Reuben speaking in his native tongue, too, and them boys were just as attentive to what he was saying as if he'd been spouting the King's English.

Reuben purely loved those times. Being a daddy sure agreed with him.

I knew my friends in town would of liked to have a stroke if they'd known about it, on account of what Reuben was doing was teaching our boys the Osage religion, but of course I wasn't about to tell anyone. In the first place, I hadn't been to town in ages, and in the second place, I figured them Osage stories and the Osage language were at least as good a place to start understanding the world as what the folks in Chautauqua would come up with, especially since the milk of human kindness didn't seem to run too deep in that bunch.

For my part, I just hummed along, feeling the life stirring inside me, looking after Reuben and the boys as best I could, cooking when it wasn't too hot and cleaning our clothes by beating them on a rock in the stream flowing so near our door. Doing laundry that way was hard work, but no harder than sweating over a tub of blistering hot soapy water at the Chins', and that's a fact.

And then, just when I figured trouble with the Daltons was behind us, it started again when a whole posse of law from north of the Line came thundering into our little village one day.

There were six or eight of them including Sheriff Taylor and some deputy or another, all loaded down with weaponry and in such a hurry their horses were lathered and panting. Seems there had been another train robbery, and this time the miscreants had done a sight more than just rob the mail coach. They'd shot a conductor and terrorized a carload of passengers, which included the United States Congressman from that part of Kansas. After that, they'd ridden into the little village of Elgin and held two families hostage for several hours, demanding supper, threatening to have their way with the women, and stealing just about every last thing of value them poor folks had squirreled away.

The long and the short of it was that the State of Kansas had put a price on their heads, as had the Pinkerton Detective Agency on behalf of the railroad, and that posse was determined to catch the Daltons and collect on the reward.

Reuben talked with them for some time and agreed to pass the word among the Osages that they should look to keeping loaded weapons on their person day and night, which wasn't the usual way of things no matter what the movies may say.

When that posse thundered away, Reuben just shook his head. "They'll kill their horses, pushing them that hard," he said to Caleb. But then he gave me a look, mounted his own horse, and rode off to pass the word amongst his people to be careful.

It didn't do much good.

Throughout the summer, the whiskey kept flowing, and if anyone did challenge one of the gang or drive them off with whatever old blunderbuss they had on the place, they were as like as not to come upon an accident of some kind within a day or two, generally involving a runaway team of horses. If that didn't discourage the good folks the gang had it in for, you could bet a barn would catch fire or a prize mare would wind up shot dead in the pasture.

Reuben spent his days investigating the "accidents" that left busted up Osage men unable to work or chasing down missing stock that everybody knew would never be found on account of they were already wearing a new brand if they hadn't been slaughtered and skinned. Of course, them kinds of depredations went on north of the Line, too, the only difference being that when a Kansas rancher lost stock, he was likely to send his own hands acrost the Line to gather replacements from Osage herds, which just doubled the amount of work my man had to do.

It was a trying time, and that's for certain.

As summer ripened and started to slip toward fall, Reuben even had a run-in with a Dalton that he actually told me about.

Seems he was chasing after some Osage beeves that had wandered north with considerable help from some stripe of Kansan, and he'd come upon Grat Dalton just south of the little burg of Caney, which is slap on the Line between Chautauqua and Coffeyville. Reuben had heard sometime earlier that Grat had beat up a Caney woman of low repute, knocking out several of her teeth and breaking her cheekbone on account of she wouldn't give him none of her services for free. Things like that infuriated my husband, so when he came upon Grat, he asked him whether he'd struck any defenseless women lately. Grat just smiled, Reuben said, and asked whether his own family was enjoying the warm weather, tipping his hat as he said it. Seen any Osage steers north of the line? Reuben asked. Nope, Grat said, but he'd surely keep an eye out. And for a while the two of them sat their horses and smoked roll-your-own cigarettes and jawed about the hot weather just like two old friends.

But shortly after that, the potshots started.

At least that's what Reuben called them.

He was riding home from Pawhuska one night, following a little creek bed so he could water the horse when it needed

it, when a bullet whizzed by so close to his head that he heard
the buzzing before he heard the report. He wheeled around to
see who'd done it, but there was only a sliver of moon, and
after a couple of minutes, he just gave up. Another time, when
he was sitting in his chair in front of the Pawhuska jail,
somebody took a shot at him from behind the barber shop
twenty or thirty rods away, the bullet lodging in the door-
frame a couple of feet from his chair. That time, he got a
glimpse of the culprit, who was whipping his horse acrost
open prairie to get away, but couldn't recognize him from that
angle. Then just a day or two later, while he was out looking
for some miscreant over toward the broken country on the
western edge of Osage territory, his horse got shot out from
under him. He managed to grab his rifle and spring from the
saddle before the animal went down. Whoever it was that
done it must of figured it wasn't a good idea to mess with my
man when he was armed like that, because Reuben sat there
for an hour alongside his dying horse, and it was as quiet as if
he was the only living soul for miles around. He walked ten
miles through dark night to the home of a friend, expecting to
get ambushed every step of the way, but the culprits left him
alone.

Reuben didn't tell me about that one for several days, and
I'm sure there were other incidents he never did mention. But
I could tell when something was bothering him, and when I'd
ask outright, he wouldn't lie.

Our hope was that once the weather cooled, so would the
troubles afflicting our region. After all, there was so much to
look forward to. Our few crops were almost ready to harvest,
and it looked like we'd all be feasting on squashes and corn
and fat hogs by and by. A spell of cold rain hit in the middle of
September, but once it passed, the most glorious weather I'd
ever seen came upon us in the blink of an eye. The sunflowers
fairly exploded along the roads and the thickets of Osage
orange began to add their clean scent to the air. To top it off,

I was past the punies at long last, and with my belly swelling and my appetite returned, I positively felt like I would be on top of the world if it wasn't for my concerns about my husband's safety.

So it was that when Reuben announced he wanted to go in to Chautauqua for supplies to tide us over through the winter—which meant he wanted to take me to town, since anything we truly needed was generally available in Pawhuska, and at a better price—I reckoned I was plenty fit to go along. A little outing would do us all some good.

It was the 19th of September, a Monday. We left sometime after sun up on what a body could just tell was going to be a gloriously beautiful late summer day. The air was crisp and clean and just warm enough that we were comfortable in shirt sleeves. Just a mingled hint of late season wildflowers and woodsmoke from the cooking fires gave the air a tang that made me feel as if life just couldn't get any better. To top it off, we had both boys with us. Though we could of left them with their aunts, it was just a few weeks before Caleb's ninth birthday, and Reuben had promised that child a treat in town as a sort of advance birthday present. For my part, I was plumb excited, and I'll confess it was mostly because I wanted to have a nice long visit with Francine and also show off my swelling belly to the Chautauqua biddies, rubbing their noses in it, you might say.

So all in all, we were in a festive mood. The plan was to get Caleb his treat, do a little shopping at the general store, then spend the night with Francine. Being Indian, Reuben knew that he'd probably have to sleep out of doors, but that would be okay with him and Caleb both. Francine might let that boy of hers play with Caleb, or she might not, but either way my older son—for such is how I now thought of him— would be with his daddy, who was the most important person to him in the entire world. Meanwhile, I could snuggle into a half-way decent featherbed for one night while them two men of mine slept on the ground with a wash of stars overhead for company.

Like I said, it was a slap perfect day. There were thousands of butterflies in the long grass, and the edge of the road was positively choked with black-eyed Susies showing their faces to the sun. I was about six months along now, so Reuben wouldn't let me ride horseback but instead had harnessed our horses to the old democrat wagon he used from time to time even though it belonged to one of the other Osage families. I sat in the back, resting on a blanket and holding Donald. Caleb was up on the wagon seat next to Reuben, and the two of them were chattering away. I nestled lower and crooned a little tune to Donald.

Somewhere a mile or so south of the Line, a shadow passed over us, and I thought it might be a cloud, but when I looked up, I saw it was a turkey vulture, all black with a naked little red head, soaring not fifty feet overhead. I never have liked them things, and it gave me a shiver.

"Whyn't you shoot that ugly old thing, Reuben?" I said to my husband.

He turned. "What thing?"

I pointed to the bird, which was still close by.

"No," he said.

"They scare me," I offered.

Reuben actually laughed. "Nothing scares you, Evarae," he said.

"Them vultures do."

"Well, they clean up dead things and they aren't good to eat, so there's no reason to shoot one," he said.

Of course, he was right, so I shrugged and let it go at that and tried to pick up the little tune I was sharing with the baby. After a minute, Caleb and Reuben started in on their own conversation again.

"What are you going to name the baby, Momma Eva?" Caleb asked suddenly, turning to look down on me.

"Land sakes, child, I haven't give it a minute's thought," I said.

"It's a girl, you know," he said all serious.

"And how do you know that, Mister?"

He gave me a sly grin, the happiest look that boy had had since I couldn't remember when. "I just do."

"Your papa told you that," I said, nodding at Reuben's broad back. He just flicked the reins, but I could see from the way his shoulders shook that he was laughing silently.

"Maybe he did," Caleb said. "But it's a girl all right." He sounded so sure and so grown up.

"Well, since the two of you have decided, what do you think about a name?" I called up to the both of them.

Reuben laughed out loud now. "I leave that to you."

"Men!" I said, and I laughed along.

"Come on, Momma Eva. What will you name the baby?" I believe it was the first time in his life that Caleb had actually teased me.

"I'll have to think on that," I said, although I already knew in my heart what I would name a girl child—the only name I'd ever really considered for a girl. If it was going to be a boy, I'd have to ponder on it some, but if it was a girl...

"Now you just leave me be and let me take a little nap before..."

What happened next still seems more a dream than anything, all these many years later.

Before I could even finish that sentence, Reuben gave a little snort, stood up halfway, and just toppled back into the wagon box on top of me. Just like that. No warning, no reason. Somewhere in the middle of that two seconds of movement, we heard the sharp report of the rifle.

Donald, startled, started to cry. I pushed hard to get toddler and me out from under my husband. That was when I felt the warm sticky ooze of blood and realized it was pulsing over me.

At almost the same instant, there was another crack of gunfire, and the horses, with no one holding onto the reins, bolted.

Somehow or another, I managed to stand upright in that rocking wagon box with the baby held under my arm like a sack of spuds and ordered Caleb to grab the reins. He was wide-eyed in terror, mostly I suppose from the bright red smear that covered my shirt and had spread onto my face and arm. I was in danger of getting tossed right outen that wagon, but calm as could be I told him again to grab the reins, and he did. I stepped over my husband and took them leather straps in my left hand and hauled back, slowing the runaways until they stopped.

"Hold them tight!" I ordered, handing the reins back to the boy. When he took them, they were sticky with blood.

"But Momma Eva..."

"No talking!" I commanded. "You just hold them horses." Then I turned and knelt over Reuben.

He was already dead. That much was clear without my giving it a moment's thought. The bullet had struck him in the left side of his neck, severing an artery, and already his heart had quit pumping the spurts of blood outen a hole the size of a fifty cent piece. That wagon box was positively filled with his gore.

I was dumbfounded. I believe I actually slapped myself in hopes that I'd awaken from that terrible dream, but of course I did not. The baby was caterwauling fit to be tied, and then Caleb started in, not screaming, but moaning, low and painful, the awfulest sound he'd ever made in his life, and I just stood there, looking down on Reuben's body.

I remember thinking, standing there, how could it be that he was dead when he'd been so alive just a minute before? I must of sunk down beside him, for the next thing I can remember was shooing late season flies away from the wound while I smoothed his black hair.

After a while, Caleb's moaning died to a sort of long groan, and once when I looked up at him, I thought for a second he'd been shot, too, as pale as he was, gripping them reins so tight it would of taken a strong man to pry his hands loose.

But always it was the same thing in my mind: how could it be that my Reuben was dead?

And who had done it?

After a time, I scanned all the land around, trying to see whether I could spot the killer. There were open spaces like little meadows, stands of bur oak, and the gentle roll of the land, but nothing else. By that time, the whole countryside was as utterly empty as if no human being had ever even been in them parts. It was just me, the boys, the horses, and the flies.

Whoever done it had vanished as completely as a wisp of smoke on a blustery day.

Sometime later, I don't know how much, I clumb outen the box and took my husband's seat, managed to free the reins from Caleb's hands, and chucked the horses into motion. Instead of town, I turned around and headed home. It was full night before we got there, and I don't need to tell you how them Osages greeted Reuben's passing. They were as shocked and saddened as I was, for they had loved him, too—not as well, perhaps, but for many a year longer. The men laid him out on a piece of planking, and his sisters commenced to fussing over his body, replacing his worn and bloody workaday clothing with the ceremonial garb of his tribe. They let me and the children be, and somehow or another I managed to get us outen them gory clothes and put a little soup on for Caleb, though he didn't have no more appetite than I did. Donald, who of course didn't know any better, wolfed down the fatty pudding and fry bread I put before him, then promptly went to sleep. I laid him in his little bed, the one that Reuben had carved outen a cottonwood stump, then I went outside and sat on the ground with my back against the side of our house just the way Reuben had most of the nights of our short three years together. Caleb curled up beside me. It took him a long time to go to sleep. I'd never seen that child shed a tear, and he didn't that night, neither, but watching him twitch and moan as he laid there touched me almost as deeply as had the sudden death that afternoon.

Here I was, twice a widow and only just twenty-four years of age, and here was Caleb, four times an orphan at eight. Good God Almighty, I didn't know how I could stand it.

How I got through the next days I will never know, and I wasn't alone. Reuben's sisters slashed themselves until the blood ran down their arms and set up a keening that I swear would of given wolves the heebee jeebees, which of course was their custom. The men had already seen to it that word traveled to Pawhuska and the other Osage villages on account of the high regard all them people had for Reuben, so I wasn't surprised when relatives and friends from among the Osages came to pay their respects.

However, I was surprised by a visit from Horace Taylor late in the afternoon the day after Reuben died. Though from north of Line, Horace told me how very sorry he was, and he swore he'd do whatever he could to help the Osage Nation find and punish whoever it was that had done this terrible thing, though my first suspicion was that he'd likely come mostly to be sure the shooting hadn't happened in his jurisdiction since he didn't want trouble with anyone from down in the Nations.

Nonetheless, he was right solicitous of my feelings.

He asked me if I had any idea who had done the deed, and of course I had to say no, although I told him there had been bad blood between Reuben and Bill Doolin and maybe the rest of the Daltons for some time. I told him about the pot-shots, too. Just the mention of Doolin made Horace's wattles turn red, I'll tell you. He said he didn't think Doolin would do something that foolish and said he was of a mind that it must of been some Indian Reuben had arrested, but he thanked me for the information and said that he would most definitely look into it. I told him straight to his face that I knew no white Kansas lawman was going to waste time trying to bring an Indian's killer to justice, particularly if it meant running up against ruffians like Bill Doolin and his cowboy gang. He got a touch indignant at that, but after a moment or two, he allowed as how I was entitled to my opinions given the circumstances.

So he offered condolences again, promised to move heaven and earth to find Reuben's killer, and rode off into the early evening.

Anyway, the next day, the Osage elders saw to it that Reuben was buried in Pawhuska after the white man's fashion, but with the proper Osage ceremonies, which were as solemn and impressive as any white man's funeral I ever attended.

Like I said, his sisters had slashed their arms with cooking knives until the blood ran and Helen had chopped off her hair in mourning, but once the funeral was over, they let it go at that. I suppose they'd seen so much killing down through the years that they just couldn't be overly affected by one more murder, even one that took such a good man from their midst. Reuben was gone, just like many others, and that was that.

Now, by the time that funeral ended and the boys and I were on our way back to our village, I'd come to my senses enough to know that if anyone was going to see justice done, it was probably going to have to be because I made it happen. I figured I knew who'd done the killing, or at least who was behind it, and I was slap ready to find the Daltons and Doolin myself and gouge their eyes out or worse. So by the time I got home from the doings in Pawhuska, I had a plan already beginning to take shape in my head that had me cleaning and oiling Jack Ross's old revolver, putting my boys in the care of

Helen and her sisters, and riding north alone until I found them scoundrels and blew their lights out.

I'm sure I would of done it, too, though as it turned out, the good citizens of Coffeyville beat me to it two weeks after we committed Reuben's earthly remains to the ground.

The Daltons, apparently thinking themselves to be the greatest bad men since the James-Younger gang, decided to rob the C.M. & Condon Company and First National banks in Coffeyville, both at the same time. In spite of their wearing fake beards, the townsfolk recognized them easily enough, and this time the good folks didn't scurry for cover. Instead, they grabbed their rifles and shotguns and started shooting. In the ensuing gunfight, four of the townfolk gave their lives, but Bob and Grat Dalton and a couple of other miscreants were killed along with them, and Emmett Dalton got pretty shot up, though he still managed to live a long life, first in prison and then out in California, where he made money from his infamy by writing books and appearing in motion pictures.

Now, Bill Doolin, who I suspicioned was Reuben's actual killer, wasn't in Coffeyville that day—or if he was, he got away clean and ran for the hills, which probably wasn't that hard what with just about every lawman in eastern Kansas being too busy having their pictures taken with dead Daltons to try rounding up any missing members of the gang.

Anyhow, my plan for revenge never got off the ground.

Then, while all of that foofaraw up in Coffeyville was still going on, my youngsters and I got booted outen our home. Seems that no sooner was Reuben in the ground than the elders of our village got together and decided it was time to ask me politely to leave.

It was Helen who had to break the news. It wasn't anything personal, she said, but I wasn't Osage. Had I been, I probably would of become the wife of one of Reuben's cousins or some such, but because I wasn't an Indian, the Osages didn't feel any obligation to me and mine the way they would of otherwise. As for Caleb, no matter how he thought and how he acted, he wasn't Osage neither. Donald and the baby inside me were surely at least part Indian, but it was my responsibility to look after them, and the Osages figured that since I needed to go back to my own people, then that's where they would have to go, too.

Well, the shock of that was about enough to finish me off on top of the grief I was already bearing, but truth to tell, after the first little bit, I came to see their point.

Had they let me stay, I wouldn't of known where to begin raising them boys as Osages, and though Caleb would have had it figured out right quick, it was just as true that he was taking the loss of Reuben hardest of all, and getting him in new environs, so to speak, and back amongst his own people might help him through his grieving.

So I rounded up my few belongings, took my orphans, traded my little hut and pretty near everything in it for that old democrat wagon still stained with my husband's blood, loaded the boys into it, and made for town again, far more sorrowfully than when I'd started out so few days earlier.

When we passed the place where Reuben's killer had laid in ambush, I could see plain enough how it had happened: the road passed right by a coulee that led down to a small creek, and a stand of cottonwoods and scrub oak crowded just above the bank where a man or several men could of hid without being seen from the road. Whether he—or they—had known Reuben was coming along that way or whether they'd just seen him and decided on the spot to take whatever vengeance it was that moved them didn't matter a whit to me.

The deed was done, and like my Osage sisters-in-law would of said, that was that.

Still, as I passed that cut bank, I felt an anger well up in me that I'd never known before, and I decided then and there that somehow, some way, some day, I was going to see to it that the earth was rid of the snake that had killed my husband.

Over the next month, I settled in with Francine, who was good enough to give me a room even though she wasn't as eager as she would of been before I had a half-Indian child, and I commenced working for coolie wages for the Chins once again. Every spare moment, few and far between though they were, I made it a point to give Sheriff Taylor a good dose of what for about how he had a murder to solve.

Now, I figured that, being a relatively recent widower himself and having been so concerned about my feelings the day after Reuben got killed, he truly would press my case if only to help assuage my grief, but he did not, saying it was likely that Reuben's murderer had been amongst the dead Dalton boys. I told him straight to his face he was wrong, Bill Doolin being the one I suspected, and I actually made the trip to Sedan several times to press him on the point besides accosting him whenever he showed up in Chautauqua. It got so he would turn his horse around and gallop off in the other direction whenever he saw me coming.

Then one day long about the middle of November, I caught him where he couldn't get away so easily. I'd seen him entering the barbershop, where he was known to hold court with some of his cronies, so I followed him in and marched right up to him and stood there with my hands on my hips and my belly sticking out a foot as I told him to his face in front of a gaggle of other men how I supposed I was going to have to kill Bill Doolin myself on account of he sure wasn't getting the job done.

For a moment, you could hear a pin drop, then one of them men started sniggering, and before I knew it, all of them were guffawing like what I'd said just tickled them clear to the bone. Horace told me—for the umpteenth time—that he was sorry for my loss and would do what he could to see justice was done, but he winked at his pals when he said it, and they were still laughing and joking about me being nothing but a squaw long after I was out the front door and on my way home.

If I'd of known then what was to come, I should of used Jack's revolver on Horace Taylor right then and there, and never mind about Bill Doolin, but I'll get to that part of the story in time.

As it turned out, by that time, Bill had moved into Oklahoma Territory anyway, where he kept on terrorizing and robbing with a new bunch of yahoos. That caught the attention of some Oklahoma lawmen who had more guts than the Kansas variety, and they commenced to dog him, chasing him from one spot to another until his luck ran out. U.S. Deputy Marshal Heck Thomas, one of the best peace officers our part of the world ever produced, sent old Bill to his great reward with a blast from a twelve gauge sometime in 1895 or '96.

Good riddance to bad rubbish is all I say.

But the only thing I knew at the time was that someone had killed Reuben, and they had got away with it.

Life's just like that sometimes.

New Trials

THE FACT THAT MY SEASON of vengeance-seeking just sort of petered out didn't mean I was over my loss. Not by a long shot. In a way, it only ushered in what was to prove the hardest time of my life up to that moment.

Though I wouldn't of thought it would ever get worse than the weeks following the murder of my husband, it surely did. To put it plainly, I was lost, homeless, and overwhelmed. I felt as if I was just being ground down, being scoured by a grinding wheel that wouldn't stop until there was nothing of me left. It was like I was in some kind of terrible nightmare that I just couldn't waken from. My own black mood surely matched that of Caleb. For the sake of my boys, I tried hard not to let it show, but it took so much energy outen me that I just gave up after a while. I went days at a time when I know I neglected the care Donald deserved and didn't speak two words to Caleb, who had turned morose beyond all reckoning and unlike me was only too happy to let the whole world know it.

Francine tried mightily to keep me chipper, but her constant refrain of "time heals all wounds" and "God knows what is best for us all" and "you've got your young'uns, at least," wore me down like sandpaper would a fine-edged knife.

At least Francine had let me move back into my old room,

though of course it was a mite more crowded now with two boys and a baby on the way. For all she could cluck and scold about religion and morals in spite of her own familiarity with the ways of the flesh, I will give that woman credit for another thing: this time, she never said a word about me carrying a mostly half-Indian baby in my belly.

It turned out that letting me take that room was an act of kindness that it took me a little while to appreciate.

The truth was, she didn't need me all that badly. She still had that little Negro gal to cook, and in my absence, she'd become fast friends with a woman named Maude Calkins, a big old girl with wild red hair, a lazy eye, and a reputation for being able to do the work of a brace of strong men. Maudie could be coarse of language and uncouth in other ways, but I came to learn in the days to come that she had a heart of gold. She lived on the edge of town in a little thrown-together shack amongst the bur oaks that reminded me of my home in Missouri, with enough cats to keep the mice down all over town. Maudie was probably forty years old then, and had never been married. As far as I know, she had never even been with a man, but that didn't matter a whit to Francine and me. Maudie had been helping Francine with just about everything around the place, but once I arrived on the scene, she said she preferred the hard work chopping wood and such, and wasn't much for the finer work like dishes or cleaning. Francine had me do that easy work and claimed it was payment enough for my room. And I went to work for the Chins again (who weren't much happier about it than they'd been the last time), though I had to split what little wages I earned from them with Francine to cover what the boys and I ate.

Truth to tell, I don't think Francine could of come up with two bits to pay me for my labors if she'd of wanted to. By that time, one of the other boardinghouses had closed, and neither Francine nor the other remaining house was able to stay anywhere near full up on account of the railroad laborers had moved on to wherever the end of track now stood. Most of her old house, now three full stories tall, was vacant. Her own son Rufus, who as I said was several years older than Caleb and a good deal larger, what with running to the heavy side naturally and nourished on lots of his mother's greasy potato dumplings, had already been put to work down at the livery stable currying horses, hauling oats and such like to bring in a few extra dimes of hard cash when he wasn't in school.

So it was that we all settled down into what proved to be a hard and joyless life.

Caleb's ninth birthday came and went without much notice, and a freak ice storm the first week of November locked up our corner of the world tighter than a drum and brought on such a bad case of the croup to little Donald that I thought for a day or two it would carry him off to be with his pa, wherever that was. I was practically turning into a consumptive at the same time, what with standing outside betwixt an icy, windswept field and a pot of scalding lye water crammed with tablecloths, bed sheets and men's filthy skivvies. I was so miserable that I almost asked the Chins what it would cost me to partake of the opium that a few cowboys and what railroad hands were left still came by to smoke in the evening. To this day, I actually believe I would of done it if I hadn't been with child.

Some nights when I'd spent all day at the laundry, I'd take my aching back and swollen belly into my little room and spread out on the bed and go so sound asleep I missed supper. Most of the time, Francine didn't bother to wake me and took care of my boys herself.

I didn't see many of Chautauqua's townsfolk in them days, both on account of I was too busy and because I didn't want to listen to none of their snide remarks about me being a squaw and suchlike. I will say that when I did take the children out on the rare clement day or when I went to the mercantile to see about buying enough gingham to make Caleb a decent shirt, some people would surprise me by being more civil than I'd expected. Of course, there were plenty of the snooty ones—women, mostly—who kept their noses permanently pointed skyward, but some others acted as if they truly were sorry for my loss. They'd still say things about Donald along the lines of wasn't he going to be a heap big chief some day and suchlike, but some, at least, would give him a little pat on the head when they said it.

It beats all the way people can be downright mean one minute and turn around and overflow with the milk of Christian kindness the next.

But Caleb, poor tormented child that he was, didn't get any of that tenderness.

Even then, at that young age, I realized that some folks were a little bit afraid of that child, and it's my sorrow to this day that I was beginning to feel somewhat that way myself. There wasn't no question but that boy already had a way about him that could put fear into grownups when he was of a mind, which was getting to be more and more regular, and other children anywhere close to his age, including Francine's Rufus, who was, as I said, far bigger than my boy, positively ran the other way when they saw him coming.

Sullen didn't say the half of it.

When he was in a mood, which was most of the time, I swear he could look holes through a steel plate. I've seen grown men—including blacksmiths and other rough types brawny enough to go two or three rounds with a grizzly bear—get all confused and flustered just because that boy was giving them his "look." Here he was but nine years old, and about all he'd seen in life was good people dying, from his mother to Jack and now to Reuben. Of course, each of them deaths had hit me hard as well, and even though I was a grownup and on top of that not a weak person by nature, that last one had knocked the wind plumb outen me. Caleb sometimes worried me even when Reuben was alive. Now...

It was with some trepidation that I sent him off to school as soon as we were good and settled in with Francine, thinking that a little book learning might somehow be the tonic he needed whether he wanted it or not, but that turned out to be an even bigger mistake than I'd expected. He ran away the first day, and the second, and the third, and by the time he'd been there a week, the teacher informed me in no uncertain words that it just wasn't worth the effort, and besides, the way Caleb terrorized the other children had her worried that she'd lose all her pupils. She was a sweet-tempered girl who had finished the twelfth grade somewhere in Arkansas and had come west to find her life's adventure or some such foolishness, and from what I could tell, she wasn't cut out for dealing with a pack of energetic youngsters under any circumstance, let alone my renegade. Of course, the alternative was probably some old bachelor with a mean streak and a hickory switch, which wouldn't of kept Caleb in his seat one jot longer. So I told her it was all right, that I'd keep Caleb home and try to give him a little book learning myself and maybe we'd try it again the next year. Both of us knew that was a lie, of course; I didn't know the first thing about teaching that boy, and even if I had, there wasn't a power on earth that was going to make him any easier to handle when he got a year older. It was just one more lost cause.

Still, the boy must of been hungry for some kind of education. Somehow or another he taught himself to read a little, probably by hanging around the men in Francine's parlor who spent their evenings entertaining fellow boarders by reading outen the newspaper. He proved to have a good head for numbers, too, though a body could tell it was Indian learning, for he could count horses in a milling herd and be right on the money every time, but if he was to set down and try to work out the multiplication tables on a sheet of paper, he'd like as not throw his pencil acrost the room and stomp off all angry before he got it done.

So that dreary late autumn and early winter, while I waited for my baby, Caleb was my special burden. When I'd finally get him and Donald both to bed and I'd be sitting in our tiny room with my back aching like sin and the lantern wick turned down as low as it would go without guttering out, it would be just me and my thoughts and the occasional ripple of the life inside me.

At times like that, the melancholy would just hit me something powerful.

How could it be that here I was just twenty-four years old and twice a widow and soon to have three young ones to raise? How could it be that the real love of my life was gone so quickly? Sudden death was something we lived with in them days—much more so than nowadays—and up to then I'd done a passable job of coming to grips with it, but I just plain lost the knack that winter. There were nights when I wouldn't sleep a wink and the tears would just stream down my face. That baby growing inside me must have known something of my grief, for it turned and tumbled and kicked whenever I got blue, which seemed like pretty much a constant thing. Sometimes I actually wished I'd lost that baby, though of course whenever that thought came on, it just added shame to the grief.

Many a night, I'd sit there until my lamp burned itself out, and I'd stare into the blackness until I heard Francine or Maudie rustling about and that little cook going to it in the kitchen and I knew it was time to get up and go to work for the Chins.

The room Francine gave us—our old room—was maybe eight feet by eight feet, just big enough for a bedstead that all three of us shared along with a chest of drawers and a wash-basin and chamber pot. Actually, it was about the same size as our cabin in the Osage village, but it seemed so much smaller because the door was always closed and everything was jammed together rather than free and open the way it had been south of the Line. And because we were on the northwest corner of the boardinghouse, the wind hit us full on in a way that dug its way through every last wooden slat until I swear the room might as well of been outside. The mud hut in our little Osage village, in spite of its crude doorways and windows and dirt floor, was a good deal warmer than that clapboard sided room, and that's a fact. Some nights the drafts were so strong we'd have to pull the covers up over our heads and huddle together in a tight bundle to keep from freezing, and there was many a morning I awoke with a crust of frost acrost the tattered old quilt Francine had loaned us.

Though Donald was reasonably quiet and good enough, having long since passed the colicky stage, he was nonetheless a constant reminder to me of his dead father, particularly the way he'd tilt his head or turn his chin up just so. I can't say he looked much like Reuben, being fairer complected and still chubby with baby fat, but he already had his daddy's mannerisms. At not much over two years old, he wasn't housebroken yet, and toddling enough that he could scoot outen the room and disappear in the blink of an eye. All in all, he was a lot of work no matter how good he was. As for Caleb... well, I've already mentioned how that was going, and him being freed of schooling wasn't making him any less temperamental.

Now, boys that age will sass their elders and get a mood on, but there was a special kind of trouble brewing with Caleb, and everyone who came in contact with him could see it. Sometimes he'd have such a black scowl that it made my blood run cold, and many was the time he'd get up and leave home just the way he'd left school, no matter what the weather or time of day or night, and not come back until he was ready.

The first time that happened was on a cold and stormy night around the first of December. I was cuddling Donald, trying to keep him warm in that drafty room while Caleb sat in the corner, brooding. All at once, he stood up, snatched his ragged old coat off the rusty nail he used for a hanger, and bolted outen door.

I told myself at first that he just wanted to use the privy rather than the chamber pot. When he didn't come back right away, I figured he'd only stay outside until he'd gotten all the raw wind and spitting sleet a body could stand, but an hour went by, and then two. I was fit to be tied, I'll tell you. I wrapped Donald up as snug as I could in a comforter and tucked him in between a couple of pillows, then I pulled on my own coat and went out the back door and into that black night. Where in the world was I to begin looking? The Chins' mean little hut was closed up tight as a drum, with no light at all coming through their oilskin windows. I bent into the wind and headed for the livery stable on the off chance that my boy was searching for comfort in the company of animals. The liveryman, who spent most evenings looking for the bottom of a rye whiskey bottle, was dead to the world on his cot and the six or eight horses in their stalls were mostly asleep standing up. I looked in each stall and between the grain bins at the back, but besides the horses, the only living things around were a couple of cats that didn't appear too happy that I'd interrupted their mousing.

From there, I walked the alleys, getting colder and wetter with every step. No Caleb. I even stepped into a couple of saloons, hoping beyond hope that he'd gone toward the tinkle of an old piano or the rumble of men's voices, but other than fierce looks from men I wouldn't want to come acrost in broad daylight, I found nothing. After what seemed like hours of searching, I trudged back to Francine's. She was in the parlor in high dudgeon that I'd left my toddler and run off into the storm in my present delicate condition. Donald was asleep on her lap. I took him and went to our room, where I laid awake all the rest of that night, waiting—and fearing that Caleb was dead somewhere on the prairie and we wouldn't find his frozen body for days.

But the next morning, there he was at the little table Francine had rigged up for us near the stove by laying a couple of planks over a fifty gallon barrel. He looked none the worse for wear, but when I asked him where in tarnation he'd been all night long, he only shrugged and filled his mouth with a spoonful of oatmeal. I never did find out where he'd gone off to or what he'd done, and after it happened a time or two more, I stopped worrying too much about it. It was plain he could take care of himself.

Besides, by then I was so heavy with child and the weather was so awful that it just scared me to be out of doors alone.

Looking back on it, I should of known what was coming, but I truly didn't. I believed I was doing as fair a job as I could with them two boys under the circumstances, and though I knew at the time that I was plumb outen my depth, it just didn't occur to me that he wouldn't come around in time and be as chipper as he'd been in the Osage village.

After all, when Caleb wasn't in the dumps or running off to God knows where, he'd sometimes let me read stories to him outen an old book of fairy tales Francine had for her own son, and on some days he'd even come by the Chins and help me stir the big kettles of wash water. I always took that for a sign that he was feeling some better, even if he wouldn't speak or even look me in the eye as he did it.

Sometimes until my own condition made it impossible, I'd take both of my boys on walks around town or for rides in Francine's new buggy in spite of the weather, though I always went north, trips toward the Territories being too likely to bring back painful memories, and since I always had the boys with me, I couldn't take the risk that Caleb would run off to be with his Osage aunts.

Now, I did consider that that was exactly where Caleb really should be, and that perhaps that was where he went whenever he ran away from home, though that village was a fair piece even for a body on horseback.

To this day, I can't say if he ever went south of the Line. My guess is that he sometimes slept out of doors no matter what the weather, and sometimes spent the night in some rancher's stable, and sometimes he maybe didn't sleep at all—as I didn't—but just walked, brooding about all the folks he'd looked up to and lost, mostly meaning Reuben and to a lesser extent, Jack. Maybe his mother, too, though in all the years we were together, I can't remember him talking about her except the once, which I'll come to in time.

Francine, of course, was scandalized by that boy and his actions. She let me know in no uncertain terms that her own son, who was troublesome in his on way, mostly on account of he wasn't very bright and was the object of bullying by some of the other boys in town, was an absolute paragon compared to Caleb, and more than once she allowed as how it'd be best for all concerned if I'd ship him off to the Kansas Orphan Asylum up in Leavenworth, which she'd learned about from a Quaker woman who'd boarded for a few weeks while I was off with Reuben. To hear Francine tell it, that place was absolute heaven on earth for children who'd lost their folks, but I wasn't having none of it, no matter the assurances that Quaker lady had given Francine. I told her flat out that Caleb had a ma, meaning me, and that was that. If she wanted to send some child to the Leavenworth orphanage, she could start with her boy Rufus. She harrumphed and fussed at that, and for some days thereafter, we weren't hardly on speaking terms to the point that I was afraid she'd boot me outen her house, though it never came to that.

Still, I believe to this day that if Caleb had failed to come home some time when he did one of his runaways, Francine would of rejoiced.

Then came Christmas and New Year's.

And Dell.

***

It was a hard delivery, the very hardest of the three children I bore. She wanted in the worst way to come out backwards, and I'll tell you, I struggled. For all her pettiness and fussing about my morals, Francine was a Godsend on that occasion. She didn't have anything like the knack for nursing that my former Osages sisters-in-law had, but I swear she worked harder at it than any woman alive. When it was clear that the baby was going to come one way or another, that woman plumb took charge. She banished all the men from her house and grabbed Caleb and Donald and her own son by the scruff of the neck and marched them over to the Chins and demanded that them Chinese take the boys in until she was ready to take them back and if they messed around with opium—the Chins, I mean—she'd have their hides. When they refused, she simply set the boys down on the Chins' earthen floor, crossed her arms, and said she'd skin all of them alive—boys and the Chinese alike—or better yet, render them into soap and candles if she so much as heard a peep outen them. The Chins, and probably the boys, too, were dumb-founded with Francine showing that kind of gumption, and they all did as they were told. Then she het water, brought every scrap of linen she had into my small room, piled pillows around me to make me as comfortable as possible, and sat with me, waiting.

After I'd been working for some hours and it become pretty clear to us that both babe and I would die unless something else was done, she called out into the street and sent a passerby for the doctor, though of course Chautauqua didn't have a regular sawbones nor a decent midwife, neither, and the doctor up in Sedan was a notorious drunkard. It being the middle of winter, there was no hope for getting someone down south of the Line to fetch one of Reuben's sisters, neither, and they probably wouldn't of been able to come, anyway. All of which meant the best we could come up with was the livery stable owner who naturally had considerable experience doctoring animals. He was a big, brutish looking fellow with a brusque manner and the smell of horse piss in his clothes, but at least he hadn't been drinking that night, and he did know about delivering foals and calves. He had a surprisingly gentle touch, probably on account of it embarrassed him half to death to have to do what he did. But somehow he and Francine managed to turn that baby so she could come out the right way. I was afraid he was going to reach up inside me to pull that child out the way he might a mare, but it wasn't necessary: all of a sudden, she just came, and that was that. Ever afterward, though, that gentleman would tip his hat to me and blush crimson as a boiled beet whenever we'd pass on the street.

Anyway, I was worn to a frazzle, but it still made my heart leap to know I'd had a girl. Though her hair was dark and her skin was olive like her daddy's, I named her Dell Christine after my darling fair-haired sister.

That baby and I were both so tuckered out by the long struggle that we just curled up in that rumpled bed together and slept for I don't know how long. Luckily, she was a good deal stronger than either of my boys had been, and once I got her to rooting for the breast, she just perked up to fairly brimming over with life.

It wasn't until her third day, once I was up and doing a little for myself, that Francine let the boys come home. She threatened to whip the older ones with a switch if they made any noise or bothered me in any way, and they took her at her word, even Caleb, which surprised the daylights outen me. I ate my first meal of solid food with them, having subsisted on clear broth and dry toast since the baby was born, then I tidied up our room and went digging in a box of things I'd brought from the cabin to see what I might be able to cobble together for a little dress for that child.

That was when I found the box Reuben had made and

hidden inside a rolled up old homespun shirt I'd probably come dangerously close to throwing away. It was a small thing, about four inches on a side, made of red oak he'd sanded and polished to a high luster. The cover was held fast by a small brass clasp, and inside was a brooch he'd apparently fashioned from a black-and-yellow box turtle shell, carving it into a miniature version of the animal itself. I pinned Dell's blanket around her with that turtle brooch, and that was the way I showed her off to the town in spite of temperatures near zero most days and spitting snow that the wind drove like tiny needles into exposed flesh.

Now, some of the biddies who'd actually been polite a few weeks earlier stuck their noses in the air because it was clear as could be that she was a dark-skinned half-breed, but the better folks, which was frankly more likely to include dance hall girls than church people, were real kind.

A couple of weeks after Dell was born, a blizzard struck the likes of which I hadn't seen since the Gove County days, leaving drifts up to the second story windows on the north side of Francine's boardinghouse and all but burying the Chins. Ranchers round about lost countless head of cattle, and there was even talk that some of the horses in town might starve because the hay supply was buried and nobody could get to the storage bins on the west side that held most of the town's oats. Two children lost fingers and toes to frostbite right there in town when they got lost going to the privy, and out in the country there were one or two folks who died of the cold.

Thanks mostly to Maudie Calkins, we managed to dig enough of Francine's woodpile outen the snow to keep a fire going in the cookstove, but that only barely kept the kitchen above freezing, and with the boarders being unable to work, they got first crack at sitting closest to the stove. It liked to turn my heart to stone to see them fat, blustering men sitting there with their boot soles steaming from the heat and their faces red as September apples while Caleb and Donald shivered under a pile of blankets outside the kitchen door.

Only Dell seemed not to notice, but that was because she was cuddled at my breast.

Now, for all the cooing and oohing that Francine and Maudie did over my new baby, my boys didn't take to her, particularly Caleb. Donald had what I suppose is the usual jealousies that caused him to pester her something awful in the early days, but Caleb flat out acted as if she didn't exist. I would of thought he'd be protective of the girl, especially since she was named for his momma, but maybe that's where it went wrong. Maybe whatever he could remember of his mother wasn't a comfort, and being reminded just turned him even more sullen than he was already.

Or maybe it was because her looks reminded him too much of Reuben. I don't know.

All I do know is there was something about me having that baby that made his black moods even blacker and led to my first serious trouble with him as soon as the weather broke enough that he could get outen doors without risking life and limb.

This time, the trouble wasn't running off. This was him doing things he knew were genuinely wrong, like catching two cats, one a stray and one of Maudie's that might as well of been a stray the way it hunted all over town for mice. Somehow or another, he managed to tie them two cats' tails together and dump them into a burlap bag, which he carried down to Johnson Street, where he tossed them out near a hitching post in front of the general store. Naturally, the cats commenced to fighting and squalling, and the horses tied there went half crazy from the racket. A couple of them tore their halter ropes loose and stampeded. By the time the bystanders got things settled down, two cowboys were left afoot on account of their horses were gone, one cat was dead from getting squashed by an escaping horse, and the other needed to be put outen its misery from the slashing it had taken from the other's claws. The wife of the banker brought Caleb home pulling him by the ear, which showed a mite of courage on her part since that boy was putting on both height and weight and could of made her pay for her impertinence had he been of a mind to. While I didn't take very kindly to the way she abused the child, there was no question that he'd done something awful and she was more than within her rights to be upset. I whipped him and put him to bed without supper, which of course I knew would only make him madder. Sure enough, sometime in the night, he got up, slipped out, and wasn't there the next morning in spite of the night turning cold enough to put a skim of ice on the water in my wash basin.

I knew in my bones that this wasn't going to be one of his usual runaway spells, neither. Not after the beating I'd given him. Of course, I was both worried sick and furious at myself for raising a hand to the boy. Reuben would not of done that, but then Reuben wasn't there.

Just before noon, Horace Taylor brought Caleb home tied to the saddle on a pack horse like a sack of spuds. My boy had made it all the way to Sedan on foot in the darkness and, when the sun came up, was found throwing rocks at somebody's chicken coop and generally making a ruckus fit to raise the dead. Horace left Caleb on the pack horse and clumped into Francine's kitchen where he warmed himself by the stove for a few minutes without bothering to take off the greasy hat he'd tied to his head with a wool scarf to keep his ears covered, then commenced to lecture me on what I needed to do to take care of that child, complete with how I oughten keep him tied to a bedstead if I couldn't keep him from running off. Then, when he was done, he untied that scarf, took off his hat, and asked me if I would do him the honor of letting him keep me company some evening—with Francine there to chaperone, of course.

If that didn't beat all. I was so flabbergasted I couldn't hardly speak, and from the look on Francine's face, I knew she was just plain mortified. Somehow, I managed to thank him, tell him that I wasn't interested in keeping company with any man, and how I appreciated what he'd done bringing Caleb back.

He just cinched that hat back onto his head, trundled outside, cut Caleb loose, and dragged him to the back door by the shirt collar.

"Mebbe 'nother time, then," he said, nodded to Francine, and clumb back on his own horse and headed north.

"What on earth..." I said, watching him go.

Francine started to say something, broke out in tears, and fled to her bedroom, leaving me alone in the kitchen with a half-froze boy who didn't look a bit happier to be standing next to a warm stove than he did sitting a pack horse in a freezing wind. It dawned on me that Francine had been hoping to pick up with Horace Taylor right where she'd left off with old Cummings, but I didn't dwell on it. She could have him if she wanted was the way I looked at it.

I had my own worries.

So I stood there, looking at Caleb and wondering what I could possibly do to make him pay for his sins.

This time, I spared the rod and simply hoped it would blow over, which it seemed to do after a few days, though I kept an eagle eye on him day and night. But two weeks later, a goat the Chautauqua banker's family kept for milk had it's throat slit, and though there were plenty of folks who didn't like that man on account of the interest rates he charged and how high he lived on other people's money, I know for a fact it was Caleb who did the deed: he claimed that very day that he'd lost his shoes in spite of the freezing weather, but Francine found them in the garbage pile out on the back lot line, all sticky with blood. Thinking again of what Reuben would do, I let it go, though in my heart I knew I shouldn't—

and I wasn't altogether sure Reuben would of, either. Being cruel to animals is something I believe every boy does once or twice, but this was taking that cruelty to a higher level.

I've thought of that many a time down through the years, wondering if I could of turned Caleb to a better path if I'd done something different or found a way to make him see the errors of his ways. But I didn't even try, I'm ashamed to say, and I've been paying the price ever since.

From that point on, life settled into a drudgery that made time pass in a peculiar way. What with the hard work I was doing every day for the Chins, the necessary mothering I tried to do each night keeping my little boy and baby daughter cleaned and fed, and worrying about what Caleb was apt to do next, the days and weeks seemed to drag on forever, but in a funny way, the seasons and even the years passed in a flash. Winter turned to spring, and spring to summer, then autumn and winter again, and before a body knew it, the whole she-bang happened all over again. It wasn't no time at all, it seemed, and Dell was walking and talking, though she never talked much. She'd sometimes sit for hours, silent as a stone, with them dark eyes of hers just darting every whichaway, watching. It was the Osage in her, I suppose. For his part, Donald was turning into a polite little man, though with a stubborn streak. Caleb would be good for a while, and then a neighbor would complain of chickens with their necks wrung, or somebody's fence would be cut and a milk cow would have its bag slashed with a razor, or a patch of dry brush would catch fire and threaten to burn down the town.

It was an existence with more fear than joy for me, I'll tell you.

In them days, life in Chautauqua and our whole end of Kansas was changing, too. The railroad boom was over for certain, and gandy dancers and railroad big shots alike were gone or going fast. With the end of track somewhere miles and miles farther on, the roundhouse on the edge of town fell apart from disuse. The trains still roared through, but they didn't even stop to take on coal or water anymore, the stops being limited to dropping off the mail or picking up the occasional passenger who was leaving our country for good. That meant Francine didn't get business from the railroad men, and while there wasn't any danger of getting axle grease on her horsehair divan, the rooms were mostly empty. Acrost town, the fine houses that five or six years before had been home to important men with muttonchop whiskers and round bellies behind their waistcoats and watch fobs were just sort of melting back into the prairie. The windows in them houses were broken or stolen, sapling red oaks grew up betwixt the front porch floorboards, and bats, mice and owls pretty much had the places to themselves.

In what seemed the blink of an eye, the railroad had become just a whistle in the night, with nothing to make a body even think about it if it wasn't for an occasional grass fire set off by sparks from the smokestacks.

By that time, yeomen farms that had dotted the countryside when Caleb and I first arrived had pretty much given way to ranches. Ten or fifteen people could run a spread that forty families might of homesteaded once upon a time, and the farmers who sold out moved on somewhere else—Coffeyville, Independence, Wichita, or even Colorado and California—leaving the small towns that had depended on them simply to shrivel up. The truth of it is, that shriveling is still going on to very this day, fifty years and more later. I don't think there's maybe half as many people in Chautauqua County now as there were in them days, and there are a whole lot more funerals than birth announcements, I'll tell you.

But it was more noticeable back then. What had been all exciting and new and fresh, even if it was mighty rough around the edges, had begun to go to seed.

And I felt like that, too.

I was certainly feeling old beyond my years. Oft times I thought of my ma, and how haggard she looked when I was a sprout, and though I hadn't had near as many children as she had, what with the hard work and worry, I knew I was on my way to looking just the same.

It didn't help that the only two friends I had in the world were Maudie Calkins and Francine, and Francine had begun to change, too.

For one thing, she was drinking some, which when it started was only noticeable late in the evening. She'd get a little unsteady on her feet and give off a faint aroma of whiskey just like the men in the parlor, but otherwise a body couldn't tell there was any real problem. Thinking back on it, I'd always suspected she tippled a little at night, which with her being Irish was probably about as natural as breathing, but suddenly it just sort of took her over completely. In no time at all, that sharp smell was with her when she got up in the morning, and she'd frequently disappear for long stretches during the day. Taking naps to ward off headaches is what she said, but I knew different. She got to abusing that boy of hers, too, hollering at him day and night and accusing him of abandoning her just like his daddy had, which turned into a prophecy fulfilled once he'd had all he could take and moved outen the house and into the little shed behind the livery stable where he worked. I reckon she took her sharp tongue to the stable, too, because shortly thereafter, he quit that job and Chautauqua altogether.

One day when I asked her about where the boy had gone, she said he'd gone to see his pa—by which I assumed she meant that railroad man Guthrie, wherever he was—and let me know I wasn't to bring it up ever again. She got roaring drunk that night, accused me of all sorts of mischief and said ugly things about my half-breed children right in front of the three boarders we'd managed to snag somehow, then held it against me when two of them moved out on account how embarrassed they were. I thought for certain that she would kick me out after that, but she didn't. Though she let me stay, I decided right there that I shouldn't ever bring the matter up again. Even Maudie, who could of taken care of herself in a fight with a gandy dancer, started giving Francine a wide berth.

Then some weeks later, while she was sitting at the kitchen table with a wet cloth wrapped around her head to cure the headache she'd had since breakfast, she just blurted out that Rufus wouldn't ever be coming home. And he never did. It wasn't his pa, she said. He was just gone. He wasn't but fourteen years old.

There was rumors years later that he'd wound up in St. Louis running a real hotel, but I never put much stock in that on account of I didn't think he had enough common sense to run a two-horse stable let alone a real business.

I'm not certain whether it was having her boy run away—or driving him away, whichever way you look at—or something else altogether, but after that, Francine's decline started picking up speed in earnest. Maybe it was having so few boarders that she had to let the Negro girl go, and the ones she did have were just the dregs—men who chewed snoose and spit on the floor without even trying to aim for the cuspidors and ruined her dining room chairs with their spurs and broke wind right in front of the children. Maybe it was just the way of it, with no real reason to be had.

Anyway, the spring of 1895, shortly after Dell turned two, was a dry one, with the tall prairie grass never really turning green. Thunderstorms set off grass fires that would burn for miles, with clouds of smoke turning the sun red in the daytime and forcing folks to breathe through wetted handkerchiefs to keep from choking. It was but the smallest hint of what was to come during the Dust Bowl years, but in them days, it seemed like the end of the world. Wheat fields and pasture burned alike. Bobwire fences didn't stop fire any better than they stopped cowboys with wire cutters. I know for a fact that the fires swept away whole home places just as clean as a twister would do, and many a rancher or farmer's wife and children who wouldn't or couldn't outrun them fires lost their lives. The Bible thumpers amongst us swore it was God's vengeance, but the more charitable Christians just said their prayers of thanks that our towns didn't fall victim to the flames.

Of course, the cattle suffered worse than the people. Hundreds were caught by the flames, and once the fires passed, the ones that didn't get roasted alive commenced to starving because there was nothing left for them to eat. Cowboys from all over that part of Kansas and Oklahoma Territory did the best they could to move them poor beasts to new pasture, but too many animals on too little dried up land took its toll. It was a sorrowful thing, seeing cows and calves standing in parched fields with their ribs showing and their tongues hanging outen their mouths with clouds of gray dust swirling around with every step they took.

Chautauqua turned from a dying railroad town into a cattle town that summer when some of the outfits decided the best way to cut their losses was to send whatever stock they could round up north to the slaughter houses. I'd stand on the front porch at Francine's and watch them long dusty strings of bawling beeves marching up Johnson Street to get loaded onto the boxcars. I swear the flies were thick enough to carry away small children, and you could smell the sourness of scared animals for hours after they'd been herded onto the cars and the trains had pulled out. They said it was ten times worse in Coffeyville and some of the bigger towns.

The losses ruined many of the smaller ranchers, and a good chunk of them pulled up stakes and headed for greener pastures just like the farmers they'd replaced, which in them days was just about anywhere they could run stock, but especially Colorado or even Montana, leaving the big operators to get even bigger. In the end, that dry season was just a tick of time, though. The rains returned, and the grass with it, and the herds once again grew thicker and thicker even as the human population dwindled.

As much as I hated having strings of cattle churning up the dust and leaving cow pies everywhere, Caleb loved it. Or, more precisely, he loved the cowboys. When he'd see them small, dirty men all dressed up in leather chaps and greasy hats with their sunburnt faces making them darker than any Indian I ever knew, he'd stand and stare just like that day Reuben faced down Bill Doolin in Pawhuska. His hands would twitch and turn, and I'd see that he was making the same motions as some rider adjusting the reins where he sat in the saddle. When one of them boys would spit into the street, Caleb would turn his head and spit in the same direction. When he'd hear one of them cussing a blue streak, the next thing you know I'd be washing his mouth out with soap.

The funny thing was, he never fought me on that one. He was getting big enough now to pretty much have the better of any tussle we'd get into, but when I'd scold him for swearing and warn him I'd tan his hide if I heard that language around the little ones, he'd just give me a sort of half grin and line right up next to the wash basin, chew that bite of old lye soap, spit it out, and go about his business.

I only wish everything with that child would of turned out so easy.

The black moods and troublemaking I'd hoped he'd outgrow had become part of his nature. On his good days, he'd be spooking horses tied up on Main Street just for the fun of seeing them run, and never mind that their riders swore they'd tar the daylights outen him if they ever did catch him. Or he'd follow some woman with a baby carriage, and just when she was stepping off the boardwalk to cross the street, he'd swoop by and give the carriage a shove, dumping it and the baby into the mud. It was just like Bill Doolin would of done. One tyke came away with a nasty cut on its forehead from one of them incidents, and the mother reported it to Sheriff Taylor, who paid me a visit to warn me that he'd arrest Caleb and make him spend a night in the county jail if he did it again, and never mind that he wasn't but eleven years old. Other times, Caleb would swipe some little trinket from the mercantile and throw it into the privy just for fun, or he'd take night soil from the slop jars and sprinkle it into the gravy Francine was making for breakfast so she'd have to throw the whole pot out.

Once when he did that, she actually took matters into her own hand and let fly with a cast iron skillet, putting a deep bruise onto Caleb's shoulder, which of course he deserved. I was afraid he'd retaliate, but just like the lye soap mouth washing, he seemed to take it in stride.

I know, too, that it wasn't long after that, when he was maybe going on twelve, that he stole a gun somewhere and started teaching himself to shoot. He'd come home smelling of gunpowder, with black burns on his clothes and blisters on his hands. I never found out where he got the gun. Stole it, I suppose, or traded some trinket he'd swiped from the mercantile to some cowboy, and likely came up with the ammunition in the same way.

Where he went to do his shooting was a mystery to me as well. There were reports of an occasional steer or yearling calf getting gunned down for sport, which may of been Caleb or may of been somebody else just out for a hooraw with a belly full of whiskey. A sign the town fathers of the nearby village of Caney put up advertising their Masonic and Odd Fellows outfits got shot to pieces, but again, that could of been just about anybody. I figured he went south of the Line to some little draw he knew about where nobody would be likely to hear him and plinked away at old bottles or some such bits of trash. At least that was my hope, and I confess I really didn't want to find out if he was getting into worse mischief than that.

It scared me that he was learning to use a gun, but in them days, most of the men around town owned some sort of firearm and knew how to use it, and all of the cowboys Caleb was so fond of were plumb weighted down with iron. So, just as with most of the other things he did, I let it slide.

Then there was the matter of the girls.

Like just about every other boy who ever breathed, Caleb became fascinated by girls his age blossoming toward womanhood. Now, homespun and calico didn't show much of a girl's shape, which was just fine with all right thinking fathers and mothers, but Caleb was determined to see what was under them garments, whether the girl in question wanted him to or not.

Needless to say, that brought trouble down on our head, once again in the form of Sheriff Taylor, who showed up at Francine's one early autumn day on a lathered horse with a legal document of some kind all wadded up in his big hand.

"I told you it would come to this, Missus," he said to me. "I got a warrant for your eldest boy's arrest." He clumb down offen his big old gray gelding, who looked mighty relieved to be shed of the weight. "Seems your boy assaulted Miss Penelope Cleaver in her person yesterday out along Caney Creek near Butcher Falls."

That was some ways northwest of Sedan—a far piece for a boy afoot, even one as used to wandering as Caleb. "I doubt he did it," I said, brushing the hair off my sweaty forehead with a hand roughened to sandpaper by laundry water. I hoped I sounded like I meant it.

"The girl says he did."

"That's quite a hike for a boy without a horse."

"She says he had a horse. She says he took her picnicking and they rode out to the falls and he tried to have his way with her."

"He was here in Chautauqua all day yesterday with me," I

said. It was a lie, of course. I had no idea where Caleb was or what he'd been doing the day before, which was pretty much the way it was every day.

"The Cleaver girl says the opposite."

I nodded at the crumpled paper in his hand. "So you're going to lock him up?"

"That's about the size of it."

Now, I confess I'd known it would eventually come to that, as much trouble as Caleb seemed determined to get himself into.

"Then what?"

"I suppose it'll be up to the girl's parents. Depends on whether they want to go to trial and all."

"Trial?"

He nodded. "Charge like this is important."

"He's not even thirteen years old."

"Old enough to try to have his way with the girl. So like I said, it's up to her folks whether there's a trial, which right at this minute they say they want."

"What would make them change their minds?" I asked. "Would they put their girl on the witness stand?" I was thinking just then what I'd do if I was in their shoes, and of course I'd want to see the miscreant pay for his crime, but at what price?

Sheriff Taylor's sunburnt neck turned an even deeper shade of red. "The girl does say she loves your boy," he said.

"She says he assaulted her, but she loves him."

"That's about the size of it. But it don't matter one way or t'other. I got to take him in now."

I just shrugged. "If you can find him, I don't suppose I can stop you."

"No, ma'am, you can't. Just wanted to let you know."

And that was that. He got back up on that poor horse and rode off, with that paper still clenched in his fist.

He did find Caleb—rolling dice and smoking hand-rolled

cigarettes with a couple of older boys behind the mercantile. Caleb made a run for it, but as I heard the story, Sheriff Taylor somehow managed to get his horse into a stiff trot in spite its burden, and when he caught up with Caleb, he just bent as low as he could, snatched at his britches, and lifted him clean off the ground. I heard that Caleb fought like a wildcat, but Horace Taylor was a strong man and just hung onto them britches until Caleb had swung and clawed himself limp.

Fortunately, the girl's parents did change their minds the next day about there being a trial on account of how poor Penelope wept over having her little boy lover in jail, and Caleb came home in the darkest mood I'd ever seen.

"Never again," was all he said when he saw me.

"I should think not," I said, though I was afraid to ask him what he meant.

Penelope Cleaver got herself with child a year or so later at the tender age of fourteen, and from what I heard, there were at least a half-dozen cowboys around Sedan that were scared outen their wits that they might have to marry her, so apparently Caleb wasn't the only one who ever took her on a picnic, but that's not to make light of what he did.

The simple truth is that what effort I was putting into being a mother—and it would only be honest to admit that it wasn't much, on account of the hours I put in slaving for the Chins all day and Francine at night—mostly went to that boy and not the other two, and it apparently didn't come close to being enough. Donald was a placid enough child that he didn't seem to need much mothering. Just feeding and cleaning and tucking in at night was about all he ever seemed to want. Otherwise, he pretty much took care of himself. Dell was the more active of the two, getting into things, crawling or walking off and showing up in the men's rooms, where she'd sometimes wake them fellows up laughing at the whip-saw sound of their snoring or the way their bare toes stuck outen the holes in their socks. I'd chase her and bring her back to our room, but before long, I'd be somewhere trying to find Caleb, knowing he was getting into real trouble, and Dell would be off again, rooting around in the flour bin or pestering Donald. She'd look at me outen the corner of her eye sometimes, and I'd swear it was disapproval, or like she was trying to figure me out. Or when I'd pick her up to hug or cuddle, she'd stiffen and fuss to be put down, so I'd just let her be. Even from those very early days, Dell pretty much raised herself, which I suppose is true for lots of children, but I'd never thought that one of mine would fall into that category, especially with there only being three of them.

Francine told me—over and over and over—that there would be hell to pay over that girl child as much as over Caleb, but usually she smelled of whiskey when she said it, so it was easy to ignore. I actually took to mocking her to her face, which didn't make things go much better betwixt us, but I just couldn't put up with being criticized by a woman drunkard who'd lost her own son.

Anyhow, that's how things went along, day after day, week after week, until another season passed, and then another year. It wasn't long before Donald was old enough to start school, though he didn't seem interested in much except sitting by himself playing with whatever old toy he might be able to get his hands on like an old limberjack or wooden blocks that had belonged to Rufus or even a piece of crumpled paper. Dell was dashing here and there, grimy as a pig in a wallow most of the time, with matted hair and a face so dark with dirt she looked more like a minstrel show performer than a little girl.

And there I was, ignoring the both of them so I could work sun up to sun down and spend the time in between trying to stay one step ahead of whatever real trouble Caleb got into next.

Two old derelict houses burned down in Chautauqua in July of '96, one of them being the very place where Mr.

Herbert Wilbertson of the A T & SF Railroad had tried to put hands on me what seemed like a lifetime before. No one was living in either place, and except for the worry that the fire might spread to the whole town, there wasn't much point in putting them out. So the volunteer firemen just kept their noses to the wind to sense a change in direction and the nearby grass as wet as they could with old gunnysacks soaked in well water and otherwise let them fires burn.

The only problem was that everyone in town knew the fires had been set deliberately, and most everyone suspected the same person I did. Caleb allowed as how it couldn't have been him because he was off sparking another girl, except it turned out that the girl he said he'd been with was visiting an aunt in Emporia who had money and a nice home to spend the hot summer months in.

Sheriff Taylor came to visit me after them fires, as I knew he would. By that time, he was riding down to Chautauqua every other week to lecture me about Caleb.

Anyway, when he showed up at Francine's that day, he told me straight out right in front of our one and only boarder that my boy would go to prison for certain—or get himself and someone else killed—if he didn't straighten up.

"He needs a father," that big, blustery old man said, pointing his thick finger right into the space between us. "A father who'll beat the daylights outen him when he needs it."

"He had a father, and I good one," I said, standing up as tall as I possibly could. "His trouble is he lost his pa—two of them, in fact—and not that he needs another."

"No, ma'am," he said, shaking his head so the jowls swung back and forth. "He needs a pa. Ever' boy needs a pa. So's that younger one. 'Thout a pa, he's going to turn out as bad as his brother. Or a sissy, which is worse. And Lord knows what will become of your daughter."

"Well, sir," I said, "their getting a pa isn't likely to happen any time soon, is it?"

He licked his lips. "Could."

"How so?"

"I'm asking to marry you."

Now, you can imagine I was absolutely thunderstruck at that. I'd plumb forgotten he'd asked to spark me once already. "You?"

"Yes."

"No."

"You think on it. 'Twould get you outen here," he said, with a sweep of his hand that took in Francine's dilapidated place and the Chin's laundry and opium den. "You wouldn't need to slave for a couple of Chinks and a drunkard, and it would see that your older boy got the discipline he needs."

"He doesn't need discipline, Sheriff," I said. "He just needs not to have anybody die on him for a while."

Horace hawked phlegm and spit it onto the ground at his feet, just barely missing my shoe as he did so. "You think on it, Missus," he said. "'Fore it's too late."

Then he turned on his heel and stomped off.

"The idea," I said, and I went back to whatever it was I'd been doing.

Of course, Francine heard the details from our boarder. Later that night, after the dishes were done and I'd put the little ones to bed, she called me down to the kitchen. She was sipping outen a tea cup, though I know for a fact it wasn't tea she was drinking.

"You ought to do it, Eva Rae," she said, taking a big swallow and smacking her lips. "He's a steady man. Best I could of hoped for," she added sadly. Then straightening up, she said "If he's asking for your hand, you oughten give it."

"He's a big old brute," I said.

"He's not so bad. Make you a good home."

"I doubt it." I gave her a hard look. "Besides, who'd look after you?"

She sort of straightened up in her chair. "I don't need any

looking after, Sister." Then she slumped again. "With business the way it is, there ain't any reason I can't take care of everything around here myself. Me or Maudie, one." She took another drink. "Besides, unless you send that boy of yours off to that Leavenworth orphanage asylum before he brings disgrace or worse down upon all of us, I'm going to have to insist you leave."

It wasn't the first time I'd heard her say that, but this time, I could tell she meant it.

"Well, I'm not going to be married to that fat old bag of wind."

"You'd best think on it, girl," she said, echoing both the sheriff himself and something that nagged deep in my own heart—my own growing fear for Caleb.

So, against every shred of my better judgment, I did.

A Father for Caleb

THE NEXT TIME I SAW HIM was in Sedan. I'd taken Francine's buggy north to pick up the supplies we couldn't get at our little store in Chautauqua. Somehow, word of my visit must of preceded me—I've always suspected that Francine sent word to the sheriff through some cowboy or some such—because I hadn't any more than turned that buggy onto Main Street than there he was.

"Well, look who's here," he called out from the boardwalk in front of the sandstone opera house.

"Sheriff," I said, as noncommittal as I could while giving a little flick of the reins to keep the horse moving.

But he was fast for a big man. He stepped into the street and grabbed the halter, stopping the buggy. "Nice to see you, Miz Eva," he said with a big grin. "You brighten up our little town."

"Thank you," I said, forcing a smile, although just the way he said it made the hairs on my neck stand straight up. "If you don't mind, I have business at the mercantile."

"Why, certainly," he said, sweeping off his hat and exposing a round bald spot that was red as a beet and sparkling with sweat. "If I may, I'd like to come along. Never know when a woman of your quality might need protecting, and besides, I'd be honored to show you the sights once you've finished."

"Suit yourself," I said, though I couldn't for the life of me think what the sights might be, me having already seen just about all of that burg, which wasn't a whole lot bigger than Chautauqua. As for protection, I reckoned the only protecting I needed was from him.

It turned out, the sights meant the squat yellow stone jail two blocks north of Main and his office in the basement of the wood and brick courthouse.

We left the buggy hitched in front of the mercantile and walked the short distance. He pointed out where he'd kept Caleb overnight, making sure that I knew it was the roomier of the two small cells, and the only one with a small slit of window so whatever prisoner might be inside could get a breath of air. Then he led me out to the grassy courthouse square and pointed out the Baptist church acrost the street and where the Methodists hoped to build their meeting house alongside the Baptists.

"We're getting to be quite a metropolis," he said, and from the way he pushed his chest out when he said it, you'd of thought it was all his own doing. "I'm rooming at the hotel at the present time, but I have my eye on a little house over on Elm Street."

"That's nice," I said. I tell you, I was itching to get away from that man. I thought about asking him didn't he have a house when his wife was alive, but my better judgment kept me from it on account of I didn't want to put us into the same fix—widow and widower—right then and there.

Still, he must of read my mind.

"You're welcome to come live with me soon as I buy the place," he said, then he instantly turned crimson. "As my wife, I mean."

How I longed to be in that buggy putting miles between me and Horace Taylor! "I thank you, sir," I said as evenly as I could, "but I'm content with my life the way it is."

"Your boy needs a father. The other two children, too. Them being Osage don't bother me."

"Half Osage," I corrected. "Like I said, thank you, Sheriff, but..."

"I won't quit asking."

I'm sure I sighed loud enough to be heard all the way to Chautauqua. "No, I don't suppose you will."

He didn't, neither.

From that moment on, there wasn't a week that went by that he didn't show up at Francine's on some pretext or another—he was chasing a miscreant who'd stolen a pig or he was looking in on a sick friend or some other nonsense—and every time he stopped by, he'd ask me that question all over again, sometimes right in front of Francine, who had clearly given up any hope of catching him for herself and so badgered me just as bad as he did about how I ought to take him up on his offer. The both of them always made it a point to remind me how it would be the best thing in the world for Caleb, and as soon as he rode away, Francine would start dropping hints about sending Caleb to Leavenworth again.

Of course, just the thought of sending my boy to an orphanage weighed like a stone on my heart, though I was beginning to wonder how I could avoid that trouble—or worse. I was still clinging to Reuben's wisdom about not using harsh discipline on a child, but more and more I wondered if sparing the rod wasn't spoiling that child beyond redemption what with all the serious trouble he was getting himself into. Though he was small for his age, he was coming on to adulthood, and any chance I had of putting him on the right path would be gone soon, if it wasn't already.

Finally, there came the night in late July of 1897, nearly five years after Reuben was killed, that Francine invited Sheriff Taylor to supper.

"He's a nice man, and we don't get many nice men here

any more," she said when she told me. I said she could have him all to herself if she wanted to, on account of I would rather eat oats with the horses and mules over at the livery barn than sit down to table with that man, but she just pooh-poohed me like she always did.

When the day arrived, I was still set on taking off somewhere to avoid him, but Francine announced she had a terrible headache and couldn't possibly fix supper and Maudie Calkins was off somewhere visiting shirttail relations. The headache might of been real on account of her having polished off a fair amount of moonshine whiskey so rotten my old Daddy would of been embarrassed to serve it to his pals, but truth or lie, I knew I was stuck. My children and I were living free of charge except for the work I did, and I'd long ago promised her out of gratitude that I'd handle the cooking when she or Maudie couldn't.

So there I was. I had to cook for that man, and I'd have to serve as hostess to boot. I do confess that I didn't exactly put my heart and soul into the victuals that night, though. I've never been the best of cooks, so it didn't take much extra effort to make the dumplings a little gluey and the chicken not quite done. Nevertheless, the sheriff, who arrived smelling of rosewater and talcum powder, pronounced them fit for a king and helped himself to seconds and thirds just to prove it. I sat silent as a church mouse, mostly just watching him shovel it in. Between bites, he inquired about Francine, said he was sorry she was feeling poorly, told me to please call him Horace instead of sheriff, and asked if we had any fresh buttermilk to wash down the chicken. My children—that is, Donald and Dell, Caleb having slunk off somewhere the minute he found out who was coming to supper—watched from their little table in the kitchen. As young as they were, I think they could tell what was going on.

After Horace finished off the dumplings, drank half of a second glass of buttermilk, and let out a huge belch without begging my pardon, he got right down to business.

"I suppose you know why I come, Evie," he said. "May I call you Evie?"

I shrugged.

"Well," he said, looking at me over that glass of milk. "Will you? Marry me, I mean. I've been asking and asking."

Somehow or another, I had to answer his question, so I posed one of my own. "Why on earth would I want to marry you, Horace Taylor?" I wiped a sleeve acrost my brow. It seemed awful hot in that old house just then. What I mostly wanted to do was fling my plate right into that fat old man's face, to tell the truth.

"I'd be good to you, Evie," he said. "I'm God-fearing and hard working. I bought that house, and I'm fixing it up just for you, and I'm on the right side of the law, which I know is important to you."

That gave me the shivers in spite of the heat as I thought about poor Reuben, then Caleb quickly in turn, but from the guileless look on his face, I didn't think he meant anything by it. "I appreciate that," I said as evenly as I knew how. "It's just that I ain't particularly looking to hitch up with a man again. I've told you that over and over. Being a widow twice over and not yet thirty leads me to think maybe marrying isn't something I especially want to do." I sort of surprised myself being that long-winded.

"Well, I know it's a big decision. It took me the longest time to get over the loss of my late wife," he said, dipping his head as if in a moment of prayer. "But she always said life's for the living, and I finally come around to her point of view. That's why I've asked you so often to be my wife," he said, and he drained his glass, smacked his lips, and wiped them with the back of his hand in spite of having one of Francine's few remaining good linen napkins right there beside his plate. "I've given you lots of time to think about it. Now I'm asking as best I can would you please consent to marry me?"

"Thankee for the offer," I said, trying to be polite.

He grinned. "That's the best I've gotten out of you yet, and I reckon I'd normally settle for that, but not this time. I'm asking again, and I'm going to keep asking until I get the answer I want." Apparently, putting his proposal as a question wasn't but a formality in his mind, leaving no room for an honest answer. "Marry me. For the sake of your children," he said.

"Now what would I want with a big old windbag like you?" I said, straight out.

That didn't seem to faze him. "Well, I'm going to adjourn to the parlor and have me a see-gar, and when you're done with the dishes, I'm going to ask you again," he said.

Which he did. Twice, before I finally told him straight out that he wasn't going to get any answer he wanted to hear that night and the more he asked, the less likely it would be that he'd ever get a different one. That turned him a mite sullen, but he said he guessed he knew which way the wind was blowing and would be back the next night after I'd had a chance to think it over.

Of course, I was determined NOT to think about it all, but that was about as likely as having the sun come up in the west the next morning. I couldn't think about anything else as I tossed and turned that night, and it didn't help a lick that Caleb never did come home from wherever he was catting around.

I told myself that Horace's proposal was just so much wasted breath, and that nothing at all had really changed. But of course it had. I'd had a serious proposal of marriage—or close on to forty of them, if you counted every time he asked—from someone who wasn't going to give up and who had to be taken seriously even if I wasn't the least bit interested in being his wife.

And in my heart, I knew there was some truth in what he was saying: there I was with three rambunctious children to raise, one of which was turning out to be more troubled and troublesome with every passing day, and no prospects except for endless drudgery in a Chinese laundry. My own heart's ambition was maybe to buy an interest in Francine's boardinghouse, and she and I had even talked about it some, but there wasn't a way in the world I could scare up enough cash money to do it, and it didn't take a genius to figure out that owning part interest in a ramshackle boardinghouse without boarders in a town moving in the direction of extinction wouldn't leave me and mine a bit better off.

By the time dawn came, graying the sky enough so I could see my two little ones sleeping in the bed beside me, I'd decided I'd done worse than Horace Taylor. Or at least so it had seemed at the time, when Daddy sold me off to Jack Ross. Jack had proved to have some real redeeming qualities, deep-in-the-bone decency being the greatest one.

Didn't that prove that any man could turn out a good deal better than first impressions?

As for Reuben...

Well, Reuben was the love of my life, pure and simple, and there wasn't nothing in the world going to change that. He had been strong, noble, kind, brave, and loving. Most of all, he had been a good and gentle man through and through. But Horace's wife's admonition was true enough: life was for the living.

As for the children, Donald and Dell sure enough could use a daddy. No child should grow up with just one parent if there's a way around it. Caleb was another matter altogether, of course, but perhaps Horace was right that what that boy needed most was a man's strong hand before he was so far gone into a life of trouble that there would be no rescuing him.

Still, just to think of lying in bed with a snoose-chewing three hundred pounder with a reputation for having a serious mean streak made my blood run cold.

I got up, dressed, tucked the children in tight for another bit of sleep before it was full daylight, and went to the kitchen to light the stove for breakfast.

Caleb was sitting in the corner by the back door, all crusted with mud and dried blood. His face looked like he'd been kicked by a mule.

"What on earth happened, child?" I asked as I knelt to examine his wounds. Besides bruises, it appeared he had a broken nose.

He jerked away from me. "Got in a fight, Momma Eva," he said, though it was jumbled some on account of a swollen lip.

"I can see that. Are you all right? Let me take care of your bruises."

He twisted some more so that I couldn't see his face.

"Caleb, are you all right?"

He stiffened a little. "I'm fine, Momma Eva."

Just the way he said it gave me the shivers. "And the other fellow?"

He said nothing.

"Caleb, I'm talking to you."

But he just hunkered down, refusing even to look at me.

"Did you do something really bad this time?"

He mumbled something.

"What?"

"I said it wasn't my fault."

That's all I could get outen him, no matter how hard I tried. He wouldn't tell me more, nor would he let me help clean up. After a time, he just got up, went outside again, and I didn't see him for another two days. I reckon he straightened his own nose, no matter how much that must of hurt. I hoped against hope I wouldn't hear that some poor cowboy had gotten himself killed in a fight with my adopted son, and fortunately, I didn't, but then there were so many fights and shootings in them days that folks didn't take much notice unless someone important or well known got hurt. The cowboys were usually drifters from Texas or Arkansas, oftentimes without last names that anybody knew, and if one of them disappeared, the assumption was that they'd headed home, not that they were lying dead in a gully somewhere. Still, the worrying absolutely made me sick, and it started to tip the scales in the direction of giving Horace Taylor a reluctant "yes," though I'm not sure I even admitted that to myself at the time.

I also held off for a while on account of Francine stuck her nose into it even more than she'd done already, telling me what a wonderful idea it was and how I ought to be proud having such a fine man setting his cap for me and otherwise driving home the point every last chance she got. Nor did it help that he was true to his word about coming to town, showing up every single day to repeat his proposal of marriage, and before long, Francine wouldn't let an hour go by that she wasn't harping on how Horace Taylor was the grandest catch in the history of the world. It was Horace this, and Horace that for days on end until I liked to went crazy. In later times she would of made a good used car salesman, the way she was so intent on making sure I knew the good points of that man almost every second of every day we were together, and where he didn't have good points, she made some up. If I was helping make the beds, she'd be going on about how Horace had a little money which he'd inherited from his first wife and I'd be able to hire what help I needed. If we were peeling spuds and boiling cabbage in the outside kitchen, she'd be saying how easy it would be to prepare a meal for one man rather than a boardinghouse full, though she didn't have much of a comeback when I reminded her that a man of Horace's girth could pack away a powerful lot of victuals and besides, we didn't have but a handful of occasional boarders.

It finally got so bad I accused her of being in his employ on the subject, and though she let out a "Well I never!" and claimed to be mortally wounded by the accusation, she never entirely denied it, neither. All of her prattle was hogwash, of course, but the more she said it, the more she believed it and the more determined she became to seeing that I was matched up with him. She'd simply decided that my marrying Horace was the smartest thing in the world.

Some women are like that, intent on seeing that every other woman on the planet is situated in marriage even if the only eligible marriage partner is a skunk.

Finally, there came the night when we were slaving over a hot tub of soapy dishwater, cleaning up after a mess made by a couple of boarders who had dined on a pot of stew that had left Francine's chipped old china covered with grease. It was hotter than blazes, and we were so soaked with perspiration that them little white moths that are forever flitting around on an early autumn night were sticking to us like glue. In the dim light of the back yard, we looked like two children who'd been in a fight with a ripped up old feather pillow. We started laughing and shooing bugs and having a high old time in spite of the wickedly hot work.

Then she said it.

"Eva Rae, I can't put you up any longer. You have to leave."

Just like that.

"What?" I said, brushing fluttery moths outen my eyes.

"You and the children. You have to go. I love you like a sister. Better, in fact. But my business is all but lost on account of that boy of yours. You know as well as I that he scares away the boarders."

"Oh, he does not," I said.

"He certainly does," she said. "I've had three different men move out the last six weeks on account of they said they're afraid of him."

"He's only fourteen," I said.

"Well, when a grown man admits to being afraid of a

child, no matter how old he is, you know it's bad."

"Maybe you need to find a braver bunch of boarders," I said, trying to make it sound funny, but the way my voice cracked told us both that she'd hit home.

"Eva Rae, he scares me, too. I've told you that for years. It's hard to say this, but he's going to turn out just like that Dalton trash. Unless some righteous man takes charge of that boy, he's going to do murder, if he hasn't already. I can't have that on my conscience."

I ached to be able to tell her exactly how wrong-headed that notion was, and how Caleb was going to turn out just fine, thank you very much. But there was no getting around the truth of what she said.

"You need me, Francine," was all I could utter. I was on the cusp of telling her that without me, her drinking would be the ruination of her business a whole lot faster than would Caleb's shenanigans, but I decided against pressing my luck, which was a good thing, because she started to cry. Even in the darkness, I could see the streaks of the tears on her cheeks.

I actually put my arm around her. "How long do I have?"

"I don't know. Not beyond the end of next week. I just can't stand to have that child around any more."

I shuddered. She was deadly serious. And right.

God help me, but I knew in that instant what I had to do. Maybe what Francine called a righteous man wouldn't even be enough to prevent the coming tragedy I feared deep in my bones, but without the firm hand of a no-nonsense man, I knew Caleb didn't stand a chance in the world. Horace certainly wouldn't of been the one I would of chosen if I'd had a say in the matter, but it was crystal clear that I really didn't have a say at all.

I stood there for some time with my hands in that dishwater, thinking. Then I excused myself and went to bed without saying another word on the subject.

I tossed and turned all night long. There I was with three kids, the oldest coming on to a manhood that promised to be short and brutal. What Francine had put into words was something I'd been carrying locked away in my heart. For all I knew, Caleb had already committed rape or murder, and if he hadn't yet, it would only be a matter of time.

The simple truth was that I loved Caleb with every ounce of strength I had, but he was beginning to frighten me, too.

Anybody with a lick of sense could of raised my younger children. Dell was too little to be a bother, and Donald was so even-tempered a child that if I'd of told him to stand in the corner on his head, he'd of done it for half the day.

But saving Caleb was going to have to come through Horace Taylor one way or another, with him being either Caleb's daddy or his jailer.

I got up the next morning about half sick to my stomach at the thought of what I knew I had to do. I helped Francine with breakfast, though neither one of us said a word to the other, and we stuck to that silence all that day and the next while I thought and thought till I was afraid my head would bust open. Then on the third day after Francine told me we'd have to leave, I washed and dressed and walked the two long blocks to the livery stable, rented a pony and buggy and rode alone all the way to Sedan.

I intended just pulling that buggy up to the sheriff's office and going in and saying it right out, but my nerves got the better of me, and when I reached the little cemetery on the edge of town, I stopped and let the horse crop the grass for a while. It was peaceful there, and quiet, and the only person I saw was a gravedigger who doffed his hat and said "Mornin'" and then went about his business. Though I knew I couldn't put off what I'd come for forever, I truly feared that the twenty minutes I spent just sitting there was going to be the last peaceful moment I was likely to have in this life.

And for many a year, it was.

Anyway, I finally screwed up my courage, flicked the reins, and found the sheriff's office at the courthouse. Again, I sat outside for a few minutes, then I clumb down and headed for the door. My knees were like jelly. I knocked on the door and opened it and went inside without being invited.

There he sat, sweating in a faded red union suit without a shirt, though of course he was wearing trousers. I thought he'd hurt himself he jumped up from behind his desk so fast.

"Miz Eva," Horace said with a nod and a half smile, as if he knew what was coming. "What brings you here?"

I told him. Just blurted it out. He just stood there looking like a man who'd been pole-axed. I was beginning to think he'd changed his mind and regretted the offer when he let out a war whoop and grabbed his hat off his desk and threw it in the air and did a little jig, which set the floorboards to bouncing so hard I thought his three hundred pounds was going to go straight through to the ground a couple of feet below. Once he'd got over the initial excitement and caught his breath from a round of wheezing, he got all serious and told me he couldn't show me that little clapboard house on Elm Street on account of he was on duty and due in court to testify in a few minutes and had to freshen up, which I presumed meant he was going to put on a shirt, but would I wait around and let him show it to me after?

I swallowed hard and said I would.

As I sat there in that sheriff's office, wondering how I'd gotten myself into such a fix, time just plumb came to a standstill. That two hours was the longest of my life since the morning I'd waited to make good on my betrothal to Jack Ross.

At least the house, which he showed me when he came back from court, really was a nice little place. The undertaker had lived there for about a year with his wife, but when that woman died of the ague or some other melancholy disease, he'd moved into a room off the embalming parlor in his storefront mortuary. The house still had a bit of a woman's touch with doilies on the furniture the undertaker didn't want, lace curtains with precious few flyspecks, plank floors that had been scrubbed on hands and knees, and whitewashed walls inside and out. There was a sitting room and separate small formal parlor, although neither was big enough for Horace to do much more than turn around in, and two small bedrooms—a whole room just for the children, Horace said. The room that would be ours was about the size of the one I had at Francine's, and just the thought of being cooped up in there with that mountain of a man gave me a case of the heebie-jeebies, but I had to admit that that little house was purely a palace compared to anywhere else I'd ever lived. There was a small barn out back, with enough ground for grazing a horse and maybe even a cow.

"Real nice, ain't it?" he asked as we stood in that itty bitty parlor. "Nicest little place to be had in all of Sedan."

I allowed as how he had to be right about that and thanked him again for thinking of me and mine.

"I just want you to be happy, Miz Eva... Evie," he said, and then he spit onto the floor without benefit of cuspidor or nothing and ground that brown stain into the planking with the heel of his boot.

Somehow, I found the courage to hold out my hand, which he took in that big, sweaty paw of his.

So it was that I became formally betrothed to Horace Taylor.

I told myself I still had a choice, that I could get outen the deal if I just couldn't make my peace with it, but then Caleb ran off for three straight days later that week, and between sleepless nights worrying about that boy and wondering what I'd do when he did come home, I just gave up. If Horace could make that child toe the line, then whatever I had to put up with was nothing.

After all, hadn't I put up with worse?

Horace was never going to be equal of Reuben White-snake, but just maybe, I said to myself, I'd get another Jack Ross into the bargain—someone who wasn't so pretty on the outside but turned out to be decent and loving on the inside.

Well, I'm here to tell you that just because something works out once doesn't mean it will a second time. But I'll get to them details presently.

Horace and I tied the knot on the tenth day of October of 1897. He was forty-eight years old and looked every day of it, and I was twenty-nine, twice a widow, and if I'm going to be honest about it, I probably looked just about even in age with my new husband. It was a church wedding, the only one I ever had, though that Methodist church in Sedan wasn't nothing but the front parlor of a house belonging to the gentleman who ran the drygoods store and his biddy of a wife on account of the preacher rode the circuit and they didn't yet have a congregation large enough to pay for a proper building, though they had big plans for that parcel of land acrost the street from the courthouse.

It was a new preacher to me, too, the Reverend McGee who had spliced Reuben and me having up and left the country, reportedly to open a gambling hall up in South Dakota because he'd decided he wanted to die rich and being a Methodist preacher wasn't going to get that done. I've always hoped that story wasn't true but have no way of knowing. Anyway, this new preacher was a spindly little fellow with a shock of dirty brown hair, a chicken neck and an Adam's apple that bobbed up and down when he talked. He appeared to be frightened of my husband-to-be, which was pretty much the case with most every regular citizen in them parts but was especially true of the drygoods man. I had the impression that that gentleman had prodded the preacher to get through the ceremony as fast as ever he could just to get Horace outen his sitting room.

Still, the church ladies, most of whom I did not know, had decked out that parlor with an altar and a cross and a couple of brass candlesticks, and the woman of the house had decorated altar and walls with so many fall flowers—the last of the season's sunflowers, mostly—that I got a sneezing fit right in the middle of the ceremony and brought the whole shooting match to a dead standstill while I tried to get rid of the sniffles. I'm sure some of the ladies thought my sniffling was on account of the high emotion of the day, but it was really just them flowers.

Horace was sniffling some, too, but I figured that was from the rosewater he'd sprinkled so liberally on his head that he smelled like a lewd woman. He was outfitted in the cleanest clothes he owned, which I will give him credit for. His shirt and coat were a couple of sizes too small, having been bought in his younger days when he hadn't yet put on all the weight he now carried, and while I sneezed and sniffled he stood there getting progressively redder of face both from the perfume he'd doused himself with and how his collar was choking him. I wore a pale blue gingham that Francine had loaned me for the occasion. I'd taken it in considerable, but there was still enough dress there to hold me and about a half another one just like me. We must of looked a sight, that overstuffed man towering a foot over a scrawny woman in a blue dress borrowed from a bigger woman. Still, everyone who crowded into that parlor—and it seemed like most of Sedan was there because it was their sheriff getting married and they probably figured they had to—said we looked a picture. I know there were a few people who didn't come on account of they couldn't countenance their sheriff bringing half-breed kids into his home, but that didn't seem to bother him.

Anyway, afterward, Horace treated the men to beer brought in buckets from one of the outlawed saloons on the outskirts of town while the ladies sipped lemonade in the shade of a couple of cottonwoods in the mercantile owner's yard, made small talk, and pretended not to notice what their husbands were doing out back. Of course, anyone buying or drinking that beer was subject to arrest, our state being officially dry, but since it was the sheriff doing the buying and most of the drinking, all the other fellows figured they could enjoy themselves without much fear of the long arm of the law. The reverend said grace for us ladies, then sat with us looking as nervous as a cat. He studiously avoided the men, probably out of fear that someone would hand him a beer and then he'd have to decide whether he wanted to offend the groom and be sent straight to the pearly gates right then and there or take a nip and put his soul in dire jeopardy at some later date.

During all of this, my children appeared pretty well bewildered, which was only to be expected since I felt the same way, though I tried not to show it. My younger ones were in Francine's care both during and after the ceremony, and she kept them occupied as well as she could, which generally meant leaving Donald to his own devices, being the prim and proper little man that he was, and chasing after Dell every ten seconds to keep her fingers outen the frosting, first on the little cupcakes someone had contributed as a wedding present, and then the larger white cake that I'd bought with the few dollars I could scrape together.

Caleb was another story altogether. He hadn't said six words to me in the days since I told him I was going to wed Horace, and I believe to this day that the only way I actually got him to that ceremony was by threatening to chain him to his bed if necessary, then staying awake two nights running to keep an eagle eye on him. He had sat in the first row of chairs through the ceremony, but he'd spent his time with his head cocked to the side looking out the window. His face had an expression that I thought at the time must be like someone in prison wears when he thinks about freedom. I was just grateful that he didn't bolt right in the middle of things. After the wedding, when everyone stood in line to congratulate the bride and groom, he still sat right there with his arms crossed over his chest and his eyes closed. Then once the partying commenced, he just plunked down in the shade of a box elder tree and drew little designs in the dirt with a stick. I suppose he didn't take off on account of he was trying to be respectful of me, but nonetheless, he was the saddest looking thing in Kansas that day, and it like to broke my heart. I went over to him once and knelt down beside him to see if I could cheer him up, but he just turned his back to me.

"Missing Reuben won't bring him back," I said, but that brought no reaction whatsoever, and before I could go on, someone called me back to the table with the eats.

Well, once the feed was over and the men were tipsy on beer and the women sated on lemonade and cupcakes, Horace began shooing folks away. He stuffed a five dollar gold piece into the pastor's vest pocket, pumped the hand of the mercantile man, and led me and my little brood toward that tiny white house he was so proud of.

I was in a state, I'll tell you. I was half sick with worry about what Caleb was going to do and half sick with thinking about spending my first night with that huge old man.

Turned out I needn't have worried about neither of them things.

Caleb wasn't in any better a mood, but he'd apparently made enough peace with the situation to decide he wasn't going to be a burden to me, at least for that one day. He took the little kids offen my hands as soon as we got indoors and proceeded to get them ready for bed and even told them a story about cowboys and Indians and such, which I presume was something he made up on the spot. Then he tucked them into a little trundle bed in that second bedroom, washed up, and said good night just as calm and pleasant as if nothing had happened. I was amazed but of course more concerned than ever that he was planning on running away.

Horace, on the other hand, fell asleep in our one decent chair in the living room while trying to read the newspaper by lantern light, and when I wakened him, he allowed as how he'd just as soon sleep sitting up on account of how bad he snored. That part turned out to be the slap truth, too, although I couldn't prove it that first night, because I left him in the chair right where he was and so spent my first night as Mrs. Horace Taylor alone in the bedroom, writing a letter to my mother and trying to make the news sound cheerful.

That night was the first time I'd slept totally alone since I was thirteen years old, and it was wonderful. It didn't last, of course, but for that one night, I was in heaven.

I was right about Caleb. Two nights after the wedding, after he'd tucked the little ones into bed, he went outside as if to use the privy and the next thing I knew, I heard a horse galloping away in the night and knew it was him going somewhere. I told Horace right away, but he pooh-poohed it and said the boy just needed some air and that he'd be back when it got cold, which it was certainly doing most nights now that fall was upon us. If worst came to worst, the horse knew his way home, Horace said, which told me that Caleb being gone didn't matter to Horace half as much as that horse being somewhere other than in his stall. That came as quite a surprise, given all the blustering Horace had done about how the boy needed a man's steadying hand and how Caleb was going to turn into some kind of outlaw and all that.

Well, Caleb didn't come home that night, nor the next day and night, neither. The horse did, true to Horace's prediction, but the boy didn't come with him. I was half crazy with worry, but once again, Horace seemed not to think much of it. "Boy's got to find his way," he said over supper, then he took himself another slab of cake left over from the wedding, leaving crumbs for the little ones. "You want me to go looking, I will tomorrow."

"I'd like that," I said, although I sure as the dickens wanted him to get up outen that chair and go looking that very minute. He scowled at me, then gave me a sort of laugh.

If I hadn't realized it before, I did right then: if I'd made that marriage to keep Caleb out of trouble, I'd made a serious mistake.

It turned out there wasn't any need for Horace or anyone else to go on the hunt, for Caleb returned home sometime after midnight. I heard him rooting around in the fruit cellar for something to eat and got up and lit a lamp with the wick turned way down low so as not to wake my new husband. I wasn't worried about making too much noise on account of the racket that man put up with his snoring. Anyway, I found Caleb a piece of bread and some cold ham and buttermilk that one of the neighbors had given me for the kids, Horace not having bothered yet to get a cow. That boy wolfed the food down like he hadn't had a bite to eat since he ran off, which I supposed was the case. He was shivering with cold and filthy dirty, too. I started a fire in the big old cast iron stove to warm him up. When I tried to talk to him, telling him how scared I was for him and such, he just glared at me.

"You didn't need to marry that man," he said at last around a mouthful of bread and ham. He gave a nod of his head in the general direction of the bedroom.

"What I did or didn't have to do regarding Horace is no business of yours, Caleb," I said with a whole lot more starch than I felt. "He'll be a good father to you. You just have to let him."

His dark eyes narrowed until I could hardly see them in the dim coal oil light. "Reuben was my father," he said softly. "Won't be another."

"Give Horace a chance, boy," I said.

"Reuben was my father," he repeated. "Only one I ever had." Then he wiped his mouth with the back of his hand and headed toward his own bed.

I wasn't going to argue with him on that score, at least not on behalf of Clement Handley. If Jack Ross came up short in Caleb's eyes, it was probably just that he was too young to remember much about him. "You best clean up," I said. "I'll put some water on the stove to heat up." Though I didn't expect him to do it, he turned around and came back into the kitchen and waited dutifully while I het water and found a bar of soap.

"Good night, then, son," I said, and I patted him on the arm. I could feel a shudder run all the way through him.

"Good night, Mother Eva," he said in such a cold way that it brought a sudden burst of tears to my eyes and I had to hurry off to bed so he wouldn't see me crying.

After that, the days and weeks just sort of ran together. Horace worked long hours at the sheriff's office, sometimes even taking his meals there, which I had to carry to him in a tin pail as quick as ever I could so the food wouldn't get cold. I kept the house, which wasn't much of a chore compared to all the work I'd done at Francine's, and the little kids settled well enough into our new life. Donald took to climbing onto Horace's lap when that man read the newspaper, and Dell did, too, though she seemed a good deal more timid than Donald around her new daddy, especially when he went to tickling her or asking for a kiss.

For his part, Caleb grew quieter and quieter, until I was half way to my wit's end trying to think of something that would cheer him up. Maybe Christmas would do it, that holiday being just a matter of weeks away by then. The only bright spot was that my eldest stayed home most nights, and even had started going to school, though the teacher, a Presbyterian gentleman with weak eyes and rounded shoulders, said he was a hopeless case for learning since he had no interest in it and a will too strong to be cajoled by use of the willow switch.

Then came the day a couple of weeks before Christmas when all hell broke loose.

It started over boiled potatoes.

We'd just sat down at our little table to a supper of potatoes and canned chicken and kraut donated by a neighbor on account of our own larder was mostly empty. As he usually did, Horace just mumbled a couple of words of grace nobody else could understand and tucked into the spuds, filling his mouth till his cheeks bulged out. I was mashing up a bit of potato for Dell when outen the corner of my eye, I saw something fly by.

Horace looked up from his plate. "What in tarnation was that?" he asked, spewing bits of food as he did.

I looked at Caleb. He was staring at his plate. Calm as anything, he reached out, picked up a quarter of a potato, and hurled it as hard as he could into the wall.

"By God, boy, what's the matter with you?" Horace thundered, spitting even more potato onto the table.

Caleb just looked at him, picked up another bit of potato, and let fly all over again. "They're cold," he said, looking straight into his stepfather's face.

Well, that did it. Horace was up and around that table so quick it was like magic. When he got a head of steam up, he could move with amazing speed for such a big man. Anyhow, Caleb jumped outen his chair sideways to avoid a swipe from Horace's big right paw, which whistled by the boy's head by inches. Horace lunged again, and this time, Caleb wasn't fast enough to escape. Horace's open hand caught him on the side of the jaw and sent him spinning around like a top.

In a heartbeat, I was up and trying to get between them, but not in time. Horace knocked the chair outen the way and slammed into Caleb before the boy had a chance to recover his balance. This time, my husband backhanded him hard enough I was afraid he was going to knock teeth loose. But Caleb wasn't one to quit in a fight, neither, and somehow or another, he brought up a knee into Horace's crotch, which ended the fight, at least for a moment.

I yelled for them to stop it, but by then there was no need for that. There we were: Caleb sprawled against the sideboard with a fair gusher of blood running from his nose, Horace crumpled up on the floor groaning, both little ones squalling like they'd been stuck by hat pins, and me not knowing which one to go to. So I just started picking up the broken crockery and spilled food.

"You ever do that again, boy, I'm going to kill you," is what Horace wheezed when he'd caught his breath enough to talk.

"Not if I kill you first," that boy said.

It was plain as anything that the both of them meant exactly what they'd said.

This time, I fairly screamed "Stop it!" and, dropping the shards I'd been scooping up, I got between them in hopes of preventing murder right then and there. I confess I was shielding Caleb from Horace more than the other way around, which brought the blackest look from my husband that I've ever seen on a human being.

"You going to let that boy sass me like that?" Horace barked, though there wasn't much power behind it on account of he was still bent over in pain.

"You're the one threatened murder first," I said.

"It's a father's right."

"You ain't my father and never will be, you fat old pig!" Caleb shouted from behind me.

Well, I had to do something at that. I spun and reared up to give that boy a cuff of my own, but thought better of it when I saw that blood all over his face and shirt. Instead, I took him by the shoulders and shook him. "You mind your mouth, son, or I'll get the soap."

"Soap! Soap's too good for that one!" Horace said with as much sarcasm as he could.

I saw Caleb was about to say something else, but I put a finger to his lips and looked him straight in the eye, and for the moment, at least, he held off.

By this time, Horace had managed to pull himself up and was reaching around me, trying to grab ahold of Caleb's arm or shirt. Somehow or other, I had the strength to keep him away. Keeping myself between the two, I steered Caleb back to my own chair and pushed him into it.

"Now you eat them spuds," I said, pointing to the little pile on my plate.

He looked up at me.

"Eat them," I said.

After a second or two, he nodded, picked up my fork, and put a quarter of a potato into his mouth. Then I turned around to face my husband.

"Don't you ever strike this child like that again," I said.

That appeared to flummox Horace for real. "You're siding with the boy?"

"No, I'm not. He's eating the spuds. But I'll not have talk of murder in my house!"

He just blinked at me and stood there for another minute with the color rising to his face and his jaws working till I was sure he'd crack his teeth. If ever I've seen the look of pure murderous violence in a man's eyes, it was in Horace's at that moment. I was convinced he was going to take a swipe at me. He didn't though. Instead, he just kicked at one of the bits of potato that Caleb had thrown, swore under his breath, and stomped off. A couple of minutes later, I heard the front door slam, and I knew he was headed to the office, where he'd likely spend the night.

"Don't you ever do that again," I said to Caleb, who was now picking through the kraut, eating a little here and there.

"He ain't my pa," he said.

"So you've told me. But he's all the pa you're going to get. Don't do it again."

He looked at me. The blood had dried into a crusty brown smear on his face, and I could see his right eye was beginning to blacken. I confess I was hoping to see tears, but there weren't any.

"Yes'm," he said softly.

It was the last time he ever threw potatoes, too, but it wasn't close to the last time them two men of mine went at it hammer and tong with me in the middle. Christmas was a grim affair, and no sooner had the children opened their little presents—I'd bought Caleb a whole box of pencils in hopes that he'd take more interest in school and I'd managed to carve a little horse for Donald outen a piece of stovewood and stitched up a corn husk and gingham doll for Dell—than Caleb went outside to use the privy and once again took off with Horace's horse. This time, Horace swore up and down if that horse wasn't home by daybreak the next day, he was going to get the judge to swear out a warrant and have Caleb hung for a horse thief. Fortunately, the horse was back before dark, but Caleb didn't come home for four days. The weather wasn't so cold that I worried about him freezing to death, but there was a cold rain and then mud everywhere, so when he did return, he looked like a pig that had spent days in a mud puddle. He caught his death of cold from that escapade, which kept him from running off yet again at least until after New Year's.

For his part, Horace just quit talking to the boy or even about him. When the two of them were together, Horace wouldn't look at him, and instead lavished his attention on Donald and Dell, bouncing them on his knee and acting for all the world like them two kids tickled him plumb to death, all the while making it a point to let one and all know that as far as he was concerned, Caleb didn't even exist.

By that point, I'm not certain the boy cared one way or the other. I begun hearing whispers about some things that were happening when he ran off, and there wasn't any of it that was good. I'd of settled for him playing boyhood pranks turning over privies and such, but I also had to admit he wasn't a boy any longer, and though it broke my heart to think it, he'd graduated to thefts and worse. Yearling bulls shot through the spine so they'd suffer while they died, barns set afire that burned up a family's whole remaining hay crop, family dogs poisoned with strychnine and other such depredations seemed to occur at exactly the same time as Caleb's absences. I hoped against hope that it wasn't him, that this was all some kind of terrible coincidence, but I reckon I knew better. Of course I didn't tell Horace, but then I didn't have to. As sheriff, he was charged with investigating them crimes, and a blind man could of seen that he had his own suspicions who the culprit was. Turned out that most of the folks in Chautauqua County felt pretty much the same way.

At first, it did seem that as long as no person got hurt directly, Sheriff Taylor wasn't going to work too hard at publicly dealing with the situation. Whether that was Horace's way of trying to be kind to me or whether it was because he, too, was afraid of Caleb at some level, I do not know, since we never discussed it. He would huff and puff about how criminals were taking over the county, and on the rare nights that Caleb came home for supper, he'd grill him about where he'd been and what he'd been up to and what did he know about so-and-so's corn crib catching fire without ever making a direct accusation.

That all changed the day Lemuel Magruder's wife took a spill outen her buckboard and broke her shoulder so bad she never again had the proper use of her left arm. Someone had sawed the front axle nearly in two so that the first hard turn that buggy made, the axle snapped and tossed the driver out onto her head and shoulder. The Magruders ran the apothecary, so they were amongst the cream of the social crop, you might say, and her being so badly injured was absolutely the talk of the town. What was also part of the chatter was that Caleb had been seen hanging around the Magruders' shop, asking if he could do little chores in exchange for a few pennies in payment. Several folks had seen Lemuel shoo him away more than once, and others had been present when he told my boy in no uncertain terms that his kind wasn't wanted there and he wasn't to hang around the store ever again or he'd have him arrested for loitering. The mishap with the buckboard occurred the very next day.

That was it: Horace had to do something. Even I knew that. Caleb was home that week, or at least he was taking his evening meals at home and sleeping in the second bedroom with the little kids, and the very night I heard he was being tied to the accident, I took him aside before supper and told him that if he'd done the deed as it was being talked about, then he should just confess and take his medicine. While I surely didn't want to see him get arrested, which I figured was coming, neither did I want to see him bolt town and be chased down by some blood-thirsty posse.

"It's all right, Mother Eva," he said, and he patted my hand, like he was trying to gentle a colt.

Somewhere off in the distance, I could hear Horace's horse come clopping along, bearing its burden toward our little stable. Our new cow mooed, too, by way of a hello to her stable mate. Cool as could be, Caleb washed his hands in the basin by the back door, dried them on a towel, winked at me, and grabbed his coat offen the hook, it being the middle of a cold and blustery March. "Don't wait supper on me."

"Caleb, don't," I said.

But he just winked again, and before I could say another word, he was gone.

And right into the teeth of trouble, which he must of known. It wasn't two seconds before I heard Horace's booming voice, then Caleb's thinner tenor. I grabbed my own wrap off the hook and headed outside. There they were, Horace astride his mount, not three feet from Caleb, and both of them yelling at the top of their lungs. Before I could get to them, Horace pulled his revolver, bent over, and backhanded my boy with the barrel, sending him sprawling. In the next second, Horace was off the horse, holding the cocked gun pointed directly at Caleb.

"Dear God, no!" I shouted.

"You stay outen this, woman!" Horace shouted back without even looking at me. "Last time he's ever goin' to sass me!"

Caleb tried to move, but Horace swung the gun again, cracking him in the back of the skull. He raised the gun for yet another blow, and I dove straight at him, hitting him in the midsection and knocking him back against his horse's barrel. The animal sidestepped, and Horace fell. I was on him like a panther.

"Run, Caleb," I shouted, but only once, as Horace cuffed me with his free hand, tossing me aside like I was a rag doll. Then he was up and standing over the boy again. Like I said, Horace could move fast for a big man when he wanted to.

He cocked his pistol. I shouted something, but the gun went off. The yellow lick of flame from the barrel headed skyward: Horace had fired into the air.

"Next one goes in your ear, youngster," he growled, and he pulled Caleb to his feet by the scruff of his neck. Caleb just hung there, limp.

"He's hurt," I said, scrambling to my feet.

"Lucky he ain't dead, Missus," Horace sneered. "He ever sass me like that again, he'll wish I'd killed him this time. And you, too."

With that, he tossed Caleb over his horse's withers, clumb on himself, and turned the animal back in the direction of the courthouse.

"We'll finish our discussion when I get home," Horace said, and he put spurs to the horse.

When I went back into the house, there was Dell, standing in the middle of the kitchen, all big eyed and serious looking. Donald was already sitting at the supper table with his bib tucked into the collar of his shirt.

"Ain't Daddy coming to supper?" that boy asked as if for all the world nothing had happened.

All I could do was weep.

A Troubled Time

FROM THAT MOMENT ON, I don't know which I was more scared of—Caleb's violent, senseless crimes, or my husband's swinging fists and readiness to pull a gun.

Truth to tell, I was on the receiving end of far too many blows from Horace's big ham hands, mostly when I defended Caleb or roused his anger in some other way. Looking back on it now, I know I should of just gotten shed of Horace right then and there and took the kids back to Chautauqua, or Missouri for that matter. But I didn't. It was as if I just gave up, and I've been paying the price for that ever since.

Caleb did his time in jail over the Magruder's buggy accident. Though he never admitted doing the deed, and there was never a trial of any sort, Horace kept him locked up for two weeks, giving him only bread and water and keeping him in a cell so cold there was a sheet of ice on the wall every morning where his breath froze to the stone. Horace went on and on about how he'd called in a favor from Judge Ezekial Latham up in Elk County, who was traveling the circuit in them days and serving the Chautauqua County court when Caleb was arrested. According to Horace, Judge Latham, being a Masonic pal of his, agreed not to send the boy to prison on Horace's assurance that he'd personally keep him from any more mischief. Of course, there was also the matter of some payment to the Magruders, which Horace said he'd take outen my hide by making me take in wash for the neighbors.

"I heard you were pretty good at it when you was working for them Chinks down to Chautauqua," he said, making a lewd gesture as he did so. "Reckon you'll be happy to provide them services here to one and all if it keeps that precious kid of your'n from making the trip to Lancaster," he added with a laugh, meaning the state prison.

What was I to say? Working my hands raw with near boiling water and lye soap was, indeed, a small price to pay. So that's how I came to being more charwoman than ever I'd been at Francine's, working from sunup to sundown boiling laundry for what seemed like half the town of Sedan, and for certain all of the really uppity folks that Horace wanted to impress. Sometimes I'd meet one of the ladies I was doing the laundry for, and often as not, she'd look right past me like I wasn't even there unless Horace was with me, in which case there would be pleasantries all around.

It wasn't my first lesson in how folks can be, and it wouldn't be the last, neither. In my experience, men are often crude and thoughtless, but women go outen their way to be rude to folks they think are beneath them.

Anyway, when Caleb came home from that two week stint in jail, it was certain that he'd changed. I could see that jail had made him absolutely terrified of Horace, which broke my heart on account of I couldn't remember seeing him afraid of anything or anyone before that. What Horace did to him while he was locked up, I don't know to this day. Neither of them ever spoke of it, at least not to me, but it must of been something terrible. I do know that Caleb had purplish welts all over his body, and he walked with a little limp ever afterward, as if his left ankle hurt him.

Then there was the subject of school.

Now, book learning never was his strong suit, and having missed school during his time in jail, that weak-chinned old

Presbyterian school master made it plain that he wasn't welcome to come back. I pretty much gave up on having the boy ever go to school again, what with he at least could read and write and was fourteen years old with a changing voice and a shadow of dark hair coming on his upper lip, but for reasons I couldn't fathom, Horace started to harp about how education was what Caleb needed to set him on the straight and narrow. Given that the local school didn't want him, I said I didn't know what we could do, but Horace assured me he could get the boy into a school up near the town of Independence, north of Coffeyville, where the schoolmaster was expert at handling tough cases. When I asked around, all I heard was that the gentleman in question was known for using a horse whip on troublemakers, and that one of his young charges was blind in one eye from a beating. Whether he knew the first thing about teaching the three R's, I could not tell.

Of course I balked, and so did Caleb.

But Horace wasn't having any of that. With his newfound zeal to get Caleb what he called a proper education coupled with the boy's fear of him, Horace was holding all the cards. So one day he just said flat out at a breakfast Caleb happened to be attending that the two of them were going to ride up to Independence to see about getting into that school. I thought sure as shooting the boy would run, but he didn't. He just sat there stirring his oatmeal and looking for all the world like a child who had lost every last friend on earth. I tried to argue that we needed to think on it some, but that didn't faze my husband, who just wiped his mouth on his shirtsleeve and told the boy to get ready. Ten minutes later, the two of them were mounted up, Horace on his big gelding and Caleb on a young mule that didn't seem too happy about it.

"When will you be home?" I called after them, not exactly knowing which one I was addressing.

"Supper tomorrow," my man said. The boy just looked

over his shoulder at me, then hunkered down into his coat.

It was the last time I would see him for three weeks, and when he did come home, it was clear that the stories about that schoolmaster being a brute were true.

It was midday in early April if memory serves, and about as beautiful as a day can get in them parts, which means it was near on to heaven. Flowers were in bloom, birds were chirping in the yard, and even the cow looked happy as she cropped the bright green grass of the side yard. I was doing my usual chores, which meant I had the washtub full of hot water, soap, and the townsfolks' unmentionables while another tub of water was heating up on a wood fire nearby. I was fixing to make soap, too, so I had water trickling through a box filled with yesterday's ashes to collect the lye I'd mix with bacon grease and such other fat as I could find. It was devilishly hard work, but on a day like that I didn't hardly mind.

Then, just like that, there he was, standing in front of me, as if he'd appeared outen thin air.

"Momma Eva, look what I brought you," he said as if he'd only been gone a few minutes, and he handed me a small grass basket with three peeping chicks inside. "Meadowlarks," he said. "I think a cat got their mother."

He tried to smile, but had a tough time of it. He'd lost weight in the weeks he'd been away, and from bruises on his face and hands and the rends in his shirt and trousers, it looked for all the world as if he'd been in a tussle with a bear.

"What happened to you, boy?" I said as I put down my stirring stick and rushed to him. He stiffened when I took him in my arms and gave him a hug, though I don't know whether out of embarrassment or pain. When he did so, I could see a mark on his neck like a burn, as if someone had laid a hot iron against his skin.

"Nothin'," was all he said as he tried to pull away.

"You come inside and let me clean you up."

I stepped back and took a longer look at him. There was a mat of dried blood in his hair, and the Lord Himself only knew what marks were covered up by the clothes that hung on his scrawny frame. "And maybe get some bread and ham into you, too."

He just shook his head. "Ain't staying," he said. "Just wanted to see you 'fore I left."

"Caleb, you're not leaving. You're hurt."

"Yes I am," he said. "Leaving, I mean. You take care of these, please?" he said. He tipped his head toward the little nest of meadowlarks in my hand, gave me a look that liked to broke my heart, and turned to go.

But I was quicker. I dropped the chicks and snatched him up, and in spite of the boy's size, he just sort of melted in my arms, he was that weak. I carried him into the house, set him on a footstool near the wash basin, and wet a rag to see if I could clean him up some. I expected him to bolt the minute I turned my back, but there were tears in the corners of his eyes, and he just let me work. The little kids, who had been napping in their bedroom, had awakened and come out to watch us, too. Donald looked for all the world like a child watching a grown-up curry a horse, with sort of a mix of curiosity and boredom. Dell, when I glanced at her, had a dark and brooding look, as if she was angry about something, but neither of them made a sound.

I was still tending the boy's injuries some minutes later, trying to get some kind of word outen him about what had happened, though with absolutely no results, when the front door burst open like someone had set off a bomb on the other side. I jumped so that I spilled the basin, but Caleb just turned and looked at that door almost like he'd expected it to happen.

It was Horace, of course, and I have to say, never in life up to that moment had I ever seen a man look madder than he did. His face was the color of boiled beets, and I could fairly see his heartbeat pulsing in the veins of his neck where it overflowed his buttoned-up shirt collar. Compared to what followed, the fight over the spuds at Christmas wasn't nothing but child's play.

"Boy, you have some explaining to do!" Horace roared, and he crossed from that front door to the kitchen in about three long strides and snatched Caleb by the scruff of his neck.

"You stop, Horace. He's injured," I said, or rather started to say, because I finished that short speech on my back on the floor, where I'd been sent when Horace cuffed me. Before I could get to my feet, my husband had Caleb lifted clean off the ground and was carrying him like a rag doll back toward the front door.

Caleb must of had more strength than you could image would exist in that slim body of his, especially as beat up as he was, because somehow, he pulled away and actually punched Horace hard enough in the stomach to bend him over with a sort of whoofing sound as the air went outen him. But he didn't let go, and he caught Caleb acrost the face with the open palm of his free hand.

"Stop it!" I screamed as I clambered onto my feet and went charging toward the both of them. "The boy's hurt!"

By this time, Caleb was swinging wild, and Horace, not to be caught by surprise again, was holding him out at arm's length. He turned his big body to block me from reaching Caleb, and then just flipped the boy away, sending him crashing into the wall.

I tried to get around Horace, but he put one of them big paws on me and held me back.

"He's hurt!" I said as I tried to get a good look at Caleb, who had crumpled into a heap on the floor. "Can't you see that?"

"Not as hurt as he's going to be, Missus," Horace said, still blocking my way. He was already stripping off his belt, which he doubled up. "The sonofabitch run off from his schooling."

"He's been abused!" I shouted, but Horace just flipped that belt backward toward me, and the sting of leather acrost my face sent me reeling. Almost instantly, I could feel the trickle of blood start from my nose.

"He's ungrateful and he's a thief, that's what he is!" Horace shouted back at me.

Grasping the two ends of the belt in his right hand, he bent over and advanced on Caleb. When he was within range, he started to swing. That belt made a popping sound almost like a whip against Caleb's thin shoulders and back. I tried once more to get past my husband, but he swung his left hand and swatted me clear into the kitchen. I fell onto my backsides, but almost instantly I was part-way to my feet again.

Horace must of known it even though he was bent over Caleb, because he whirled and came at me again with that belt. He held it high but this time didn't bring it down on me.

"I'll whip you till you can't stand up straight if you give me any more back sass!" he shouted, and it was clear he meant it. I swear there was murder in his eyes. Spit was coming outen his mouth, and I more than half expected him to have a stroke right on the spot. But once the threat was made, he whirled again and commenced to beating on Caleb. He swung that belt time after time, each blow landing with a pop, and he only let up when he was gasping for air from the exertion. He stood over Caleb for a minute, then threaded the belt back into his trousers, almost as dainty as if he was getting ready for church, and then kicked him hard with the toe of his big brogans.

"You ever run off again, you little sonofabitch, I'll hunt you down and kill you dead," he said with a snarl. "And this time I mean it. No child I'm responsible for is ever going to make a fool of me!"

"Go to hell," Caleb said almost softly, and that belt come outen Horace's trousers again as fast as a whip and popped again and again on the boy's back and shoulders, until Horace was so winded he had to lean against the wall to catch his breath. "You're going to jail this time, boy, and not for no two weeks, neither." He kicked again, then turned to me. "Woman, you get him cleaned up, so he's presentable before the judge!" And with that, he stomped outen the house, slamming the door behind him.

I don't believe the whole thing took five minutes.

I crawled over to Caleb and cradled him in my arms. His shirt was torn through, and there was blood on his back and on one ear and an angry red welt already growing along the side of his jaw that seemed to match the mark I'd already seen on his neck.

I couldn't do anything more than just hug him closer.

At one point, I realized that the little kids were still standing in the kitchen watching us, but I couldn't even bring myself to look at either one of them.

"Ma, I got to use the privy," Donald said after a time in a sort of a whine. "And your nose is bleeding." I answered something—I don't remember what—and wiped at the blood on my lip and mouth with the back of my hand. Dell just watched for a minute, then turned around and went back to her room and shut the door behind her. Donald came back in a few minutes later with a mess of muddy grass in his hand.

"Look what I found," he said softly.

It was that forgotten bird's nest, smashed flat and dripping blood where Horace must of stomped on it. Caleb took one look at it and tried to reach for it, but I held him back in a tight hug, the tears running down my cheeks and wetting my collar.

"Donald, take it outside," I told him. "It's just birds," I said to my other son.

Caleb let out a deep groan as little Donald left with the bloody mess.

"What was it that you did?" I asked after a while.

"Nothing. Just left," he said through lips already swelling

to twice their normal size. "You ever let that bastard hit you again, I'll kill him."

I let it go, not knowing how to respond. All these threats of murder scared me to death, because I knew both of them meant it.

"You didn't do anyhing?" I asked, as if his last statement had never happened.

"I mean it, Momma Eva."

"I asked you a question, Caleb. What did you do?"

He sort of shrugged there in my arms. "Just left. That's all."

"Did you steal anything?"

He shook his head, but he couldn't look me in the eye, neither.

"What did you take?" I asked.

"Pocket watch," he said under his breath.

"You stole the teacher's pocket watch?"

"Bastard hit me with the fob. Big old lump of brass. Just swung it at me."

"Watch your language," I said, but without much force behind it. "You shouldn't steal, Caleb." That sounded even weaker.

He took a deep breath. "He got mad at me, pulled out that watch, and just swung it into my ear. I grabbed the chain, jerked it outen his hand, and ran."

"Where's the watch?"

"I threw it away."

"Where?"

"I smashed it on a rock and threw it into the Verdigris River. Bastard ain't never going to hit no one with that fob again."

There was something in his eyes that just suddenly made my blood run cold. "You did more than that, didn't you, boy?"

"What if I did?"

"What did you do?" I'd grabbed ahold of his arms so tight

I must of stopped the blood.

He just pushed himself up to standing. "Nothing. Absolutely nothing. I can't help it if you don't believe me." He positively looked like a different person what with the fire in his dark eyes and the way his face was swole up so bad. "Now I'm leaving, Momma Eva, and you can't stop me."

And I didn't even try, to my undying shame.

On his run from that schoolyard up near Independence all the way down to Sedan, Caleb had cut fences, spooked cattle, thrown rocks through windows, and committed just about every other kind of petty destruction he could think up. I don't know that he harmed man nor beast directly, though he might of. What had made Horace so angry was certainly the shame of "his boy" running off from that teacher, but probably more so the need to pay back all the folks who had seen Caleb doing the devilment as he ran back to us—to me. And see him they had. It was as if the boy was slap bent on making certain that every person he caused trouble for knew exactly who'd done it. More than once, he even trotted up onto a front porch, knocked on the door, and waited to heave a brick through a window until the lady of the house was standing there watching.

So it was at our house. All these years later, I've come to understand that Caleb showed up at home more with the intent of provoking Horace than saying good-by to me, and of course that big lummox of a husband more than obliged.

Horace swore out a warrant for Caleb's arrest that very afternoon and went into a fury when he came home and found the boy gone, though he must of known that Caleb would run off and perhaps even hoped he would, especially because of what happened next. He threatened to whip me again, then tossed over the laundry tubs in the yard just so I'd have to start over on cleaning all them clothes. He ranted and raved and came at me once, actually swinging his big fists. I picked up a stick of firewood the size of a man's forearm and threw it at him, clipping him on the left cheek and drawing blood under his eye. I was certain he'd beat me senseless for that, but instead he backed off, and in that very second, I realized my husband was just a coward who could be mean as a rattlesnake in August right up until somebody called his bluff.

Which, I'm sorry to say, pretty much set the pattern for our lives together from that time forward.

Why I didn't leave him right then, I'll never know. I'd like to think it was because I wanted a proper home for Dell and Donald, but I'm not so sure of that. I could of moved back to Francine's yet again, or I could of packed up kit and caboodle and headed somewhere else—back to Missouri, or even Gove County, I suppose—but I'd put down roots, after a fashion. I had acquaintances if not friends, I had children to look after, I had a dead husband in the ground thirty odd miles to the south, and a live one right there. Though we never shared the marriage bed ever again, nor hardly spoke a civil word to one another from one day to the next, we were married, and that meant something to me. Maybe to the both of us. I don't know.

Or maybe I was just as big a coward as Horace was.

Anyway, our life settled into a dreary pattern. I'd launder for the folks around, squirreling away the occasional nickel or dime that came my way as a sort of tip from the handful of ladies who knew what I was up against and apparently felt sorry for me. At first, I wouldn't take them little coins when I'd drop off their clean unmentionables and their husband's shirts and socks and trousers, saying that what they were paying Horace was money enough. I didn't want their charity, you see. But after a time, I decided it wasn't charity at all, but rightful payment for the work I was doing for them.

That's what Charley McGuane said, anyway. He was Horace's young deputy. He and his wife were Scotch from back east somewhere. Why they'd come to southern Kansas I never did know, but they were decent, kindhearted people who didn't put on airs. So when Charley whispered that I'd earned the extra nickels when I took him his trousers and the missus's fluff, I believed him.

I never asked for money from the McGuanes nor anybody else, but I surely did take it when it was offered, and I always made sure it was put away someplace where Horace wouldn't find it.

At home, I'd cook breakfast, get the children dressed and put to doing whatever little chores there were to do or send them off to school in the winter time. Come supper, I'd feed Horace, who'd taken to eating alone, then I'd feed the children, then finally sit down myself and eat what might be left. When Horace and I talked at all, which wasn't often, it usually turned into an argument, and frequently enough, into a fight with him shoving or slapping and me letting fly with whatever might be at hand. I got good at ducking his fists, and he got good at ducking cups and saucers and, more than once, kitchen knives.

Dell and Donald just took it all in, wide-eyed. There was fretting and tears at first, then not much of that.

As time went on, it was clear that Donald had picked sides in the fight. He craved Horace's attention and would sit at his feet when my husband read the paper or just snoozed in his chair, and whatever Horace did around the house (which wasn't much, I'll tell you), Donald would stand there in awe, as if watching a man pound a nail or chop a bit of kindling was some kind of magic show. For his part, Horace would wink or pat the boy on the head once in a while, but for the most part, he just ignored him.

Not so with Dell. As she grew, Horace seemed to take real delight in Dell. He would bounce her on his knee or tickle her on the soles of her feet, and he always asked for a big hug and kiss before she went to bed at night, calling her his little Indian princess. Strange as it seemed to me at the time, all that attention only made her more aloof when it came to her step-daddy. I do believe that Donald would of killed for the attention his little sister was getting, though he appeared not to hold that against Horace, while she ignored the man who showed such delight in having her on his lap.

It took a long time for the citizens of Sedan to get over what had happened to Mrs. Magruder and the vandalism Caleb had committed after running away from the schoolmaster up in Independence, but eventually I do believe they forgot about them things, or at least put them outen their mind as long as there weren't any other depredations. The townsfolk were just happy not to see hide nor hair of that boy, and from what I could tell, that included my own children, for neither Donald nor Dell ever asked about him, not even once, which liked to broke my heart.

Where he went, I did not know then and do not know now. I've always presumed he went south, into Osage country, where he would of felt most at home, though he could of gone all the way to Texas or even Mexico for all I know. That first spring and summer after he left, I'd occasionally ride down to Chautauqua or even acrost the Line to our old home village looking for him, but no one in Chautauqua nor none of Reuben's family, either, had laid eyes on him, or so they said. It was like as if he'd just disappeared from the face of the earth.

I can't begin to tell how many times I cursed the decision that had taken me outen Chautauqua and put me into Horace Taylor's home. Though I knew in my heart that if I'd of kept on working for Francine and the Chins—and if they'd of let me—Caleb would of continued to be a problem with no right end in sight, I was absolutely certain that my marriage had only deepened the trouble and hastened the day I'd lose my boy. Francine always told me it was for the best that he was gone, though she was kind enough not to say "and good riddance," which was always on the lips of the biddies in Sedan.

As summer turned to autumn, then to winter, then another year was upon us and yet another and another after that, I spent less time searching and more time praying for the return of my lost lamb. I'd never been the religious sort, exactly, no matter how many Sundays I sat in the pew and listened to the sermon. In my experience, church people were only better than the run-of-the-mill unchurched citizen for about an hour a week, or maybe two if you threw in Sunday School, but with the burden of Caleb on my heart, I just naturally turned to the Good Book and the Lord for help, though there didn't seem to be any heavenly help forthcoming, at least not so as I could tell. Not that I really expected any.

After a time, I just figured that if my boy was alive somewhere, that was about all the answered prayer I could hope for.

Meantime, the throwing and ducking at home just went on and on, with the two little kids growing like weeds but keeping mostly to themselves.

At long last, we did hear something about Caleb, though the news was far from good.

There had been some trouble over to Bartlesville, some miles east of Reuben's little Osage village. Some big shots in that town had recently drilled an oil well, then another and another, which was bringing a whole new class of folks into the region. Them smelly black gushers were making money hand over fist for the gentlemen that put up the money, and that in turn made one of the Bartlesville banks a whole lot more flush with cash than were most banks in them parts. Well, where there's banks full of money, there's just about always a pack of scalawags waiting to steal it, and that's just what some fellows did. One of them got shot up in the process and another got arrested, and only the boy holding their horses managed a clean getaway.

Although that boy's description could of fit a thousand young'uns in that country, the Oklahoma Territory authorities south of the Line had wanted posters with Caleb's name on them distributed throughout the country roundabout quicker than you could blink. I've always suspicioned that Horace was the one who suggested Caleb's name to the sheriff in Bartlesville, but whether that was the case or not, he did get his hands on a stack of them posters and brought one home to show me. I thought he was going to go apoplectic he was so worked up over it.

"Surprised it took this long, but there it is!" he thundered, shoving a poster under my nose for the hundredth time. "There's your precious boy, with a price on his head!"

When I pointed out the price was only fifty dollars, that made him spit and sputter, and it wasn't any time at all before we were heaving things at each other and scaring the daylights outen the children. Of course, it hurt me to the quick to see that reward hanging over Caleb, no matter what the size, but by then I was determined not to let Horace nor anyone else see my shame. I took to walking as tall and proud as I could and greeted the biddies with a hearty "Good morning, ladies," even if I knew they were talking about me behind their hands. In secret, though, I was worried sick that Caleb would be arrested and sent to prison—or worse.

The next time we heard of him was later that year, or maybe the next—it's hard to remember. That came in the form of another wanted poster, this one made out by the chief constable of Wichita. Caleb had gotten himself arrested for vagrancy there, and in the course of his time in jail, they'd found out he was wanted in Oklahoma. Since Oklahoma Territory didn't have a proper prison, they were fixing to transfer him to the Kansas State Prison in Lansing, but he managed to escape. Though he was sixteen or seventeen at the time, apparently he was still slight enough of build to slip through some gap in the bars or climb over a wall. Either way, he was gone. Horace sputtered some more, and I said my prayers real hard, hoping Caleb would go somewhere far away and reform from his life of lawlessness.

Of course, it was not to be.

As time went by, it seemed there were always rumors of Caleb running with this gang or that wild bunch. There were reports of horse theft, which Horace was certain were true on account of the boy having taken his horse back in the early days of our marriage, never mind that the animal always came back on its own. There were stories of Caleb rustling stock, and even shooting an Indian woman in Pawhuska, which was the one tale I was sure was absolutely false. There was no way that young man, having spent the only happy days of his life in an Osage village, surrounding by loving step-aunts, would of harmed a hair on an Osage woman's head.

There were even rumors that Caleb was heading up his own gang of desperadoes, robbing anyone who had a nickel to his name, but I took that with a grain of salt as well on account of Caleb had always been a loner, and a loner he was likely to stay. He was certainly capable of thievery or outright face-to-face robbery if it came down to it, but I couldn't imagine him with the patience or temperament to work in cahoots with any sort of like minded bunch, that bank robbery in Bartlesville notwithstanding.

Every time Horace would come home huffing and puffing about some miscreant who'd stolen a horse or burned a barn or robbed a bank, I could see in his eyes that he was taking pleasure in my torment, for such it was. Even if the criminal in question turned out to be a renegade from south of the Line or some poor homesteader done in by rotgut whiskey, the simple truth was that it just as easily could of been my boy. Of course, I'd never give Horace the satisfaction of thinking he'd gotten under my skin, but he did, and there were plenty of nights that I'd lie awake staring at the ceiling, wondering over and over what I could of done different to save that boy from his demons.

Thus the old century died and a new one was born.

As far as I was concerned, the twentieth century didn't hold a lick more promise than the nineteenth had.

I continued slaving over the laundry tubs, warred with Horace, did what I hoped was my best with the two little ones I still had—though they weren't so little any longer—and kept my eyes and ears open for news about the boy I most longed to see. In my head, I knew Caleb had turned bad, but my heart was a mother's heart. I hadn't given him birth, but he was my son nonetheless, and I yearned to be able to take him in my arms and comfort his hurts and make all the sorrows go away.

As for Donald and Dell... what is there to say? Donald grew into a serious little man who continued to adore his stepfather for reasons I will never fathom, did tolerably well at school though he made it clear from the get-go that book learning was never going to be much use to him, and otherwise generally kept to himself. It was plain as day that he was going to grow up to work with his hands, because even as a little shaver, he could spend hours on end with a piece or two of wood and a bit of twine, putting them together into different shapes that didn't appear to be anything in particular except that they made him happy. When he got older, he discovered a hammer and some rusty nails in the stable, and before you knew it, he'd hammered every one of them nails into the side of the house in a little X pattern, then yanked them out, pounded the bent ones straight, and did it all over again. I thought sure that Horace was going to skin him alive for that, but by then, my husband was losing interest in both home and family except for Dell, whom he had taken to calling his little papoose even in public, so when he saw the nail holes in the clapboard, he just grunted once, told me it was my job to patch up the damage, and went about his business.

Dell was the one I confess I understood the least. She'd been a quiet child from birth, and she got quieter as she grew. It was her Indian blood, Francine said. She would watch me at the wash tubs without ever asking a question or saying a word, or at night she'd sit on the floor pretending to read from a tattered old Mother Goose book I had, or put up with being on Horace's lap without a smile or a sound when he scooped her up offen the floor. He'd tickle her or tousle her hair, but she'd just turn and stare out the window. And she just slap ignored her brother, acting for all the world as if he didn't exist, which of course was fine with him.

Dell was a bright thing who did well once she started school, and it was clear she was going to be the closest any member of my family would ever came to being a scholar. She played with dolls some, but preferred to read books once she learned how, and though all we had to read on the premises other than the Mother Goose was the weekly newspaper and a tattered Bible that had belonged to Horace's first wife, she would spend hours and hours at a time parsing the words. I believe she had whole chapters of the Bible memorized by the time she was ten years old, with her tastes running to the Old Testament Book of Ruth and the Psalms. Whether she understood the language, I do not know, but it was something to behold when that small, dark child commenced to reciting scripture, and she was all the rage at the Methodist Sunday school, I'll tell you.

My friendship with Francine continued through all them years, though in truth it did fade some. Her drinking had really gotten the best of her shortly after the time of my marriage to Horace. Luckily for her, Maudie Calkins proved to have more saint in that big Irish body of hers than anyone would of expected, and she'd taken it upon herself to keep Francine away from spirituous liquor altogether, with occasional success. Francine always said she appreciated Maudie's efforts, at least when she was sober, and the two of them got closer and closer, until you couldn't even think of one without the other. My laundry work kept me from visiting Chautauqua, and they almost never made the trip north to "the big city" of Sedan, so months at a time would go by without Francine or me laying eyes on one another. When we did, we discovered we had less and less to talk about. I suppose I was embarrassed for her on account of her drinking, and she was embarrassed for me on account of Caleb's exploits and what the gossips all said about the fisticuffs and broken crockery in our home. I heard through the grapevine rather than from Francine herself that her boy Rufus had come down with tuberculosis—what we'd called the consumption when I was a girl—and had left St. Louis to come home to Chautauqua, but had gotten himself waylaid by a lewd woman before he got there and moved with her to the mountains of Colorado to take the cure. Shortly thereafter, all Francine could talk about when I did see her was how she was going to pick up stakes and move to Colorado Springs, which, to hear her tell it, was so close to heaven on earth that God himself walked the streets sprinkling gold dust and granting passersby with eternal life. She never did go, though. For one thing, Maudie Calkins wouldn't of left Chautauqua if you'd of lit a stick of dynamite under her, and by that time, them two were insep-arable. For another, Francine's prospects of selling the boardinghouse were somewhere between slim and none, what with the population of the town skidding to record lows and most of her customers being foul-smelling tar-covered work-ers coming from the new oil fields sprouting up all over Oklahoma Territory, and without that, she didn't have enough cash money to buy a train ticket to Wichita, let alone Colo-rado. Besides, the way I heard it from Maudie, her boy Rufus let it be known he wasn't the least bit interested in seeing his ma.

Truth to tell, life was lonely for me in them days, though I'm not complaining. That wouldn't do any good, and besides, most of it was of my own making. I just couldn't cotton up to the biddies.

It's for certain that Caleb continued to be the cross I bore, even though I went years without seeing him.

Then we got word that Caleb had been arrested, all the way over to Hot Springs, Arkansas, and it turned out to be over a woman. Seems he'd struck up a friendship with the wife of a rancher from somewhere some miles east of Coffeyville, which surprised me on account of I had believed Caleb had long since quit our country. Anyway, the two of them had run off together. Naturally, the rancher didn't take kindly to losing his bride, and gave chase. When he caught them, he threatened to kill them both, but Caleb got the drop on him and instead it was the rancher that took a ball. It didn't kill him outright, but it smashed his knee and he likely would of bled to death except that his wife apparently had a fit of remorse and stanched the bleeding and picked up her husband's gun and shot a time or two at Caleb herself. She missed, probably on purpose, and my boy decided to light outen there, as you can imagine. The woman told the law that the two of them had been planning to run off to Hot Springs, and for some reason, Caleb kept going that way. Sure enough, when he got there, a party of lawmen were waiting.

There was considerable confusion about where the crime had happened, or whether it even was a crime. The rancher swore he was in Kansas when he was shot. Caleb told the Arkansas lawmen who arrested him that he was ten miles inside the Cherokee Nation. At first, the woman agreed with Caleb, then decided her husband was right, then changed her mind again and said it was actually on Shawnee land, and she proved just as fickle on the question of whether Caleb had fired in self defense or whether he'd meant to kill the rancher.

Well, after some head scratching, there wasn't much them Arkansas boys could do but let Caleb go, though with a stern warning that he was to stay outen their state forever and steer clear of Kansas, too, if he knew what was good for him.

I thought Horace was going to have a stroke over all that business. The pure glee in that man's eyes when he thought Caleb was going to be tried for attempted murder in Kansas was enough to make me sick at my stomach, but at least I got the guilty pleasure of seeing him go all apoplectic when the state of Arkansas let the boy go.

Anyway, after the business with the rancher and his wife, I hoped Caleb would take the Arkansans' advice and be gone to Texas or New Mexico or some such place for good. I did send him a telegram when he was in the jail in Hot Springs offering advice along those lines, but if he ever got it, he didn't bother to respond.

And so, like I said, the days passed into weeks, the weeks into months, and the months into years.

Before I knew it, my other two children were grown plumb to adulthood. It was as if I just wakened up one day in the summer of 1905 and found Dell blossoming toward womanhood and Donald starting to grow a scraggly little mustache and talking about some girl he was sweet on.

Dell was as much a mystery to me as ever. I had hoped she would outgrow the "quiets," but she never did. Sometimes she'd have such a faraway look in her eyes that I wondered whether her mind was sound except that she was doing so well at her schoolwork. She took to trying to wriggle outen Horace's grasp when he'd pull her onto his lap, which only made him bluster and blow and get angry with me, but she never said a cross word to him, neither, and would go what seemed like weeks on end without a word of any kind to me.

Donald quit school in the seventh grade to go to work for Delbert Sweet, who ran the livery stable and wagon shop near the corner of School and Main Street. I fretted some, for I'd been hoping that my boy would at least go to the tenth or eleventh grade, but Horace pointed out that once a young man could cipher and read and write, there wasn't much more practical learning to be gleaned from sitting in a school-room, which of course was just the opposite of what his argument had been with Caleb. And besides, he said, we could use the money. By that, Horace meant that he expected Donald to turn over his pay each week and put it into the china bowl on the mantel where all our money went, excepting of course the few dimes of tip money I hoarded in a tin can I buried behind the barn. You could tell that Donald didn't think much of that idea, but he done as he was told, mostly because he held Horace in such reverence.

Work seemed to suit him, to tell the truth, and that more or less surprised me. Naturally, with all the worrying I'd done over Caleb, I hadn't given a whole lot of thought to Donald, so I suppose any way he'd turned out would of been a puzzlement to me.

Anyway, he seemed to take to the repair work at the wagon shop, and when Emil Danker, the wheelwright, announced he was going to open his own place and repair windmills and other metalwork, Donald went along with him. Donald's main job was to drum up business for the old German, and he did a fair job of it by all accounts, riding all over the county, visiting farmers and townsfolk alike, and while doing that he came to know just about every man, woman and child in Chautauqua County. By that time, he also had become plumb smitten with the internal combustion engine, and though I always thought the noise and stink of the few automobiles around our parts was likely a sign that they were a visitation from Hell itself, Donald's eyes would just light up whenever he saw one, and while he was working for Mr. Danker, he managed to bring in a little work for himself when folks would let him tinker with their horseless carriages.

Of course, it turned out that my boy had more on his mind than just work when it came to Emil Danker.

The Danker clan was a big one. Emil hailed from Ohio—Cincinnati, I think, though I don't suppose it matters. He'd come to work on the railroad back in the boom days, and he'd married a Frommelt girl, whose people were of German extraction, same as him, who farmed over near the town of Caney. It was a fact that her people weren't much good at raising crops, but they were first rate at raising as many kids as humanly possible, and Emil's wife took to that chore like a duck to water. They had better than a dozen children spread out over eighteen or twenty years, all of them scrawny little blue-eyed blondes like their mother rather than being squat-tish and black-haired like their father. It was one of them kids, the middle child named Lydia, that had caught Donald's eye.

Now, at first, I liked Lydia well enough. She was polite and clean and well spoken when Donald brought her by for a Sunday supper four or five months after he and old Emil set up shop together. She laughed a little too much at Horace's jokes, which tended not to be funny, but I chalked that up to nerves. She did offer to help with the dishes after supper, which was about all I needed to put her down as all right in my book.

Except that from that day on, them two weren't outen each other's sight but to sleep at night and at church on Sunday, the Dankers being dyed-in-the-wool Lutheran and therefore having a low opinion of Methodists, a sect which they considered several steps too close to Popish for their tastes. Anyway, Lydia worked at her father's shop as a bookkeeper or some such, having just finished the eighth grade herself, so she and Donald were together during the workday and took their lunches together sitting on the back stoop. After a few months, I asked Donald if he wanted to bring her by again for Sunday supper, and a "nope" was all I could get outen him. The two of them would drop by the sheriff's office at the end of the day and listen to some wild tale or another that Horace cooked up to entertain them, but they wouldn't set foot in our house together, and in fact Donald commenced taking most of his evening meals with the Dankers.

Naturally, that pleased Horace no end since we didn't have to provide victuals for the boy, who was, like most young men his age, able to eat enough for two threshers and still have room left over for a half a pie.

That summer that Donald started keeping company with Lydia Danker and Dell grew ever quieter as she began to bloom was also the summer that Caleb came back into my life and—just like that—slipped away again.

This time, it was the Osages who caught him. The one thing I would of bet my life on was that Caleb would steer clear of trouble with the Osages, which of course was why I didn't think he'd been involved in the shooting of that Osage woman I mentioned before. Turned out, I was wrong. I suppose that by that point in his life, raising Cain had become such a part of Caleb's nature that it didn't matter to him what he did—or who he did it to.

So it was that one day Horace came home at noon, which was unusual for him. He preferred having a sandwich and a beer with his cronies in the court house. But on this particular day, he had a telegram to show me. It had come from the tribal police in Pawhuska, and it was addressed to me.

I've never forgotten what it said.

CALEB WHITESNAKE IN OUR CUSTODY STOP WILL CONSIDER RELEASING HIM TO YOU STOP PLEASE ADVISE STOP

That was it.

"Boy's name ain't Whitesnake," Horace grumbled as I

read them few words a second and third time. He slurped his soup and belched. "And bring me more coffee."

"He's got as much right to the name Whitesnake as any other. More, if you want the truth," I said, though it did bother me that Caleb had chosen to besmirch the name of the one person who had done more good for him than any other.

He waved his hand as if to brush away a pesky fly. "Well, I say if they want to string him up, let 'em. For whatever'n hell he's done."

A shiver ran through me, and I traced my fingers over the yellow sheet of flimsy paper yet again. "It doesn't say anything about hanging." Just mention of the word liked to take my breath away. "Do you know what they say he's done?"

"No."

"Can you find out?" I asked.

"Why bother?"

"Because he's your stepson."

"Not mine," he said. "I disavowed any kinship with that one long ago."

"You never had any kinship with him, but that ain't what I asked. Can you find out?"

He wiped a big paw acrost his lips and sucked on his teeth. "Suppose I can."

"Then do that, please." It hurt my sense of pride to be the least bit polite to that man.

"It'll cost money. Western Union won't let me send a telegram for free to the Nations."

I figured that was a lie, but I let it pass. "I'll give you money from the cookie jar," I said, and I took the crockery jug offen the top kitchen shelf and dug around for some spare change. I came up with six bits.

He glowered. "That's money meant for other things."

"Then I'll repay it by taking in more wash." I thrust the coins at him again.

He took it. He cocked an eye at me and said "You ain't

thinking of bringing him back here, are you?"

"I might be."

"If you do, I'll have a dozen outstanding warrants ready to arrest him on." He was grinning as he said it.

"I want to see my boy," I said. I didn't—wouldn't—tell him that I had no intention of bringing Caleb north of the Line.

It turned out that the Osages wouldn't tell Horace what it was that Caleb had done, neither, saying only that out of respect for Reuben Whitesnake, they were willing to free my boy, but only to me. I had our little buggy readied within the hour and asked the Methodist minister for the loan of his horse for a few days to pull it and headed for Pawhuska at first light the next day.

I wasn't a mile outside town when Horace came thundering up on his big bay gelding.

"You ain't invited," I said.

"My sworn duty's to keep miscreants like that boy outen Chautauqua County or arrest 'em when they come in," he said, giving me a grin that made me want to take a swipe at him with my buggy whip. "So I'm coming."

"Go to hell," I said.

That brought him up short.

"What did you say?"

"I said go to hell. Look after the children while I'm gone, if you're man enough to do it."

I flicked the reins to send the horse into a trot. Horace, apparently still flummoxed by my cursing him, just sat there. "You keep that boy outen Kansas, or I'll see the both of you behind bars!" he shouted when I was almost beyond hearing.

The sun was nearly down by the time I rode into Pawhuska. The town had grown some since I'd last seen it, and it had come to look even more substantial and prosperous than Sedan. The old Osage police office, which had been little more than a mean shack when Reuben was alive, was a nice stone building now.

In spite of the hour, I drew the buggy up, clumb down, and went inside.

The lawman on duty wasn't anybody I recognized, but he seemed to know me right off. He said he couldn't tell me anything about Caleb, but if I came back first thing in the morning, his boss would be there and would take me to my boy. That surprised me, on account of I had expected Caleb to be in the little jail out back, and I said so.

"No, ma'am," the policeman said. "He's not here, but we'll take you to him in the morning." He gave me directions to a nice little boardinghouse within site of the big cemetery where Reuben was buried. I offered to help cook the next morning's breakfast to pay my way, but the little lady running the place, who appeared to be full-blood Osage, wouldn't hear of it when I told her I was Reuben's widow, which I must say warmed my heart.

I headed back to the police office shortly after first light. This time, an older officer was on duty.

"What's my boy done?" I asked.

He just shook his head. "I'll take you to him."

"What's he done?" I asked again, but still I got no answer.

So off we rode, me in the buggy with the tall, thin police officer clopping along in the lead.

We rode into the ring of hills that overlooks the town to the south and west. Up through one long ravine, over a ridge, and down into a shaded valley we rode, then up another ravine so steep it made my horse blow and into a little clearing in the oaks.

There stood a low-roofed log hut in the middle of the clearing, with an Indian policeman standing in front of a plank door secured with a padlock. He had a rifle crossed over his big chest.

"She's come for her boy," my escort said to the man with

the rifle.

The guard lowered his weapon and pulled out a big skeleton key, which he used to open the lock. It must of been rusty, the way it squawked when he pulled back the hasp. He shoved the door open and motioned me inside.

I stepped past him into the cool of that hut. It smelled of damp earth and mildew and man sweat. The policeman who had brung me stepped inside with me.

It took a moment for my eyes to adjust after the blinding brightness of the day, but when they did, what I saw broke my heart.

Caleb was trussed up like a Christmas goose, with hands and feet bound and pulled so he wouldn't have the use of either. Coils of rope snaked around his chest, pinning his arms to his side. I could tell from the stink of the place that he'd soiled himself. But the worst of it was his face, which had been pounded almost past recognition. One eye was closed behind an ugly black bruise that had puffed his cheek out, and his nose was pushed sideways and leaking blood that had caked on his chin and filthy shirt. His hair, wild and dirty, showed a shiny crust of dried blood just back of his hairline.

Incredibly, he smiled at me. "Momma Eva," he said with a nod through swollen lips.

"What have you done, son?" I asked.

For a split second, I thought I saw something that looked like a mix of fear and hatred contort Caleb's broken face, but maybe it was just the play of poor light and shadow. Then he gave me a lopsided grin. "They say I stole two mules," he said. "Resisted arrest."

"That all?"

"That's about it."

"Did you do it?"

Before he could answer, the Osage cleared his throat. "There was another crime," he said very slowly. "He took a young woman from the village on Cedar Creek."

"She came along voluntary," Caleb added, more to me than to him.

The policeman turned to me. "She was the wife of an important man and daughter of another. She would not disgrace her clan in such a way."

So once again, Caleb had apparently taken to stealing a woman who didn't belong to him.

"She come along on her own!" he said right forcefully.

"Caleb, you be quiet!" I said louder than I knew I should. Softer, I added "If you know what's good for you, please quieten down."

"Aw, Momma Eva..." But he could tell from the look I gave him that I meant business.

The policeman scowled at the boy. "The whites would hang him for his crimes," he said, "but we have decided to return him to his mother, who was wife to our friend Reuben."

"Why are you holding him here?" I asked.

"If we take him to town, we cannot be responsible for what happens," the policeman said flatly. "He has many enemies."

"Well, thank you, then," was all I said.

The policeman produced a bowie knife from a sheath on his leg. He waved it in Caleb's face as if he meant to do him grievous harm, but then with two quick swipes of that blade, he cut the bonds tying Caleb's arm's to his sides. With another, he freed his feet, leaving only his hands tied. Then he sheathed the knife and jerked the boy upright.

"Take him," the policeman said. "Keep him out of Osage lands forever. You stay away, too. You are not welcome here ever again." Then he spun on his heel, nodded to his companion, and just like that, the two of them were gone, leaving us alone.

I rushed to Caleb and turned him over. He had other wounds I hadn't yet noticed, including a twisted shoulder and a broken collar bone. The smile he'd forced in front of his captors was still there, but I could tell how much he was hurting.

"Momma Eva," he said softly. Then he gritted his teeth and closed his eyes.

"You can't come back to Kansas," I said. "Horace will arrest you the second you cross the Line."

"Not if I kill him first," he said so flatly there was no doubt in my mind he would do it.

That purely made my breath catch in my throat. "Don't you talk that way. No matter what he's done. But that's beside the point now. You have to go away. Far away. California, maybe. And never come back." I sat in the dirt and took his hand. My own were trembling. "Don't you see, that's the only way it can be. You can ride in the buggy with me until we're out of the Osage Nation, and then you're on your own. But Caleb, don't come back. I mean it."

He just nodded.

So we did just that. It was early evening by the time we reached Kaw country some miles to the west. I'd brought what little savings I had and used most of it to buy an old sway-backed gelding from a farmer. The rest I gave to Caleb. He gave me a hug and clumb onto the gelding bareback.

"Momma Eva, I'm sorry the way everything turned out," he said, looking down on me in the twilight.

"I don't never want to see you again, Caleb," I said, trying to make the lie sound as true as I could. "If you ever come back to Kansas, you'll wind up in the penitentiary or at the end of a hangman's noose. That would kill me." I paused, then said the other thing that weighed heavy on my mind. "And please quit using Reuben's name. It dishonors him."

He gave me a look that hinted at violence, but only for a moment before it melted into something like sorrow. "Then it's good-by," he said. And without a hug or a touch or another word, he turned the horse toward the setting sun and rode off.

I thought my heart would break.

I spent the night dozing in the buggy in the tiny village of Washunga, which was so small you could of put three towns that size into Chautauqua and still had room left over, then headed north shortly before dawn. That trip home took me two days, and I was so lost in thought I can't even remember what the countryside looked like.

I arrived home late in the afternoon of one of them hot, sticky days that makes a body feel certain a terrible storm is on the way, and just sat down at the kitchen table and cried. Dell came into the room once and stood looking at me, but when I called her to me, she just turned and walked away. For his part, Donald fussed about needing to go to work, and then he was off, likely as not heading for the Danker place to spoon with Lydia.

I was as low as a body could get. There I was, living with a man I despised and who, from all appearances, despised me even more. My best loved child was a thief or worse who appeared determined to remain an outlaw, which would surely bring him to a terrible end. My other children didn't seem to have any feelings for me one way or the other, though I figured I deserved that on account of how little attention I'd given them in all the years I'd been fighting for Caleb.

Life didn't hardly seem to be worth living.

And then, right in the midst of all that self-pity, there was a knock on my door. I pulled myself to my feet, dabbed at the tears with the corner of my apron, and went to the door. When I opened it, my first thought was what is this old tramp doing on my front porch with his hat in his hands. Then I took a closer look at the creased black face, the strong white teeth and the bowed legs.

"Howdy, Miz Eva," Marcellus Robinson said with a big grin.

Friendship and Sorrow

Hᴏᴡ ᴏɴ ᴇᴀʀᴛʜ can a body go from just about the worst kind of grief and worry imaginable to pure joy in the blink of an eye? I do not know, but it happened to me at that instant. There stood my dearest old friend just at the very moment when I needed friendship the most. It was as if a black angel had descended from Heaven itself!

I must of stood there with my mouth open for two whole minutes, because after a time, he cocked his head and asked me if I was all right.

That brought my wits back, and I told him I was fine and of course asked him in.

His own grin faded a bit. "Is your Mister at home?"

"No," I said. "Not right at the moment."

"Then I best wait," he said. "Probably it would be best if you introduced us 'fore I come into your house."

I started to ask him why on earth that was so, and then I remembered back to our first meeting. A black man coming into a white woman's home without any other man around could do a sight more than just cause tongues to wag. Instead, I pointed him to one of the caneback chairs sitting on the porch. "Rest a spell, at least."

"I'll do that," he said with a chuckle as he settled into the chair, "though I been settin' in a railroad car for nigh onto two days, so I don' need to set all that bad, neither."

Turned out he'd sold such herd of cattle as he had and left his old homestead in Gove County—me and Jack's old one, that is—some months before and had gone to Colorado to look into homesteading another piece of property down along the Purgatoire River—the Picket Wire, he called it. But he decided that country wasn't any better for raising cattle than right where he'd spent all these last years, and he said at his age he didn't have the gumption to start over from scratch. So without cattle to tend and a few dollars in his pocket, he said he just hired out to whatever outfit needed him to help with calving or the spring roundup, and when that work more or less petered out, he figured a little vacation was in order and decided on the spur of the moment to come see me. How he learned where I was he wouldn't say, although it must of taken quite an act of detective work. I do know he went to Chautauqua first to ask after me, and we must of come within a mile or so of one another, him going south and me going north as I made my way back from the latest loss of Caleb.

I learned later that Francine was slap beside herself about a black man asking after me, but it was Maudie Calkins who told him where he could find me, and it was likewise Maudie who warned him to watch out for my husband.

Which was a good thing, as it turned out.

Marcellus and I were still sitting on that porch, talking like a couple of school girls, when Horace staggered into the yard, having spent the best part of the afternoon drinking beer with his court house cronies. He came weaving up the lane, mostly staring at his feet, but when he glanced in our direction, he just stopped dead still. He blinked a time or two, then came on, marching as straight and fast as a belly full of beer would allow. When he stopped short a few feet from the front steps, he had his hand on his Colt's revolver.

"Horace, I'd like you to meet an old friend of mine," I said, sweet as anything.

Marcellus whipped off his hat and stood. "Sir," he said with a nod.

I smiled so wide I thought my face was going to crack. "This is Marcellus Robinson. He's a dear friend from my days back in Gove County," I said. "He plumb saved my life a time or two." I couldn't remember if I'd ever told Horace about Marcellus, but from the look on my husband's face, I assumed I hadn't. Or at least I hadn't told him that Marcellus was black. "Marcellus, this is my husband, Sheriff Horace Taylor."

"Pleased to meet you," Marcellus said with another nod.

Horace squinted at Marcellus, then turned to me.

"You didn't bring that boy of yours from the Nations, did you? 'Cause if you did, I'm goin' to lock him up."

"I did not," I said. "I believe he's on his way to California."

Horace just harumphed at that, then returned his attention to Marcellus. "Boy, you best get offen that porch," he said, and he lifted his revolver a few inches from his holster before settling it back into the leather.

"Now, Horace..." I said.

He just waved a fist at me. "Now!"

Marcellus nodded and stepped around me, almost daintily. "Yes, sir. Meant no offense, sir."

"Git offen my porch and git offen my place!" Horace growled without even giving Marcellus time enough to climb down the steps.

Well, I naturally hadn't expected Horace to be all sweetness and light, but I surely hadn't expected him to be that rude, neither, and I wasn't going to put up with it. I'd had all the heartache a body could stand the past few days, and I didn't intend to have any more.

"Horace Taylor, you mind your manners," I said. "You're drunk as a skunk, and you need to know right now that Mister Robinson is a friend of mine, and he's always going to be welcome in our home." I stood up as straight and tall as I could. "In fact, I've invited him to supper. It ain't the first time, neither, and it won't be the last."

Both them men turned a puzzled look on me at that, and Horace started to sputter some nonsense about no darky going to cross his threshold, but I just glared at him with the coldest, hardest look I could muster, and after a time the air went outen him and he shook his head and turned on his heel.

"Well, don't wait supper on me!" he shouted over his shoulder, and then he was gone.

So it was that Marcellus had supper at our house that night, and the next, and the night after that. When it dawned on Horace that he was going to have to pay for his eats downtown pretty near forever unless he gave in, he slunk on home, shook hands with Marcellus like he was grabbing onto the business end of a rattlesnake, gave me an evil look, and tucked into the victuals whether there was a black man sitting at his table or not.

I don't believe he ever said more than two words to my friend in them first days, which was just fine with me.

Marcellus hit it off right well with the children, which certainly came as no surprise. Or at least I should say he did with Dell, who warmed up to him in a way she never had with Horace—or even me, for that matter. She was twelve years old that summer, and I'd come to believe the hang-dog look that was always on her face was going to be permanent, but she took such pure delight in Marcellus you'd of thought she was a different person altogether whenever he was around. He'd show her little tricks with his hands, making coins disappear then magically reappear in her ears, or he'd make a sort of hat by folding up last week's newspaper and putting it on her and telling her she was a proper lady, and she'd strut around just oozing superiority until she'd collapse into a fit of giggles. She called him Mister Marcellus, and he called her Little Miss. They were thick as thieves from the get-go, and after a while, it dawned on me that whenever Marcellus came by, it was as much because that child tickled him as it was to see me.

Which was entirely fine by me. Him brightening Dell's mood helped take a load offen my own heart.

Donald was another matter altogether. Though he wasn't outright rude, it was plain as day that he was cut from the same bolt of cloth as Horace even though their kinship was only circumstantial. He'd never been one to cotton to strangers or folks who were the least bit different, and that proved to be doubly true when it came to Marcellus. Donald would glower when Marcellus would ask him to please pass the peas, and when my friend tried to make conversation about Donald's job or what his plans were, he'd just give a one or two word answer and clam up tighter than a tick. Once Horace returned home, Donald made it a point to ask him how his day had gone and then kept the conversation going with his step-daddy as if the rest of us weren't there. On the nights when Marcellus wasn't there—which turned out to be most nights after that first few days on account of he'd told me straight out he had no intentions of wearing out his welcome—my two men, meaning Horace and Donald, would play checkers or work together in the stable fixing tack or currying the horse. When Marcellus was there, Donald would just adopt whatever grumpy look Horace had and mimic him right down to the way he'd slurp his coffee or shovel the biscuits into his mouth whole. It would of been funny if it hadn't been so rude.

It was the absolute truth, though, that Marcellus's company eased the sorrow in my heart.

It turned out he had a thousand stories about Gove County folks I couldn't but just barely remember, and thousands more about drouth or cyclones or grasshoppers or blue northers or rattlesnakes or coyotes and all the things that made life on the high plains such a challenge. It seemed like he was a natural born story-teller who'd had them stories bottled up for years on account of having no one to tell them to, and now, with an audience of two, they just rolled outen him, to Dell's and my delight. To hear him tell it, he'd had some tough scrapes trying to make a go of that homestead even once he'd given up trying to raise a crop and turned instead to running beeves, there still being something of a market back East for Kansas cattle in spite of all the new railhead towns like Caney and Elgin and a hundred others.

Based on Marcellus's testimony, it was absolutely certain to me that had Jack Ross lived, he would of failed miserably at making a go of that patch of burnt-over prairie. I didn't miss that country one bit, and I told him so. He didn't, neither, he said, on account of how hard he'd worked to own that sorry bit of ground and how little he had to show for it.

Turned out Marcellus was every bit as good a listener as he was a storyteller, too, and he'd sit on our porch for hours while I told him about my early years in Chautauqua or life with Reuben. When I'd come near to tears over what had become of my eldest child, he'd just pat my hand and say "That boy was star-crossed from the start," or some such thing. He was there with a kind word and the soft pat of a hand, too, when the letter from my brother James came and told me Ma was dead.

After a few weeks, I decided to ask him if he was staying in Sedan. "Just passin' through, Missus," is what he said, but in no time at all, it was obvious that the opposite was true. He'd taken a room of sorts, moving into a shed behind the post office that the postmaster let him use for two dollars a week on account of no one would rent him a decent place because of his race. I would of been glad to put him up, but we didn't have anything other than a crude stable, and besides, both of us knew without having to say it that we'd be pushing our luck with Horace far past the breaking point to have Marcellus living that close.

Anyway, he cleaned up that shed and bought himself a little Franklin stove, and what with the bedroll and other traps he'd brought with him from Gove County by way of Colorado, he managed to turn it into a snug little home. He had enough pocket money to last him for a while, especially since I insisted on feeding him as often as possible—which was a small price to pay for good company, I'll tell you—and after a month or so, he took on a job helping the livery man. It was the kind of work that Caleb had done for a while before Horace shipped him off to that school in Independence, and though Marcellus was an absolute genius when it came to horses, I know for a fact that he didn't get but half the wages my boy had. He seemed not to mind as long as he had a few nickels in his pocket and a warm place to sleep.

The liveryman was clearly glad to have him around in spite of the poor wages he paid, and pretty soon word got out that Marcellus could do just about anything with a horse that a body could want—word that was spread by Horace's deputy, Charley McGuane, who had taken something of a shine to Marcellus, probably on account of Charley didn't know the first thing about horses and marveled at them who did.

Anyhow, even though he was long past being a young man, Marcellus could break the meanest bronc, and he never seemed to care how many times he got thrown. Sometimes, school kids and loafers would gather at the corral out behind the livery stable just to watch Marcellus work with a horse somebody had brought in to be broken, and often as not, they would start taking bets on who would give up first, man or beast, but it wasn't long before only strangers or the mentally deficient would bet against my friend. One time, a rancher sent word that he needed help gentling a young mare about to give birth the first time, and Marcellus offered to go. He saved both mare and foal, and after that, his reputation spread so fast he actually got offers from as far away as Independence and Arkansas City to come stay at the bigger spreads, with ranchers competing with one another for who could book his services in advance of the next year's foaling season. Why, it wasn't no time at all before Marcellus was making fair wages for his efforts, black skin or no.

He did other work around town, too, such as odd jobs for old ladies and general clean-up around the Baptist Church. The congregation voted against letting him actually sit in a pew during services, but on account of all the work he did there, they let him stand at the back when the weather was poor, or sit outside under an open window on better days so he could hear the preaching. That seemed fine with him, though I thought it showed a lack of Christian spirit. Of course, the Baptists didn't ask my opinion on the matter.

Horace never did take a shine to him even if most of the rest of that town did, and the more time went on, the more them two men would eye each other with mistrust on Marcellus's part and pure hatred on my husband's. It made for some unpleasant mealtimes, but I had resolved not to let Horace's animosity ever come betwixt me and my dear friend.

Still, I wasn't prepared for what happened next.

I'm not entirely certain when it started. Horace would say hurtful things about Marcellus all the time, and I mostly just ignored him, but I do remember one warmish day in late autumn. I'd given myself the luxury of taking off early from my laundry duties and instead had begun sprucing up the yard a little, hoeing weeds outen my garden and bringing in the last of the squashes before the nights got so cool as to spoil them. As I bent over a squash vine, I heard a horse come thundering up our path and Horace calling my name.

"You seen that nigger pal of yours?" he bellowed as he brought the horse to a full stop.

"Please don't use that word," I said, wiping my hands on my apron. "And no, I haven't seen Marcellus."

"How 'bout your daughter?"

"Dell? She's not home from school yet."

"You think she's at school?"

"Of course."

He snorted and pulled a plug of tobacco outen a shirt pocket and bit off a chunk. "You best keep them two apart, Missus, if you know what's good for her. Can't have no daughter of mine spoilt by the likes of him!"

"What on earth do you mean?" I asked.

"She's taken to visiting that cabin of his."

"They're friends," I said.

He gave me a look that fairly turned my heart to stone. "*Friends!*" he barked. And with that, he jerked on the reins. The horse, startled, reared up and nearly threw him, but he gave a savage yank to swing its head around and pounded down the path the way he'd come.

I confess I just stood there with a sudden cold chill up my spine. What on earth...

There couldn't be anything to worry about. Dell wouldn't be thirteen for a few months yet, and Marcellus was sixty if he was a day. He was a good man. They were friends...

Still...

It's just that easy to put poison into the human mind.

When Dell got home, I determined to ask her was there anything to be worried about when it came to Marcellus, but it took some doing, her having gotten good at avoiding me. I'd follow her into the parlor and she'd scoot outen the door saying she had to use the privy. I'd wait for her by the front door and she'd come in the back. I'd try to catch her in the kitchen and she'd head for the parlor again.

At last I managed to grab her arm and hold her.

"Sit down," I said.

"Why?"

"Just sit. I have something to ask you."

She sat, but there was a black look on her face that made me shudder.

I took a deep breath. "Your daddy came by this afternoon and said I should ask you about Marcellus."

She blinked. "You mean Horace? He's not my daddy."

I waved that off. "So I'm asking about Marcellus. Is there something I need to know?"

She shook her head.

All I could think of were the times them two would sit knee-to-knee while Marcellus told her some story or showed her a coin trick, and how she'd laugh with a little bubbling sound that I'd never heard come outen her mouth until my friend showed up. "You sure? You're not doing something to be ashamed of, are you?"

The blood drained outen her face. "With Marcellus?"

"Look into my eyes, child," I said.

But she was up, dancing away from me, and out the front door again, and she didn't come back until way past dark.

I couldn't sleep nor eat for days. Dell avoided me like I had the pox, Marcellus didn't come by, and though I tried a couple of times to get up the nerve to walk over to the post office to confront him, I just couldn't bring myself to do it. Horace was the only one who seemed to want to talk on the subject, though it was mostly snide remarks such as had I seen my nigger friend lately or "what's that daughter of your'n see in a black buck anyway?" or "I heard them darkies are hung like stallions—you reckon that's true?" and suchlike trash.

It just slap made me sick to my stomach.

So I took to spying on my daughter. Like many young girls, she'd kept a diary once she'd learned to read, and when she was off to school, I'd hunt everywhere I could think of to see if I could find that book, but she must of kept it with her or hid it really well. I checked and rechecked the little chest of drawers that held all her worldly possessions to see if there were any clues—though of course I had no idea what I might be looking for—and after she went to bed at night, I even searched the tattered old schoolbooks she brought home and read the little pencil notes in the margins.

There wasn't anything to find.

Thanksgiving came and went, and still no Marcellus.

Then the first week of December he showed up on my doorstep with a big grin and a headless turkey dangling from his hand.

"Been workin' over to Independence," he said, "or I'd of brung you this bird for the holiday." He thrust it toward me. "Better late than never, I always say!"

I guess I took the bird, but his smile faded in seconds. "Somethin' wrong?"

"You have any explaining to do about my daughter?" I said, just blurting it out.

He looked purely puzzled. "'Bout what?"

"You and Dell are close, ain't you?"

He grinned again, but only for about a half second before he caught my drift. He stepped back a little, opening up the distance betwixt us. "What you sayin', Miz Eva?"

I had to swallow the lump in my throat. "I don't know, Marcellus. Just tell me how close you and my daughter are."

"She's a frien', like you."

"She's not even thirteen years old."

He seemed to think on that for a long time. "'Bout the same as you when first we met," he said. "You was a chile, an' so's she. I don't take advantage of chil'ren, if that's what you're drivin' at."

I just stood there, and so did he. After a while, he just touched his fingers to the brim of his hat. "Guess I be goin' then," he said. "You enjoy the bird." He turned and stepped off our porch and started down the path to the street.

"I believe you!" I shouted after him, but he didn't stop, and I didn't try to stop him, neither. I knew as sure as I've ever known anything in life that I wasn't going to be seeing Marcellus Robinson again for a long, long time.

Well, I didn't think there was any way I could of been any more miserable than I was right then, and from the way Dell moped through Christmas and into the new year, I figured whatever kind of friendship she had with Marcellus was over, too. That girl made it a point of avoiding me, and any time Horace would grab at her to pull her onto his lap for a tickle, she'd twist free and run into her little room and slam the door. Whole weeks went by that she didn't say a single word to either of us.

I wanted to talk to her, to ask her what had happened, but could not. Somewhere along the way—all them fights with Horace or watching two husbands die or whatever—had just taken the starch outen me and I couldn't do it.

Then in the middle of a March cold spell, my miseries deepened in a way I'd been both dreading and expecting for years.

Caleb was in trouble again, and this time it was murder.

I knew it was bound to happen sooner or later. I confess that some part of me had known that he would come to a bad end since the day we buried his ma and pa and took him away from that horrid dugout in Gove County. No matter how much I had loved that boy, no matter how much I tried to mother him, he truly did seem to be star-crossed, and there was always that dangerous part of him that just couldn't be reached, at least not by me. Another, better mother might of done it, but I couldn't. Had Jack lived, he might of survived his torments, and certainly Reuben had stood a fine chance of turning him around, even if he turned him into full Indian in the process.

But with both of them fine men gone, Caleb was a goner, and probably had been from the get-go.

Still, the way it ended truly did break my heart.

Instead of leaving Oklahoma the way he should of, Caleb managed to get mixed up in a string of crimes all over the territory from the Red River to the Cimarron Strip, using several names with various different gangs of thugs. Apparently, he was thieving regular, just like it was a job, and now he'd added deadly violence to his crimes. Every time his name came up as a suspect, Horace would tell me all about it with a look of sheer glee on his face.

There was the report of a bank teller shot and gravely wounded by a lone gunman who maybe fit Caleb's description and maybe didn't. A white church woman in Tulsa was raped by a bandit who'd tied up her husband and robbed the family of its silver and jewels, and that got attributed to Caleb, too. But the most serious charge was murder of a police officer in Claremore on a blustery March morning. The officer showed up at the local bank while a lone gunman was still inside stuffing bank notes into a horse's feed bag. When the officer challenged the culprit, the robber wheeled and fired, sending one bullet into the lawman's fore-head, then calmly finished filling the bag, tipped his hat to the ladies, and made his getaway.

There were a dozen eyewitnesses to that crime, and every one described the killer exactly the way I would of described Caleb myself. Every lawman in two states was looking for him.

But weeks went by, then months, and we heard nothing. I prayed that maybe he'd left the country at long last, that perhaps someday I'd get a letter from Canada or Mexico or Guatemala or some such place where a tormented soul could maybe live in peace, though at the same time I felt shame for hoping my boy would elude capture and what was surely his just punishment.

Then, in the late summer of '07, they got him. Horace told it over supper one night, just as matter-of-fact as if he was telling a story about someone catching a stray dog. According to what he'd heard from his lawmen pals, Oklahoma's most famous U.S. Marshal, Bill Tilghman, and a posse of trained deputies had finally run Caleb to earth in the wild country of the Ouachita Mountains. They had hauled him to McAlester, where they were about to put him on trial for various crimes including the rape of the church woman and the murder of that Claremore policeman. After the initial shock passed, I begged Horace to let me go to the trial, but he said nothing doing to that, and he hid the cookie jar where we kept our money so I couldn't buy a railroad ticket.

It would of been over by the time I'd gotten there, anyway, the whole thing lasting not two full days. From what I learned later, there wasn't any defense to speak of, Caleb's entire case being his own word that he didn't do it, and after that church woman took the stand and described how the defendant had brutalized her and them dozen witnesses to the Claremore bank robbery and shooting told how certain they were that my boy had been the one who shot that constable in the head, Caleb's word wasn't worth a plug nickel. The jury spent more time eating the free lunch the Territory provided than they did deliberating the fate of my boy.

The verdict was guilty on all charges. The judge sentenced him to be transported to the Kansas State Penitentiary, Oklahoma Territory not yet having a prison of its own, and to die there by hanging. Since Kansas had a full slate of its own punishments to mete out, the judge set Caleb's date with the hangman for the day after Christmas.

I've never seen a man happier than Horace was over Caleb's misfortune when we heard the news. He actually danced a jig right there in our parlor.

"Good riddance to bad rubbish!" he fairly shouted as he waved that telegram in my face.

As sick as I was, grieving once again for one of mine, something inside me snapped. "I wish he'd killed you instead of that Claremore policeman!" I yelled, and I charged at him, my fists raised. "I wish I'd killed you myself!"

Well, that removed the twinkle in Horace's eye, I'll tell you. He stopped stock still, with a rush of blood to his face that gave him the color of cooked beets.

Then I was on him, pounding his chest with my fists. "I wish he'd killed you, you fat old coward!"

That did it. He swung that big right paw of his around so fast I didn't have time to duck. It caught me flush along the jaw and sent me crashing acrost the room and into the china cabinet. I saw stars and slid onto the floor. Then he was on me, swinging again, filling my mouth with blood. In what seemed like a half-second, Dell was there beside him.

"Don't!" she screamed.

Horace just looked up at her. "You stay out of this, Missy, or I'll kill the both of you!" he hissed.

So she did.

How I got through the next months, I'll never know. I did my best to stay beyond Horace's reach, but he'd still find ways to trap me in a corner and give me a cuff. I stopped fighting back out of the sure knowledge that it only made things worse. I was so bruised and battered that people turned away when they saw me on the street so they could pretend they didn't notice. Even Charley McGuane and his wife would step off the boardwalk and cross the street when they saw me coming.

More than once I thought about digging Jack Ross's old Navy Six outen my traps stashed away in an old valise in our stable, but then I would remember my sister Dell and how it was that the beatings and abuse drove her to madness and murder, and I determined not to come to the same end.

Instead, I laid plans to go see my boy one last time, for it was the sorrow over Caleb that weighed heaviest on me, even more than the regular beatings I was getting from Horace or how I'd lost my way with my other two children. For all he was not my natural child, I had to admit that I loved him better than I loved either Donald or Dell, yet he'd broken my heart at every turn. I mostly blamed his daddy for that, of course, for however Caleb turned out, he'd been set on that road long ago by Clement Handley's strange and violent ways, but I couldn't help but blame myself for an awful lot of it, too, especially for taking him into Horace Taylor's home so soon after Reuben's murder.

We should of stayed in Chautauqua, or gone to Missouri. But we hadn't. We'd stayed in Sedan, in the house where Caleb wasn't wanted no matter what Horace had said to trap me into marrying him. Except that I wasn't trapped. I did it of my own free will, and I'd stayed there in spite of I could of—should of—walked out at any time and taken my children with me.

And Caleb paid the price.

That is a burden that even today, after all these many years, I know I'll carry to my grave.

So I laid my plans, waited for the slow turning of the seasons, then with winter coming on, packed my bags, and sewed what little money I'd squirreled away into the hem of my heaviest dress.

Then early one morning the week before Christmas, I confronted Horace as he spooned globs of oatmeal into his mouth and told him I was going to see my boy.

I expected a fight, but he just paused, looked up at me for a moment, then commenced eating again.

Once he'd stomped off to work in the pre-dawn darkness, I roused Donald and Dell, fixed them their own breakfast, and explained that I was going on a trip and would be back in about a week or so, that they were big enough to take care of themselves, and that I loved them. I told them I likely would not be home before Christmas, but if I wasn't, I promised to give them the presents I'd made when I did return.

Donald never said a word.

"You're going to the hanging, aren't you, Mother?" Dell asked.

It caught me by surprise. We hadn't spoken of it even once since we heard the news.

"Yes," I said.

She just nodded and went back to eating her breakfast.

I told them to mind Horace, and took off for the railroad depot on foot, lugging my bag behind.

Within the hour, I was aboard the train and on my way.

The miles that passed between Sedan and Lansing, where the state penitentiary was, were grim and dark, I'll tell you. Winter had turned the land the color of old ashes, and of course my mood was darker still. Though it was just four o'clock in the afternoon when we pulled into the Lansing depot, it was dark as night and spitting little balls of sleet. I trudged to a small boardinghouse the railroad clerk told me about and got myself a room.

The place smelled of mildew and dead mice and the old woman who ran it had her own odor of rosewater and filthy undergarments, but it was cheap and practically within the shadow of the prison where Caleb was waiting to die.

The next day, I screwed up my courage and walked the few short blocks to that grim place with the intention of talking my way in to see Caleb.

The penitentiary was as ugly a building as I ever saw, with grimy sandstone blocks like some old castle looming over everything, and miles of rusty, tangled-up bobwire and guards on horseback riding the perimeter. They passed me through the main gate and two other locked doors into a waiting room. When the warden came out, he was pleasant enough until I told him who it was I'd come to visit. Caleb had been hard to handle, he said, and wasn't taking his sentencing well, and a visit from his foster mother wouldn't make things any easier. So he sent me away, saying he was sorry but suggesting I go back to Sedan on the first train.

I was back on his doorstep the next morning, with a loaf of bread I'd paid dearly for at the boardinghouse so I had something to eat even if the powers that be made me wait all day and all night, too, which is what it looked like the warden was going to do. I sat on an old oak bench in a long stone hallway all morning and into the afternoon and practically until suppertime before the warden came outen his office and told me to get out or get arrested.

But I was back the next morning, and the next after that, and finally I guess he figured I wasn't going anywhere and the thing to do would be to let me see Caleb and get it over with. He ushered me into his office and sat me down in front of his big oaken desk.

"Since it's Christmas Eve," he said, "I suppose I'm bound to do the Christian thing and let you visit with the prisoner."

I started to thank him, but he held up his hand.

"Fifteen minutes. That's what you have. After fifteen minutes, you have to go." Then he told me to wait while they got Caleb ready.

A half hour later, two burly guards who looked like roughnecks from the oil fields took me to a small room with a solid steel door and a single window not much bigger than a shoebox with four iron bars in it on an outside wall. There was no glass, and the sleet and snow that had continued to fall every day had found a way to angle in through that window so one stone wall was coated with a thin layer of ice. It was cold enough that I could see my breath.

After I'd been waiting another ten minutes or so, that steel door opened with a clang, and in came a guard, dragging Caleb.

He was shoeless and wearing the ugly black-and-white striped uniform seen on prisoners in them days, and they had big iron shackles on his legs with about ten inches of chain between them so he had to shuffle when he walked. His hands were cuffed, with the cuffs chained to a stout leather belt around his middle that buckled at the back, where he couldn't get to it. They set him down in a straight-back chair and took another piece of chain and bolted one end to a ring in the floor and the other to that belt. My boy couldn't of moved more than two inches in any direction unless he had a stick of dynamite.

But I confess I wasn't looking at all that rigging.

I was focused on his face, or rather the deep purple bruises and welts that disfigured him so that, along with signs of premature age that I hadn't expected, I wasn't sure I would of recognized him if I'd of bumped into him on the street.

"What happened, son?" I asked as soon as all the buckling and clanking stopped and the guard stepped away, though he kept a wicked-looking twelve-gauge shotgun pointed directly at us.

Caleb glanced at the guard and then down at his feet. "Nothing."

"You been hit. Many times."

He shrugged. "Guess so."

"Why?"

"He's a wild one," the guard said with a sneer.

I could see Caleb wince at that, and I reckon I did, too.

"Forget it, Momma Eva," Caleb said. "It's not important." His eyes twitched at the corners, and though his glance flicked acrost my face, it didn't hold. Instead he appeared to be interested in something down around his naked feet. "You been hit, too."

I didn't say anything to that.

"Well," he said after what seemed like a long time, "you shouldn't of come."

"I had to see you again."

He shrugged as best he could weighted down with all that iron. "Forget about me is my advice. You've spent too much time worrying about me. Look after the little kids instead."

"They're not so little any more," I said.

"Well, look after 'em just the same. Forget about me."

The way he said it brought tears to my eyes. "I love you, Caleb. You're my son, just as much as Donald. More, if you want the God's honest truth. I know I didn't do right by you a lot of times, but..."

He stopped me with a jerk of his head. "Don't you say that, Momma Eva. You're the rightest thing that ever happened to me. The only right thing that lasted. If it wasn't for you, I'd of been dead before I even had a chance at living."

I swallowed hard to keep my tears under control. As I looked at him, all them years just melted away, and I could just picture him in Jack's lap, or standing alongside Reuben, taking in the intricacies of the way Reuben would weave the little strips of leather for a quirt. "You lost too much in your life," I said. "I'd give my own life in a minute to change that."

"Can't be helped."

"No, it can't."

I looked up at him, knowing the red rims of his eyes reflected the welling tears in my own. "If you'd of just been a cowboy. Something useful..." I let the words trail off.

He actually smiled. "I'm not exactly the kind who works for wages, Momma Eva."

"No," I had to agree. "But still, a body can wish."

He put his head back and looked at the low ceiling, and I knew he was wishing, too, though for what I couldn't rightly say.

I never did ask him whether he'd done the terrible things he'd been convicted of. The murder, at least, I reckoned was on his conscience, and probably most of the rest of it had been his doing, too. Instead, I filled what little time we had left by telling him how Dell was turning into a fine young woman and Donald was making his way in the world, leaving out the part about running off to Chautauqua over that Danker girl every chance he got.

"How's Horace treating you?" he asked once I'd run out of chatter.

"Fine," I said, as chipper as I could.

"You're lying, Momma Eva. Like I said, you been hit."

I sighed. "He's a hard man, Caleb, you know that. But he means well."

He laughed out loud. "Meaning well doesn't enter into it. He's a cruel sonofabitch, and you know it. The knocks they're giving me in here, I deserve. You don't deserve to have a single hair on your head harmed. Get shed of him first chance you get is my advice." He licked his lips and his left eye twitched. "Though I reckon my advice ain't worth much."

I took a deep breath. "Caleb, I'm so sorry. Sorry for what you've been through that I didn't have any say over, and sorry for what you've been through that I did."

"You saved me," he said. "Or tried to."

I had to pull a hanky outen my bag to dab my eyes.

He took in another breath and looked up at the ceiling. "Momma Eva, tell me about it. You never have."

"Tell you about what?" I asked.

"My mother and father. What happened." A little smile flickered acrost his face. "You'll never get another chance."

Well. That struck me to the quick. I reached for his hands, to hold them, but the guard stuck out the business end of the shotgun and glowered at me. Caleb pulled back as much as he could and shook his head.

"Just tell me, Momma Eva."

So I told him. Everything. How that rude hole in the ground and a worthless husband had robbed his mother of her sanity, how she had killed his father and then herself, how much I wished I could of done something to stop that terrible double murder.

"I don't really remember Jack Ross," he said softly once I had finished. "I wish I did."

"He was a good man, Caleb. You had two good fathers."

"Yes," he said. Then he looked me square in the eye and said "I told you, if it wasn't for you, I'd of had no life at all. What's been good in my life is because of you. What's been bad ain't your doing. But starting tomorrow, just forget about me. Please."

"Caleb..."

He gave me a sort of crooked smile. "Funny, isn't it. How both my ma and me will end up the same way."

I tried to speak, but no words came. Then, just like that, our time was over and the guard told me I had to leave.

"I'm staying in town," I managed to get out as they started to unchain Caleb from the chair. "Until after Christmas." Them words caught in my throat enough to choke me.

"Go home, Mother," he said. "Please."

That gave me a start as it was the first and only time in his life he'd called me that, just *mother*.

"No, I'm staying." I didn't tell him it was my plan to take his body back to Pawhuska for burial next to Reuben. I tried to reach out, to touch his face, but that guard with the shotgun got betwixt us.

"I love you, son," I said, but he was already shuffling out and didn't say another word. I watched him go, loaded down with iron and chains and stoop-shouldered like an old, old man. I blew a kiss after him, and then they rounded a corner and he was gone.

I spent the loneliest Christmas Eve of my life in that town. It stayed cold and damp, with a leaden sky that matched my mood. I kept to my room, which I had to share with an old woman with no teeth and a snore that I swear rattled the window loose in its frame. Though I'd paid for two meals a day, I had no appetite, and I certainly wouldn't of appreciated the company at the boardinghouse table, anyway. In spite of the holiday, several of the gentlemen boarders had come to town for the express purpose of watching the hanging. Most were old bachelors or widowers without kith nor kin, I suppose, though one was the bank owner from Claremore, who'd come all that way just for the pleasure of seeing my boy die.

It made my flesh crawl.

How was one family's tragedy going to make amends for another? He didn't know I was related to the prisoner, which was just as well, and from the way he went on at the top of his lungs about it being blind justice and about time Oklahoma got serious about getting these criminals behind bars or swinging from a rope, I doubt it would of made any difference to him.

On Christmas morning, I tried to visit Caleb again. The deputy warden was on duty, the senior warden having the day off, and it was clear he didn't want to do it, but apparently his boss hadn't actually said I was to be prevented, so I prevailed on his Christian spirit and he sent word to the cell block once more that I'd come to see my boy. This time, Caleb told the guards to let me know that he wasn't up to it, which disappointed but didn't exactly surprise me. I went back to the hotel, and the rest of the day, I just sat on the edge of my bed, lost in memories.

Was there anything I could of done different beyond keeping him outen the clutches of Horace Taylor? Short of killing Clement Handley myself so my poor sister didn't have to do it, I didn't suppose there was. What Marcellus had said was true: Caleb had been star-crossed from the very beginning.

It started to snow hard about dark, with a wind that cut straight through that drafty old lodging, but I scarcely noticed.

I laid awake all that night and past dawn the next day with my stomach tied into a knot so tight I almost wondered if I was having a heart attack. The men who had come to see the hanging were up early, clumping up and down the halls and shouting at each other in the dining room to please pass the ham and gravy. They were right jovial. It was a Thursday morning, and they were going to a hanging. What could be better than that? All of them took off for the prison together, and only then did I go downstairs for a cup of coffee. The mistress of the house must of figured by then what I was up to, for she stuck her nose in the air and wouldn't talk to me, as if it was my fault that my boy was about to die at the hands of the State of Kansas, on behalf of the people of what had just become the State of Oklahoma.

Well, maybe it was my fault.

She poured me some coffee, tossed the back of her hand in the general direction of the few cold biscuits her boarders hadn't wolfed down, and left me to my own ends.

I sat at a small table in the kitchen, jumping every time I heard any sound, all of them seeming to me like the thud of a trap door being sprung.

How can I explain the emotions I felt as I sat there, waiting for that boy to die? I can't. Some things are beyond description.

I tried to pray some as I sat there, but it wasn't anything I'd ever been much good at, at least when the chips were down. Praying's easy when there ain't nothing serious to pray for, but when your favored child is about to die...

Anyway, it was too late for prayer to do any good. I asked God to forgive Caleb if He would, and to forgive me as well. I added my sister Dell into the bargain, but I couldn't bring myself to ask for forgiveness for Clement Handley. Then I just ran outen steam and sat there staring into that coffee cup like some kind of lunatic or something. Sometime around eight-thirty or nine o'clock, I felt a breath of cold wind, and from its place in a box of rags by the potbelly stove, the landlady's old cat woke from a deep sleep, hissed and pawed at the air.

I knew at that moment it was over.

By ten o'clock, the men came drifting back in, and I'll say this: at least they were suitably somber, having seen a thing that no right-thinking person could enjoy even if he did consider it justified. More than one of them men was ashen faced and trembling, which told me all I ever needed to know about what they had witnessed.

I pulled together all the courage I had, walked past them men and that un-Christian lady of the house and stepped outdoors. The day was fierce with needles of wind-whipped snow and so gray it was as if God himself had drained all the color outen everything in Creation. I walked through the biting wind to the prison, and there I made the arrangements to pick up Caleb's body that very afternoon, explaining that I intended to have it loaded onto the afternoon south-bound train. I think they were relieved they didn't have to bury him in the prison's potter's field, most likely because that ground was iron-hard with frost and it would be some weeks before they would of had a prayer of busting through the sod to put in a coffin.

It cost me five dollars to get my boy's body, which was what they figured that pine box was worth.

A prisoner they trusted outside the walls wrestled the coffin into an old wagon, then he clumb up onto the seat next to me and we rode through the streets of town to the railroad station. He put the box with my boy in it on the siding along with all the other freight, touched the brim of his old slouch hat, and headed back to his prison home. I found a bench inside, curled up, and waited with nothing but my misery for company.

The train was late on account of the weather, but by early evening, we were rumbling south, me in a passenger car with wooden slat seats and Caleb in that five dollar plain pine box in the baggage car.

I guess that was where I got God's answer to my feeble prayers, which was simply this: in the end what happened to Caleb was his choice. He was the one who dropped the hammer on that Claremore policeman. He was the one who robbed them places. He knew better, but yet he did it. And now it was over. What his pa did to his ma, what she did to him, what Fate and family—and my own failings—did to that boy and then what he did to others was all in the past.

Let the dead bury the dead is what the Bible says.

Somewhere, deep into the dark hours, I started to cry as I

had never cried before.

I'd bought a ticket for Chautauqua instead of Sedan, and when I got there early in the morning, the same old liveryman Caleb had worked for once upon a time gave me the loan of his wagon to haul my sad cargo south, back into Oklahoma where my son's happiest and meanest days had been spent. He did me the kindness of loading the coffin, and Caleb and I headed for the Line together one last time, and never mind that the powers that be had told us both we weren't welcome.

I found some of Reuben's cousins in Pawhuska. One, an old man who'd been to my wedding, solemnly agreed to take the body and wrap it. He had an ice house where he could keep Caleb's body until the ground thawed, and he likewise promised to bury my boy next to Reuben when it was possible to do so. I took him at his word, for I'd never known one of them full-blood Osages to lie, at least when it came to something as serious as sending a body into whatever was waiting for it in the hereafter. I told him that the Osage policemen might not think kindly about that on account of what they'd said when they released Caleb to me in the hills above town, but he just smiled and said there wasn't no Osage that would hold a man's past sins against him in death.

Well, that comforted me mightily, and after sitting alongside that pine coffin for a few hours on a bitterly cold afternoon, I said my good-byes. What I said I reckon is my business and no one else's, no matter who it is that's reading these words.

Then it was over, and I bundled up against the chill and turned the wagon north.

I've not been back to Pawhuska since.

As I made my way toward home, lost in thought as I was, I scarcely noticed the weather or even the time of day. The old slat-sided horse the liveryman had lent me knew the way home, and that was enough for me. The rolling country and the gray winter sky that nearly touched the earth were invisible to me, even the wicked outcrop where Reuben had died.

So it was that I practically rode past Marcellus just south of the Line without even noticing, never mind that he was hallooing and waving at me. If my horse hadn't stopped because of the commotion, I don't think I ever would of seen him.

"Glad I found you," he shouted, waving at me. "I was hopin' you'd come this way."

It had been so long since I'd laid eyes on that man I thought he'd left our territory, and under the circumstances, I wasn't all that keen on talking to him, what with my grief over Caleb weighing me down, never mind the suspicions Horace had planted in my brain.

Still, I steered the horse in his direction.

I reckoned he'd been waiting for some time from the looks of the campsite he'd spread out in a cluster of bare bur oaks a few yards off the track. He had a little tent pitched as a combination shelter and windbreak, and there was a remnant of an old campfire. An ancient mule browsed nearby where he'd picketed it near a copse of cedar.

He took off his hat as I drew close, and I was astonished to see his face. It was bruised and swollen, with the left eye practically closed and clotted blood marking a wicked slash on his cheek.

"Whatever in the world happened to you?" I asked as soon as I had my wits about me.

"Never you mind, Miz Eva," he said with a small bow. "You the one that's had it hard."

"Life is hard, ain't it, Marcellus?" I said back at him.

He allowed as how that was surely true.

"Why're you out here in the middle of nowhere?" I asked, knowing it sounded curt.

"They's some trouble in town, Missus," he said, pointing

north.

From the looks of him, I figured it was serious trouble, indeed, and a shiver went up my spine. Surely he hadn't done some awful thing to my child and come here expecting forgiveness. "What have you done, Marcellus?" I asked, sounding cold and intending it so.

"Not me," he said. "Mister Horace." He lifted his head. "I got to leave. Got to get outen here. But I need to tell you what happened 'fore I do."

I stood in the buggy and looked around, half expecting to see a posse come thundering over the top of the nearest hill, even though we were still in Osage country. "What did you do, Marcellus?" I said again. "You didn't kill him, did you?"

"Oh, no'm," he said. "Should of, but I didn't."

And then, just from the look he was giving me outen that good right eye, I had the first inkling of what I'd been too stupid to see before. My blood ran absolutely cold.

"Marcellus... my children..."

He swallowed hard. "They's all right. I brung Dell to Miz Maudie for safe keeping."

"Safe keeping?"

"Mister Horace... he... what I mean is, that's how come him and me got to fighting."

It took me a moment. Then I knew it all, as plain as day. "God in heaven." I slapped the reins over that old horse's back, startling it awake. Marcellus stepped forward and grabbed the poor animal's halter.

"Miz Eva, whyn't you set a spell?" he said without letting loose, and pointed me toward his little camp. "Let me explain?"

"I have to get to my children."

He held tight to the halter. "Your chil'rens are safe. Let me explain," he said so quietly I could hardly hear.

It was the least I could do.

***

What he told me as we crouched next to his little fire in that slow, steady way of his just added to the anger boiling within me so that I was afraid I'd explode or, more likely, go crazy betwixt it and the sorrow I was already close to smothered by. The thing I'd feared—and had been too ready to blame on Marcellus, thanks to Horace's poisonous accusations—had come to pass while I was away.

On Thursday last, even as I was waiting to pick up Caleb's body, Horace had gone to where Donald was at work on somebody's flivver and paid the owner a dollar to let the boy take off early on account of it was the holidays. Of course, Donald immediately headed for Chautauqua to be with Lydia Danker, leaving just Horace and Dell in the house alone.

By the grace of God, Marcellus was having a bite of lunch given to him by the Baptist parson's wife in the spirit of the season, though of course being a black man, he had to eat it at her back door rather than at the table with the other Christians. Anyhow, Marcellus saw Donald ride down Elm Street on his way outen town, and just like that, he said he got a bad feeling and decided to pay a visit to our house.

"To tip my hat and wish your Mister a happy belated Christmas if everything was all right," he said, squatting on his hind quarters on the cold ground there in the shadow of his little windbreak. "Maybe to he'p out if things was amiss."

I couldn't hardly control my rage at what I knew was coming next.

"Well," he said as he traced figures in the winter-dry dust with a gnarled finger, "of course they was. Amiss, I mean."

He swallowed hard and looked up at the gray sky for a long time, trying to put the words together. Then he just blurted it straight out: he said he could hear Dell screaming before he came within ten rods of the place. He broke into a run, went around back, and banged on the door.

"'Mister Horace! What's wrong with that chile' is what I shouted," he said. "Of course, the hollerin' stopped right away, so I knocked again. Wadn't but a second or two before she must of broke away, because she hollered out my name, and then I heard a crash." He paused, licked his lips, and touched the bruise on his face. "So I bust the door open."

I scarcely heard what he told me next I was shaking so hard, but the gist of it was that he saw a naked Horace standing over Dell with both her shirt and skirt wadded up in his hand, having ripped them off in their struggles. Horace was red faced and breathing hard, and Dell was bleeding some from the nose and mouth. Marcellus took one look and lunged for Horace, tackling him and knocking him off Dell and into the parlor.

"I tole that chile to git outen there while Mister Horace and me commenced to poundin' on one another," he said. "She done as she was tole."

"He must of gotten the best of you," I said, inspecting his wounds. Horace was fat and got winded quick, but he outweighed Marcellus by at least a hundred pounds, and as I knew very well, he had a powerful wallop.

He shook his head. "Would of, I suppose. Except I managed to knock his head against a table leg. That took the starch outen him." For just a moment, his good eye shined. "So I did it again."

With Horace out cold, Marcellus said he figured it was time to get shed of that place in a hurry, what with being a black man who'd just broken into the sheriff's home and fought him to a standstill. So he tied my husband to a parlor chair with a strip he tore from my curtains in hopes of slowing him down once he came to, then he lit out for safer pastures. He said Dell was still in the yard, half undressed and with a pitchfork in her hand in case it was my husband who came outen the house first, so he wrapped her in what was left of the curtains, saddled Horace's big old horse, adding horse thievery to his crimes, and the two of them rode double all the way to Chautauqua where Maudie took them in, or Dell, rather. For his part, Marcellus headed straight for the Line because he knew he'd be the object of a manhunt as soon as Horace managed to get free. Maudie had given him the loan of a mule and a rusty pistol and told him she'd keep Dell safe from Horace if it took a shotgun to do it.

"Miz Maudie's watchin' to see if you come through town, but I set up camp here because I jus' knew you'd come this way," he said.

"So will Horace," I said, and I took him by the hand. "You're in mortal danger, Marcellus."

He nodded. "Could be. Ain't too worried on it."

"Well, you should be. You go fast as everything to the Osages. They'll look after you." For my part, I ached to jump into my wagon and race to Chautauqua to see my daughter.

"No'm," he said. "I'm goin' back to Gove County."

"You won't be safe there. You won't be safe anywhere in Kansas." *Or anywhere on the face of the earth* was what I was thinking. "Besides, you sold the place."

"That's all right. Peoples know me. 'Sides, it's home," he said. "I know that now, if I didn't 'fore I went to Colorado." Then: "Come back there wit' me. You an' the chile. They's a pretty little boardinghouse in Grainfield I believe could be had for a song, and it does nice bidness from the railroad. I'll take care of the place an' you kin run it." He gave me a weak smile, twisted as it was by the swelling in his face. "Jes' like we did when Mister Jack died."

I reached out and touched my fingertips to the black clot on his cheek. He backed away almost as if he'd been burned.

"I can't, Marcellus. My home is here. And I still got my children to consider. Besides, what would folks think, me taking off with a black man?"

He looked away as he spoke. "You know I didn't mean it that way. We's friends is all, and it seems to me you could use a friend."

"Marcellus, you're the one that needs a friend," I said.

"Please go to the Osages."

"No'm."

"Then run. As fast as ever you can. You've waited far too long already."

His good eye slowly came up and met mine. "Yes'm, I s'pose so" he said. He reached into his pocket and handed me a twenty dollar gold piece. "Tell Miz Maudie this all I got to pay her for the mule."

"I'll tell her, Marcellus."

And with that, he gathered up his few belongings and was gone.

Horace

WHAT HAPPENED OVER THE NEXT DAYS seems more like nightmare than reality all these years later. I stopped for Dell at Maudie's. Francine was there, helping to serve as a look-out, and even the Chins had posted themselves near the corner of Olive and Johnson Streets where they could keep an eye on the road from Sedan.

To her everlasting credit, or perhaps to Maudie's, Francine was sober as a judge. She had an old shotgun some boarder had left behind long ago all loaded and primed and standing in the corner just in case Horace showed up, which he had not. Maudie said Dell had taken to bed and wouldn't talk to nobody. Of course I raced upstairs anyway, calling her name as I ran so she wouldn't think it was that no-good snake I called a husband that had come to get her. She was cowering in the corner with a pile of quilts around her, and though I was hoping she'd talk to me, she just rolled away and faced the wall. I sat on the edge of the bed, looking down on her for the longest while, until I swear I could hear both of our hearts beating. I asked her flat out if her daddy'd had his way with her, and all she said was "My daddy's dead," meaning Reuben, of course, and echoing what poor Caleb had said so often all them years ago. I tried to pet her hair, but she shuddered under my touch, and at that moment it seemed plain as day I'd lost two of my children in the same week.

So I told her I loved her and that Francine and Maudie would take care of her and I'd be back in a couple of days, once I finished with the business that needed doing in Sedan.

Then I sped north, growing angrier with every mile.

When I got there, Horace was gone. The word all over town was that my black friend had tried to rape my daughter, that her step-father had fought him off until knocked sense-less by treachery, and now he and a posse were searching for the culprit with the express purpose of stringing him up. The Methodist pastor's wife told me this straight to my face, and she couldn't help but sneer as she told it, looking down her nose at me as if to say I ought to be dangling on a rope with my friend. There wasn't a bit of concern about was Dell all right, no matter who it was that had tried to despoil her. Just outrage that poor Sheriff Taylor had been treated so badly at the hands of a black man.

Most of the folks in that town were mighty poor judges of character, I'll tell you.

Even Donald gave me the cold shoulder, and though he knew better, it appeared he'd begun believing the tall tale being told. In the course of a heated exchange with my son, I pointed out that none of this would of happened if he'd stayed home where he belonged instead of sashaying off to Lydia's house, but that just prodded him into accusing me of being the one who'd left the both of them alone and spoiled Christ-mas into the bargain.

Which stung all the more because it was the truth.

All I could do was try to put the house back together, about half our meager supply of furniture having been busted up in the fight. What little crockery we had left was smashed to smithereens, and there were dried blood splatters every-where and a gouge in the parlor wall where something or someone had hit it hard enough to bust the plaster.

So I worked like a demon and, like Francine, kept a

loaded weapon with me at all times in case that sonofabitch I was married to came home.

It was the longest week of my life.

I had to eat my words about Lydia and apologize to Donald and ask him to make his trips to and from Chautauqua just so he'd deliver a daily letter to Dell and let me know how she was doing.

She was fine enough, he said. She'd begun helping Francine with the chores around the house—same as I'd done more than twenty years before—and otherwise kept to her room. Donald said she looked good, though his thoughts were so full of Lydia that I wasn't sure he'd of noticed if his sister had been struck by leprosy.

Dell didn't answer to my letters, but Francine did. I could practically hear her cluck-clucking and see her finger-pointing as I read how my daughter needed a change of scenery and good Christian care and that a good mother would set up housekeeping so she could care for her daughter.

I burned them notes in the cookstove and fretted about when that despicable so-and-so of a husband of mine would come home.

Which at last he did.

It was the third day of January, 1908, the day after Dell's fifteenth birthday, which of course I'd missed, and cold enough to turn the slops in the night jar to stone. Sky and earth both had the same gunmetal color, exactly matching my mood. I was scrubbing something in the dishpan and watching the yard darken to dusk through the little kitchen window when I saw him ride into the yard, so bundled up in an old buffalo robe that he looked like a bear sitting atop a horse. I confess that it was all I could do not to take Jack's old Colt's revolver, which was within arm's reach on the drainboard, and send him straight to hell right then and there.

Donald had arrived home from his trip to spark Lydia and deliver my letter not a half-hour before and was not having much luck trying to piece a table leg together so it would hold.

"Son, get outen here this minute!" I said as I watched Horace dismount.

Donald looked up at me.

"Your father... Sheriff Taylor's home. Get outen here."

"Ma..."

I whirled on him. "Go. I don't care where. Go back to Miss Lydia's, for all I care. Just go. That way!" I pointed toward the front door. "Don't talk to him. Don't stop. Just go."

"Ma..."

I must of brandished the gun, because he grabbed his coat and bolted outen the front door.

Then I turned my attention to the big man outside.

He was moving slow, like his body hurt, and he took his time getting the horse rubbed down and fed, which of course wasn't like him at all. He knew I was home, for he kept looking over his shoulder in the general direction of the house. As I stood there at the window, my hands shook so they actually made a knocking noise on the drainboard, and when I saw him turn at last and start trudging for the door, I slipped that Colt's revolver into my apron pocket. The weight nearly pulled that apron offen me, but I cinched the tie tighter and turned to face the door and braced myself.

He opened the door real careful, as if he expected me to take a shot at him. The cold swirled into that room like a knife, and as nervous as I was, my teeth began to chatter. He stepped over the threshold, took one long look at me and at the heavy lump in my apron pocket, shut the door, and stripped off that big old buffalo robe, which commenced to steaming in the warmth of the kitchen.

I pulled the revolver and thumbed back the hammer to half cock and held it out in front of me with both hands so it pointed straight at Horace. It surprised me how steady I held that gun, but at that moment I could of killed him and not skipped a beat.

"You going to shoot me, Evie?"

"It'd serve you right."

"How so?" He had a half-smile on his face, but he didn't move away from the door, neither, which I took to mean that he was weighing the odds and leaving himself an escape route if need be.

"You know damn well how so," I said.

"Seems to me like you're the one ought to be punished," he said evenly. "Taking up with that nigger the way you did, and then him trying to rape your daughter." He smirked as he said it.

"'Twasn't him trying any such thing."

"That so? I come upon it and seen it. If I'd of been a minute later, he'd of had his way with her, and God knows what would become of that child then."

"You don't give a hoot in hell for that child, Horace. Never have." I swallowed hard. "Except as the object of your own evil lust. I should of seen that years ago, and it shames me I didn't."

"You're crazy, woman. I wouldn't harm a hair on that girl's head, but that black bastard sure as hell would."

"Ain't the way she tells it."

"Then she's touched in the head. Same as you." He actually chuckled, as if what I'd said was some kind of joke. "Probably accounts for your being attracted to the darker races. I been thinking about having you committed to the insane asylum, if you want to know the God's honest truth. The way you put up with that murdering nephew of yours, then keeping company with a black man. And now this."

"Dell told me the truth," I said, surprising myself at how easily the lie came. "She said you did the despoiling."

Suddenly, he was dead serious. "Then maybe I'll have to have the both of you put away."

"What about your posse?" I asked, wiggling the gun.

There was that smirk again, almost big enough to be

called a smile. "Caught us a nigger, all right."

"Him?"

"Why you want to know? You thinking of joining him?" He made a lewd gesture.

I thumbed the hammer to full cock. "Was it him?"

"Don't reckon I know. Can't tell the difference one from other with them black boys. 'Specially when they're so scared they pee their pants. The one we caught's a couple of inches taller than he used to be, is all I know. If you get my drift." And he laughed.

That did it. I squeezed the trigger. The hammer dropped, and that big old gun roared, knocking me backward and filling that little kitchen with blue smoke. I caught my balance to keep from falling and brought the gun up and cocked it again. My ears were ringing so bad I was sure I was going to be stone deaf.

I'd missed him, more's the pity, but I did put a hole in the wall not two inches from where his head had been. The bastard's grin was gone, I'll tell you that, and all the blood had drained outen his face.

"You git, or I'll kill you for certain," I said. I meant it, too.

He must of believed me, because he reached behind him and snagged that buffalo robe offen the hook.

"I'll see you in the insane asylum for sure, woman!" he said, and I heard it plain in spite of the ringing in my head.

"Git!" I aimed the gun carefully this time, and found that I was even steadier than I had been before.

He got.

I watched him saddle up and go, then I blew out the kerosene lamp, stoked the stove to keep some kind of warmth in that drafty old house, and slumped to the floor and sat there the whole night long with my back to the wall. The shakes had come back so hard I thought I'd come apart.

Just thinking about Marcellus strung up somewhere, Caleb in his grave, and both my other children driven away by my neglect and the evil I'd allowed my husband to bring into our home made me think more than once about turning that old gun on myself except I wouldn't give Horace the satisfaction.

Sometime near to midnight, Donald came creeping back in and went straight to bed. I never said a word and don't know to this day whether he already knew about me taking a shot at his stepfather, though he surely figured it out the next day from the silver dollar sized hole in the kitchen wall. Around midnight, I could hear the wind come up and thought I could hear Horace's horse nickering in the yard. I got up and peered out the kitchen window, but there was nothing there. I put more wood in the stove and sat down on that cold floor again, and there I was when the sun came up.

Word got around town fast that I'd driven Horace off. He kept to the sheriff's office while I packed up my few belongings and prepared to move back to Chautauqua permanently.

Surprisingly, I discovered it pained me to leave, what with that house had been my home for ten years, and I dawdled. I could of been ready to leave in a few hours, but instead it took me two days—partly, I believe, because something inside me was daring him to come back and have it out one final time.

During them two days, Horace, the coward that he was, stayed outen my way. Donald, being Donald, spent more time at the sheriff's office than he did at home, and it was plain as day whose side he took in the whole affair. I begged him to stay away from Horace, too, but I knew I was just wasting my breath. Instead, he announced he'd go where he pleased, and that he was taking a room at the Danker place. To tell the truth, I was relieved. Let the Danker clan expend the energy keeping him and Lydia apart if they could, and if they couldn't... well, so be it. I had my own worries.

Anyway, I took my time packing an old valise I'd had

since Jack Ross and I left Missouri with what little I owned outright, and I raided the old cigar box under the bed for whatever cash Horace had stashed there. He must of done that himself before the posse went out in search of Marcellus, because there wasn't but four bits in hard money and a couple of two-dollar greenbacks. I rolled the coins inside the bills and stitched them into the hem of my drawers. They chafed a bit, but at least I knew exactly where that money was.

I even got up the gumption to push my luck by going downtown to buy a few necessaries (carrying Jack's Colt in my handbag just in case). From the looks the local folk gave me, it was pretty obvious they'd taken sides, too, and weren't going to miss me when I left town. The Methodist parson's wife, as always the town's biggest gossip, made it a point to scurry over to the mercantile just so she could tell me in no uncertain terms that folks had had about enough of all the high anxiety over Caleb's crimes, the shame of his hanging, and me cavorting with a Negro. She did allow as how she had some sympathy for Dell having been nearly raped, though of course since it was that black friend of mine that had tried to do the deed, the good folks of Sedan would just as soon she stayed in Chautauqua, or better yet leave the county alto-gether so they wouldn't have to be reminded of that particular brand of sin every time they saw her.

To top it off, she told me it would be best if I didn't come to Sunday services any more, in Sedan or Chautauqua either one.

What the parson's wife, nor anyone else, wouldn't or couldn't tell me was anything about the black man that Horace and his posse may of lynched. The livery man, who had no ax to grind with Marcellus, did say the posse had gone northwest, toward Wichita. If Marcellus had headed straight for Gove County once he left me, it could well of been him they caught, but the fact that Horace hadn't bragged straight out that it was Marcellus, who of course he knew by sight in spite of what he'd said, gave me some hope on that score. Still, when I saw Charley McGuane standing on a street corner as I headed home, I asked him right to his face was it Marcellus that was lynched. He just turned red, stammered something, looked at his pocket watch, and took off like someone had lit a fire under his behind.

It wasn't an hour later that I got the visitors that nearly scared the life outen me and convinced me I'd pushed my luck too far hanging around Sedan.

I was just coming back from the fruit cellar, where I'd gone for spuds to make up a bit of supper, when I heard the sound of hoofbeats on the still-frozen ground. I managed to get just inside the back door and throw the bolt before two men on horseback rode into the side yard. I could see them through the tiniest crack between door and jamb.

One was Judge Latham, an old reprobate from up in Elk County who was a poker player and drinking chum of Horace's—the same one who Horace had always claimed had done him a huge favor keeping Caleb outen prison over the Magruder buggy deal. The other was a big bruiser of a fellow I didn't recognized, but his horse was weighted down with saddlebags that scarcely moved when that horse stepped, as if they were full of lead.

Judge Latham pulled out a huge old bandana and blew his nose into it. "Eva Rae Taylor, you come out!" he called once he'd stuffed that rag back into his pocket. "We know you're in there."

The other fellow clumb down offen his horse and opened one of the saddlebags and what he dragged out froze my blood: manacles and chains attached to long strips of leather just like what I'd seen Caleb wear. He dangled them from his big hands and turned as if to come toward the door, but the judge called him off.

"What you want to do, let her see that kit afore you're ready?" the judge asked, though soft enough that I wouldn't of been able to hear it if I hadn't had my ear pressed against the door.

The big fellow just shrugged and stuffed the shackles back into the bag.

"Come out, I say!" the judge thundered again.

"Mebbe she ain't to home," the big man said.

"She's here," Latham answered. "Horace says she don't leave 'ceptin' to use the privy. An' even then, she carries a big old Colt's with her."

"I heard she was downtown just this afternoon."

"Well," the judge snorted, "she probably had the gun with her then, or we would of taken her. I had that Scotchman McGuane on the lookout."

That gave me a queasy feeling, I'll tell you. I looked over my shoulder to where I'd left the gun sitting on the kitchen table.

The big one got back onto his horse. "You never said nothing about her having a gun. I didn't come all the way down here to get shot at."

"Crazy people always have guns, don't they?" the judge asked.

"Some do and some don't, Judge. Depends. Most are just as apt to claw your eyes out with their fingernails or stab you with a kitchen knife as use a gun."

"Well, this one uses a gun."

"Whyn't Sheriff Taylor take it away from her?"

Judge Latham snorted like he was exasperated having to answer an idjit question like that. "Because she'll shoot him if he tries."

"Oh."

The judge hollered to me again, and yet again. In the meantime, I was thinking just what I could do to get away from them. Suddenly, he called out "Consider it a warning, then, Missus. You best be ready to come out when we come back. And we will be back."

Then they left. Just like that.

I'll never know for certain whether Horace put them up to that just to scare me out so he could come home or whether they really would of put them chains on me had I stepped outside, but either way, it didn't take a genius to figure out that the big fellow talking about crazy people was from the insane asylum, and Judge Latham for certain had the authority to send me there. The asylum was in the town of Osawatomie, which was famous for having been the place where John Brown butchered a bunch of the pro-slavery folks during the Bleeding Kansas days, and it was known as a grim place, indeed. Once you went in, you never came out. Most of the folks there were said to be women gone crazy from loneliness or loss, just as my poor lost sister Dell had. It sure wasn't a place I had any interest in ever seeing the inside of.

So if I wanted to keep outen a straightjacket and away from the company of lunatics, I was going to have to vacate my current premises as fast as ever I could.

Once I was sure they were gone, I tucked that revolver in my apron pocket and collected my valise and a few other belongings which I bundled up into a pillowcase. I cut the handle off an old broom, tied the pillowcase to the end of the handle, then slipped outen my housedress and into a pair of Donald's trousers and an old work shirt he'd outgrown and sat down, nervous as a cat on a stovetop, waiting for dark.

When it came, bringing a cold wind outen the north with it, I pulled on a cap Horace used to keep his bald spot covered when he used the privy, jammed the Colt's into the waistband of the trousers I had cinched up with a piece of twine, and stepped outside. With that stick and pillowcase over my shoulder, the valise dangling from my left hand, and all them man's clothes, I looked just like some old tramp. At least I hoped I did.

It hurt like sin that I was letting Horace win, driving me outen my home. What hurt far worse, though, was the certain knowledge that he'd never pay a price for what he'd done to Dell and maybe Marcellus, leastwise not this side of the Pearly Gates.

But just then, my main job was keeping him and his pals from sending me off to the asylum.

Cold logic told me that Chautauqua might not be much safer than Sedan, but on the bright side, it was just a hop, skip and jump from Oklahoma, where I might be able to beg some sanctuary with my old Osages in-laws, leastwise until I could figure something else out.

It was time to hit the road.

As I walked south that night, keeping to the shadows as best I could and getting colder by the step, I couldn't help but think of all I'd lost so recently.

Losing Caleb him for good on Christmas had put an ache in my heart that would never heal. Then to come so close to losing Dell, to lose my home, and to face a grave risk of losing my very freedom all within just a matter of days seemed more than a body could bear.

But bear it I must.

Maybe I could win Dell back was my only hope if I could somehow make amends for not seeing what that snake I'd married was up to. It was about all that kept me trudging along on that bitter winter night.

So it was that I wound up back in my old room offen the kitchen at Francine's, where I kept my valise packed in case I needed to make a break for Osage country in a hurry.

Lord knows, there was plenty that needed doing around her place.

The boardinghouse had fallen into serious disrepair in the years I'd been gone, probably on account of both her drinking and the boarders being oil field roughnecks. The third floor was closed off entirely, given over to bats and birds, the second floor sloped off to the side worse than ever, and everything smelled of must and the congealed black grease the men tracked in.

Still and all, them oil men did bring in the business.

In them days, oil drilling rigs were sprouting up all over like sunflowers in August. Oil men, like the railroad boys and the cattlemen before them, found Francine's place to be a convenient, if somewhat down-at-the-heels, abode. Once I moved in, with Maudie Calkins's constant urgings and at least some encouragement from me, Francine actually let up on the drinking a bit, and together, the three of us got the place spiffied up so it was almost respectable.

Of course, no matter how much we cleaned, the drillers and muscle-bound laborers sitting down to dinner acrost from the money men and prospectors who scouted the countryside looking for likely places to drill left such a stink of oil in her parlor that even Francine's heaviest gravies tasted of the stuff. Her chairs took on a dark sheen, and try as she might to protect her things with doilies, that oil just oozed on through. She complained about it something awful, but them fellows' money was good, and she wasn't about to kill the golden goose by kicking them offen the property.

For a while, she even took up with one of the money men, but it turned out he had a wife in Tulsa and another one back in Pennsylvania somewhere, so in spite of the gold double eagles he kept stacking on her bureau, she told him to get out. I know it was hard for her, and though I'd never taken her for a woman of very strong morals, it appeared that putting up with philanderers had become an embarrassment for her, especially as she aged. Anyway, her next beau was a rough-neck who had to be fifteen years her junior. He wasn't the brightest of gents, to put it kindly, and he certainly wasn't rich, but he was a big, strapping fellow with rippling muscles and a nice smile. He was always polite with women, too, which is more than I can say for most of the better educated men I met down through the years. I do believe Francine actually fell in love with him even though it was a lead pipe cinch with his looks that he had other ladies in other towns. But she claimed to be happy, which was good enough for Maudie and me.

Anyhow, it didn't take long before Francine's place felt as much like home as it ever had, and after a while, I didn't worry so much about Judge Latham and that asylum fellow. By the time winter began to peter out and spring was coming on, I decided if they were coming for me, they'd of been there already.

Meantime, I kept busy helping around the place, Dell had a cot in the corner, and we shared a small chest of drawers that I think had belonged to Francine's son Rufus once upon a time. Dell even started back to school, though that only lasted a few weeks. The teacher was a cross little thing who hadn't but barely gotten through high school herself and didn't know much more than Dell, and she was forever turning up her nose and grumbling about having to teach a half-breed, so one day Dell announced she was finished and said good-by to her formal schooling, having gotten most of the way through the ninth grade.

During all that time, I just couldn't seem to close the distance betwixt my daughter and me. She and I didn't talk much, and that's putting it mildly. We'd never been close, me being too intent on trying to keep Caleb outen trouble, and now she just seemed to tolerate me because she had to. I tried more than once to get her to tell me what had happened that day when Marcellus rescued her from Horace, but she'd go all stony-faced and pouty. If I point-blank asked her had Horace ever hurt her, she'd just look away and put her hands to her ears as if just the sound of his name was painful. So I figured I knew all I had to and let the matter drop.

More and more, she spent her free time at Maudie Calkins's little place, helping Maudie with chores and whatnot but seldom talking. Maudie, great soul that she was, said I should just leave her be, that Dell needed to find her own way. I supposed that was the way it was going to be even if it did make me feel as if I'd abandoned my child at the moment when I should of been making up for lost opportunities.

Anyway, in what seemed like no time at all, it was almost as if we'd never lived in Sedan, though every time I looked in a mirror, I could see the permanent welts that proved I'd been at war with Horace. I also kept my valise packed so I could make my break for the Line if the need arose.

Turned out it was Charley McGuane who told me the coast was clear, at least for the time being.

It was late March or April sometime—I know the crocuses had already bloomed and the lilacs were sweetening the air— when Charley appeared at Francine's front door. I was in the back cutting up chicken for supper, and when she called out loud enough that I could hear it "Well, Deputy McGuane, what brings you here?" I skedaddled for my room, thinking maybe I could get outen the back door or even climb through the window to get away. I could hear voices in the parlor as I checked the load on the Colt's.

Then it was quiet for a spell, and finally I heard Francine at my door.

"Eva Rae, Charley's here to see you," she said softly through the closed door.

I pulled up the sash on my window and got ready to make my break.

"He says he's only here to talk and has no interest in arresting you or otherwise taking you into custody," she said.

I took a deep breath. "Do you believe him?"

"I do."

"Is there anyone with him? Like a big man on a weighted down horse?"

"No," she said. "He's alone."

I thought for a moment about going out the window, just in case. Instead, I put the Colt's into my apron pocket and opened the door a crack. Francine was still there.

"You sure it's safe?" I asked.

She nodded, and from the look on her face, I could tell she meant it. "He said if he had wanted to arrest you, he would of done it that day in Sedan," she said. "Whatever that means."

True enough. I stepped into the hall and followed her to the parlor.

Charley was standing there looking as nervous as a cat in a room full of rocking chairs. He always wore a little bowler hat, which he was turning in his hands. He smiled when he saw me.

"Eva Rae, it's good to see you."

"Charley," I said.

He glanced at the weight in my apron. "You won't need that. I'm just here to bring you some news."

"Oh?"

"Your husband..." He blushed crimson. "I mean Sheriff Taylor... he's had a heart attack."

In spite of my absolute hatred for Horace, that struck me to the quick. "Is he...?"

"He's alive, praise be," Charley said, "but he's in a bad way. His horse threw him right on Main Street. We thought he must of busted some ribs, but it turned out his heart almost gave out on him. Doc Claymore says he'll be laid up for..." Charley paused and looked down at his shoes. When he looked up again, I could see there was a tear in his eye. "Well, it could be he won't make it."

"I'm sorry," I said, though honestly I wasn't at all.

"Anyway, Miz Taylor... Eva Rae... he's asking for you."

That pretty well stunned me. "What on earth for?"

Charley shook his head. "Don't know. He just said would I fetch you."

I thought for a moment. "No," I said. "There's too much bad blood betwixt us. I don't have any interest in being seen in Sedan, and if I did go, we'd just argue, which might just kill him, which would satisfy me no end except I'd only wind up with it on my conscience." I figured there was also the possibility it was a trick meant to put me into the clutches of Judge Latham and his asylum man, no matter what Charley said, but I stayed mum on that.

He looked at me, and I looked back at him, and I swear he almost smiled. "I told him that'd be the way of it," he said. "Sorry to bother you." Then he did a little bow to Francine and me, turned on his heel, and clumped outside.

Francine started to say something, but I just turned my back to her and went to my room.

Turned out that Horace had the constitution of an ox, and in no time his ticker was sound enough for him to be up and around, and by late summer he was back on the job as if nothing had happened. I kept to Chautauqua, he kept to Sedan, and life went on about as normal as it could.

For a while, I toyed with the notion of going back to Gove County to see for myself if I could find Marcellus in case it wasn't him the posse had strung up and maybe look into that boardinghouse in Grainfield he'd spoken of, and I even considered heading for Callaway County to see if one of my Cumberland relations might take me in, but in the end, it was just too much work to think about moving on. Besides, I knew that at least one of my children wouldn't come, him being so smitten with Lydia Danker, and as for the other, it was becoming clearer and clearer every day that we just didn't even know how to talk to one another.

I still kept that valise packed through the summer and into the autumn, but once the weather commenced to turning crisp again and it had been nine months since my visit from the Judge, I figured it was safe enough to settle in and not worry any more.

Besides, I had a new concern, which was that Dell had a

beau.

The first I learned of it was when she announced to Francine one night at the supper table (she just talked past me as if I wasn't there) that she was in love.

Well, who was it, Francine asked.

David Branch, she said, and then she gave me a look that was pure challenge, as if she dared me to say a word.

"David Branch," I said, looking away. I took a bite of peas. I knew in my heart that Dell was grown almost to womanhood, and I'd seen young Mister Branch around town with his clan many a time. He'd been all arms and legs and foolishness as a youngster, but it was true that he'd grown tall and handsome and had good manners and the bluest eyes you ever saw, so it only stood to reason that any girl of Dell's age would swoon over him.

The trouble was, he came from a big family of no-accounts who were well known for being long on looks and short on brains.

"We'll talk on it later," I said without looking at my daughter.

"Nothing to talk on," she said. "David and I are already keeping company."

Just like that.

When just the two of us we were doing dishes later, I brought the subject up once or twice, but Dell acted like she didn't hear.

It wasn't exactly that I didn't approve of David. He was mannerly enough. I just thought Dell was too good for him, and the truth was that I was worried about how maybe Horace had spoiled her in some way.

I couldn't tell her that, of course, but over the next weeks, I did tell her for certain that she wasn't but fifteen years old, and unless she wanted to wind up with the endless drudgery of a farm wife, she should get outen Chautauqua County and see the wide world before she settled down. I also told her I didn't want her to miss out on the things a young woman of her qualities by rights should see, nor did I want her to get trapped into marriage the way I had. If she got hitched to a Branch, there'd be babies and hard work and growing old before her time, and someday she'd look at that boy acrost the kitchen table and he'd be an old man, used up by chores and the lack of common sense that ran in his family, and she'd be worn to a frazzle and too tired to do anything about it. Lord knows, I hadn't done nothing in life to give her hope for anything else.

Naturally, I could tell from the hard look on her face every time I brought it up that I might as well of been talking to the wall. So after a time I let the matter mostly drop, though I couldn't help but give her my two cents' worth every once in a while.

From what I could see, the Branches were a dim bunch, and that's putting it mildly. Their good qualities—natural politeness and rugged good looks—never quite made up for how singularly unsuccessful they were. Poor as church mice didn't say the half of it: that family could go from one month to the next without ever coming within spitting distance of a plug nickel. The kids—and there was a lot of them—would wear their clothes until you could practically see right through the parts that weren't patched with whatever kind of fabric that happened to be on hand, and I know for a fact that the boys went years without a proper pair of shoes, keeping the winter rains and snows offen their feet by plugging the holes in their brogans with bits of cardboard or folded up newspaper. Their homestead, which was about halfway betwixt Sedan and Chautauqua along a salt creek, didn't seem to grow anything but prickly pear and weeds, and I swear even their chickens starved to death most winters. Everybody liked them, they being a particularly friendly lot, but everybody pitied them at the same time. David's pa was a drinker, too. He was a pleasant sort for a drunkard, but a drunkard nonetheless, and a lame one to boot, having gotten busted up so bad he couldn't work at all when a wagon overturned on him one night coming home from the saloon. David's ma, who I will say was a good Christian woman who always smiled and tipped her hat to me even when most of the biddies wouldn't give me the time of day, didn't have the knack for running that place on her own nor making her kids do the necessary work, so the whole shebang just sort of dwindled away to nothing. It actually made Ma and Daddy's place in Callaway County seem prosperous by comparison.

Then there was another bunch of Branches, cousins, who had the wildest streak I've ever seen. They weren't mean like the Daltons had been, but every now and then, they'd get a bee in their bonnets about something, usually over some remark somebody had made about them being poor, and the next thing you'd know, there would be somebody's fences cut and a dozen heifers run into a wheat field or their outhouse would be burned down or their front and back doors would be nailed shut so folks would have to come and go through a window for a day or two.

Wouldn't you know but Dell would take interest in one of that clan.

But my two cents had no impact at all on my daughter. She'd set her cap for David, and that's all there was to it.

Then came the afternoon when Francine announced she'd invited David for supper that very night.

Well, I was furious at both my daughter and best friend for flouting my wishes, but what was I to do? I welcomed him, though with what I was sure was a steely glare, and sat there while them two chatted merrily away like a couple of school kids, which of course they pretty much were. After all the years of silence between us and Lord knows how many meals she'd just stared down at her plate without saying two words, having Dell talk about anything and sounding so gay into the bargain should of been a welcome thing, but it grated on me like dragging rocks over a washboard.

I did have to admit that David was about as good looking a young man as there was in them parts and probably for a long way beyond, though of course I've never been one to put much stock in looks, Reuben Whitesnake notwithstanding, probably on account of what picking a pretty boy did to my poor sister. Anyway, David was tall and slender except for wide shoulders, with a straight nose and them piercing blue eyes and hair the color of buttermilk that he greased and parted down the middle after the fashion in them days.

Turned out that unlike the rest of his family, he fancied himself to be smart as a whip, too.

"Mrs. Taylor, I'm going to go to college," he said to me as Francine and Dell were clearing the dishes and bringing in slabs of pie for dessert.

"Pardon?" I said.

"College," he said, and he gave me a smile that would of melted stone. "Once I get the money together, I'm going to the Kansas State Normal School in Emporia and become a teacher."

"You don't say." I almost laughed. Getting the money together was going to take a genuine miracle given his family's poverty. Going to college was practically unheard of in our neck of the woods, anyway, even for folks who actually did have the brains and a dollar or two squirreled away. In my heart, I figured David was just play acting at being smart for my benefit.

I just couldn't let Dell waste her life on that boy, so that's when I said something I shouldn't of in hopes it would make him change his mind.

"You know Dell's half Osage."

He got a startled look for a few seconds, then blushed and said "Oh, I know that. It doesn't matter a whit to me. Heck, my grand-dad on my ma's side was part Cherokee."

Well, that shamed me, I'll tell you. Now I'd just insulted

both him and my own child into the bargain.

Anyway, after the pie, he announced he was departing for home, took my hand and shook it like a gentleman, thanked Francine, smiled at Dell, and was gone.

Francine said she'd do the dishes on account of maybe Dell and I wanted to talk, but I told her in no uncertain terms that my daughter and I would do the cleaning up, thank you very much.

This time, I told her straight out that I did not—could not—approve of whatever she had in mind with David Branch.

She stopped right in the middle of lifting a plate outen the soapy water and gave me a look that would of stopped a charging bull in its tracks.

"You've got some nerve, Momma," she said, talking at last but spitting out them words one at a time.

Now, that put my hackles up, and I had to bite my tongue pretty hard. "I'd maybe feel differently if he wasn't a Branch," I said. "I'll admit he's a nice boy, but..."

"Whether you approve or not doesn't have a thing to do with it," she shot back.

"Now, Dell..."

"I'm almost sixteen, Momma. How old were you when you got married? The first time, I mean."

"That was a different time, child," I said, "and you know it wasn't my idea."

"How old were you?"

"You know I was thirteen."

"Yes. And you didn't even love him. You thought he was a mean old crusty no-account loafer—don't deny it because you've said so yourself—and you and him turned out all right, except that he died."

"Got nothing to do with whether you're ready..." I tried to put in, but she had a head of steam up.

"But I'm almost sixteen and David will be nineteen next month and he's going away to college to be somebody."

"How on earth is that boy going to afford college? If you scraped together every penny his family has, he couldn't afford to buy shoe strings."

"I'll work. I'll take a job at the mercantile or clean houses."

That absolutely shocked me. A young woman working! Of course, I had worked—was working still—but that was different somehow.

"I forbid it!" I fairly shouted, and before the words were outen my lips, I knew I'd made the second terrible mistake of the evening. She just glared at me for a minute, then set that plate down in the dishwater as daintily as I've ever seen it done.

"Forbid all you want, Mother. I'll do as I please." Then she whipped off her apron, tossed it onto the butcher block next to the stove, and stomped out past Francine, who had been listening from the dining room, and through the front door.

That was that, and I suppose both of us knew it. Dell had a mind of her own, and when it came to picking a man, there wasn't much likelihood that she was going to pay attention to anything I said under any circumstances.

Though I continued to try. But any time I mentioned the failings of the Branches, she'd just turn her back to me and pretend I wasn't even there. Sometimes when I was harping on the subject, she'd even get a faraway look in her eye or give me that little smile that said she knew something I didn't. I more than half expected to hear that they were betrothed or—God forbid—that she was in a family way.

I was plumb working myself up into a fine frenzy over it until Maudie Calkins sat me down one day and told me I should just let it go.

"The harder you push, the more that girl's going to dig in her heels," was the way Maudie put it, and though I wanted to argue, I had to accept that what she said was probably true.

Besides, another matter raised its ugly head.

Horace. Again.

He had another heart attack just after Christmas, and though he recovered once again, this time it was certain that he'd never be the same. I had biddies clucking to me about how I should go back home and look after my man until I was ready to scream.

"The milk of human kindness don't run through you the way it should," one said. Or another would add "Whatever you think he done, it's you that should be finding some forgiveness in your heart now that he's so sick." Of course, to their way of thinking, he hadn't done anything bad at all. It got so that by the time warm weather came, I actually figured I had to go to Sedan and look in on him just to shut up them cackling hens, but one thing and another came up, giving me some excuse or another, and I didn't get it done.

Then, in October of 1909, I heard that Horace was sinking fast. He'd managed to get through most of another year, but the end was coming.

At least that's what the gossip said, and this time, when Charley McGuane came and told me that my husband was asking for me and wanted to apologize, I went. To this day I don't know why, but I did.

The ride into Sedan in Maudie's buckboard, with Maudie and Francine at my side for moral support, was like a dream. It was coming on to two years since I'd left. The biddies on Main Street looked shocked when they saw me, but once they'd come to their senses, they still turned up their noses and gave my friends looks that would curdle milk. It bothered Francine, but Maudie, bless her, just thought it was funny.

We stopped first at the sheriff's office, where Charley was ensconced behind Horace's desk. He rose, tipped his bowler to the three of us, thanked me for coming—"It'll be a blessing to your husband," he said—and added that he would be pleased to escort me to my old house. The ladies were surely welcome to come along, but on account of the delicate condition of the patient, they would have to wait outside, and since it was a warm Indian summer day, surely they'd prefer to repair to the hotel for a refreshment. Francine was just about to agree, but Maudie cut her off and said no, they'd be fine waiting for me in the yard.

"So there aren't any shenanigans," she said, giving poor Charley her fiercest stare.

After he got done blushing and stammering that no, ma'am, there wouldn't be no shenanigans at all, we "repaired," as Charley had put it, to where Horace lay dying.

What I found in that little house shocked me. All a body had to do was open the back door to know it was as filthy as a pig sty, and it reeked of human waste. It turned out I wasn't the only one who had abandoned him in his hour of need. During that last couple of months, all the old pals had stopped coming. His Masonic friends, his beer drinking chums, the courthouse gang—everyone except good old Charley. Maybe Horace's condition embarrassed them, or maybe he'd driven them all off in one way or another, or maybe they'd only pretended to be his friends on account of his position as sheriff, but in any case, they were ignoring him. Even Donald, who had snuck into Sedan to visit his stepfather many a time when he thought I wouldn't find out about it, had stopped coming. If it wasn't for Charley looking in on him twice a day, he could of been dead for a week before anyone would of noticed.

"We got to clean this place up," I said from two feet inside the back door. I could hear snoring coming from the bedroom, and a thousand old memories and some not so old came flooding back. What I really wanted to do was run, though the way my knees had turned to jelly, it was unlikely that I could of managed it.

"Time for that later," Charley said, and he pushed me forward. I stepped a couple of feet and stopped.

"I don't know," I said.

"It'll be all right," he said. "I'll waken him." He left me

standing there while he went into the bedroom. A few seconds later the snoring stopped, and right after that, Charley beckoned to me.

I took a deep breath and clumped acrost the parlor and into that small, dark room. The stale air smelled of unwashed man and sour breath and witch hazel.

Horace was propped up on the bed. I could see even in the dim light that filtered through the filthy curtains that he had lost a great deal of weight. His cheeks were sunken and covered with a scraggly growth of beard, and the grayness of his skin told me right away how sick he was.

"Howdy, Sure Shot," he said, using what was of course the old-time nickname for Miss Annie Oakley, who had become famous touring with Buffalo Bill and his Wild West show. He sucked in a breath and attempted a smile. "Ain't seen you since you took that pot shot at me." Just that bit of talk clearly took all the strength he had.

I acknowledged him with a nod. "Horace."

"Thank you for coming."

"Charley said you've been asking."

He closed his eyes, and I thought for a moment he'd drifted off. "Charley's a good man," he said.

I agreed. Then, as I stood there, he did slip into a slumber, but a rasping snore wakened him. He licked his lips, looked at me, and seemed surprised that I was still there.

"Charley said you wanted to apologize," I said. "Otherwise, I wouldn't of come. You know the bad blood between us ain't never going to go away."

He held up a hand. "I know." And again, the eyes closed and I thought he'd drifted off, but he gave a little start and looked me square in the eyes.

"You've got a lot to apologize for," I said.

"We'll get to that," he said. He reached for a glass on the little table beside the bed, but his big paw just bumped it and it fell to the floor. Without thinking, I stepped over beside him, picked it up, and hurried it out to the kitchen. The water bucket in the sink had moss in it.

"I'll fetch some fresh," Charley said, lifting the bucket and heading for the door.

"No, I'll get it," I said. The truth was, I had to get outen that house, to fill my lungs with clean air and see if I could get shed of the hatred that had started to suffocate me the moment I faced that man again.

Maudie had clumb down from the buckboard and scared up some oats from the stable, which she had poured onto the ground for the horses to eat. Francine had sort of sprawled on the wagon seat and shaded her eyes with her bonnet. They both eyed me.

"It's filthy," I said as I flung what little water there was in the bucket into a patch of dying weeds where once I'd grown pansies and asters to add a bit of color to the place. Maudie took the bucket from me and carried it to the pump. She worked the pump handle a couple of times and gave up.

"Needs priming," she said.

I shrugged and went back into the house and told Charley about the pump.

"So there's no water for him right now."

Charley mumbled he'd take care of it and would I please go back in and talk to Horace as he'd hollered out he was afraid I'd left.

I steeled my nerves and went back into that bedroom. Horace's face actually brightened some when he saw me.

"It'll be a while getting you a drink," I said.

He waved it off. "I was trying to apologize, like Charley said."

"Go ahead."

"I done some awful things in my life."

Even in the dim light, it seemed to me like he was smiling. "That's for certain," I said. "You tried to have your way with your own step-daughter. And don't you deny it, because

I know it's true. Are you going to apologize for that?"

Slowly, his eyes came up to mine, then darted away. I thought I saw him nod, but I wasn't sure.

"Say it."

Again, he smiled and licked his lips. "I apologize," he said with a shrug.

"Don't sound like you mean it."

He took a deep breath. "Well, hell, there was that nigger she was always cozying up to. A redskin and a nigger! I figured she needed to be taught by a white man."

If I'd of had my gun at that very moment, I would of blasted him to Kingdom Come. "You evil bastard."

He coughed, reached for the glass again, and gave me a hard look when he realized it wasn't there, as if I'd taken it from him on purpose.

"Well, I apologize if she got her feelings hurt. Didn't mean her no harm."

I truly wanted to kill him. "If that's all you had in mind to apologize for when you called me here, you shouldn't of wasted your breath."

"Oh, there's more," he said.

My own heart skipped a beat. "Marcellus."

He twisted under the bed clothes like he was squirming to get away from something. "No."

"You didn't lynch him?"

He waved it off. "Not important."

"Of course it is," I said, but again, he waved his hand again as if flicking away mosquitoes.

"What then? You asked me to come here. If there's more, now's the time to say so, for I'm never coming back."

He rubbed a hand over the stubble on his cheeks and tried to push himself up in bed a little. He licked his lips and gave me a quick glance in the eye, then looked away. Finally, he said right out, clear as a bell, "Your man. That Indian."

It took me a moment. "Reuben?"

"White woman like you shouldn't of got spliced to a redskin. Ain't fitting. That's what got him kilt."

"He was ten times the man you ever thought of being," I said, "and color didn't have a thing to do with it."

"Well, it's what got him kilt. You begged me to find his killer, but I didn't have to."

"Why not?" I asked.

He licked his lips again. I waited.

Then, in an instant, it hit me. "Oh my God!" My knees started to give out and I had to clutch at the door frame to hold myself up. "Dear God, tell me it wasn't you."

"You thought he was better than the rest of us. Thought he was something special. So I had to prove he wasn't."

"You bastard!" I screamed, and I started for the bed, ready to beat him to death with my fists.

He held up his hand. "You strike a dying man, they'll send you to the asylum for sure." And he smiled.

That stopped me.

"Anyway, that's what I wanted to tell you," he said. "I'll apologize for the other, just so Charley's not made out to be a liar, but that's why I really asked you here. So you'd know." Somehow, he managed to laugh. Then he turned his head away. "Now get outen here and go back to them mongrel kids."

As I stood there, he drifted off to sleep and started snoring just like nothing had happened.

Well, as clear as the memory of him lying there telling me that is to this day, I scarcely remember what happened next. Somehow, I got outside. I think I was sick to my stomach and when Charley tried to help me, I know I slapped him because Maudie told me later that I did it and commenced to screaming at him, accusing him of knowing it all along, but I have no recollection of that, either. She said it took both her and Francine to hold me, and it was a long time before I calmed down.

I do remember Charley standing beside the buckboard once they'd gotten me up into it.

"Most nights, I've been at his bedside reading to him outen the Bible," Charley said as if it was Horace I was grieving for. "He likes the first few books of the Old Testament, which is pretty dry going, but that's what he wants."

"I hope you been reading the Ten Commandments to him over and over," Maudie said, for she'd already guessed the gist of what I had learned. "Especially Number Five." Then she snapped the reins and wheeled that old box around. Charley stepped away, and let us pass.

I sat there, watching as Deputy McGuane and my old house got smaller and smaller, and then we turned for home without saying one word the whole way.

Now, I've been told that a good Christian woman would of forgiven him on the spot no matter what he'd done on account of it was clear that he was going to be dead in no time, but them who make statements like that weren't in my shoes that day. I couldn't forgive him, and I never will.

If that's a blot on my own soul, so be it.

Hard Times

I NEVER SAW HORACE AGAIN in life.

I wanted to. I truly wanted to kill him, and I plotted a hundred ways to do it when I'd be lying in bed at night, I was that consumed with hatred. Just the thought of that man still being alive with my Reuben nearly twenty years in the ground made me absolutely ill. It didn't help that Francine swore she didn't believe it and insisted that Horace had only told me that to get my goat. Maudie took my side, but it was she who warned both Francine and me to keep the whole matter to ourselves, saying that Horace was absolutely right that if we spread the tale around, it would only get me sent away and I'd wind up spending the rest of my days amongst the lunatics. She actually told Francine she'd do her bodily harm if she breathed a word of it to anyone else, knowing how Francine could spread gossip with the best of the biddies.

I decided on my own not to tell my children on account of there wasn't any reason to burden them with that awful news. Donald wouldn't of believed it anyway, and as for Dell... well, we weren't exactly on speaking terms anyhow. I'm sure she could see how consumed with anger—hatred—I was, and I suppose she thought it was aimed at her for sparking with David Branch, for she started sending black looks to me that were identical to what I saw in the mirror every morning. All I could do was get through the day as best I could and, in the darkness of night, imagine ways to make Horace pay for the evil he'd done just to give him a foretaste of what he faced in Hell.

Of course, Horace rallied once again. I don't know how, but he did.

Autumn turned to winter, then to spring and early summer once again, and that Godforsaken excuse for a man was still with us. Rumor had it that some time after my visit, he'd found the strength to get up and around and had actually cleaned up the house a little. In time, he even managed to get himself over to the sheriff's office, where he tried to lord it over Charley McGuane. At least I was able to take some small comfort in learning that he'd not won back any of his old cronies on account of how he'd belittle everyone he talked to right to their faces, even old Judge Latham, who got Horace booted outen the Masons.

In the meantime, I kept outen sight, just doing my chores for Francine and wishing I could get on better terms with my daughter.

Then, in July of 1910 came the news I'd been more than half expecting, though not in the way it was delivered.

Donald and Lydia came by one Sunday afternoon and announced they'd gotten married. After all that long engagement, they'd just up and taken one of Emil Danker's buggies over to Coffeyville and gotten themselves married by a retired Lutheran minister. There was no hoo-haw for them at all, and no honeymoon, neither. Emil and the missus and that passel of kids cleared out of the family home for one night so the newlyweds could get started without any company, then moved back in the next morning. They'd been married a week before they got around to telling me.

"We're going to Sedan to tell Pa," Donald blurted out once we'd pretty well run out of other things to say, which hadn't taken very long.

"Pardon?" I said.

Just like that, Lydia's look went from sweet to sour. "We would of had a proper wedding," she said in a tone that made me wonder if she thought she was talking to a child, "but you and Sheriff Taylor being on the outs made us decide against it."

"So it's my fault you eloped," I blurted out.

A flush of red came to her throat, and she started to say something, then stopped and just looked away, as if something on the far side of the room had caught her interest.

Donald tried to smooth it over. "We're just going to share our news with Pa. That's all." He took his wife's hand and squeezed it. "Then we're going to look for a little place, and I'm going to set up my own shop. Mr. Danker—Pa Danker, that is—says I'm better with engines than he'll ever be, so he's going to help me get started."

The way Lydia looked at him, suddenly all aglow, you'd of thought he'd just got elected President or something.

"Well, if you need a place to stay while you're looking..." I said.

"Oh, we couldn't possibly live here," Lydia said with a little laugh that made me want to slap her.

And they didn't. They bought a drafty little clapboard cottage over on Elm Street. It wasn't much more than a lean-to with a chicken coop and an outhouse in the back yard and a summer kitchen off to the side. It reminded me of a smaller version of the rattletrap old place I grew up in. Lydia didn't like it at all—you could tell that from the patch of color on her throat that returned whenever I asked her about it, which I confess I did fairly often once I realized it got her goat, but Donald thought it was just the best. "We're snug as a bug in a rug," he'd say, all grins, then he'd give Lydia a little squeeze, which made her blush even more. By then, of course, she was with child, which I suppose didn't put her in too good a mood on account of she got the punies right off, or said she did, and she stayed sickly right up until the baby was born, which kept Donald at home looking after her. The baby, a boy, lived three days, then went home to the Lord. Donald took it harder than did Lydia, and it wasn't long before she was expecting again.

But I'm getting ahead of myself.

To this day, I don't know how their visit with Horace went. Of course, I was hoping he'd curse at them or belittle Donald the way he had his old pals, but I never asked. They did see him a time or two after that, and Lydia always called him a "fine old gentleman" in my presence, which nobody in their right mind would of actually thought about him, so that was just to take a jab at me.

Meanwhile, Dell continued to work silently alongside me at Francine's, then got a paying job at the general store on Main Street--to save money for David's schooling, she said. I learned that them two were formally betrothed, though she never did tell me outright, letting me hear about it through the biddy grapevine, and when I asked her about it, all she said was that it wasn't none of my business.

Whole weeks would go by where we wouldn't exchange two words beyond "Morning, daughter" or "Good night, Mother." When she wasn't with David, she spent all her free time over at Maudie Calkins's place, which hurt some, though at least I knew Dell was in good hands, never mind what the biddies said about that woman's habits.

Good is good, no matter what polite society says.

Finally, the following winter, came the news I'd been waiting for—hoping for, to tell you the truth.

Horace's constitution finally failed him.

The Methodist preacher called on the telephone on the tenth of December to tell me that Horace had died, but telephones being scarce in them parts, he actually had to put the call through to the Chautauqua bank, and the banker came and told me. It snowed that day, with a sharp wind that blew the snow into knee-deep drifts, so I had more than enough excuse to stay away from Sedan.

I do confess to a peculiar mix of feelings as I sat in Francine's parlor that day watching the snow drift and settle after I'd trudged back from taking that phone call at the bank. I didn't have the least bit of fellow feeling for Horace on account of the terrible things he'd done, and the fact that he was dead didn't change that one whit. We'd been married going on fifteen years, though sometimes it seemed more like a hundred. Of all the endless loss I'd seen, from Daddy to sister Dell, Jack and my little baby to Reuben and Caleb, this was the one I couldn't mourn. Yet, somehow, I felt sad, if only for the lost years.

At its very best, our marriage hadn't been but what polite society would call a marriage of convenience, pure and simple, and in the end, all that was left was hatred—me for him certainly, for how could it be otherwise, given what he'd done to me and mine?

I told the children, of course. I trudged through the snow to Donald's little home to deliver the news. He wept, then took off for the Danker place, saying he needed to help old Emil shovel out. I didn't see him again for two days. Dell just turned away and went about her business as if it wasn't of any consequence even though Horace had been the only daddy she'd ever known, never mind about the worst kind a child could want.

Three days later, I made the trip to the mortician's parlor in Sedan alongside Donald and Lydia. As far as Donald was concerned, I was doing my duty, but in my heart I confess I mostly just wanted to remember Horace the way he was now: dead. Besides, I figured that whatever threat that old man posed to me had died along with him. Dell would not come, nor did I try to make her.

The funeral was a sparse affair, I'll tell you. Charley McGuane, who was now the sheriff in name as well as fact, and his wife were there, along with a scattering of old timers.

The undertaker had done his best, but Horace was down to about ninety pounds when he died, which was long past skin and bone and into skeletal for a man of his size. The Methodist preacher, who was new to the church since last I attended, read from the Psalms and said a few words about Horace's long service to the people of Chautauqua County. Donald sobbed out loud and Lydia dabbed at her eyes though they looked dry to me.

We followed the hearse to the cemetery, the pastor said a few more words about dust to dust and ashes to ashes, and then it was over. He was to be buried alongside his first wife, but as the ground was froze solid, they propped his coffin up on a couple of saw horses in a little shed, where it would stay until they could dig a proper grave come the March thaw.

Afterward, we rode back to the courthouse for the reading of the will. A new lawyer in the county who couldn't of been a day over twenty explained that Horace had instructed that the house and all his property was to be sold at auction, with the proceeds to be sent to an orphanage back east I'd never once heard him mention. Me and mine weren't to inherit a thing, which didn't bother me one whit, though I could tell that it troubled Donald.

On the way outen town, we went by the house so Donald could sniffle a little, then we rode home and ate fried chicken and biscuits that Francine had prepared.

So time passed.

In the peculiar way of things, it seemed as if the days dragged by and the weeks would never come to an end, yet the years themselves came and went so fast that it was like I'd slept through them.

I admit that the more I got to know David, the less I could stay angry with Dell. There was something about him, something that for certain made me think he'd somehow been adopted except that he looked like all his brothers. He loved a good time like the rest of his clan, but there was a serious side to him, too, that you didn't see with his brothers or cousins. He even told me one night when I relented and let Francine invite him over to supper that he had his college plans all worked out, that he'd farm through harvest, and then begin his schooling over to Emporia. He said that even working every free minute, it would take him longer to finish college than most, and he was sorry about that, because it meant he and Dell would have to put off the wedding awhile on account of he just couldn't burden a wife with that kind of sacrifice. I saw her nearly come to tears at that, but I also saw they'd talked about it already and David, bless him, had had his way.

It gave me a new sense of confidence in the boy, I must say, because if he could win an argument with Dell, he had to have some kind of backbone that the rest of humanity lacked. Still, I took that whole discussion of college for so much hot air, mostly because I didn't think them two young ones could live apart that long, but I held my tongue and let him have his dreams.

Well, it turned out that David was as good as his word. Their betrothal lasted dang near five years, proving me and probably everyone else in Chautauqua County wrong. Dell bore up well enough, and when he was in college, she moved to Emporia to be near him, but they kept separate quarters and near as I could tell never did a thing that either of their mothers would be ashamed of. She drummed up work cleaning house for various bachelor professors, and although I worried that she'd get the same kind of treatment I did from that nasty Herbert Wilbertson back in the old days, if she did, she never let on, and I reckon she was tough enough to handle her own business on that score, anyway. David worked two and three jobs the whole time, too, mostly as a night watch-man at the rail yards and selling books in a store during the day so he could read most of his college texts for free, and I gather from the stories I heard later that he'd maybe go two or three days with no sleep at all. It must not of hurt him much, for he did well in college.

Their wedding was at the Methodist parsonage in Sedan on a rainy Saturday afternoon in November of 1915. Dell was twenty-two, and her new husband was twenty-five. I was glad for that, at least. By the time I was her age, I'd been wife or widow for nine years. I know the biddies around town were clucking about how she was so old only a Branch would have her, but I let them cluck. Donald felt the same way, of course, though he wouldn't say so out loud to me or his sister.

In my mind, Lydia proved that just because the bride was under twenty didn't mean she was any prize.

Anyhow, I don't believe a handsomer couple than David and Dell ever drew breath. David's ma and pa, Donald and his little brood, and I were the only folks there, though a bunch of the Branches promised a chivaree for the newlyweds when they showed up at the little hired man's house David had rented and fixed up pretty as a picture for Dell. Of course, them two knew what was coming, so it was in high good spirits that they left the parsonage after a round of handshakes with the pastor and Donald and kisses for the women. David even lifted me clean off the floor and swung me around in his strong arms and gave me such a kiss on my forehead that I know I turned the color of an overripe tomato. Dell managed a smile, though I could tell she was thinking "I told you so."

Then they were gone, bouncing toward that party like a couple of kids going off to the candy store.

I only heard about it later, of course, but that must of been some doings. I understand that a bunch of the Branch boys flat kidnapped the bride while they were still a mile short of the house and took her over hill and dale, riding ten miles to get to a one-room schoolhouse that wasn't but a half-mile from the kidnap site. There they put Dell for safe keeping and padlocked the door to keep David out. The groom had chased them every step of the way once he'd unhitched a horse from his buggy, of course, and now they attempted to jump him and tie him up or some such, but he was too fast and too smart for them. At the end, he hove a rock through that schoolhouse window and snatched Dell up right through all that busted glass and pulled her onto his horse's back and rode hell-bent for leather home. Of course, since it was all in fun, David had already set a keg of illegal beer to cool in the little spring behind the house, and once everybody showed up, one of David's brothers who could fiddle a bit started in playing jigs, the kidnappers' wives and sweethearts appeared, and the whole bunch danced and partied until noon the next day. I even heard tell that David's father stayed stone cold sober and still proved to be the life of the party.

Such was the joy with which my daughter entered married life. The truth of it is, I wished just one of my weddings had been that much fun.

David taught school in Sedan in the beginning, and from what I heard, he was good at it. They didn't have any children right off, which surprised me, though of course I never breathed a word of it to Dell, mostly because the two of us still weren't talking, but also because her loud-mouth brother was enough for her to deal with on that score, him acting as if the ability to breed on a regular basis made a person more worthy. I could of told him my own Daddy had proved that notion false.

Then came the war.

Of course, we'd been hearing about it for some while and reading about it in the papers, but France and Germany and England were far off, and the troubles them little countries were having with one another wasn't of much account in Kansas. Woodrow Wilson was President, and though he was a starchy gentleman who didn't generate much fellow feeling among poor folks in the middle of the country, he had promised to keep us outen the war, and we believed him.

That all changed in 1917. Suddenly, Army fellows were showing up in town recruiting the young men, and the ones that didn't enlist were drafted. Many a farm boy clumb down from his daddy's wagon and took up a government rifle in them days. Whole tent cities devoted to turning them boys into soldiers started sprouting up, and a body couldn't go any-where without bumping into ruddy-faced young men in wool uniforms just itching to get at the Kaiser and his henchmen.

Donald didn't have to go on account of by then he had four little ones crawling around the house, but he did serve a stint on the county draft board. I asked him once how he could send other young boys off to fight when he wasn't going to have to go himself, but he just gave me a queer look.

Dell's David did go.

Though married men generally figured out a way to stay home and work the farm or whatever, David wouldn't have any of that. In August of 1917, David's number came up, and off he went. That's all there was to it. Because he was a col-lege educated man, the Army men who set up the 17th Kansas Infantry Regiment elected him a lieutenant and sent him off to Camp Funston up at Fort Riley to learn to lead other farm boys.

Right from the start, David was a natural, though in the beginning, being a leader amounted to marching them boys up and down dusty wheat fields and teaching them how to keep the sand outen their rifles.

France was a different deal altogether, which I only learned years later. Some of the boys in David's charge went crazy from the sound of them big guns almost as soon as they hit the trenches, and before they'd even had a chance to catch their breaths, they were right in the thick of what came to be known as the St. Mihiel drive. The kind of killing them boys took part in—days on end of fighting and killing and dying—just boggles the mind. David led them through that whole shebang, and I know he wrote personal letters to at least twenty mothers from Chautauqua and surrounding counties explaining how courageous their dead sons had been. I saw some of them letters, and I saw how his handwriting changed over the weeks and months, from the beautiful curlicues of a formal well-trained hand to a jagged scrawl with little tics that I could only imagine came when a bullet whizzed by or one of them big German guns sent over a shell. Long years after, David had regular nightmares about what them boys did that would have him awaken screaming.

Dell fretted every single day he was overseas, though she was a brave soldier, too, knitting socks for the boys over there, holding war bond rallies in the schools, and taking training as a nurse in case David and others returned with wounds that needed looking after.

The war took a lot outen both of them, but it made them what they became, too, for when the war was over, David wrote to say he would be staying in Europe a while to help Herbert Hoover and his commission look after the refugees in France and Belgium. I couldn't imagine a boy from our county, let alone a Branch, helping the starving millions, but that's exactly what he did.

What the soldier boys who had fought so hard came home to was the Spanish flu. Some said it actually started in Kansas in spite of its name, though I don't understand how they could know such a thing. I do know that many of the boys at Fort Riley who never did get overseas were stricken, and many died. All through 1918 and into 1919, people all over the country would be fine one morning and be dead by nightfall of the following day. That's what happened to my brother James, at least according to the nice letter I got from his wife. Quarantine signs went up on every other house, it seemed like, but none of it helped. Small children and old folks didn't seem to be hit especially hard, but many a strong man or woman in the prime of life was felled. No one had ever seen anything like it. A mother and older child might succumb while a father and a baby were spared. A neighbor one side of you might have nothing more than a case of the chills while the neighbor on the other side died an agonizing death.

Francine was one of them.

Now, ever since Horace's demise, Francine and I had been at crossed swords. Even though she never kicked me outen the house, it was clear that she didn't approve of the way my life had turned out. Having been sweet on Horace herself once upon a time, she'd taken to believing I'd intentionally ruined her chances and spoiled him into the bargain. Her drinking didn't help, neither. When the last oil field worker to take a personal interest in her left a note on her bureau and said he wasn't coming back, she took to her bed with a jug of whiskey and got so drunk I thought she'd die right then. She didn't, of course, but her mood stayed so black for weeks that I was afraid she'd harm herself.

Then, in February of 1919, the flu struck our little town with a vengeance. Maudie caught it, though she recovered. I spent a couple of days in bed with the chills so bad I thought my very bones would crack from the shaking. A whole family on a farm a few miles from Sedan died in the space of three days. The banker—the same one who had brought me the news about Horace—died, as did a doctor over in Coffeyville who had worn himself to a frazzle trying to help the sick, proving that the flu was no respecter of social position.

Through it all, Francine seemed fine. She'd hung a little bag of camphor around her neck, saying that was all the remedy a body needed. But a few weeks after the worst of the epidemic had passed, she came to me one morning while I was washing sheets, complaining of a headache. Of course I assumed she had a hangover, but within an hour, she was screaming in pain and burning up with fever, and by the time night fell, she had soiled herself and was turning blue.

Well, I was terrified. I cleaned her up as best I could and ran to Maudie's. She had a telephone by then, so we called the doctor in Sedan. He said he'd come as quick as he could, and we ran home to see if we could make Francine comfortable. By the time the doctor got there sometime well past midnight, she was coughing so hard it sounded like the baying of a hound and blood was actually oozing outen her ears. The doctor took one look at her, shook his head, and asked me if I'd mind putting on a pot of coffee, for it would be a long night.

We took turns sitting with her. I was with her just as the dawn was beginning to lighten the sky, when she motioned to me to sit beside her.

I did.

"Top bureau drawer," she said. "Something for you." Then she was plumb carried away with a fit of coughing that I thought would tear her in two. She never said another word and died at a quarter to ten o'clock that morning.

We buried her in Oak Hill Cemetery, which wasn't but a few blocks from the boardinghouse and by that time already had more Chautauqua people in it than the town did. Maudie and I were the only mourners. We sent a telegram to her son in Colorado, but never heard a word from him.

It was only after the funeral that I actually looked in that top drawer, and there I found an envelope addressed to me. Inside was a short note saying how much our friendship had meant even though she had never been able to tell me so to my face, and the deed to the boardinghouse. She had signed it over to me.

So it was that at a month shy of turning fifty-one years of age, I became proprietor of the last remaining genuine boardinghouse in Chautauqua. Donald thought I was crazy to keep it, but keep it I did.

I was just getting my feet under me and beginning to feel

like I was meant to be mistress of that old house when David returned from Europe late in 1919 and I faced another loss. He asked Dell to come be with him in Washington, D.C., because he'd taken some fancy job with the War Department. While the other doughboys had mostly mustered out and were trying to get back to the life they'd known before the killing, David had decided to stay in the Army. His school teaching days were over. He was a major or some such rank, and the big shots liked him.

We said our good-byes at the train station, Dell and me, with Maudie Calkins in attendance. She had tears and hugs for Maudie, but my daughter and I just shook hands rather than embrace, and off she went, head held high and ready for a new adventure with her man. I know it embarrassed Maudie something awful, but I allowed as how it wasn't her fault, gave her a wink, and then went home and spent the night crying in my room, I was so low.

It dawned on me right then that the only person left in my life whose love I wanted—needed—was the daughter who rightly held everything bad that had happened in her life against me. I couldn't of been prouder of both her and David, but it cut me to the quick to know that I really didn't have anything to do with the way they had turned out.

I was never so lonely in my life.

Of course, I did have Donald, at least after a fashion. He lived and worked nearby, but somehow that didn't make up for the loss of Francine and Dell. Donald was... well, I guess the best you could say is he was being Donald, which wasn't much more than ordinary in my sights. I suppose I should of been happy for him, or proud or something, but that boy— that man—just didn't seem to have gumption, which had surprised me when he was a boy and surprises me to this day given who his momma and daddy were. I think Lydia has had a lot to do with that, though of course that sounds catty to say out loud. She just never has gotten over being a sour little thing, and the way them kids came regular as clockwork didn't put her in a better mood, neither. The only good thing all them kids did when they were little was keep their dad outen the war, if you want my opinion. I'd say they were just a bunch of wild Indians, but that would slander the good people on their grandfather's side of the family.

Mind? Not that bunch.

Many's the time I heard them sass their pa enough to make me want to grab a switch and go after them, no matter what I'd learned from the Osages, and I can only imagine how much worse it was when I wasn't around. Of course, I believed then (and I believe now) they got that from their mother. It drove me crazy the way she'd snip-snip-snip at Donald day and night and in front of folks, too, but he just took it and kept coming back for more. Evie, the middle child, was the only one who I never heard sass her father or throw a fit when asked to do something, but of course I'm prejudiced when it comes to her. She's been my favorite since the day she was born. It's not right having a favorite, I suppose, but that's the way it is.

Anyway, when it comes to Donald, I suppose he's like a lot of folks who just plain seem to like getting abused. At least he did manage to make a little money running his business. He truly had taken to automobiles like a duck to water, and when someone needed their flivver fixed, which was just about every time they went for a drive, it was Donald who got the call. The fumes from working on them engines gave him splitting headaches that sent him to bed right after supper most nights, but he'd be up and at 'em the next morning, pulling on his greasy old coveralls and lumbering off to work with a lunch pail under his arm while Lydia stood in the doorway, nagging him until he was past hearing.

Meanwhile, I just kept to myself, ran the boardinghouse, and watched the seasons pass.

Sometimes I did enough business that I needed to call

upon Maudie for help, and once, when some new strike brought a passel of workers to the nearby oil fields, I even had to get the Chins, who were still at it in spite of they were getting on in years, to help with the laundry. But most of the time, it was just me and one or two boarders. An old maid school teacher stayed for most of a year, but when she wasn't carping about the food, she was trying to whittle me down on what I charged her, so when she moved on, I was glad for the peace and quiet. Sometimes the oil field roughnecks would sleep in the camps but sign up for Sunday dinner so they'd have at least one decent meal a week, and a couple of widowed old timers from the railroad days would stop by now and again for supper, which mostly just paid for the food with a few spare coins for my trouble. I usually kept the second floor closed on account of the sag had gotten worse with the passage of the years and I didn't have to burn so much coal in the cookstove to keep a little warmth in the place in the winter with the stairway door shut.

It didn't help business that Chautauqua, like most of the villages round about, was truly dying. The population had been going downhill ever since the railroad shops moved on, but after the war, prices for good Kansas wheat collapsed, and most of what other farmers grew followed suit. Farm folk had had high times during the war, getting good money for their crops, but that came to an end with the Armistice. Suddenly, they couldn't sell their crop for enough to buy coal or stove wood, and they took to twisting knots of wheat straw to burn on cold days, just like their daddies and granddaddies had burned buffalo chips. The oil business still paid, but more and more of that money was going south, to Tulsa and Texas, and the roughnecks went with it.

Hard times eventually hit the entire U.S. of A., of course, but money men jumping outen windows in New York City and people selling apples on street corners and such wasn't a bit worse than what we'd been going through for some years. By the time the Depression hit back east, hard times were old news in our part of the country.

If some duffer died, his children would abandon the old homeplace rather than try to keep a losing proposition going. Folks who had bought more land during the flush times couldn't make their payments, and the banks foreclosed. The trouble was, there wasn't anybody willing or able to buy that land from the banks, and pretty soon they were in trouble, just one or two at first, but then a whole passel of them failed in quick succession when crowds of scared folks tried to draw out their life savings all at once. A few people like Donald, who hadn't never trusted banks in the first place, looked smart as whips all of a sudden for keeping their savings in a mason jar or old coffee can buried somewhere in the yard.

So people started to pack up and leave, first just farmers going to town in the hope of finding paying work, but then leaving Kansas altogether when the jobs in town didn't pan out. Most of them didn't even have a clue where they were going. I've seen families of ten or twelve packed so tight in an old Model T or busted up mule-drawn democrat wagon that kids were hanging onto the fenders or standing on the running boards as they jounced down the road.

Charley McGuane was still sheriff in them days, though he was getting a little long in the tooth, and I know for a fact that it liked to killed him having to deliver the bad news about a foreclosure. When he had to do it around Chautauqua, he'd sometimes stop by for a cup of coffee afterward. He'd tell me how he'd seen the look of pure terror in the eyes of worn out women with a half dozen young ones hanging onto their skirts and their menfolk trembling with emotion, and it would bring him to tears, too.

More than once, some farmer would go out into the field after Charley had delivered the bad news and blow his brains out or take a turn over a barn beam with a stout piece of rope rather than face the loss of his home place. There isn't much in life sadder than that.

Then on top of what was already hard times, drouth and the Dust Bowl hit.

We didn't face the worst of it. Our yards and fields didn't blow away like they did in western Kansas and Oklahoma, but we still saw plenty of black sky filled with what had blown off other folks's land, and many a morning there would be a thick coating of brownish yellow dust all over everything. It'd come seeping in under the doors and through the cracks in the window frames and settle down the chimneys. Sometimes them dust storms would come with lightning that'd crash and sizzle like the world itself had slipped into Hell, only there'd be nary a drop of rain. I remember once in one of them storms, a bobwire fence just down the road from my place started to glow with what somebody called St. Elmo's fire, but it looked like Hell its ownself and liked to scare the bejeebers outen me.

Still, I hung on through all of that, even though there would be weeks on end when I wouldn't have a single lodger, what with all the drummers just giving up and staying home when it was obvious they couldn't sell their wares to people who were flat busted, and sometimes when I did have one, I'd find out at the end of his stay that he couldn't pay and had sneaked out in the middle of the night, leaving an IOU on his pillow, though I knew as well as anyone that them promises to pay weren't worth the scraps of paper they were written on.

And then we had our first bank robbery. Wouldn't you know, it was the Grange Bank in Sedan, one of the very few that had weathered the worst of the run. A whole bunch of townspeople who mostly didn't have but a few nickels to rub together lost what little they did have when that bank went down. The kid who did it was just a big old barefoot farm boy from Arkansas who'd been hanging around Chautauqua and generally making a pest of himself enjoying the services of one of the few remaining ladies of the evening who hadn't been driven off by hard times. Nobody realized what was up until the day he borrowed a car from somebody or another, gave his lady friend a great big kiss right on Main Street in front of everybody and took off for Sedan. Once he got there, he threatened the bank teller with a rusty old shotgun that likely would of blown up in his hands if he'd pulled the trigger. The teller, who was a family man, wasn't taking any chances. He cleaned out the safe and stuffed what cash they had into a canvas bag and handed it over, then walked over to the sheriff's office to report the robbery.

Still, it scared the daylights outen people, never mind leaving them even poorer than they were already, and it made me heartsick to remember how Caleb had done even worse by the people of Claremore and God knows where else.

Anyhow, Charley McGuane scouted up a posse and took out after that Arkansas kid, but he had too long a head start and was probably half way acrost Oklahoma before they got organized enough to follow. Charley told me later he'd heard that the kid had a high old time at Hot Springs, taking the waters and whatever young lady wanted to be treated to a good time until the money ran out, which of course also reminded me of Caleb.

That was in 1929 or '30.

After that, it was quiet again for a while, but only for a while.

Before long, it seemed the only folks doing well in our neck of the woods were the outlaws and bandits. Most were no-accounts you never would of heard of in better times who turned into stone cold thieves and killers. It was just like the days of the Doolins and Daltons—and Caleb, sad to say—all over again.

Charlie Floyd, who the rest of the world knew as Pretty Boy, came and went in Chautauqua County pretty much all the time in them days. He lived just down the road a piece in east Oklahoma, and when he wasn't hot-rodding all over the

Midwest going from one bank robbery to another, he was hiding out somewhere in our neck of the woods. He wasn't as bad as that Frank Purvis and the G-men said, but he wasn't any Robin Hood, neither, no matter what the songs say.

I actually had a chat with him one day at the Silver Dollar Cafe on Main Street. I was there nursing a cup of coffee and talking with Ruby Fields, the owner. She was a widow woman from somewhere over near Wichita originally who'd been in Chautauqua nearly as long as me. I liked to sit and talk with her of a morning, and she seemed happy enough to oblige on account of I always left a nickel tip on a nickel cup of coffee whenever I had it, since I knew she needed the money even worse than I did. It was about the only money she was likely to see from sun up to midday when two or three bachelor farmers would come by for one of her cold meat loaf sandwiches.

Anyway, one day while Ruby was chopping carrots and onions for suppertime stew that likely would have no takers, this big black Chevrolet pulled up out front and a fairly stout fellow clumb outen the passenger side and came in. There were two other fellows in that car, but they waited out there with the engine running like they were in a hurry to go somewhere.

Right away, I recognized Charlie Floyd.

His picture had been in the papers for a year or so by that time. He'd gotten himself blamed for absolutely every stickup from Dallas to Kansas City and half of the rest of them all the way east to Indianapolis or some such place, and there he was, clicking a pinky ring on the counter to get Ruby's attention. There was a bulge under his coat on the left side, and I knew well enough what was in there. Now if life was like in the movies, I'd of thrown scalding coffee on him or something and wrestled him into custody while Ruby called the sheriff, but a foolish thought like that didn't even occur to me. I had no respon-sibility to the law, I was old and slow and a woman to boot, he hadn't done anything to me that I knew of, and all the coffee I had was dregs and it was stone cold.

So I just said "Morning," and smiled at him.

He cranked his head around and glared at me, then softened his gaze somewhat. "Morning, ma'am," he said.

"You'll have to wait till Ruby finishes. She's slicing carrots and onions in the back, and if I know her, she won't want to stop. She's a little late getting the stew on."

"That so?" he said. "I'm in a hurry, though."

I stood and walked around the back of the counter. "Maybe I can help. I don't work here, but she won't mind."

"Yeah, okay." He was looking at the piece of greasy old blackboard hanging on the back wall that served as the only menu in the place. "How about three pieces of apple pie and three cups of coffee? Can you make that to go?"

"We got any pie, Ruby?" I shouted over my shoulder.

"Nope," came the answer from the back room. "Gladys Goodrich is on vacation if you can believe it."

"Gladys is the lady from over to the Baptist church that makes the pies," I explained to him. "Don't ask me why she's the only one that does it, but that's the way it is."

"How 'bout some cookies, then."

I craned around to get a look at the big old glass cookie jar Ruby kept near the cash register. It was about a third full of cookies that looked like they'd been there since Harding was president. "Oatmeal raisin, it looks like." I was hoping the raisins weren't really bugs.

"Gimme six. And the coffee if you have paper cups."

"I think so," I said. I dug the cookies outen the jar and wrapped them in a piece of wax paper, found the stack of thick paper cups, shook out the top one in case there were roaches or some other critters inside, and lined them up to fill. "You fellows must be in a powerful hurry," I added with as sweet a smile as I could muster.

He laughed at that. "You know who I am?"

"Sure do, Charlie," I said.

He positively beamed. "I thank you for not using that nickname, ma'am."

"You're welcome."

"I'm paying cash for the cookies and coffee, too. This ain't no stick up."

"Didn't figure it was or else it would of already happened."

"True enough," he said, and he started to dig around in his trouser pocket.

"That'll be forty-five cents," I said. "A nickel apiece for everything."

He pulled out a fistful of money, bills and coins both and slapped it down on the counter. I could see thousand dollar bills in there, but he fished around for silver and came up with four nickels and a two bit piece. Like I said, he wasn't exactly a Robin Hood. I scooped up the money and dropped it into my apron pocket.

"Thanks for your business, Charlie."

He touched the brim of his cap. "Sure. Say, you wouldn't be thinking about snitching on me, would you?"

I shook my head. "Why should I? As long as you take them cookies and hit the road, you were never even here as far as I'm concerned."

He cocked his head as if truly trying to figure me out. "Well, all right then," he said, and he pushed the paper lids down on the cups so he could stack them up, grabbed the wax paper bundle of cookies, and headed out the door. Just as the screen was about to slam shut, he stopped and turned around.

"Say, ain't this the burg Caleb Handley come from?" he asked.

Well, you can imagine the lump that came to my throat. "It is," I said, then added "though most folks roundabout don't like to claim him."

"I heard he was one hell of a bad character," he said with a grin. Then he turned again, the door banged shut, and within seconds, he'd clumb into that Chevrolet and they went roaring out of there.

A couple of minutes later, Ruby finished her chopping. I handed her the forty-five cents.

"That's for three coffees and a half dozen cookies to go."

"Oh, I wouldn't a sold them cookies," she said. "They're so old they'd be like eating shingles."

I tried to laugh, but the memory of Caleb wouldn't let me. "I don't think them fellows care."

"Who was it?" she asked. "Somebody from around here?"

"Pretty Boy Floyd and his gang," I said.

Her face fell until I thought her chin would hit the floor. "Well, why didn't you call me out here to meet him?"

Then there was that Clyde Barrow and Bonnie Parker trash. She was maybe the single most evil human being I ever met in my life including Bill Doolin, which is saying something. And meet her I did. Twice.

The first time was in the summer of 1931 or maybe 1932, before they were famous as outlaws. They drove up from Oklahoma and actually spent the night at what passed for a hotel one floor up from the mercantile. Mousy little Lucille Macomber owned it. She did more business than I did, but made even less money on account of most of her clientele was either ladies of ill repute or greasy gents just a step or two away from becoming hoboes. But one day these two young slickers showed up and more or less took over Lucille's place, riding roughshod over her and scaring away the one or two other customers she had.

I'd already heard about it before Lucille appeared at my back door the next morning to see if I'd maybe help her get rid of them. Donald was there having breakfast on account of Lydia had gotten into some snit or another and refused to make him his morning victuals. Anyhow, I asked Lucille couldn't she do it herself, but the blank-eyed stare and shudder she gave me told me that whoever was there was scaring her half to death.

Now, if you think about it for a minute, you'll probably wonder what on earth a five foot tall woman in her sixties could do about evicting unwanted hotel guests, and why I'd want to take on such a job for my competition, anyway, but Lucille had got it in her mind that I was just the right person for the job. Donald liked to have a stroke over it, but I just laughed and told that poor woman I'd see what I could do. My thinking was I'd talk to them and they'd probably leave on account of knowing they weren't wanted, and that would be that.

But I had no idea who I was dealing with.

When I got to Lucille's, the first thing I saw was this young woman sitting on the boardwalk with her chair tipped back against the wall and her feet spread wide for balance, just like a man. On top of that, she was smoking a cigar. She wasn't but about twenty years old, and not very big, maybe just an inch or two taller than me, with dishwater blond hair and a plain face marked some with acne scars, but what I remember the most was her eyes: small and gray and keen as a wolf's. I never saw another soul in my life that young that had that kind of evil look. She was fanning herself with one of them cardboard fans they give out at church—the ones that say "Jesus Saves" on the back.

I clumped up onto that boardwalk, introducing myself as a friend of Mrs. Macomber's. "Eva Rae Taylor," I said, holding out my hand. "Hot enough for you?"

"Bonnie Parker," she answered, although she made no move to shake. Of course the name meant nothing to me then.

I just said straight out that Lucille was wondering if she and her man friend might be interested in moving on.

"What's wrong with us staying here?" she asked without

taking the cigar outen her mouth.

"Not a thing in the world. It's just that..." I let my voice fall to a whisper and I leaned in toward her all conspiratorial like. For some reason it didn't surprise me one bit that she smelled like she hadn't had a bath in two weeks. "...it's just that Miz Macomber is a bit peculiar, if you want the God's honest truth, and sometimes she just doesn't take a shine to her customers. It ain't personal."

"So we're supposed to just up and leave."

"There's another hotel up in Sedan," I said. "To tell you the truth, it's a lot fancier than this place. Has indoor plumbing and everything."

She gave me a narrow-eyed look that made my blood run cold. "We like this one," she said.

Just then her man came outside. He was just a kid, too, of medium size, with slicked back brown hair and a round face with a nose sort of pushed over to one side like it had been broken a time or two. He was wearing a white shirt that had gone all wilted and wrinkled in the heat, with big sweat stains circling his armpits. In spite of that, he had a necktie snugged up against his throat.

"S'matter, Bonnie?" He leaned against the wall next to her and gave me the once over.

"This woman says the landlady doesn't want us here, Clyde. Says we need to move on to the next town over."

"Well, maybe we should. There sure as hell ain't nothing special about this dump." He made a sweeping gesture, which gave me to understand that he meant the town and everything and everyone in it, including me.

"It's the principal of the thing," the woman said.

"Hello, my name is Eva Taylor," I said, holding out my hand to the man.

He just nodded without making any effort to shake. "Clyde Barrow," he said. "Ever heard of me?"

"Can't say as I have," I answered.

He grinned, showing a mouthful of bad teeth. "You will. Bonnie and me are going to be famous."

"What for?" I asked.

The grin widened. "You'll see."

Bonnie Parker, sounding irritated, interrupted him. "She says the landlady doesn't like us. Don't that beat all?"

"It's not that she doesn't like you," I said. "She's just..." I touched my forefinger to my temple and said a silent prayer asking the Lord's forgiveness for making it seem like Lucille was touched.

"Well, I wouldn't want to stay in a house run by no crazy woman," Clyde said.

"She's not exactly crazy, neither. It's just..." I thought for a moment about what to say, then just gave in. "Aw, hell, if you want to stay, go right ahead. I'll square it with her."

Bonnie leaned forward and her chair thumped down onto the porch. "Why didn't you just square it with her in the first place instead of trying to roust us?"

I could tell she was madder than all get-out, but her man put his hand on her shoulder as if to hold her back. "It's all right, Bonnie."

"The hell it is. I don't take to having folks treating me like I was some kind of white trash."

"You'll get used to it," he said with a little chuckle. "Once we're famous." With that, he pulled a handkerchief outen his hip pocket to mop his face. "Now come on, Miss Bonnie. Let's take us a walk around this burg and see the sights. I got some things to show you."

Turned out that what he wanted to show her was any-place that might hold the promise of easy cash. I know that, because I watched as they took their little tour. At the filling station, they jimmied a soda pop outen the cooler without paying for it and Clyde offered it to Bonnie with a little bow that made both of them laugh. From there, they sauntered up the street to the bank before circling back to the dry goods store downstairs of the hotel. Twice Clyde stopped and pulled out his handkerchief just to wipe the dust offen his patent leather shoes.

I found Lucille still at my place.

"They're staying," I said.

She gave me a look of pure terror.

"It'll be all right. They won't hurt you. If you want, I'll stay the night with you." I didn't have a single boarder of my own, and since Miss Parker and Mister Barrow now knew poor Lucille didn't exactly cotton to them, I figured it was the least I could do.

"I'd like that," she said.

So I did, spending the night sitting in Lucille's little parlor two doors down from where them two criminals cavorted, banging into the walls and making the bed squeak like crazy. I told her they were just acting that way because I'd mishandled the situation and they wanted to make a point, but every time that bed would bump, Lucille would jump as if somebody had fired a gun.

Next morning, they were gone, and we figured good riddance and forgot about it.

But in early November a year or so later, they came back, and by this time, Clyde Barrow's prediction had come true. They were famous. There had been a lot of talk about the Barrow gang for some while, and Bureau of Investigation people clear from Washington had come to town a couple of times asking questions and warning that the gang would surely come back, which scared the daylights outen Lucille so badly she just abandoned that dismal old hotel and headed for the East where she had people.

Now they were back, just like the G-men had predicted, and this time, they stayed with me.

They had another fellow with them, a mean-looking customer with a thick brow and big hands who parked their big Buick out back and demanded a room on the second floor overlooking that car. I already had a customer in that room, a railroad detective who drank himself to sleep every night, but after one look at that brute, I gave in and packed my boarder off to Maudie's with a little note asking would she please take him in as I wasn't feeling well.

I actually gave a minute's thought to whether I wanted to alert the sheriff, but by then it was some idiot named Munn Bandy who'd taken over, having defeated Charley in the last election by spreading rumors that Charley was senile. Munn was mean as a snake, and I wouldn't of snitched on the Devil himself if it meant a feather in his cap. Besides, in the time it would of taken him to get there, that gorilla in my second floor room could of killed me ten times over and cut me up into little pieces, so I just decided to make the best of the situation.

Well, that bunch disappeared upstairs, and I didn't hear a peep outen them while it was still daylight. Come evening, I lit a coal oil lamp or two in my parlor. Donald had prodded me into putting in electricity, but all I had was a couple of bulbs dangling from the ceiling, and I hadn't used them ten times since they'd put them in. Anyhow, once the lamps were lit, I went to the stairway and called up that I'd have supper ready in a half hour.

It wasn't but a few seconds before Bonnie appeared at the top of the stairs. She had one of them tommy guns in her hands, with the business end pointed straight at me.

"No call for that," I said, though I'll tell you it took some doing to get the words out. In two heartbeats, my mouth had gone as dry as a wad of winter corn husks. "I just want you to know that I'll be fixing supper, Miz Parker."

"You know who I am." It wasn't a question.

I swallowed hard. "Yes'm. We met a couple years ago."

She gave me a squinty-eyed look. "I don't recall that."

"Well, we did. Up town. You were staying in the hotel. A friend of mine owned it."

"You called the law, didn't you?"

That set me back, what with her holding that ugly weapon. "No'm," I said.

That seemed to tickle her fancy and she laughed out loud. "No, I don't suppose you would." She wiggled the muzzle of her gun. "We won't be needing supper. And blow out that lamp, or else I'll shoot it out."

I absolutely believed her, so that's exactly what I did.

It turned out that was one of the longest nights I ever spent in my life. I wrapped an old bit of blanket around me and sat in the parlor and tried to sleep, though with them gangsters upstairs, I knew that was probably a lost cause.

Clyde Barrow spent the whole night pacing, clumping around in circles on that old plank floor. At the other end of the hall, the fellow who was keeping watch over the Buick was playing a harmonica and doing the same sad tune over and over. It would of drove a saint crazy, and it made me jumpier by the minute. Some time after midnight, I decided if I was going to die, I'd rather have it quick than being tortured to death, so I clumb them stairs and knocked on that man's door to ask him please would he stop with the racket.

Had I known what I was going to see in that room, I wouldn't of done it. Even by the light of the moon, which was the only light I had, I could see three or four shotguns, another tommy gun, and a big slat box piled high with ammunition. They had enough weaponry there to pretty much blow away the whole town of Chautauqua if they'd of had a mind. The only thing I could think of was that they were waiting for someone—lawmen chasing them, probably—and that there were even odds that my old boardinghouse was going to be the scene of a wicked gunfight before dawn ever broke.

Luckily, it was not to be. Daybreak came at last, and with it, them three criminals began to stir. While I was breaking eggs for breakfast, Clyde Barrow walked into the kitchen. He was outfitted in a dirty white shirt and necktie that made him look for all the world like an unsuccessful bank clerk on his way to work.

"Just coffee will do us," he said.

"It's no trouble to give you some eggs and toast," I said and pointed out that I already had the stove going and the bread sliced.

"Just coffee," he said, and he turned on his heel and stalked off.

So that's what they had—two cups of coffee apiece with cream and sugar, though the big fellow with them folded a couple of slices of bread and stuffed them into his coat pocket. Then the men hauled that arsenal outen the house and loaded it into the Buick.

"You won't tell we was here, will you?" Bonnie asked as she finished her coffee. The tone of it was just like she was asking a girlfriend to keep some silly little secret.

I shook my head.

"Good," she said, and that smile widened. "Because if we find out you did tell anyone, we'll come back and kill you." A blind man could of seen she meant it, too.

With that, they were gone. I watched that Buick go to the corner and turn north, toward Sedan. I put some extra coal into the stove and poured some of Francine's whiskey that'd been sitting in the cupboard for Lord knows how long into my morning coffee to quieten my shakes.

As I sat there, I thought again how there must of been folks who had the same reaction to Caleb that I'd had to that gang. I couldn't imagine being frightened of that boy, but I suppose some mother somewhere felt the same about Clyde Barrow.

As for Bonnie and Clyde, they got their comeuppance down in Louisiana some months later. Shot from ambush, they were, and the way I heard it told, the car they were in was so full of holes it resembled a Swiss cheese.

Some months later, that G-man Melvin Purvis caught up

with Charlie Floyd somewhere in Ohio and the government men shot him dead, too. I've heard accounts of how he was cursing lawmen as he died, but I can't say one way or another what's true. I know there was a big funeral for him down in Oklahoma, which made me sad remembering how I'd had Caleb laid out next to Reuben without a solitary soul paying any notice, but that wasn't Charlie Floyd's fault.

There were articles in the papers about all them hoodlums' deaths, of course, and they always mentioned the Daltons and my boy, too, noting that they were all killers cut from the same bolt of cloth.

Maybe they were.

Maybe there was something about northern Oklahoma and southern Kansas that just turned some fellows down the wrong path. Maybe they'd all had idiots for fathers and weak-minded mothers like Caleb. Or maybe it was just hard times, though there were thousands of people who suffered through the lean years without robbing and murdering.

I prefer to think that for Bonnie and Clyde, at least, it was something evil instead.

Anyway, that pretty well ended the excitement with gangsters in our part of the world. Life got just plain dull, to tell you the truth.

A couple of years later, Donald offered to have me come live with him and Lydia, saying he was afraid that old house would burn down with me in it. Though I told him no—I'd of rather perished in a fire than spend my days listening to Lydia—it was Maudie's passing some time later that made me change my mind.

Maudie.

What a dear soul. She worked so hard to keep Francine outen trouble all the years I lived in Sedan, and then harder still more or less raising my daughter them last few years as Dell and I grew further and further apart. When Francine died, I asked her did she want to come run the boardinghouse with me as part owner, but she said no, she was content in her own little place and besides, the boardinghouse wasn't bringing in enough cash money to keep the wolves away from my own door, so how on earth could I ever make a go of it with a partner?

So we just stayed friends—in spite of the hurt I felt over my daughter clearly favoring Maudie over me when Dell went to Washington. She helped me out from time to time, and whenever I could, I'd send her leftover stew or even kill and dress a pullet. She didn't have chick nor child of her own, but I never heard her complain once about anything.

At least until the cancer got to her.

It was in early 1935 or '36. She'd gotten really heavy over the years, and had a hard time walking. She was well past seventy by then, so it was coming on to her time, anyway, but nobody should have to die the way she did. She came by to visit one day, and while we sipped coffee in the parlor, she gripped at her chest and said, more to herself than to me, "This God damned pain is more than I can bear!"

Now, she'd been known to use some pretty strong language, but I had never heard her take the Lord's name in vain until that moment. I asked her what was wrong. "I hurt is all," she said, though I could see she'd gone white as a sheet. "Old lady pains, I suspect."

But of course they weren't. The pain got worse and worse, and suddenly all that weight just began to melt offen her. Her color changed to a sickly gray, and she started to hurt everywhere. I paid to have the doctor come down from Sedan—he was a young one, the sawbones who'd looked after Francine having retired—and once he'd examined her, he just said straight out that her body was full of cancer and she needed to get her affairs in order.

Though what affairs Maudie had she could of handled in a day, she kept putting it off until she got so sick she couldn't even sign her name. I wrote to Dell to let her know her old friend was dying, then closed up the boardinghouse (the railroad detective having died of a bad liver a few months before, leaving me without a single boarder) and moved into her place so I could nurse her.

Maudie's passing was about as brave as I'd ever seen, and when my time comes, I pray I can go with the kind of courage she showed, though I'd just as soon not face the pain and hardship that she endured.

She died the same day a thick letter from Dell came for her. I read the letter aloud while Maudie's body lay there cooling, as if my old friend could still hear it. There was more news there than I'd heard from my daughter in the more than fifteen years she'd been away. When I was finished, I tucked the letter into the cookstove and struck a match to it, then called the undertaker and had him come take Maudie away.

We buried her alongside Francine.

I moved back to the old boardinghouse for about another year, though I had to take a job helping the local biddies with the bolt goods at the mercantile just to pay my bills to the telephone and electric people. When the second floor stairs collapsed one day and I found out the whole place was riddled with termites, I finally told Donald I was ready to take him up on his offer to move in with them, Lydia notwithstanding. I sold the whole shebang—that rickety old place and the patch of dead grass that marked the spot where the Chin's Chinese laundry had stood—for a hundred dollars, packed everything I owned into one cardboard suitcase, and made the two block journey to Donald's home, knowing it would be my last move.

The new owners of the property pulled down what was left of the house with a brace of mules and a grappling hook, shoved it into a pile, torched it, and hauled away the ash all in the same day. Other than me, it didn't even draw a crowd. There wasn't another soul left in town who remembered or cared about what that old place had been in its heyday.

As I walked back to Donald's—home, now—it seemed as

if my life was like that pile of ash. For all the years of effort, it had been nothing but a waste.

Mrs. Branch

FROM THAT POINT ON, the years just seemed to come and go without much point.

I will say Donald was—and still is—good to me, or as good as I suppose I deserve. He's given me a place to live, refused the pittance I tried to offer to pay for room and board, and never grumbled much about the living arrangements.

Not so Lydia.

That woman could of put a circus clown in a bad mood most days just by the way she grumped and groused about everything under the sun. It was too warm, or too cold, or too humid or too dry. The coffee tasted funny, or her husband hadn't washed behind his ears (which was probably true) and didn't her children know they would surely bring shame on the family the way they acted? She crocheted almost constantly, and while she did, she mumbled under her breath complaining about the thread or her crochet hook or something. When Donald would wear through a pair of socks, she'd complain about how she had to darn them, and if he wore them holes and all, she'd complain that any decent man would ask his wife to get out the darning egg rather than showing off the back of his heel like that. When the socks were too far gone to darn, she'd complain that they couldn't possibly afford to keep buying him new ones all the time.

I didn't like her, and she knew it and made it known that the feeling was mutual. Most days, we just gave each other a wide berth and so got by without trouble. On days when we had to work together—Monday was laundry day and what with the coveralls Donald wore always getting covered with grease, the job was just too big for one person—we'd nod and point a lot rather than speak.

I'm sure Donald noticed, but in all the years I've lived with them, he's never once mentioned it.

With the passage of time, Donald got a little grayer and paunchier and ever more timid when it came to standing up to his wife. I don't believe there was ever a more henpecked man to my way of thinking, and to think he sprang from my own loins, with Reuben Whitesnake for a father... well, I just don't understand it and I don't suppose I ever will.

On the brighter side, my little Evie blossomed into a sturdy young woman with more spirit than both of her folks put together. She actually liked to hear my stories about the olden days, which I suppose was what made her decide to give me these school tablets and pencils I've used to jot down all these remembrances.

As I've said before, that Evie's a peach.

Anyway, though I've chafed under the rules set forth by Lydia, there's never been much I could do to change things, so in time, the two of us just settled into what you might call an armed truce. After all, it was their house—*her* house, as she so often pointed out—and I was there as a more or less unwelcome guest, so I just shut my trap and made do.

At least until the day Dell finally came home for a visit.

She'd been gone more than twenty years.

It was the early autumn of 1940, and times were improving somewhat, although there was all that talk about the new war going on in Europe and how maybe we'd get sucked into it same as we had the last one.

Given how we'd parted and how I'd just tried to put it

outen my mind, it actually came as a shock to me to realize how much I'd missed her until she stepped offen that train, coming through a cloud of steam and giving me a little hug and a peck on the cheek as if it had only been a week or two since last we'd seen one another.

Of course, there was a lot of old history wrapped up in that little peck. I didn't blame her for what I knew she held against me—all them years when I didn't pay her or her brother enough attention because I was looking out for Caleb, or how I'd tried to stand in the way of her and David getting married. And over and above it all, there was, of course, all that ugly business with Horace and Marcellus's disappearance. I couldn't blame her if she held a grudge. As the years had gone by, our letters, which never were much more than polite notes, dwindled to just a line or two at Christmas and Easter. Yet I realized in that moment at the train station that I'd been praying she would take after her pa—I mean Reuben—when it came to forgiveness, or that she'd learned a lesson or two in kindness from old Marcellus Robinson and Maudie Calkins, even if she was but a slip of a girl at the time.

Honestly, it struck me in that instant when she stepped outen that steam cloud that I was a little afraid of her, too. After all, she was *Mrs. Branch* now, an important woman in Washington, D.C., married to an important man. She hobnobbed with senators and justices of the Supreme Court and she even let on to others during her visit (though never to me) that she was on a first-name basis with Mrs. Eleanor Roosevelt, the First Lady of the entire U.S. of A. And here I was just a tired old scrubwoman in a no-account corner of Kansas that she'd surely spent two decades and more trying to forget.

Always willow-thin as a girl, Dell had thickened in the middle with the advancing years, and her dark hair had streaks of silver running through it, which was a surprise, too. In my mind, she had stayed the young thing who had boarded the train in 1919 to head east to her Washington adventure, and it seemed strange to look at her and see a woman well along in middle age. But then, when she looked at me, she certainly saw a woman who'd gone from middle age to old age over that same number of years. I don't remember what I said to her, nor her to me, if we said anything at all, and though I was fairly bursting to tell her things that might begin to make up for all them lost years, she spied Donald standing beside his car, and off she marched, leaving me alone on that platform. Before we even went home for the lunch Lydia had spent the better part of a week stewing over, Dell announced she had to go to the cemetery, where she shed a tear over Maudie's grave and laid a paper flower she'd picked up in some train station on the way. I reached for her hand as the both of us stood there looking down on that patch of grass, but she managed to turn just as our hands touched, and she marched back to the car without a word.

For just a moment, I confess I was so jealous of Maudie that I wished it was me lying in that grave just so my daughter would cry over me, but the feeling passed, or at least I pretended it did.

Still, I enjoyed Dell's visit. She'd taken to wearing the heavy blue woolen dresses that I suppose were what polite society in Washington, D.C., wore, and they made her look mighty highfalutin amongst the biddies who thought they were bigshots in our town. I confess to swelling up with pride just walking down the street with her, knowing how some folks would be peeking through their Venetian blinds at this fancy lady they'd once looked down upon.

It seemed peculiar to me how few airs she'd taken on. When she sat at the little table there in Donald's and Lydia's kitchen, chatting away with them like they'd always been best of friends, she drank her tea with her pinky finger poked skyward, and behind her back, Lydia commented on it with a "well-I-never," but it seemed like old times to me: that's just the way her namesake had done when we were kids all them years ago.

"Mother, you must come to Washington," she said outen the blue one afternoon while I was sitting on the porch with her and Lydia, feeling as out of place as a laying hen in a fox's den.

That was a shocker, I'll tell you, and it must of been for Lydia the way she dropped the crocheting she'd been worrying over as we talked.

I gave my daughter a look to see if she was serious, but she had turned and was watching something out in the yard.

I managed to get out "Reckon I could come to visit. Assuming Donald will let me travel alone." From the way Lydia puckered up like she was sucking on a lemon, I figured I knew the answer to that.

"It's settled, then!" Dell said brightly, though she still wouldn't look at me, and before I could think to say another word, she was back to asking Lydia about the latest gossip amongst the Methodists like I wasn't even there.

Of course, it dawned on me that she had asked me only to be polite and probably hoped never to see me again, in Washington or anywhere else, and after a time, I put the whole notion outen my head.

But she brought it up again a few days later, this time saying how very much David wanted to see me and could I come next summer? So maybe she wasn't mad at me after all, I thought. I tried to bring it up again after supper that night, but couldn't quite get the words out, and it wasn't any easier the next day.

Then she was back on that train, shaking my hand and heading east just as she'd done so many years ago.

The real invitation came in a letter at Christmas, in David's fine bold hand, though with only a "Merry Christmas" penned by Dell, and with it came money enough for the fare. Donald fussed and fumed and blustered, and I could see he had a powerful urge to get his hands on that money, but it was clearly mine, and unless I sent it back with my apologies, which I wasn't about to do if only because the whole idea of my going to Washington vexed Donald and Lydia, it appeared I was committed. I was afraid as the months went by that Dell or David would have second thoughts and ask for their money back, but they never did.

So it was that I went to visit the two of them in the late summer of 1941, taking the train through a whole half of the country I hadn't ever expected to see in life.

The war in Europe still hadn't raised much of a ruckus in Kansas on account of it was a long, long way off and nobody had taken a shot at us yet, but the farther east I rode, the more it appeared that we were already a country at war. Every other seat in the coach cars was taken by some young boy in uniform, and by the time I got to Washington, it didn't seem there was much else on anyone's mind.

Now, I don't know what I expected, exactly, but the greeting I got in that ornate old Union Station took my breath away even more than the high arched ceiling and huge statues.

It came in the form of a huge bear hug from David.

He seemed just tickled to death to see me, and even picked me up and swung me around in the air. I couldn't help but giggle. Dell gave me a hug, too—a real one this time, which liked to took my breath away—and held my hand as we drove home to their townhouse. We didn't talk much, and my first dinner (prepared by their maid—can you imagine?) was mostly just small talk about how were things back home, though David truly seemed to want to hear all the news about Donald's brood and what I knew of his old clan, he having not kept in touch with them much better than Dell had with me.

My days in that city truly were a blur, as Dell had something for us to do every day. She took me shopping in downtown Washington and we drove over to Mount Vernon so she could let me look at that big old place where George

Washington lived. Or we'd spend a morning at that Smithsonian place where they keep all the nation's old bric-a-brac, or we'd wait in line to get into some building I've forgot the name of to see the Constitution and Declaration of Independence. We took a morning and sat in the gallery above a mostly empty House of Representatives and listened to some long-winded duffer who was all in a dither go on about something or other while a handful of his pals snoozed or read the paper, then we went to a fine old hotel for lunch and exchanged pleasantries over little sandwiches the size of my thumb.

I wished we would really talk—or, truth to tell, I wished I could apologize to her for the hurts I'd been a part of—but the words would not come.

After that first evening, I didn't see much of David at all. The war business really had him hopping amongst all them military fellows in their fancy uniforms. Dell told me the first day when I asked him some question or another and he just hemmed and hawed and didn't answer that he didn't want to talk about Europe or what was happening in London or any of them things. There were things he knew he just couldn't talk about, she said, so I let the matter drop.

In the afternoons, and often on into the evening if David wasn't home, we two women would just sit on the porch and fan ourselves and sip lemonade, maybe making a little small talk but mostly just watching the traffic go by. Even if Dell and I had been the chatty type, it was so hot in that city— much worse than anything I'd ever experienced in Kansas or even central Missouri, and that's saying something—just fanning and rocking was about all a body would have the gumption to do.

So it was that a week or so into my visit, as we sat watching some little kids playing a game of baseball in the street, I wasn't expecting a thing beyond lemonade and the buzz of locusts in the trees and the sort of quiet that always settled in on us when David wasn't around.

Instead, she up and said it.

"Mother, I want us to start over."

Just like that.

"I don't know what you mean," I said, but the way my heart started beating, I think I did.

She sighed and straightened her back a little, as if she needed to find extra strength for what she was about to say. "I want us to get past what's been dividing us all these years. I haven't been the daughter you wanted, I suppose, but I'm asking you to put that behind you, just as I need to put behind me the anger I've felt toward you for as long as I can remember. I'm tired of it."

I opened my mouth, but nothing came out.

"Now, you need to know," she said so softly I could scarcely hear her, "this was David's idea. At least originally. I fought him on it, actually, but he said it was something that just needed doing. For the both of us." She took a sip of her lemonade and watched the boys play ball for a moment while I thought she could surely hear the pounding of my heart.

"You've always been a wonderful daughter," I said, but it was as if she didn't hear me.

All she said was "Actually, I didn't even want you to visit. It was David who insisted."

Well, that took some of the wind outen my sails. What so few seconds before had seemed like a sudden and unexpected answer to my prayers maybe wasn't that at all. Maybe it was just something she had to do because David had made her.

"It's all right," I said as bravely as I could. "You needn't..."

But she interrupted me. "No, Momma. He was right. It's way past time we make amends. Or at least that *I* make amends."

I just sat there. It seemed like a long time before she spoke again. "You see, I always blamed you for... well, for many things. But it's only lately that I've come to realize how hard it must have been for you with the hell Caleb put you through. And of course there was Horace, too."

As far as I knew, Dell hadn't spoken Caleb's name in twenty-five years.

"Caleb didn't put me through any hell," I said. And I repeated that she'd been a wonderful daughter.

"You didn't act like it," she said. "But what I realize now is that you simply had more than you could bear because of Caleb, who really did put you through hell whether you admit it or not." She leaned forward and put her hand on my knee without taking her eyes off them kids in the street. Her hand was cool from the ice in her drink. "We all saw that. I hated him for what he was doing to you, and for what it did to the rest of us. You, Donald and me. He took so much of your love there wasn't enough left for my brother and me, and what did he give in return?"

She took a sip and sat there so long I thought she was done. But then she said "Anyway, I've come to realize it wasn't his fault. I thought it was my whole life long—his fault and yours—but now I know better."

There was something in the way she said it, something that sounded like sorry and forgiveness mixed together, that practically brought me to tears, though I couldn't rightly say why.

"No, it wasn't his fault," I said again. "A decent person could never look at it that way. Some of it—the things he did later—I won't condone, but with what he went through as a young'un, I don't believe he could of helped turning out the way he did, and there was certainly no way I could ever of held that against him. If I spent too much love on him and not enough on you—and I know that's true—I'm truly sorry."

I paused for a drink of lemonade and a long look out at that Washington afternoon. In the distance, almost lost in the steamy haze, was the white dome of the Capitol, so much grander than that graystone dome back in Missouri.

"What was it that happened?" she asked after a time. "I mean when he was little."

"Oh, you know. Surely I told you."

"No, Mother, you never did."

It startled me to realize that she was right.

So for the very first time in her life, I told Dell everything there was to tell about her namesake, and the way she had lived in that mean hole and what she had done to her husband and how she died and how Jack Ross and I found Caleb in that dugout, and even the way he was splattered with Reuben's blood when that good man was killed. I admitted, too, to what I'd been thinking almost every day since I made that long, painful journey to Lansing—that it would of been better if Caleb had never been born. But the truth of it was that the thought of not having had him in my life—and me in his, I suppose—was too painful to countenance. It was true: the one child who wasn't mine was the one I'd loved beyond all reason. "So I ask you to forgive him and me both," I said at last. "Horace was another matter. I should of never married him in the first place. Or better yet, killed the sonofabitch, for your sake and mine."

Dell nodded and sipped her own lemonade. "Or both," she said with a little smile.

"Yes," I said softly.

I looked at her. It was time to make a clean breast of it. I told her that other awful thing, that it was Horace who had killed her daddy.

Once again, she sat there the longest time without saying a word. Finally, she stood, patted me on the shoulder and said "I'll be back in a minute."

When she came back, she had a bottle of something with her. She poured a little into my lemonade and a lot into her own. Then she sat down and said "I think we need that."

I took a sip. It burned like fire, and I thought if that was what Daddy's moonshine was like, I surely didn't understand why all them fellows found it so wonderful, but when I sipped again, I felt that warmth spreading through my body. It surprised me that it was a comfort in spite of the sultry heat of the afternoon.

After a couple of minutes, I started in again right where I'd left off. "Anyway, if I'd of known what Horace had done from the get go... well, it would of saved us all a lot of grief."

"Yes," she said softly.

"As for the other, what he tried to do to you... I should of seen that coming. For years, probably. But I just couldn't get past worrying about Caleb when I should of been worried about you, and your brother, too. Marcellus tried to warn me, but by then, Caleb was in prison and I just couldn't think of anything but that I had to go see him before..." I had to stop and take another sip of the calming fire in that lemonade. "While he was still alive. I left you in mortal danger. All I can say is I'm ashamed and sorry."

There. I'd said all of it, a third of a century too late to do any good. I took yet another big gulp of that lemonade. "It's the great sorrow of my life."

"I did hold all of that against you, Mother, for a very long while," she said so softly I could scarcely hear. "Then I realized that you'd left Marcellus to protect me... "

"That was his doing, not mine," I interrupted.

She reached out and patted my hand again without looking at me. "No, it was your doing. In that day and place, just being friends with Marcellus was something of a miracle. Anyway, you had to go look after Caleb, and you knew Marcellus would be there to keep me safe."

"But you weren't safe," I said. "Neither was he." Just saying them words brought tears to my eyes, and they spilled down my cheeks faster than I could dab them away.

She dabbed at her own eyes, then looked down into her lap as if there was something really interesting about her fingers. "Ah, and don't you see that's where my guilt comes in? It was my doing that got him driven off. Or killed."

"Oh, no," I said. "That's not true."

"But it is," she said. "You see, I believe I knew what Horace was going to try." She cleared her throat and took a deep breath. "I could have run away, but I believe that because I knew Marcellus was looking out for me, I just... let things happen. So our friend would intervene. That was what put Marcellus directly in harm's way."

"It's not your fault, child," I said, and in that moment, I truly thought of her as a child, like she had been all them years ago.

"But it's not just Marcellus I'm guilty of, Mother," she said after she'd taken another drink. The afternoon was going on toward evening, and just then David's big car rolled to a stop at the curb. He got out, waved to the boys playing ball, and headed up the walk to where we sat. He was sporting a big grin, but it faded as soon as he looked into his wife's face.

As he stepped up onto the porch, Dell said simply "We're talking," and he nodded and went into the house without a word.

Then Dell turned and reached for my hand and stroked it for just a moment. There was a look of both love and pain on her face that fairly took my breath away.

"Anyway, after we moved to Chautauqua, I did everything I could to put up a wall between us, Mother. I thought it was you who'd walled me out, but when I'm honest with myself, I know it was the other way around. All I could think of was how I'd gotten Marcellus into terrible trouble and how I blamed you for putting me in that position and for all the rest of it, too—what I took for being abandoned so you could look after Caleb."

"Oh, daughter, I never..." I started, but she shushed me.

"It's why I walled you off. Why I essentially ran away from you. I'm so very sorry for that, though I'll be eternally grateful that the man—boy—I ran to was David. What could have been the biggest mistake of my life turned out to be the greatest stroke of luck."

"Oh, Dell! I'm the one who's sorry. Been sorry every day for thirty-five years."

"Nothing to be sorry about, Mother. As I said, I realize that now."

I swallowed hard. "Then you do forgive me?"

She looked up and our eyes met for a second. This time, it was mine that darted away.

"Nothing to forgive, Mother. Nothing. There's nothing to forgive Caleb for, either. He was just a star-crossed child." Her voice cracked. "The Lord works in mysterious ways, Mother. Truly he does. If it hadn't been for Mister Ross, you never would have moved to Kansas in the first place, and you never would have been in a position to rescue Caleb."

"I didn't rescue him, child."

"Of course you did. He'd have died in that barren place if it hadn't been for you. As far as that goes, if you hadn't been in Gove County, you never would have known Marcellus Robinson, and then neither would I." She took a deep breath. "Anyway, as for holding anything against Caleb, I'm guessing if it hadn't been for him, you'd never have found Daddy," meaning Reuben, of course. "And if it wasn't for Daddy, I wouldn't be here."

"That's true," I said.

"Then," she said, raising her lemonade in a sort of toast, "let's drink to all the fine gentlemen in our lives, from Jack Ross to Caleb to Reuben Whitesnake to Mister Robinson to my David, and forget about those who tried to do us wrong."

When we'd drained our glasses, she set hers down and said "Now let me tell you something more." She reached over, and this time she gripped my fingers and squeezed them tight.

"Long ago, I decided I was going to go to my grave being angry with you over Caleb. David tried to talk me out of it—tried to talk some sense into me—but I just couldn't let go of being angry. It seemed so unfair that Caleb got all your love and did nothing but hurt you in return. Then one day Eleanor invited me to come along when she visited an orphanage. She knew the way I felt, and I think she did it on purpose."

"Eleanor? Mrs. Roosevelt?"

Dell actually laughed. "Of course, Mother. She's a dear friend. Anyway, she asked me to come along to this orphanage in Baltimore. It was the saddest thing I've ever seen in my life. I suppose the children were well enough cared for, but they looked so glum and lonely it broke my heart. So right then and there, I decided I wanted to adopt one of them."

She waited so long before going on I thought that was somehow the end of the story. "That was... five years ago now. We brought home a little boy named Robert—Bobby. He was three. His father had been a drunkard and his mother had died when he was born. He was the cutest little boy you ever saw."

I could see tears spill down her cheeks. When she wiped at them, her hand was trembling.

"You never said a word," I said.

"No. You see, we only kept him five months. It was awful. That child needed something that neither David nor I could give him, no matter how hard we tried. I wanted to be the best mother in the world, but he wouldn't let me. He'd just sit in a corner by himself and kick and scream if we tried to play with him. Whenever we took him outside, he'd try to run away. If we tried to touch or cuddle him, he'd bite and lash out. The doctors said he missed his friends at the orphanage, or that he was retarded. But it was more than that. He was like a little wild animal. We hired a nanny, then another, and then another. They wouldn't stay, and after a while we just knew there wasn't anything else we could do. So we... sent him back." Her voice broke. "Just like you'd return a gift you didn't want to the department store."

"Oh, Dell," I said.

She took a deep breath. "It broke my heart, Mother, and it made me so ashamed. Then one day David said something that just struck me like a bolt of lighting. That must have been what Caleb was like, he said. Or what he would have become if you hadn't been there to look after him. Of course he'd never heard the story of Caleb's beginning, but somehow he just knew."

She rose, went inside, and returned a minute or two later with the pitcher of lemonade. She filled our glasses half full, then added liquor again, this time a fair amount for the both of us. I did not complain.

"Anyway," she said as she settled back in her chair, "I've come to realize that you did the very best you could, Mother. For all of us. Better than I could have, at any rate. David—and of course poor little Bobby—made me see that. That's why I want us to start over."

We sat on that porch until the boys playing ball had gone home to their suppers and it was full night and the fireflies had commenced winking in the grass.

Then two days later, Dell took me up to the spare room where I was staying and showed me a beautiful gray dress she'd bought. It had black velvet on the collar and cuffs and everything.

"We're going on the town tonight," she said, "and I got that for you."

Well.

David came home extra early, for him at least, and the two of them dressed fit to kill and we took off for someplace in David's car, the both of them as happy as two hogs in a mud puddle.

I figured we were going to some fancy restaurant where I'd be as out of place as a fish at a thrashing party never mind my new gray dress, but that wouldn't of been the tenth part of what they had in store for me.

You can't begin to imagine my surprise when David turned that car in at the White House!

"Dell, you're not! I mean, we're not!" I said from the back seat, but from the way she turned and grinned at me, I knew it was true.

When a big black man about twice as tall as me, or so it seemed, opened the car door and held out a white-gloved hand for Dell, then for me, I was so weak in the knees I was afraid he'd have to carry me inside. Two soldiers all done up in fancy blue uniforms stood so ramrod straight I wasn't sure they were alive until they both moved in unison to open the outside doors, and another one in a different uniform led us down a long hallway filled with paintings of famous Americans, mostly Presidents and their ladies. I was so excited just being there I couldn't hardly breathe, and it didn't get any easier when we rounded a corner, and I practically ran smack into Mrs. Eleanor Roosevelt herself.

"Dell and David, how very good to see you!" she said in that peculiar high pitched voice of hers, and then she spied me. "Dell, don't tell me this is your mother! Mrs. Taylor, welcome to our home!" And with that, the First Lady of the United States of America took my hand in both of hers and gave it a little squeeze. I liked to fainted dead away.

"I've told Eleanor all about you," Dell whispered as she followed Mrs. Roosevelt down another hall and into the fanciest parlor I ever saw in my life.

Then I spied the President, sitting in a wheelchair on the other side of the room. That gave me quite a start, I'll tell you, on account of I suppose we all knew he was a cripple, but you just didn't think about the President that way, at least not in them days. Dell steered me over to him and introduced us. I knew I was going to swoon for certain I was so nervous. He just laughed and clasped my hand and bid me welcome in that voice that sounded so much warmer than ever it did on the radio.

"Girls, see that our guests have some refreshment," he said to a pair of dazzling young things who hovered about him. I supposed at the time they were family of some sort, though they proved to be his secretaries. "Mrs. Taylor, would you like a martini?"

Me having a fancy drink with the President of the United States. Imagine! I said I supposed I would, though of course I had no idea what a martini even was and strong spirits wasn't ever my notion of a way to enjoy myself, never mind my conversation on the porch with Dell. Anyway, before that night was over, I knew why they say drink is the thief of wit. The martini them young ladies handed me, which tasted like coal oil and to my way of thinking was an awful way to ruin a fancy olive, just went straight to my head. Before I'd had two sips I had to sit down, and I spent the rest of however long we were there just trying to follow the conversation, which appeared to be right lively between David and the President on matters involving the Army or Navy or the like. It would of been completely over my head even without the liquor, of course. Mrs. Roosevelt tried to draw me into some chat she was having with Dell about poor folks in West Virginia or somewhere, but I couldn't rightly follow that one, neither.

Every once in a while, one of the Roosevelts would say something right to me, and I'd nod or shake my head, depending, and they'd usually chuckle and the President would offer to have one of them girls freshen my drink, which of course I didn't need in the least, but freshen it they would, anyway, and I'd have another sip. Then he'd give me one of them dazzling smiles of his and jump right back into telling David how we had to help Mr. Churchill and the poor bombed-out British or some such. Dell seemed mostly amused by my feebleness, although after a while, she took my drink and set in on a little doily and patted my hand, as if to say "that's enough, Mother," for which I was grateful.

I don't remember what we had for supper at all, though it

involved more different plates and forks than I've ever seen in one place in my life. Dell coached me on how to just start on the outside and work in with that lineup of forks, though to this day I couldn't tell you what each of them was for. I do recall that the dessert was bananas that they set on fire right there at the table, which I'd surely never seen before and hope never to see again.

Then it was time to leave. The President shook my hand and said how happy he was to meet "the famous Mrs. Taylor" and Mrs. Roosevelt saw us to the door, where she gave both me and Dell a hug. A different huge black man ushered us into the car, and that was that.

Well, what little remained of that visit was something of a letdown, as you might imagine. After you've found out that all your worry about Dell holding Caleb and Horace against you was so much wasted effort and embarrassed yourself in front of President Roosevelt himself, what else is there? We did see some more sights and David took my picture standing in front of that big statue in the Lincoln Memorial, which of course would of given Daddy a stroke. Dell and I talked like we hadn't talked all her life, though none of it could come up to what we'd said to one another that afternoon watching them kids play ball.

Anyway, after a couple of weeks, Dell took me to the train station and gave me a real hug that brought tears to both our eyes, and I went home to Kansas and told Donald and Lydia all about it, leaving out only that afternoon conversation with Dell. Donald listened politely and said how nice it was that I'd had a good time, though I could tell that Lydia thought I'd made up the whole thing about the President.

From then on, Dell's letters started coming every week— sometimes even more often—and in each and every one, she kept asking me to please come back to Washington, not just to visit but to live with her and David. But then the war came at last, and talk of me going back East dwindled, then ground to a halt altogether. David got some new assignment helping mobilize, and he spent weeks on end crisscrossing the country by train meeting with the businessmen who were going to be turning out guns and bullets and tanks and planes. For her part, Dell took on so many volunteer projects, from serving tea and cookies to soldier boys to packing bandages for the Red Cross, that she was working even more hours than David. Still, there was always at least one letter a week, delivered on Mondays as regular as clockwork, but where they'd been newsy three- and four-page epistles in her tiny hand, they shrunk to a page or less in an almost manly scrawl she was in such a hurry to get them dashed off and on their way. I kept her up to the minute on the doings in Chautauqua County, though I don't suppose she cared much. Besides, what little I could tell her must of seemed pretty unimportant, what with she'd had a chance before long to meet Mr. Churchill of England and she and David hobnobbed on a regular basis with who knows how many generals and other such high person-ages.

The war came to Kansas, too, of course. Many and many a boy got called up to go fight for the country in the same way David had in the First War. Donald was on the draft board again, but at least this time he was too old to go no matter how many kids he had. Sometimes the high school band would play when them young boys who'd gotten drafted or volunteered got on the train to head for wherever it was they were going to be turned into soldiers, and sometimes it played when they came home on furlough.

I don't recall the band ever showing up when the broken boys came home, though. Those men—they weren't kids any longer, I'll tell you—who oftentimes needed help getting down offen the train because they were blind or their legs were gone could of used a little music, but most us turned away, being embarrassed to see somebody's son or husband or brother reduced to being a cripple. The band never played for the mothers who had the service flags hanging in their windows with one star for every son in the war, neither, and certainly not for the gold star mothers who got those awful telegrams telling them their boy was dead. Everyone followed the news reports of faraway places we'd never heard of a few brief months before, and somehow we always pretended that it was like in the movies, where the Americans never got killed, and there was never any blood. We'd seen the newsreels from Pearl Harbor, and we saw the pictures from those horrid little islands off in the Pacific somewhere, and Africa and Italy and then that terrible D-Day invasion, and all along we pretended not to know how bad it must of been and kept on praying for the war to end.

And then I got my own notice.

The surprise telephone call came in the middle of the night early in October of 1944. They say no good can come of a telephone call in the night, and when it's coming from Washington, D.C., to our little corner of Kansas, that's doubly true. The urgency that made David want—need—to talk to me in spite of the expense and difficulty in arranging a call like that told me all I needed to know even before I heard his voice.

"Mother Taylor, Dell's been hurt," he said in a tinny faraway voice that I suppose was the result of so very many miles of copper wire.

I felt my knees give out and would of sat down except Donald didn't keep a chair anywhere near the telephone. "Hurt? David, it's two o'clock in the morning..."

"I know," he said. "She was in a car wreck. It's raining here, and her car skidded on wet pavement and she slid into the path of another car."

I took a big gulp of air, and I know I closed my eyes. "Is she dead?"

"No," he said, and I could hear his voice break. "But it's

bad, Mother Taylor. Her head went through the windshield..."

I didn't want to hear any more. "You keep me posted, then," I said, and I think I told him to try to get a good night's sleep. I hung up the phone and trudged off to my own bed to lay awake for what was left of the night, staring at the ceiling.

The final word came the way it always does nowadays. An earnest young man on a bicycle fought his way through several inches of fresh February snow to bring me the Western Union telegram. I know lots of mothers got those telegrams during the war, and I imagine they took the news even worse than I did, it meaning their young boys had died in some far-off land, probably of some terrible injury, and would never be coming home for a proper burial. And of course, those deaths had been at least somewhat unexpected.

We had known Dell's death was coming ever since the accident. She had lingered for months, in and out of con-sciousness, wasting away. I said my prayers morning and night, and David kept me informed, mostly by telephone, which was a terrible waste of money but it was undoubtedly easier on him than sitting down of an evening and having to write the details. Besides, he was still busy with his important work when he wasn't at the hospital, there being a war to win no matter whose personal grief got in the way. At first, I had hoped against hope that she would rally, but it didn't take us long to realize that it wasn't meant to be.

The funeral would be on a Saturday morning, the tele-gram said, and David promised to wire the money if I needed assistance for the trip. He just assumed I'd be coming.

I folded that telegram and slipped it into the Bible Evie had given me for my seventy-fifth birthday. I haven't looked at that scrap of paper since, and don't plan to. Sometimes things just hurt too much.

Donald argued against my going, of course, and said it was too much for a woman in my condition to take on, by which I guess he meant that I was getting old. That was the truth, but for all I'd failed to do for my daughter when she was a youngster, and especially because she'd forgiven me for my greatest sins, I vowed that I was going to make that trip to say good-by no matter what anyone thought.

Perhaps that would make up for at least the smallest part of what I owed her.

When I told him that, Donald still insisted I was plumb crazy to travel alone in the middle of winter and God only knew what might become of a woman of my advanced age crossing half the country alone, but I countered by reminding him I wouldn't be on my own if he'd come along to help bury his sister. Of course, Donald was both too busy and too poor, or so he said, to make the trip. When he argued money, I reminded him of David's offer, which I was sure was generous enough to cover both mother and brother if it came down to it. Lydia butted in, taking his side, and I just swung around and told her to shut up since it wasn't none of her business. Hearing that took the starch right outen the both of them. Anyway, in the end, Donald just gave up and allowed as how I could go if I was going to be that stubborn, as if he'd ever had any real say in the matter.

That train trip was the loneliest three days of my life, even worse in some ways than waiting for Caleb's execution. I didn't see none of the country. It was there, rolling by outside my train window, mile after gray wintry mile, but though I sat staring out at it, I didn't really look. My eyes were turned inward, thinking back on all the years of Dell.

Dell, who in the end had so much more strength than her namesake in spite of the frightful things she'd had to endure and without any trace of the craziness of that poor woman's final years. Dell, who should of been by rights the favored, well-loved child but who mostly got ignored and still turned out so shiningly well in spite of it.

David met me at the train station in Washington. He was grayer than I remembered, and the ramrod stiffness had given way to a stoop-shouldered, slouching way of walking, as if the burdens of the last months had worn him down almost as much as it had Dell, though I'll never know how hard the war work must of been on him, too.

We drove through the streets of the capital in a black car driven by some nice young soldier from the War Department, David not saying a word except to point out all the extra buildings they'd put up to accommodate the thousands of soldiers and sailors who'd crowded into Washington during the war, but of course that didn't mean nothing to me since I'd only seen it the once. I was still so lost in my own memories I hardly noticed the big dome of the Capitol itself, nor did I pay much attention to the White House. All of them beautiful stone buildings were so much dross to me with my daughter dead. David hinted as we passed the President's house that Mr. Roosevelt hadn't looked well the last time he'd seen him, but I recollect thinking that given what David had been through, everyone probably looked peeked at best. Of course he must of been right, since the President died just two months later.

We spent a long evening at the funeral parlor, alone with Dell's body.

Now, I'd seen far too many dead folks over the years—three husbands and now three children among them—but for some reason, this one was the hardest of all to look upon. She was beautiful in the way a china doll is beautiful: porcelain white, perfectly done up, and cold as stone. I thought my heart would break gazing on her, but then after a time, I just said to myself that Dell wasn't really there. Whatever it was that had made her Dell—her spirit, I guess you'd say—was gone. It wasn't a comfort, exactly, but it took some of the sting outen the thing.

The next day dawned cold and rainy, with a touch of sleet

in the air. We dressed, David having bought me a beautiful black dress and shoes, and once again that black car took us to the funeral home. The city was as gray as a scene in some black and white movie. From the funeral home, we rode on to a big Methodist church that looked more like pictures I'd seen of some old Greek building than a proper church, though it was beautiful inside. One of those huge stained glass windows depicting some Bible story or another provided the only true color to the day. The place was packed with more black-clad folks than I could count, most of whom must of been pretty important judging from the traffic jam that developed outside. They all greeted David and told me they were so sorry for my loss when he introduced me, and as a testament to Dell, I could tell that every one of them fine, important people truly felt they'd lost something, too. Mrs. Roosevelt was there, but only for a minute, and she gave me a hug and told me how much she missed Dell already.

Then the casket was wheeled in, and the minister said his piece. Some senator or another delivered a eulogy I didn't pay any attention to, and just like that it was over. We rode to the cemetery and stood in the sleet while the reverend committed Dell's body to the ground, and David took me home where I napped some before it was time to go to the train station to commence the long ride home.

Just before I boarded the train, David took me in his arms and gave me a hug the like of which I hadn't had since Reuben died.

"You're still more than welcome to come to Washington to live with me," he said. "I mean that."

I was thunderstruck by the offer, but shook my head. "My place is in Kansas, with Donald and his family," I said.

"Your place is wherever you want it to be, Mother," he said. "You'd be a breath of fresh air among the stuffed shirts in this town." He actually smiled, and I reckon that was the first time that had happened since Dell's accident. "What I mean is, it would mean a lot to me if you were here."

"Thankee, David," I said. "Son," I added.

He hugged me again and handed me a small package which he said Dell had asked him to give me, blew me a kiss, and strode away into the darkening Washington afternoon.

I didn't open that package until that train was well to the west, chugging acrost some part of Virginia.

It was that fine black and yellow brooch carved in the shape of a turtle. The one from Reuben.

Only then did I cry.

I Make My Peace

NOW I RECKON IT'S TIME for me to make my own peace and get ready to go.

Nearly ten years have come and gone since Dell passed, as amazing as that seems, and well more than forty since that terrible Christmas when I lost Caleb. These last years have been empty ones for me, I'll tell you, and I've had altogether too much time and too many chances to look back and see how it might all of been different, as this tall pile of tablets will attest.

Might of been, but wasn't.

Chances missed are chances gone forever. I can't turn the clock back, nor undo the things I did wrong all them years ago.

I suppose I'm no better nor any worse than most. I'm just a common woman, who's lived a common life and made plenty of mistakes, which I surely do regret. In much the same way as my Daddy tried to make up for the lost cause of the South's defeat by lynching defenseless Negroes, I tried to make up for the lost cause of Caleb by lavishing my attention on him while ignoring the two children I should of been trying to save. Dell was right about that even if she did come to feel differently about it in her final years. And I've come to see, too, that Donald has paid a heavy price for that ignorance on my part, and the fact that Dell also paid that price but came out of it all right doesn't absolve me of my crimes. She pulled her ownself up by the bootstraps, you might say, and I'll die proud of that.

Her and David, that is, who turned out so fine in spite of my worrying. I never deserved the loving kindness I received from the two of them, but I'll take it thankfully to my grave.

David is dead now, too, of heart disease and, I suspect, pure loneliness at the loss of his beloved. He never did come to see me, and of course I never took him up on his offer to live in Washington, D.C., neither. Truth to tell, an old Rebel like me wouldn't of fit that town, and that's for certain, even with a Missourian like Mr. Truman or a good Kansas boy like General Eisenhower in the White House. I voted Democrat every chance I got except the first time, when I voted for Warren Harding and damn sure lived to regret it, and the last time, when I cast my vote for General Eisenhower on account of him being a war hero and a Kansan, and besides, that Mr. Stevenson was too bookish for my taste.

But politics didn't have nothing to do with me not wanting to move back to Washington. It just wasn't home— not with Dell gone, for certain—and it never could be. The noise and stink of all them automobiles would of driven me crazy, and I've grown too accustomed to being able to see all the way to the horizon just by stepping outen my front door. David never quit trying to lure me, God bless him, and the news that he'd passed on so suddenly struck me almost as hard as the news about Dell. Though this time my own infirmities kept me from making the trip, I'll say right out that I really wanted to go—not to see the sights, but to say good-by to that wonderful man.

Anyway, I'm still with Donald, who's probably a better man than I've given him credit for. He's certainly been more than decent to me—better than I deserved, to be honest. Even Lydia for the most part continues to put up with me, as I do her. At long last, we've grown used to one another in our old age, tolerating each other pretty much the way a body tolerates the arthritis that makes your joints burn and your back stiffen when you try to do the work that once came so easily you didn't even think about it. You wish it was different. You wish the pain would go away, but you just give up on expecting it and go on about your business.

As I write this, the first snowflakes of winter are dancing around the yard, hovering in swirls like so many summer moths looking for a place to alight on the half-frozen puddles edging the dirt road that runs past the house. The wind that comes in through the crack under the door has an edge to it, like a knife made of ice, and I've had to wrap an old shawl around my ankles to keep the chilblains at bay.

This tablet is about full and ready to add to the stack that's already too high as it is, too much having happened in my life that's had too much pain attached. I guess the truth is, I haven't the energy to keep the story going, but then there doesn't seem to be any more story to tell.

Maybe it's just as well.

Writing's getting harder and harder, anyway. Come late afternoon, my eyes give out and I can't see without a brighter light than ever I needed as a young woman. Sometimes Donald has to whistle for me to hear that supper's ready, and sometimes he doesn't—or I don't hear—and I go from noon dinner to the following breakfast without victuals. Sometimes in the evenings, I sit square in front of that teevee or whatever it's called with my nose practically on the glass to see what's going on there, which is usually nothing but silly people doing silly things. It's sad my life's come down to that: loafing in the living room and being entertained by a flicker of pictures on a box. Though I confess I do enjoy watching the Friday night boxing fights. Something about them half-naked men pounding on each other just tickles me for some reason. Maybe it reminds me of watching Daddy and Jack Ross go to it in our yard back home the day Ma spilled the beans on Jack and me not having shared the marriage bed.

Truth to tell, I've been thinking about the old home place more and more now that I reckon I'm soon to die. Kansas has sort of grown on me over the years, but there's still some part deep down inside that wants to climb that old chinaberry tree and look out over the rolling green of Callaway County to the graystone dome of the Missouri capitol just once more. I'm sure that old tumble-down shack where I was born is gone, but some things worth seeing probably will still be there.

So I believe I'll tell Donald he has to take me there for one last look-see and maybe a visit to Ma and Daddy in that glade where the deer feed of a soft summer's evening amongst the twinkling fireflies. He'll be madder'n a hornet and give me his usual thousand reasons why he can't take the time to go, or I shouldn't travel, or some such nonsense, but I reckon I've still got enough spunk to take him down a notch or two if he gives me any sass even if I am already a shade past eighty-six years old.

Yessir, I reckon I do.

I won't make him travel in winter, though, what with bad weather and the holidays coming on. But I'll not allow him any excuses as soon as the spring storms pass. Hell's fire, it won't take but a couple days by automobile, a trip that would of taken two weeks in the old buggy Jack Ross and I drove to Sedalia where we caught the Southern U.P. Line for Gove County.

That Godforsaken place.

Just the mention of Gove County puts me in mind of Jack. Poor Jack, who was twice the man he thought he was, and a darn sight better a human being than most I've known who were of higher station. And Marcellus, that other good, good man who happened into our lives in that most forlorn of places, then came back suddenly so many years later.

I owe him so very much. I've waited and waited in hopes

of hearing from him, but I reckon it's not to be. He'd be past a hundred now, so I suppose he's long since dead even if he escaped the clutches of Horace and his posse. I've always imagined that perhaps he went to California and found himself a good woman to bear his children. I hope so, for he would of made a wonderful father.

I think of Dell these days, too. Sister Dell, I mean, who seems more real in some ways than my own darling daughter, and I always wonder how she would of turned out if it hadn't been for crazy Clement and that dank cutbank hole he made her live in.

Of course after Gove County, there was Reuben—always Reuben!—and Caleb, God rest his tormented soul.

It'd be a blessing to be able to visit all their resting places, too, though I know I'll never get that job done. Reuben and Caleb, so close in miles, might as well be on the far side of the moon when I mention it to my sole surviving child. Ain't no power on earth would get Donald to see to that trip. I do understand that he has no memory of the one and only painful recollections of the other, so I guess I don't blame him too much.

Instead, I'll just have to say my good-byes to all them good people in my mind, and even Horace, too, though I don't miss that old cuss the least little bit. I confess I was downright happy when that murdering sonofabitch left this earth, and there's been nothing in the intervening years to make me rethink that notion. I'm only glad I had him buried next to his first wife so nobody has to fret about how I ought to be spending eternity three feet away from the likes of him.

Then again, maybe good-byes aren't what's called for. Maybe it's high time I put my faith in being able to see the good ones again in some better place if the rumors of Heaven prove true. If they ain't... if death is just an ending and a nothingness... I guess that will be all right, too. I'm pretty much ready, either way it goes.

For now, I just need to settle on being able to get back to Callaway County before I call it quits.

There's Donald, whistling for supper.

I believe I'll tell him of the plan tonight and let him sputter awhile before I put my foot down and let him know my mind's made up.